Dead Ringers

Sherlock Holmes Stories

By

Robert Perret

Paperback ISBN 978-1-78705-518-6
ePub ISBN 978-1-78705-519-3
PDF ISBN 978-1-78705-520-9

Published by MX Publishing
335 Princess Park Manor, Royal Drive,
London, N11 3GX
www.mxpublishing.co.uk

Cover design by Brian Belanger

To

Jennifer,

my only motive

Contents

Forward

Lost and Found

This is a story about a Great Detective and a hiatus and Bohemian outsiders and things once forgotten coming to light. It is a tale that doesn't get told often and it just may be that you haven't heard it at all. It is apocrypha, taking place between the chapters of the stories we tell about Sherlockiana. Let us take a step back in time, not to the 1890's but rather to the 1990's. The much beloved Granada series had ended in 1994, and had arguably petered out in cultural currency earlier than that. The most recent Sherlock Holmes craze would begin with the Robert Downey Jr. film in 2009. Some readers will likely insist upon the BBC series that began in 2010 as that flash point instead, but either way there was at least a 15 year hiatus from Sherlock Holmes in the zeitgeist (sure there were a few odds and ends in the meantime, but even avowed Sherlockians often don't remember Matt Frewer or Jonathan Pryce as Holmes). The most impactful Holmes of this hiatus was likely the animated one who solved crimes in the 22nd century. What do these fifteen years encompass? A lost generation of Sherlockians: my generation. Too cynical and anti-establishment for scions, but existing before social media as we know it today. There were Usenet groups and listservs and zines, but for the most part we were feral and lonely.

Some of us still are.

We are the Generation X Sherlockians, and as in all areas of life, we have long since lost the cultural war. Boomers shake their fists at avocado toast and bitmoji resumes, while Millenials and Gen Z bemoan the gig economy and the dinosaurs who have long since pulled the ladder up behind themselves. Hardly anyone else has anything to say about or to Generation X, save when the Boomers mistake us for senior Millennials, or Millenials lump us in as basically-Boomers.

We are a generation without an era. We are Sherlockians without a Sherlock.

Sure, some of us have adopted Jeremy Brett or Benedict Cumberbatch, or someone else entirely (personally I find Ben Syder to be the most Generation X-worthy choice), but those Holmeses aren't our Holmes, the way that Gilette, Rathbone, Livanov, Brett, or Cumberbatch have defined their respective eras.

I discovered Sherlock Holmes in a library, in a Doubleday edition of my grandparent's vintage. Rathbone and Brett made irregular visits at odd hours to my local Public Broadcasting Service station. They were still out there, still sleuthing, but in the shadows and just around corners; elusive and fleeting. I read that Doubleday Edition over and over again, and myself and that book were the entirety of my Sherlockian society. It seems there was a scion in the nearest major city, but I never heard of it at the time, and I don't know how I ever would have back then. Later I would find those early-Web oases, but this was a time when internet access was tied to a bulky desktop and a dial up modem, and not everyone even had those. The formative years of my Sherlockian vigil were in solitude: Holmes, Watson and I became a bit of a trio, and had many adventures that existed only in my head.

So it was that Sherlock Holmes made me a story teller.

I told myself stories. I told myself a lot of stories. I didn't think of myself as an author. I could also draw, a little. Enough that I became interested in comics. Not just superheroes, and not just Eisner-winning graphic novels, but also comic strips. *Calvin and Hobbes*, *Robotman*, and *The Far Side*. Here was a medium in which I could see myself, and so I drew and wrote and created comic strips for both my high school and college newspapers. Of course, newspaper strips weren't cool, and so I also picked up comics like *Spawn*, *Scud the Disposable Assassin*, and *X-Force*. I began to see myself there as well, in some bullpen somewhere churning out startling adventures of serial characters. My art plateaued but my writing continued to develop, and so I wrote a handful of spec scripts and sent them to independant comic studios, often never hearing anything back at all. And thus ended my career as a creator, and began my journey in home security, selling cutlery, temping in offices, a brief foray as a call center stock broker, and any number of other jobs. Not quite the gig economy my juniors complain about, but certainly not the careers my seniors enjoyed.

I didn't write or draw anything for well over a decade. That was my hiatus, my lost generation.

And then I came across a *Complete Stories of Sherlock Holmes* volume at Costco, and on a whim I bought it, and read it, revisiting Baker Street for the first time in a long time. By then, social media did exist, and searching online for Sherlock Holmes was an entree into the world of virtual Sherlockiana. Of course there were deep wells of scholarship, and exhaustive discussions of every Sherlock Holmes production, but what really affected me, what really reinvented me as a Sherlock Holmes fan, were the pastiches. People were writing their own Sherlock Holmes stories and my mind reeled. I had honestly never thought of putting the stories I had told myself onto paper.

Now, I could think of nothing else. I found a call for submissions and I write a story tailored to it. It was accepted and the editor, A.C. Thompson, was a wonderful person to work with. So I did it again. I found a call, and I wrote and submitted. I was lucky early on - I had three or four stories accepted before I met rejection. I had already been transformed.

I was the conductor of Doctor Watson's light now.

This collection includes the best of my traditional Sherlock Holmes stories to date. These aren't just stories to me. They are memories. Good memories of my friends Sherlock Holmes and Doctor Watson. We survived some lean times together, feral and lonely but also resilient and resourceful. We kept the memory green when the soil was parched. This is my Sherlock Holmes from a lost era of Sherlockiana. I'm glad you found us.

The Bogus Laundry Affair

The Foreign Office had rewarded Holmes handsomely after a bit of diplomatic business in Woking and so it was that we had spent the better part of a month loitering around Baker Street. I have had no small part in making the public aware of the fruits of Sherlock Holmes' prodigious industry, but he spent as much time in the valleys of exertion as he did at the peaks. He had thus languished in a blue cloud of tobacco smoke, calling for tea to be brought to the divan and toast to be brought to the settee. We were just reaching the tipping point I often feared, where his torpor would trickle into ennui and the needle would follow and so I was much heartened when a constable appeared in the doorway to fetch us to Inspector Lestrade.Holmes waved the policeman away. "If it were anything of interest Lestrade would have come himself."

"He is detaining a caravan and refuses to leave it," the constable said.

"Whyever not?" Holmes sighed. "Surely such a task is a particular specialty of patrolmen such as yourself."

"He doesn't trust anyone else to do it on account of there is no cause, sir."

"Lestrade is detaining a tradesman without cause?"

"Inspector Lestrade believes there should be cause, sir, but there isn't. That's why he requests your presence, Mr. Holmes; in order to find it."

"The Case of the Lost Cause, Watson. I'm afraid it is over before it begins."

"Why not, Holmes?" I said. "If it is nothing, you get to tweak Lestrade's nose. If it is something, all the better."

"I suppose."

"You'll come then?" asked the constable.

With a melodramatic sigh, Holmes stood from his seat and systematically stretched each muscle until he was as limber as a prizefighter. While this went on I donned my own coat and hat and held Holmes' at the ready. I had expected a carriage outside but instead we were lead on foot, the constable unerringly choosing the most sinister alley, the most forbidding passage, the most forsaken common, and soon we were deep within a London I had never seen. The buildings were ramshackle piles of bricks and boards peppered with grim faces peering from the darkness within. Refuse seemed to grow like a mold upon the place and living ghouls shuffled about, now gawking silently at the interlopers. It was as savage as the wilds of Afghanistan and it was less than a mile from where I lay blissfully next to my wife each night. My hand drifted to my pocket but I had not anticipated the need to bring my Webley. I reconsidered the constable but found little hope that he could protect us should these people become violent.

Ahead I heard the familiar bellowing of Lestrade, and when we turned one last corner we saw him standing knee-deep in a pile of clothes which appeared to have spilled from the back of the caravan. A scrawny fellow paced back and forth while protesting his right to conduct legal trade to Lestrade. Two more men of remarkable stature stood silently in the background. They turned towards us with the blank eyes of sharks as we approached. Normally toughs like these would be wound up for a fight, but these two seemed completely indifferent to our presence. In their pugnacious assessment, we did not rate as a threat, and I was forced to agree with them. This expedition had gone very poorly and I silently assigned much of the blame to Lestrade, who had drawn us into this sinister tableau without consideration or warning.

"Mr. Holmes at last!" Lestrade cried. "Will you look at this? Do you see?"

"There is nothing to see, Inspector," I said. "It is just laundry."

"Precisely!" exclaimed Lestrade.

"Did you expect to find something else when you waylaid a laundry van?" Holmes asked, prodding at a pile of castoff garments with the toe of his boot.

"Don't play coy with me, Mr. Holmes," Lestrade said. "If I can see it you can too."

"See what?" I said. Our presence seemed to have renewed the interest of local denizens and we were slowly being hemmed in by the gathering crowd.

"The laundry!" Lestrade said.

"Yes, Inspector, we all see the lovely laundry," I said. "Well done. Perhaps it is time to put in for a holiday."

"Don't be too hasty, Watson," Holmes said.

"You think there is something to this, Holmes?"

My friend shrugged. "You know my methods."

I could feel dozens of pairs of eyes watching me now. I cleared my throat and drew myself up before stepping through the castoff clothing with as much dignity as I could muster. I walked around the carriage, kicking the tires and buffing the painted name on the side with my cuff. I took the cart horse's head within my hands and examined its muzzle as if that would tell me something. While it was true that I was playing for time in hopes the solution would leap to my mind, I was also watching the disreputable men who had been arguing with Lestrade. It was a feint I had seen Holmes use many times - poking and prodding in hopes of provoking a reaction from the criminal. The small man just sneered and his comrades remained stoic in the face of my investigation. I walked around the far side of the cart and finally looked inside. It was a largely open space with shelves lining the sides and a simple plank for a bench at the extreme end. It appeared that Lestrade had done a thorough job of dumping the van's contents out on the rutted street.

"Everything seems to be in order, aside from the laundry itself being upset," I said.

"Indeed, I'm afraid the quality of the laundering puts our own habiliment to shame." Holmes picked up a shirt and brought it close to his face.

"I believe our charwoman is thick as thieves with Mrs. Hudson so there's little hope on that front."

"At the same time, Mrs. Eddels is quite discreet and circumspect, which suits me better than a pristine collar. There is another reason why this laundry is remarkable."

Following Holmes' lead, I plucked a white cloth from the ground which turned out to be a lady's underbodice. Fighting back a slight blush which I knew would win Holmes' contempt I held it up to examine it. It was so flawless as to be practically new, though I did detect a faint scent of lye. I continued staring at the delicate thing, my mind churning for any useful observation I might offer.

"It's not anything about the laundry!" Lestrade bellowed. "It is that it is here at all! Do you think any of these blighters are paying for first-class laundry service?"

Indeed most of those watching us were in filthy tatters and rags.

"I say!" I turned toward the small man, who was now twitching. "Where were you taking these things?"

"My clientele list is private!"

The two hulking men had now developed the clenched posture I most associated career thugs. Lestrade had been onto something.

"I've yet to see the laundry cart manned by three," Holmes said.

"I need protection in places like this," the small man said.

"If your business was legitimate it would be cheaper and easier to avoid this kind of place altogether," Holmes said. "Finally, I've never seen a launderer dressed so poorly."

"Indeed?" asked Lestrade.

"For in that trade, the commission is also the collateral. Within a matter of months, any practitioner will have developed a most enviable wardrobe from those items left behind or left unpaid for."

"Maybe I'm too honest for that," the small man said.

"Ha!" Holmes replied. "I'm afraid both the inspector and the doctor are correct. At the same time, everything and nothing are amiss here. You'll have to let them go, inspector."

"That's not what I brought you down here for. Constables have seen this caravan all over London in places it oughtn't to be. They are up to something and I mean to prove it."

"I concur completely but there is nothing more to be gained here. Send them on their way."

"Much obliged, Mister Holmes," the small man tipped his hat. His companions scooped the errant laundry into the back of the wagon and the whole enterprise trundled off.

"Shouldn't we follow them at least?" Lestrade asked.

"They won't do anything incriminating while we are trotting after them. Besides, the laundry's address was painted right on the side of the van. Keep an eye on Upper Camphor Street, Inspector."

"That's it?"

"I'll make some inquiries of my network. I have the feeling we see that petite gentleman in cuffs yet."

"You had better be right," Lestrade said, spinning on his heel and disappearing into the murky byways beyond.

The constable quickly trotted away behind him. Holmes and I were suddenly very much alone beneath the weight of a hundred feral gazes. I brought my shoulders back, hoping to look as imposing as possible. Holmes took a moment to survey the crowd before smiling to himself and, much to my surprise, moving to throw open one of the dilapidated doors on the edge of the square. The action sent a ripple through the onlookers. Holmes stepped through and now I was left on my own. To follow Holmes in would be to make myself subject to whatever might lie inside, and perhaps worse, it would likely trap us in. Yet I didn't much fancy my chances of retracing our path here, nor of being allowed to egress unmolested. I made up my mind and strutted right into that mysterious void whence Holmes had disappeared. I was relieved to see there was a bolt and as quickly as I could I closed the door and shot it home. Rarely in London does one experience true darkness but in this place it was absolute.

"Holmes?" I rasped.

There was a burst of light in the distance, which after a moment I reconciled as a struck match held by my friend.

"This way, Watson, but carefully."

"Are you mad?" I protested. "It will be trivial for that lot to wait us out. Or worse, break down the door. We could have made it out the way we came in."

"Many of those poor souls are little more than animals, relying on instinct. The moment they saw us as prey they were not going to let us go. We may have gotten a block or so but they would have gotten us before we left their territory."

"Let's hand over our valuables and be done with it. Better that than our lives."

"I fear it would not be so simple. The calculations of life and death are different here than what we are accustomed to."

The light between Holmes' fingers fizzled but I had a bearing now. Carefully I slid my feet forward until I could see his shape in the void.

"What do you mean to do then?" I asked.

With a horrible wrenching noise Holmes pried up a section of the floor. A fetid earthy breeze now washed over me.

"London is a city built on a city built on a city," Holmes said. "In these raw places, the strata are thinnest."

"How did you know to look here?"

"The masonry is characteristic of the old wards. These secret passages were common means of circumventing quarantine during the plague. The resurrection men made free use of these contrivances as well. I have an atlas of that macabre trade back at Baker Street."

The door by which we had entered splintered and buckled, casting an ominous pillar of light into the room.

"Quickly!" Holmes hissed.

I scuttled through the opening and Holmes followed, letting the trapdoor close as quietly as possible.

"How far do these tunnels go?" I asked.

"They are the streets of Old London, so as far as we need them to."

"Have you been down here before?"

"Not in some time."

As my eyes adjusted I was surprised to find myself in a brick-lined passage, and indeed the building above appeared to be an extension, almost like a turret.

"All of this is just laying abandoned down here?"

"It is not abandoned by any means," Holmes replied. "I suggest we step quickly."

We walked for several minutes through eerie silence before Holmes tugged at my sleeve and led me up an almost impossibly tight stairway which let out upon an alley. Following the city noises to the street, I was gobsmacked to find ourselves in front of Grant and Son.

"Holmes, I had my watch repaired here just last year!"

"You might have done as well fixing it yourself," Holmes scoffed.

"Do you think they know?"

"I shouldn't think so. Open portals like this are well-kept secrets. There's a thousand of these long since boarded up and bricked over. Only a scant few remain passable."

With that we made our way back to Baker Street, Holmes turning the curtain in the bow window to signal the Irregulars that they were wanted. By the time we had our tea, Samuel had appeared. He was chief among the Irregulars, a post that seemed to change every few years as the unfortunate children progressed from street urchins to whatever fate lay before them. I know that Holmes would discreetly exert his influence on behalf of those he felt held the most promise. He charged the boy with observing the laundry wagon, and most of all putting a name to the driver.

Shortly thereafter Holmes noted that there was no immediate action to be taken and he suggested I return home to Queen Anne Street.

"The current Mrs. Watson is no Mary Morstan," he observed. "If I keep you past your curfew I'll not see you again for a month."

With assurances he would not do anything that would put himself in jeopardy without summoning me first I went home with my head spinning and an unquiet feeling in my stomach. Thus it was that I expected the worst when my wife prodded me awake to tell me there was a policeman at the door. It was the constable who had come to Baker Street yesterday.

"What is it?" I cried. "What has happened?"

"I'm meant to fetch you to the police morgue, Doctor Watson."

I clutched at the doorway as the world seemed to tilt suddenly.

"Is it Holmes?" I gasped.

"Of course, sir," the constable replied.

"Of course, sir," I bellowed. "Of course it is, that dashed fool! I knew I should never have left him alone last night! Curfew, indeed."

"Are you coming to see the body, Doctor Watson?"

"Certainly, though his brother Mycroft is his next of kin. Probably can't pry the man away from Whitehall even for this."

"I wouldn't know about that, sir."

This time there was a police carriage and we rode in silence for I was adrift on a sea of remorse and self-recrimination. I was a bit taken aback to see that it was business as usual at the Yard. Holmes had not been one of that fraternity, but I would have thought him dear enough that his passing would warrant at least a pause in the business of this place.

"Ah, Doctor Watson," Gregson said as I descended into the morgue. "Have a look won't you."

The inspector's glib manner rankled me but every thought was stilled by the rough white laundry sack sat upon the exam table at the center of the room. The tiled floor felt as if it dropped out from beneath me as I stepped forward and my hands trembled uncontrollably. Close upon it now there was the unmistakable odor of human death. I fumbled at the neck of the bag as I tried to open it. Steeling myself I uncinched it and cast a steely gaze upon the tragic contents.

"This isn't Holmes!" I said.

"Of course not," Holmes laughed. "Why would it be?"

I turned to see my friend perched on a stool at the coroner's desk, papers adorned with dark smudges spread out before him like painter's palettes.

"The police came and told me I had to come down here to see a body," I stammered. "I was told it was you!"

"It was Mr. Holmes that sent for you, Doctor," the constable offered.

"I insisted upon it," Holmes said. "As per our agreement."

"I thought... you were... I've got my nightshirt tucked into my pants like a fool."

"I didn't want to say anything," Gregson said. "Since you have fallen back on writing I thought you might have gone a bit eccentric. Hard times can do that to a man."

"I have not fallen back on writing," I said. "I'm quite successful I'll have you know. Never you mind. Is there a reason beyond abuse that I have been dragged out of bed?"

"I don't think you can complain about having been drug out of bed mid-morning," Gregson muttered.

"Was the message not clear?" Holmes asked. "I would like you to examine the body."

"That is what I told him," the constable said.

"My dear Watson likes his intrigues," Holmes said. "Does this poor fellow remind you of anyone?"

"It is a bit hard to get at him like this," I said. "May I cut the bag?"

"Of course," Holmes said. "It has revealed to me all of its secrets."

"Hold on a minute," Gregson said. "I'm the Inspector here and that's my evidence."

We stood about for a moment.

"I suppose the next step is to cut open the bag," Gregson conceded.

Holmes produced a jackknife.

"No need to dull a scalpel," he observed.

The blade was keener than any I'd ever wielded. The rough cloth parted like water and inside was a man curled into a ball, packed in tight with fresh laundry.

"A transient, like the ones we saw earlier?" I said.

"So it appears," Holmes replied.

"Body snatchers?" Gregson asked.

"I think he was alive when he was stuffed in the bag," I said.

"I agree," Holmes said. "This man suffocated in the bag."

"How?" Gregson asked. "He looks hearty enough to me, and I don't see any sign that he struggled."

I pulled back his eyelid and say the trademark dilation and glassiness. "This man was plied with laudanum."

"Poisoned?"

"Surely the effect was meant to be purely soporific," Holmes said. "It is a needlessly complex scheme otherwise."

"Slavery, perhaps?" Gregson said. "Selling off transients to foreign merchant ships and the like."

"True press-ganging is rare anymore. A penny of opium would save you a pound of bother. Observe your fingers, Watson."

The grime on the man's face had easily transferred to my own. It was was less ground-in grit and more like a paste.

"Makeup?" I conjectured.

"Expensive makeup at that. I've narrowed the source down to a couple of likely candidates. Note also his shoes. While somewhat worn they are expertly constructed, in Naples if I don't miss my guess, and that pair is worth as much as every other shoe in this building combined. I'll hazard much the same can be said for his undergarments. We've all seen our fair share of the disenfranchised. Apply your senses once again, gentlemen."

We all stepped forward to look at the figure now laying slack upon the table.

"There's no smell," I said.

"There is a bit of an odor," the constable replied.

"Of death, but not of vagrancy," Lestrade said.

"While his costume looks the part, the clothes he is wearing are as cosmetic as his face."

"You are thinking of Neville St. Clair," I said. "The man with the twisted lip."

"There are superficial similarities," Holmes said, "But also significant points of departure. St. Clair essentially lived a double life. When he was Hugh Boone he was a vagabond; his clothes were filthy, his weatherbeaten features were real, and so were the begged coins in his pockets. This gives every indication of pure costume."

"Perhaps a pantomime of The Twisted Lip," I said. "There are no licensed performances but there are unauthorized adaptations of my stories everywhere."

"I commend that possibility to your attention, Gregson. It might explain the makeup and the laundry service, and perhaps even the strange locations we know that laundry van to have been."

"You sound unconvinced, Mr. Holmes," Gregson said.

"That eventuality does little to explain how this man came to be suffocated in this bag."

"Those theatre folk get up to all sorts," Gregson offered.

"I leave it in your dogged hands then, Inspector. I can suggest a few cosmeticians who might have concocted the makeup. Kindly leave my name out of it as I still avail myself of their services on occasion."

"And you, Mr. Holmes?"

"I want to know what this laundry business is all about. Leave that to me for the time being."

When we returned to Baker Street we found Samuel waiting on the stoop.

"Did Mrs. Hudson leave you out here on the street?"

"If I go in she makes me scrub every inch of myself until I shine like a penny."

"That sounds quite beneficial to me," I said.

"Yeah, well, if you live out here it ain't a favor. Besides, then she just sits there and looks at me all queer, like I'm going to make off with the silverware if she takes her eyes off me."

"I'm afraid she has had some experiences along those lines," Holmes said. "The Irregulars have come in all stripes, like any other men. What did you discover?"

"The bloke's name is Peter Grande, he's a sharpie from down south."

"Peter Grande, eh?" I said. "A pseudonym surely. He's not any taller than Samuel here."

"Still," Holmes said, "it is something we can work with. Anything else?"

"That laundry van doesn't go where it says on the side. It spends the night in a warehouse down in the docks."

"Slavers after all," I said.

"It doesn't go the right way," Samuel said.

"It doesn't?" Holmes replied.

"They pick up the laundry in posh places like Chelsea and Kensington, but they deliver it to places like Barking and Islington. Then they take it back again, one bag at a time."

"We saw the back of the wagon," I said. "It was stocked full of laundry."

"I'm telling you they only ever touch the one bag."

"How can you be sure?" Holmes asked.

"Because it is heavy. They've two large lads carrying it, and between the two of them they still stagger about."

"The bag is always heavy?" Holmes asked.

"As far as we can see."

"It begins to take shape," Holmes said. He pressed a handful of coins into Samuel's hands. "See that your comrades are well compensated."

The boy scampered off and we continued inside. "What is taking shape, Holmes?"

"Clearly the bogus laundry service is being used to transport people back and forth, but I now suspect it is with their consent.

You were very near the mark when you suggested that there was a bit of theatre at hand."

There came a knocking at the door. Moments later Mrs. Hudson appeared on the landing. "One of your gentleman friends, I presume, Mr. Holmes."

"Thank you, Mrs. Hudson, please send him in."

The figure that replaced her in the doorway was almost comic in his appearance and tragic in his mein. He wore a collection of the finest cashmere and silks I had ever laid eyes upon, but in a riot of colors and patterns, like he was the king of the fortune-tellers. Likewise, his hands were gnarled and cracked yet his swarthy face was as cleanly-shaven as a politician.

"Now this," Holmes said, "is a genuine launderer."

"You must be Mr. Holmes," the man replied. "My name is Aldridge."

"Please, Mr. Aldridge, have a seat. I take it that recent events are far beyond what you bargained for."

"Ha, I certainly wouldn't call it a bargain, Mr. Holmes. It seems that you know all, just as they say."

"It is a simple enough deduction when a man shows up on my doorstep the same day his business is implicated in a murder. You know that things look bad for you and you fear that the police will find just enough to stop looking once they have you in cuffs."

"A murder?" Aldridge cried.

"Did you not know that a dead man was found in one of your laundry bags early this morning?"

"Oh, this is terrible news."

"But news to you nonetheless. Why are you here if not for that?"

"There is no use in trying to hide any of it now," Aldridge said. "I am afraid I am at the mercy of very bad people, Mr. Holmes."

"Including Peter Grande."

Aldridge was completely shaken by the mention of that name.

"It is true, Mr. Holmes, Grande is the devil in my home. My family has been in the laundry business for generations but times are changing and we needed to change with them. We were no longer able to make a living with only a handful of workers each with only a handful of clients. Laundry, like all things, is becoming a business of scale. We needed a commercial building and washing machines and wagons and horses and so on. We took out a small loan and were able to quickly pay it back."

"From a private financier?" Holmes asked.

"English banks still see me as a foreigner, although my British roots run as deep as yours. With our contacts and reputation, we quickly needed to expand our business again, and then again. It was this third expansion that was our misfortune. We were successful enough that our benefactor accepted shares in the business as collateral. I was blind to the conflict of interest in that arrangement. I thought we both only benefited if the laundry business was successful. My whole livelihood was wrapped up in it. Of course to Lord Mickleton, my business was but one small cog among many. I honestly believe that he managed events so as to ruin my business. I found I was unable to make good on my debts, even as I was busier than ever. As one default followed another my business fell under his control. Suddenly he had his own men running their own side business, but with my name plastered all over it. That was when Peter Grande appeared. He slinks around my family, making thinly veiled threats towards me and taking an interest in my wife and my daughters that I can only describe as loathsome, and yet I am shackled to the whole business."

"Why have you have chanced to come to me?"

"Mr. Grande has a strange venture indeed," Aldridge said. "I've justified looking the other way because it has been harmless up to now."

"What has happened?"

"While I'm not sure I fully understand it, I know Grande was secreting people in and out of certain neighborhoods. To what end I'm not sure but he used my carriages to do it."

"Why would he do that?"

"I'm speculating, of course, but I can tell you no one looks twice at a laundry cart and we go everywhere in London."

"Surely not everywhere," I said.

"You would be surprised at the strange little hideaways the well-to-do have secreted away all over."

I thought about Holmes' claim to have five or six bolt holes about London. I could not imagine him sending out for laundry service, but then again I was certain that Sherlock Holmes did not do his own washing. What an interesting profession laundry suddenly became to me. Holmes smiled behind his tented fingers as if he were reading my thoughts.

"In any event, one of my tasks was to clean Grande's special laundry. The bag associated with his personal business. Every week or so there would be a collection of rags covered in filth and paint and I would personally launder them."

"But not today."

"Grande's special van just went out last night. It shouldn't have been back for days. When I asked why it was here he told me to mind my own business so I left it alone but the situation nagged at me through the night. I came in early to take a look at the wagon and I found the smoldering remains of a fire in the street."

"He burned the wagon?" I gasped.

"No, but in the coals were remnants of clothes I had never seen before. A young woman's clothes. Why would Grande be burning those? If nothing else they would be worth a few pounds. They must be evidence of a crime. Now you tell me there is a dead man? It must be true. Grande has done something awful and I am ruined!"

"Have you seen Mr. Grande, since? Or his colleagues?"

"No, Mr. Holmes, but I came here straight away."

"Return to work under the pretense that you know nothing, failing that, that you only know what rumors you have heard ing called out by newsboys. Cooperate fully with the vestigation, but leave your suspicions with me. You only ow Lord Mickleton and Peter Grande as unpleasant business rtners. We'll look into the possibility of a missing woman."

"Thank you, Mr. Holmes!"

After Aldridge had retreated I turned to Holmes. "What are u playing at?"

"As it stands there is an exposed incident and a secret one. e first was clumsy, the second calculated."

"You hesitate to say murder."

"I think the nature of the first incident is unresolved, wever, the disposition of it is suggestive. I'll wager that Peter ande is not a squeamish man. Had that body been a victim of I doubt we should have seen it again. He is already in the man smuggling business. Yet that dreadful sack was found carded on the side of the road."

"Was it? Then why is Gregson so sure it came from one of Aldridge's wagons?"

"Witnesses saw the bag being dumped from a moving carriage with Aldridge's name on it."

"That does seem a bit sloppy."

"So sloppy I'd assume it was a frame-up without Aldridge's own testimony. No, I think Grande's helpers panicked and dumped the sack from the back of the wagon while Grande was up top driving. By the time Grande realizes their horrible mistake, it is too late to recover the body. So he burns the evidence he can and hopes that no one is the wiser."

"What of the woman?"

"We know nothing of her or that she existed. A challenge even for me, but certainly far beyond Gregson, and so there was no need to tip our hand. It seems that Lord Mickleton is a cunning villain and I mean to catch him wrong-footed. While all eyes are looking one way we shall look the other."

Soon we were outside the address that Samuel had provided. I tightly gripped my Webley in my pocket but Holmes assured me the place would be abandoned. While at first glance it matched the slapdash riverside constructions around it the windows had been newly boarded up and the doors were perfectly plumb in reinforced jambs. Holmes approached and began feeling his way around the door. With a shake of his head, he then began knocking along the wall. Looking up and down the street I quietly freed my gun from my coat. I expected a gang of surly toughs to come bursting out at any moment. Instead, I watched Holmes make his way around the corner before stopping to kneel down. He hooked his fingers under the lower edge of the siding and began wrenching at it. After a few sharp tugs, the board worked free. We heard muffled screams inside. I rushed forward and the pair of us made short work of the next few boards, allowing us inside. The low hole we have just made was the only source of light. I was momentarily startled when I saw a figure lurking with a gun on the far side of the room before I realized I was seeing myself in a mirror. At the rear of the space, a woman was bound to a post. She thrashed and wheezed at us and I slowly approached her while making calming gestures. Holmes had turned to the doors, throwing the bolts and lifting the cross-arm. When he pushed it open the light revealed a strange place.

It was primarily a stable, with hitch and tack, mounds of hay and a trough still full of water. And yet there was a corner laid with a fine oriental rug, and upon that two polished wardrobes and a vanity that might have come right from the Savoy. No less than four gas lamps surrounded the small space and several canisters were piled high. I put my Webley in my pocket and again made calming gestures towards the lady. Gently I slipped the gag from her mouth and she drew in great gasping breaths.

"Where is he?" she demanded.

"Who?" Holmes replied.

"My fiance, Ronald Sumerton. He was with me."

"I'm afraid…" I began.

"I'm afraid you are the only person here," Holmes interrupted. "Do you know how you came to be here?"

I worked at the knots of the rope as she spoke.

"No. Well, I know a bit."

"Please," Holmes gestured.

"Ronald hired a driver to take us on a trip," she said with a moment of hesitation.

"Was this your intended destination," Holmes gestured. The woman's gaze drifted to the floor.

"A strange kind of elopement," Holmes said.

"How did you know?"

"When a young man and a young woman run off in secret what else can it be?"

The rope fell to the floor and she followed. Holmes offered his hand. "Miss…?"

Her jaw clenched for a moment but then she said, "Vidalia Hayes." She rubbed her arms to work blood back into them.

"Miss Hayes, why did you resort to this most unusual scheme?"

"I don't see how that is your concern, Mr…?"

"Forgive me. I am Sherlock Holmes and this is my colleague Doctor Watson."

"Is this part of it? Ronald was so secretive about it."

"Part of what?" I asked.

She screwed up her face before saying, "Thank you for your assistance, gentlemen. I hope I can rely upon your discretion."

"There will be no worries there, love," a voice said from the doorway. "Dead men tell no tales."

Grande was there, laughing, flanked by his fellows.

"We just wanted to see to the girl. What a pleasure to find a plump hare caught in the mousetrap. It weren't nothing to buffalo the Yard but Lord Mickleton was concerned when he heard Sherlock Holmes was involved. Turns out you were just smart enough to get yourself killed. Ta." With that, he struck a lucifer and tossed it into the hay. As I stomped at that the doors were thrown closed. Holmes threw himself against them to no avail.

"Barred from the outside somehow," he said.

We could hear the popping and cracking of burning wood.

"They've set the place on fire," I said. "Are they mad?"

One of the beams above us shuddered and collapsed.

"A question for another time," Holmes replied. "Quickly, back out the side!"

We turned just in time to see a flaming bottle shatter in the gap we had created, igniting the whole opening.

"There must be another way out," Holmes declared. "A rat-like Grande never traps himself in a dead-end. That's it!" Holmes threw back the corner of the rug, revealing a trap door.

"This must be part of the show!" Vidalia said. "Look, this is really unnecessary! Just take me to Ronald."

"This is no show, Miss Hayes," Holmes said. "Down you go!"

She was poised to continue her protest but Holmes swept her up and leaped down into the darkness. I grabbed the nearest lantern and followed, closing the door above us. I lit the wick and we moved further down the tunnel, fearing a fiery collapse. We found ourselves entombed in the dirt.

"This makes the last passage look absolutely palatial."

"Most of the network looks like this," Holmes said. "No one is paving the warrens of sailors and fishmongers. Quickly."

Where the other tunnel had seemed almost sterile this one was fecund, a riot of roots and mosses and stagnant puddles beneath our feet.

"It is a funny thing how our steps echo down here," I said.

"What's that?" Holmes asked.

"I mean, the dirt floor, all the foliage, should act as dampeners, but our steps are echoing up and down the tunnel."

"Those aren't echoes," Vidalia hissed.

"But that would mean we're... surrounded," I sighed.

Almost as if sprouting from the walls dark figures emerged at the edge of the lamplight, both before and behind us.

"Who are you people?" Vidalia cried. "What do you want?"

"You shouldn't have come here," said one of the figures, with an accent I couldn't quite place.

"We don't want to be here!" Vidalia said. "There is a madman chasing us!"

The shadowy figures guffawed.

I had my revolver pointed at the group behind us as Holmes squared off against the shadows in front.

"We don't want any trouble," I said. "Just let us go and we'll not trouble you again."

I found my arm wrenched around hard and my wrist on the point of breaking. My hand went involuntarily slack and Peter Grande was suddenly had me at the mercy of my own weapon.

"How?" was all I could muster.

Then they were upon us and I soon found myself pinned to the earthen wall while Holmes was being dragged to the floor. For a moment I was agog at the possibility that all of our adventures should end under these truly bizarre circumstances when Vidalia suddenly sprung into action, seizing my Webley from an unwary Grande. She waved it around frantically.

"You let me go! You let me go this instant."

"Don't shoot!" I pleaded but to no avail. Grande grabbed at the gun she pulled the trigger, missing over his shoulder but deafening us all in the confined space. My attackers dropped away and I cupped my ears, staggered by the concussion. Vidalia was scrambling down the tunnel wildly. "Don't shoot!" I begged again. She tripped and in a complete panic let off three more shots. My stomach churned and my vision swirled. Holmes, at last, was able to lunge forward and disarm her. I turned to see Peter Grande looming with a knife. Reflexively I put my knuckles to his jaw and he dropped. The four of us appeared to be alone in the tunnel now. Holmes was saying something to me but I could not hear over the ringing in my ears. He gestured at Grande and I nodded before slinging the man over my shoulder. It was no minor effort to haul him out but Holmes soon had us above ground again where the area was crawling with police on account of the fire and so the villain was in metal cuffs before he awoke.

Holmes broke the sorry news of her fiance's death to Miss Hayes while we were still at Scotland Yard. He could be inimitably sensitive and kind when the occasion called for it. I think Miss Hayes had her suspicions for she showed great resilience upon learning the truth. She was adamant upon the point of not returning to her parents, but Gregson would not hear any objections and had soon sent a constable to fetch them. While he was out of the room Holmes whispered to her and then demanded loudly to speak directly to the Commissioner. In the resulting confusion, Vidalia slipped away.

"This is unbelievable, Mr. Holmes!" Gregson said when he discovered the subterfuge. "I'll have you in stocks for this!"

"On what basis?" Holmes asked. "Miss Hayes is an adult who has committed no crime. She was under no obligation to stay here."

"So you send her out on her own, do you? She doesn't know her way about out there. She won't last a week. And what of her parents?"

"What of her parents? Do you not find the lengths to which she went to escape them suggestive? And yet you would condemn her to return to their dominion?"

"What do you know of parents and children, Holmes?"

A wry smile crossed my friend's face. For all I knew about his parents he and Mycroft were orphans. Had he too escaped his familial shackles?

"In any event," Holmes said, "she is no longer present." He produced a calling card. "I will meet with the parents tomorrow and we will see where the business stands."

"But they are on their way here now."

"I will meet with them tomorrow or not at all. Only I know of Miss Haye's whereabouts, and even then only for the moment."

As we exited the Yard Holmes waved away my many questions, asserting simply that all would be clear soon, and entreating me to be present at Baker Street at the appointed time tomorrow.

The next morning found Holmes draped across his favorite chair with an impish glee twinking in his eye. Mr. and Mrs. Hayes were stomping around the sitting room, taking turns in hurling invective at Holmes. Near the door shrugged a sheepish Inspector Gregson, who I imagine had spent much of yesterday enduring a similar onslaught. At long last, the pair seemed to run out of steam.

Holmes flicked open the Daily Mail. "I see here you have offered a reward for the safe return of your daughter."

"What else can I do?" Mr. Hayes bellowed. "A perfectly respectable girl goes missing for days, presumably in the clutches of this blackguard Ronald Sumerton. The police finally rescue her and you, a charlatan and a cad, secret her away. I can't poke my nose in every dark corner of London and clearly men of your ilk cannot be trusted. Fifty pounds will buy me every pair of eyes in the city, and I consider that cheap."

"It is a certain kind of father that spares his wallet when searching for his daughter," Holmes said.

"Don't you judge me, Mister Holmes! I'm a businessman and I'll pay what it takes to see the job done and not a penny more."

"May I ask why, in your opinion, Miss Vidalia ran away?" Holmes asked.

"She's a foolish girl," Mrs. Hayes said. "She always was. Got swept away with her romantic notions no doubt. I shudder to think about what abuse she has suffered at the mercy of that man."

"That man paid for his love of your daughter with his life," I said.

"I consider that cheap, too," said Mr. Hayes.

"I take it you had notions of a less romantic nature," Holmes said.

"I had the opportunity of a lifetime to expand my oriental trade. Those foreigners still practice their savage ways, you know. A well-placed marriage in Calcutta is worth more than catching the eye of some dangling whelp from the peerage."

"An arranged marriage, then?" I asked.

"Of course, she knows not a soul on that dark continent."

"That sounds little better than servitude to me," I said.

"Now see here, I am a preeminent merchant in this town and you will recognize your place, sir."

"The language in your advertisement suggests that any person responsible for the safe return of your daughter is eligible for the reward," Holmes said.

"So it is about money after all," Mrs. Hayes clucked. "It always is with these types."

"As much as it rankles me, I will honor the reward should you affect a reunion with my daughter," Mr. Hayes said.

"I would like that affirmation in writing, witnessed by Inspector Gregson here," Holmes said.

"The impertinence!" Mr. Hayes bellowed.

"As a businessman, you should have no objection to the formal observance of the particulars of this transaction."

"You are testing my restraint, Mr. Holmes," Mr. Hayes said.

"Let us just be through with this," Mrs. Hayes said. "Write the agreement."

"What do you have in mind then?" Mr. Hayes said.

"Nothing particular onerous," Holmes said. "Simply, I, Harold Hayes, affirm before witnesses that I shall honor my pledge of fifty pounds to any person who affects the return of my daughter, Vidalia Hayes, promptly and without reservation."

"Fine, fine," Mr. Hayes said, writing the document out upon my desk.

"Inspector Gregson, if you would be so kind as to set your signature as a witness and keep safe the document."

"You are playing at a strange game, Mr. Holmes," Gregson said as he complied.

"Do you have the cash?" Holmes asked.

"We don't walk around with that sum upon our person!" Mrs. Hayes said.

"It is held in an envelope at the National Bank, available upon reliable demand from the manager."

"The paper made us do so before it would print the ad," Mrs. Hayes said.

"Very good," Holmes said. "Everything is satisfactory," he called out.

After a moment of confusion, Vidalia appeared from my old room.

"She was here all along in this unsavory bachelor's flat!" Mrs. Hayes sobbed. "We are ruined."

"Actually, Madame, I was as surprised as anyone to find Miss Vidalia at my own lodgings yesterday evening, taking tea with my wife, who has more of a sense of humor about such things than she must," I said. "She spent the evening quite secure in a private room of my house on Queen Anne Street. My maid could testify to as much, as could my wife."

"But of course neither will," said Holmes, "for your daughter's conduct is no longer any of your concern."

"Dash it all, Vidalia, you are coming home at once."

"I loved him, father," Vidalia said. "And he loved me, more than I thought I ever deserved. He is dead now, because of some dreadful mishap, but as far as I am concerned you forced us into it and you killed him."

"Be reasonable, dear," Mrs. Hayes said. "We'll talk about it when you are less hysterical."

"I will not," Vidalia said. "I have made my own arrangements for my future and I do not believe you shall hear from me again."

"What do you mean, dear?" Mrs. Hayes said.

"Inspector," Holmes said. "Will you see that Miss Hayes receives her reward unhindered, please?"

"Reward?" Mr. Hayes scoffed. "What reward? The girl walked in her of her own accord."

"And thus met the terms of your offer," Holmes said. "Miss Hayes, I call to your attention that it is rather difficult to recall a person from a ship that is already underway, and I have noted upon this timetable some likely prospects departing within the day." He pressed a scrap of newspaper into her hand. Bon voyage, Miss. I regret that sorrow will be your traveling companion but I hope a well-earned peace will await you in your new life."

A single tear fell down her cheek. "Thank you, Mr. Holmes."

Gregson held the door for her and then they were gone. The elder Hayes quickly recovered and made to follow but with a spritely dash, I filled the doorway.

"Get out of the way," Mr. Hayes said.

"Won't you have some tea before you go?"

In response, he seized my lapels and attempted to pull me off my feet. Having learned a trick or two from observing Holmes I slipped his grasp and he himself ended up on the floor. Graciously I extended my hand to assist him up but he smacked it away and clamored up the wall.

"You haven't heard the last of this," Mrs. Hayes said as the pair scurried out.

"We weren't able to give her much of a head start," I observed.

"It will be enough," Holmes said. "Gregson is nothing if not stalwart in upholding the law, and I dare say my own name will carry some small weight with the banker."

"Still, was it wise to advise Miss Haye's of her escape plan right in front of her parents?"

Holmes smiled. "I quite enjoy the thought of Mr. and Mrs. Hayes turning the port of London upside down in an effort to shake out their daughter."

"She will not be there?"

"Indeed, what I passed to her was, in fact, the schedule of trains that will take her north where she can be on a French ferry before her parents are the wiser. From there I suggested that North America or Scandinavia were both places relatively friendly to independent women."

"Do you think she'll manage the trick?"

"I expect the memory of her beloved Ronald will carry her through the next few trials."

I regret to say that despite Peter Grande's best efforts at condemning the man, Lord Mickleton escaped the inquiry mostly unscathed. In protesting his innocence he disavowed his interest in Aldridge's business, and the eccentric launderer was so grateful he offered his services to us gratis in perpetuity. As I suspected, Mrs. Hudson had soon told Mrs. Eddels, who made it clear upon her next visit that she had seen far too much of Holmes' dirty laundry for him to ever consider giving his business elsewhere. Nonetheless, it was some small satisfaction to me whenever I saw one of Aldridge's wagons trundle by. As for Vidalia Hayes, I never heard another word about her. However, I did notice that Holmes' case notes moved from his cabinet to his lumber-room a few weeks later, which I took to mean he considered the Bogus Laundry Affair settled.

The Mystery of the Change of Art

One of the principal dangers of becoming a practicing physician is that as soon as one hangs his shingle he discovers that patients choose the most inconvenient times to be in urgent need of a doctor's care. I hesitate to even mention this, but since much is made of my willingness to abandon, as the accusation goes, my patients, to aide my friend, Mr. Sherlock Holmes, I feel it is only fair to observe in turn that the ill, the injured, and the incapacitated never feel compelled to consider the hour when pounding upon my door. Worst of all are newborn infants, who seem to take a puckish delight in entering this world in the wee hours of the morning, preferably in torrential rain or a blizzard, with not a cab to be found.

So it was that I found myself, having once again facilitated the miracle of birth and been thanked for my pains with a ruined shirt and a mother's gratitude, splashing ankle-deep up Baker Street, my mack soaked through, in hope of a cup of Mrs. Hudson's formidable coffee and an hour of respite at Holmes' hearth before facing whatever awaited me back at my surgery. I was disappointed to see that Holmes already had an early caller, for there was a beautiful carriage standing at the curb, with impeccably polished golden accents shining against the black body. The contraption was so flawless that I would have believed this was its maiden voyage into the hardscrabble streets of London. A coachman stood at attention in the squall as stoically as Her Majesty's own royal guards. Upon the first floor, I saw the light of the very fire I had hoped to dry my feet by flicker and dance in defiance of the gloomy atmosphere. All of a sudden Holmes himself was at the window. I thought perhaps he had anticipated my approach, as he had so many of our clients. Instead, I was surprised to see him slash at the window and then hold up the instrument of his assault in order to consider it in the light. He then began to pontificate to whomever his august audience was there in the study of 221B. It was one of his complexities that he so often evaded public commendation for his efforts and yet he would seize with relish these opportunities to pantomime for clients. Even I, who had seen my friend perform a hundred such routines, was ensnared by the flourishes of his hands and the drama of his postures.

The spell was only broken when a lady, hidden in a high collared coat underneath a smart umbrella, came bursting from the door above me. The coachman expertly bumped me out of her path as he opened the door to the cab. Neither deigned to acknowledge me, but I suppose I looked like little more than an itinerant idler in my sodden state. As the carriage clattered away Mrs. Hudson called to me.

"Doctor Watson, Mr. Holmes asks that you come in. I would have opened the door earlier and saved you a bout of pneumonia but the Lady was quite insistent that she not be disturbed."

"My apologies, Watson," Holmes called from upstairs. "Lady Longetine is rather skittish, in the way that all of her type is, and it would have been tiring to regain her candor with a new person in the room. I think she was inclined to put Mrs. Hudson herself out on the street, but a minimum level of decorum prevailed."

"It's none of my concern...," Mrs. Hudson began.

"And yet..." Holmes countered.

"I was surprised you took the Lady as a client. It is a trivial enough matter, even to me, and it is not like anything but her pride will suffer, and I reckon that can only improve her disposition."

"It is true the case itself offers little of interest, but her little trinket interests me."

"Holmes!" I said. "That is hardly a sentiment worthy of you, nor is it fit for the ears of Mrs. Hudson."

The landlady just tsked as she helped me shed my outer garments. By the end of the procedure, I was still soaked at the cuffs and shins, and left in stocking feet, but was otherwise much intact.

"I'll hang these by the stove," she said.

36

I entered Holmes' study to find him running a jeweled necklace between his fingers in a serpentine motion, endlessly looping round and round.

"A little sleight of hand I picked up in Morocco," he smiled. "This, of course, was the trinket I referred to."

"Holmes!" I declared. "That trinket is worth as much as this flat."

"Hardly," he said, tossing it to me. "It is paste."

"Paste?"

"Hence Lady Longetine's embarrassment. She has worn it proudly at any number of society gatherings. Worse, it is a family heirloom, worn by four generations of Lady Longetine's, and appraised at the time of her marriage. Isn't true love grand?"

"Which means the legitimate article was lost on her watch."

"And she didn't even notice until the paste stones began to spoil. Look, in the light, they have developed a prismatic sheen."

"Like a pool of oil."

"Beautiful in its own way, except that it proves a forgery."

"I've never heard of such an effect."

"Neither have I. There are a dozen easy ways to confirm a stone is paste. You saw me scratch it against the window. A diamond, or indeed any gemstone, would cut the glass. Paste does not. That proof was for Lady Longetine's benefit. Such an unusual flaw suggests a novel means of forgery, and that is what interests me. Everything else about this paste replica is flawless, the best I've ever seen. A new hand is at work which is deft at science and art!"

"How will you go about finding this new hand?"

"I suppose you are imagining boiling beakers and damning chemical reactions and the like."

"That does seem your forte."

"In a perfect world I would welcome such a battle of scientific wit and guile, but, I fear the next step is rather pedestrian. At some point, the authentic jewels were swapped for the replica. An examination of the Lady's jewelry box is called for, just as it would be with any case of a light-fingered maid. Will you come with me?"

"Of course, but will Lady Longetine allow it?"

"She does not want to be inconvenienced by my investigation and I do not want to be inconvenienced by her zealous secrecy and so it has already been arranged that I will examine the scene while she is out, doing whatever it is that society mavens do during the day. It will be a trivial matter to overcome the objections of whatever butler or maid may greet us."

So once again my critics can accuse me of abandoning my patients, if only for a few hours, but having added one new soul to the city this morning I felt I had earned the right to wander a little. My own clothes still hopelessly soaked, Holmes lent me a few items from his prodigious wardrobe.

"It is for the best," Holmes said. "Lady Longetine has not revealed her disgrace even to her own servants. I am meant to appear in the guise of an engineer plotting the installation of a personal telephone. You can play the role of my handiest linesman, whom I am giving explicit instructions to."

"Why can't I be a second engineer?"

"Do you know how a private telephone line functions? Can you convincingly sketch the blueprints of a room on first sight? Have you memorized the names of the legitimate telephone agents in case they come up in conversation? No, as a linesman all you need do is grunt disagreeably, carry a toolbox, and watch for my signals."

Despite my misgivings, I went along with Holmes' plan. To my surprise, when we stepped outside a workman's cart laden with spools of telephone wire and other bric-a-brac was waiting for us. Holmes' hopped into the driver's seat as if nothing could be more natural and we were off to the Longetine Estate through a gentling sprinkle.

Even as we pulled the cart to a halt an imperious butler came stomping out of the house, furiously waving us around the side.

It took me a moment to realize what the fuss was about, for doctors are always welcomed by the front door. In the guise of tradesmen, we were shunted round to the servants' entrance. When we stepped inside a startled scullery maid scuttled away without so much as making eye contact.

"Mr. Matthews, I presume?" The butler was addressing us from a door to the main house, set several steps about the servants' work area. "I take it you are not accustomed to clients of the Longetines' caliber?"

"To the contrary," Holmes replied with a rolling lilt, "all sorts are taking to the telephone, sir. Mark my words there will be one in every home one day."

"Absurd," the butler said. "What does the common fool have to natter on about, and who would want to hear it?"

"You may be right, sir. In any case, a telephone is de rigueur for a personage like Lady Longetine."

"Just mind where you park your cart. And wipe your feet. I'll not spend half my day cleaning up after the likes of you."

"Ta, mister...?

"The name is Goldstone, not that it will be much use to you. I expect this to be our one unfortunate meeting. Follow me to her Lady's chambers."

With that Goldstone turned on his heel and disappeared.

"There's a pleasant chap," I said.

"No doubt it takes a certain force of personality to withstand the Lady herself."

Goldstone was up the main stairway by the time we entered the foyer. Holmes took three stairs at a time to close the distance. I, lugging a toolbox that weighed at least two stone, resigned myself to ascending at the prescribed rate. By the time I had gained the landing Goldstone had already returned from where he had deposited Holmes. He turned his nose up at me as he passed as if I had come straight from working in the sewers.

"Nevermind that, Watson," Holmes hissed from down the hall. "Come here."

A short hallway opened up into Lady Longetine's chambers, which appeared to be as large as my beloved 221B. The mistress of the house was very much present, in that her likeness met my gaze at every turn. A great oil painting, nearly life-size in its depiction, took pride of place. It depicted Lady Longetine in the bloom of youth, posed like a queen, gazing across the Longetine grounds with a beatific look that I feel safe in wagering had never appeared upon her living face. Around this were a dozen photographs, some posed, some in fancy dress, all seemingly placing her in important company. Littered about were a few pencil sketches, a striking charcoal piece, and several studies in watercolor.

"Make some noise over here," Holmes said, indicating a spot of the wall next to a fine cherry wood end table.

"Make some noise?"

"Bang your tools around, knock on the wall, give the definite impression of manual labor. That should keep Goldstone at bay."

"And you?" I asked, making a production of measuring and remeasuring the wall.

"I will ply my own trade."

Through the passage to the bedroom, which had as many mirrors as this room had portraits, I could see Holmes begin by careful examination of the floor and then the windows. He then stepped to an ornate vanity and produced a vial of powder from this pocket. This he gently dusted over the contents of the vanity's top. He then produced strips of paper that became adhesive when moistened. Running them delicately across his tongue, in turn, he took impressions of the dust he had sprinkled. When he was satisfied he blew the residual powder away and gently opened the Lady's jewelry box. With an expert eye, he quickly appraised the contents, and then he closed it again.

"Well?" I asked when he returned.

"There are exactly two sets of finger marks on that vanity. One a woman's and one a man's. I think it is safe the assume the woman is Lady Longetine."

"Could the man be Goldstone?"

"Perhaps. The rugs only show one set of prints large enough to be a man, while at least three women have recently been in that room. I would hazard that her boudoir is off-limits to Goldstone, and the vanity is off-limits even to her maids."

"But if there are a man's prints then couldn't it be Goldstone?"

"More likely to be the Lord of the manor. At the same time, only one of the smaller sets of prints appears directly in front of the vanity, but there are dozens of such impressions about the room. Those I take to be of the Lady herself. Come, Watson."

To my surprise, Holmes plucked a silver candlestick from the table beside the chamber door and laid it atop the pile in my toolbox.

"What is this, some vital piece of evidence?" I asked.

"A means to an end, Watson. Shall we?"

Quietly Holmes led the way downstairs, where he proceeded directly to the front door. He knelt down and blew his vial of dust against the inside of the door around the handle. Nodding to himself he now let out a tremendous cough and began fiddling with the lock on the door. As an expert lockpick, he surely could have sprung the thing without a creak, but now he was cranking the handle about like he meant to snap it off.

"Hold it right there," Goldstone shouted from behind us. "What are you doing?"

"Never mind the rest of it now, just grab the toolbox and run!" Holmes said, throwing the front door open and letting a lump of putty fall to the ground. He dashed off and left me stammering as Goldstone gathered his nerve and stared me down. In a state of utter confusion, I fumbled for the toolbox at my feet and ran after Holmes. As I did the silver candlestick tumbled free.

"Thieves!" Goldstone called as he chased after me. I had almost made it to the street when a bullet whizzed by my head. I looked back and saw Goldstone at the front door with a rifle. From the way it swayed in his uneasy grip, I could tell he was not used to the gun. He shuffled forward onto the drive in hopes of bettering his aim. The horse drawing our cart roiled when the butler fired his second shot. As he fumbled to reload I leaped up into the seat and Holmes, already with reins in hand, whipped the startled beast into a brisk trot. We were barely around a bend in the lane when Holmes brought the cart to a halt and hopped off.

"Where are you going? We barely escaped with our lives."

"That's exactly why Goldstone won't expect my sudden return. Besides, the man is no crack shot."

To my consternation, Holmes sprinted back to the Longetine Manor. When he entered the gate he disappeared from my view. A few moments later another shot rang out and Holmes came flying towards me. Goldstone stepped out into the lane cursing the good name of the imaginary Mr. Matthews. He leveled his gun and gave one last blast.

"Tally ho, Watson," Holmes said as he swung himself up into the driver's seat. With a flick of his wrist, we were off, the furious Gladstone quickly disappearing in the rain behind us.

"What was all of that business?" I asked.

"I was taking the measure of the man, metaphorically and literally."

"Oh?"

"Yes. The finger marks on the jewelry box and the front door, where I had seen him place his hands as he chastised us upon our arrival, did not match. Further, Mr. Goldstone has the distinct amble of a victim of rickets."

"Absurd. I saw none of the hallmark deformities."

"The signs were subtle, I admit, and further I believe Mr. Goldstone takes great pains to hide them. Nonetheless, the nascent angles of caput quadratum could be seen about his temples, and the footprints he left in the mud don't lie. My first conjecture would be that the deficiency was congenital and that a corrective diet was not supplied until after infancy. I suspect we would find that Mr. Goldstone was put into an orphanage at an early age and from there taken into household service. Besides the signs of a deprived nativity, he demonstrates that unique combination of haughtiness and contempt found only in those lifelong servants accustomed to dining off of their master's silverware. No matter. He was admirable if ineffectual in defending Lady Longetine's belongings."

"From you."

"From what he perceived to be a pair of robbers. If he himself were the thief it would have been the perfect opportunity to let us go about our business and implicate us for any past crime he may have committed. He may be an ill-tempered lap dog, but he is at least a loyal one."

"So we have cleared him of suspicion."

"Indeed, the whole household, for Goldstone and Lord Longetine are the only men in residence, and the Lord would have little reason to sneak into his wife's jewelry box. Even if he meant to convert the jewels to currency he surely could have simply taken the necklace at any of a thousand opportunities. More to the point, there were half a dozen pieces more valuable at hand, and the Lord would have known that."

"Then we have little to go on. The necklace might have been switched anytime since the marriage."

"I am uniquely well-versed in the art of counterfeit. This method is new, and so must the theft be."

"So we may yet catch the villain."

"The possibility remains," Holmes replied, a lupine grin stretched taut across his clenched jaw. What seemed to me utter defeat was to him the very scent of the game. He retreated into the depths of his mental process for the duration of the trundle home and I was left to turn up my collar and lament the sodden cigarettes in my pocket.

Mrs. Hudson met me at the door of 221B as Holmes handed the cart off to a rough-looking fellow who seemed to materialize from the shadows when we halted.

"Oh, Dr. Watson, this is the second time today you have dripped all over my floor. I shan't be surprised if the boards are warped tomorrow. Nevermind that, your own clothes have dried, and cleaned as much as soap and brush can manage. You'd best resume your traditional attire. Mr. Holmes has a client waiting."

Keenly aware of the good landlady glaring in my general direction from the heart of her kitchen, I exchanged my workman's togs for my suit, which she had restored admirably, behind the cover of an open cupboard door. I hung the soaked costume up and shuffled up to Holmes' parlor with much the posture of a chastised schoolboy. By the time I arrived Holmes was sat primly in his chair as if he had been sat there all day pondering the papers and smoking his pipe. In my own chair was an agitated man turning his top hat round and round between his hands. His side-whiskers were eccentric but impeccably groomed and he wore a fine green velvet jacket atop a silk cravat pinned with some kind of heraldic crest too fine to make out in the gloom.

"My associate," Holmes gestured to me, "Doctor Watson."

"Doctor," the man touched his brow as if to tip the very hat that was dancing in his lap.

"I'm afraid I do not investigate matters of a purely domestic nature," Holmes said. "There are any number of agencies better suited. I know Barker to be a good man and can supply you his card."

"This isn't a simple domestic matter...", the man glanced at me.

"I assure you Doctor Watson can be relied upon absolutely," Holmes said.

"The drawing was one thing, but as far as it went it was a perfectly fine hobby for a girl."

"The drawing?" I asked.

"Mr. Reynold's daughter has an artistic bent and has long been sketching about town."

"I would prefer she focused on still lifes, of course," Reynolds said. "Or even landscapes, but she has always been fascinated by the people of London and by drawing what she calls 'scenes from life.' She wanders down the shabbiest streets as if that were nothing extraordinary."

"I sympathize with your concerns," I said, "But I quite agree with Holmes, there is little he can do about that."

"I have long since resigned myself to her stubbornness, her mother is much the same and, to be honest, it is one of her better qualities. I don't want a meek little mouse for a child. That said, we did come to an agreement that she would limit her wanderings to broad daylight, and remain in plain view. That, at least, she has heeded."

"Then how do you expect us to be of service?" Holmes asked.

"Her habits have changed recently. Where once she made studies of the common Londoner, street scenes and depictions of the harbor workers and so on, which could be argued to have social and artistic merit, she now draws portraits of rich idlers and heiresses. Worse, she accepts payment for it."

"There's nothing wrong with having an industrious spirit," I replied.

"She is toiling for shillings when she is on the cusp of marriage that would give her security for life."

"She has a fiancee?"

"No, but she is of age, and there has been definite interest from more than one suitor. I have had more than my fair share of success, gentlemen, and am in a position to see that marries well."

"Perhaps she prefers her independence," I said. "Some do, these days."

"I could provide for that as well, and would if it would make her happy."

"That isn't really independence," I observed.

"Tut, Watson," Holmes said. "The girl resides with her parents, takes her meals at home, relies upon the servants for her needs. This is no radical reformer."

"Yet she gathers coppers," I mused. "After seemingly abandoning her concern for the poor."

Holmes sat far back in his chair and drew from his pipe deeply. A prodigious billowing of blue smoke poured from his lips. He seemed to watch it twirl and climb before being dashed against the ceiling before he spoke. "Women often keep their secrets for good reason, though admittedly girls sometimes keep them injudiciously. I shall make a preliminary inquiry, Mr. Reynolds. If I deem that your daughter is in danger, or that there is something rotten in the business, I shall take the case in hand."

"Thank you, Mr. Holmes!"

"Yet," Holmes held up a cautioning finger, "If I find this is a silly nothing, whether on her part or yours, I shall immediately retreat. Such decision will be entirely at my discretion, as well as what if any, findings I will report back to you. If I tell you there is nothing to it that is to be the end of it."

"Very good, Mr. Holmes. I trust your judgment completely."

I showed the excitable Mr. Reynolds out before turning the Holmes. "Why take on a new case, one very much beneath you, when we have just begun the other for Lady Longetine?"

"Just as the first tantalizes me on a scientific level, this matter intrigues me on a human level. Besides, it will be an hour's work to decipher the riddle of Miss Reynolds."

As he spoke Holmes disappeared into his bedroom. Moments later she returned in crisp suit and tie.

"Whatever are you dressed up for?" I asked.

"Why, for tea at the Meadowlark, of course." He produced a gilt invitation from the mantle.

"What is the Meadowlark?"

"A charming country retreat, the summer home of some ancient duchess or somesuch. A classic example of Tudor architecture, with all of the modern amenities, of course. Mr. Reynolds' daughter, Emily, has been spotted there, applying her vocation."

"By whom?"

"As he himself indicated, he has been casting his daughter about town in hope of finding a good match. She is a bit of a celebrity at the moment in certain circles, as all eligible young ladies are in due course."

"That's a bit of a cynical view, Holmes."

"Nonetheless, we are charged with extracting her with a minimum of scandal. Reynolds is going to wire ahead to make arrangements for us as American business prospects out for a weekend at a real English country manor. He assures me it is the perfect camouflage."

"I can hardly pass for American, Holmes, particularly if there is are genuine Yankees present."

"No, but you shall serve quite well as my British secretary. Someone who knows the ins and outs of business practicalities here."

"And you?"

"I have had some small practice. We will put it to the test."

As we rode out to Meadowlark, clattering along on one of those rural lines that seem to be maintained almost as a hobby of the locals, I began to seriously wonder about Holmes' mental state. He had been eccentric as long as I had known him, but his behavior at the Longetine Manor had been foolhardy at best, and then to pivot on his heel to this bit of frivolity, it was most unlike my friend. As the train trundled up to the station, which was hardly more than a garden shed with an extended roof, Holmes executed a brief series of contortions to limber himself up and snatched his traveling bag from the shelf above. After I had stiffly levered down my own bag we stepped down onto the dirt. I had not realized how stale the air in the train had been, but the clean scent of warm soil came as a kind of shock. We had managed to leave the rain behind us and that, at least, was a relief. A little way off sat a landau the Meadowlark crest painted garishly in gold upon the doors. A pair of ladies were directing the coachman as he secured their luggage at the rear of the vehicle.

"I could not ask for better accessories to our disguise," Holmes whispered to me.

"Accessories?"

"A group of men is, by nature, viewed, however subconsciously, as a kind of invasion. The company of women tempers such instinctive suspicions. Besides, as you yourself have often proved, a beautiful woman is the best distraction, or at least the surest."

His whole body suddenly assumed a new posture and Holmes bellowed out, "Hold on there, friend! Don't forget about us!" It seemed that Holmes' had conjured the ghost of Buffalo Bill Cody, whom we had both seen at the American Exhibition. He sauntered over to the carriage with a kind of movement I would not have thought possible of my friend. Once there he slapped the back of the unfortunate driver and dropped his bag on the man's toes. "See that you find a good spot for my luggage, my good man." He then pivoted on his heel and seized one hand from each of the women. He lifted each in turn and kissed their knuckles with too much familiarity and for far too long. The ladies blushed and playfully batted Holmes away, only to titter to each other.

"I have never been so charmed," said the one on the left. Her dress was covered with elaborate frills of lace, as was her hat.

"May we ask whom we have the pleasure of meeting," said the other. While at first, her outfit seemed much more conservative, upon closer inspection it was studded with black pearls, as was her hair.

"Colonel Raymond Colburn at your service," Holmes said, leading them up into the carriage.

"My sincerest apologies," I said to the coachman as I approached. The man had a grimace of pure spite aimed right at Holmes' back.

48

"There's no more room for luggage," he spat at me. "You and your friend will have to ride with your bags on your lap."

"I quite understand," I said, stooping to retrieve Holmes' bag. When I tried to hand it up to Holmes I found him hunched deep in conspiratorial conversation with the two beauties. It was one of life's incongruities that Holmes, who had such little desire for the affections of women, was so apt at ensnaring them. With no help from anyone, I fumbled my way into my seat, where I found the view much obstructed by the pile in my lap. Holmes pounded upon the roof, and, with what seemed like an excessive cracking of the whip, we were off.

"Somewhere under there is my man in London, England, Nigel Greenstreet," Holmes said. "What are you up to under there anyway?"

"There was no more room," I managed before being cut off by the peals of laughter.

"We're in luck," Holmes said. "The girls here practically run the Meadowlark, and they are going to make sure we have a real good time."

"Now Colonel," chided the one in pearls, "you mustn't say things like that, and certainly not with that tone."

"Just because we are French in our fashion doesn't mean we are French in our behavior," said the other. "We are proper ladies and you, sir, are going to act like a gentleman."

The four of us sat in serious silence for a moment before the three of them began cackling again.

"Of course, my darling Arietta," Holmes said. "Anything for you."

"As always they pledge themselves to my sister."

"On the contrary, beautiful Minuet, I fear any pledge to behave myself with you would be tantamount to a lie."

They carried on in this fashion the whole way and to say it was a relief when at last we arrived at the Meadowlark would be an understatement. The hotel was breathtaking. There were a dozen peaked gables and a dizzying array of pattern work on the exterior. The top floor was completely ringed in glazed glass.

When the carriage came to a stop Holmes clamored out over me to help the ladies down. Again I was left to manage the bags myself. By the time I had extruded myself from the carriage Holmes was disappearing inside with one of the women on each arm. Members of the hotel staff had appeared to carry the luggage inside, and mercifully a man in pristine uniform, at last, relieved me of my burden. Just before whisking the carriage away the driver gave me a momentary look of sympathy. At my elbow, then, was a maid.

"You are Colonel Colburn's companion?" she asked.

"Yes, Mr., uh, Greenstreet, of London."

"Very good. I can show you to your room."

The stairway was remarkably constrained and by the time we had gained the second floor I was quite glad that I did not have to carry the bags up. While the room was small it had a commanding view of the hedge maze out back. A view ruined only by the sight of Holmes cavorting with the ladies we had met on the way here, as well as a number of other merrymakers.

The maid had left me with a pitcher of clean water, and after some ablutions and a cigarette, I felt restored enough to face the garden party below. Holmes was looking on as the sisters posed for a sketch by a woman who must certainly be Emily Reynolds. As I approached, Holmes stirred and took me by the arm, leading me a discreet distance away from the other revelers.

"I don't know what you are playing at, Holmes, but this charade is too much."

"I quite agree. I abhor vacuous small talk and empty pleasantries, and if I do not speak to anyone, including you old friend, for at least a week after this has concluded I hope you won't think ill of me."

"You seemed to like it well enough when you had Arietta and Minuet cooing over you."

"Ha!" Holmes said. "Nonetheless it has borne fruit."

"Yes, I see we have found the young Miss Emily. We hardly needed those women for that."

"No, but I was able to commission a sketch of them, and that has revealed at least three items of interest. Observe for yourself."

I stepped closer to peer over the artist's shoulder. Her depiction of the insufferable socialites was quite good. She clearly had a quick eye and a clever hand. In fact, she had captured something in black and white that I had failed to decipher in life. I stepped back to Holmes.

"Egad," I cried. "They aren't just sisters, they're twins!"

Holmes sighed.

"With one so fair and the other so dark I hadn't seen it before," I said.

"Again you are looking at the women when you should be looking at the facts."

"What do you see, then?"

"One, Miss Reynolds labels the drawings with names and addresses. A strange practice when she surrenders the drawing to her clients on the spot, wouldn't you say? And yet she never signs her own name. I have yet to see the working artist who does not sign her own work."

"She is an amateur, despite what her father thinks. You make too much of little things. What else do you see?"

"While her portraits are certainly serviceable, her skill only really shines in her depictions of jewelry."

"What do you mean?"

"I mean she spends more time on their adornments than their faces, and the result is practically schematically perfect."

"So she is better at drawing objects than faces. What of it?"

"I find that doubtful considering that she has spent the bulk of her career drawing people. Moreso, the motive becomes clear in conjunction with the next point."

"Which is?"

"She is using stylographic paper."

"You mean the self-copying kind?"

"Precisely."

"To what end?"

51

"That we know for a certainty."

"We do?"

"Think back, Watson. Where have you seen her work before?"

"Nowhere, before today."

"That is probably true, but not in the sense you mean."

"You are speaking in riddles, Holmes."

"Let me put the question to you another way. Where else have you seen portraiture today?"

"You don't mean Longetine Manor?" I peered at the sketch on the artist's easel again.

"Why, I think you may be right, Holmes."

"It is all but a certainty, but remains conjecture until I hold the proof in my hands."

"We won't be able to show our faces at Longentine Manor anytime soon. Particularly if you still mean to keep the Lady's secret."

"I have made the acquaintance of a score of burglars who might be up to the task."

"Holmes, you simply cannot burgle one of your own clients."

"It would be an easy thing. I took a plastic impression of the lock on the front door."

"I thought that was a ruse to goad Mr. Goldstone. Besides, you let the clay fall to the ground."

"I let the excess fall to the ground. It was as easy to take the impression as it would have been to pretend to do so."

"Perhaps we should leave the matter to Scotland Yard and keep our hands out of shackles."

"A dreary solution but perhaps Athelney Jones wouldn't make a complete hash of it."

"That's better, Holmes. I'm sure a prison cell would drive you to destruction."

"You have convinced me, Watson. I shall return to the station to wire Jones while you stick to that copy of the drawing like a stamp."

"Why you? Surely I as your secretary would handle such banalities."

"Undoubtedly, but I fear I have been far too effective in ingratiating myself with the Whitshire sisters. If you were to leave me alone with them you might well return to find me engaged, perhaps twice over. They have no such affection for you."

"What a relief," I groused.

"They are beginning to stir from their perch. I'll be back by dinner."

Before a protest could escape my lips Holmes had disappeared and Minuet and Arietta were upon me.

"Where has the Colonel gotten to?" Arietta asked.

"We wanted to show him our charming portrait," Minuet said.

"I'm afraid he had to see to some pressing, personal, business," I said.

"Oh dear!" Arietta said. "He is returning is he not?"

"Quite soon, I'm sure," I said. "In the meantime, I would be happy to be of service."

In response, the sisters simply wandered away. After a long moment of consternation, I snapped to attention when I realized I had already failed to keep an eye on the duplicated drawing. Emily Reynolds had packed up her supplies, and her satchel and easel were propped against the side of the hotel. I chanced to see the girl disappearing into the hedge maze with her portfolio precariously clutched under one arm. If the thing hadn't slowed her down I might never have seen her at all. Having, by some instinctual means, been deemed beneath the notice of this august company I easily slipped through the throng and stepped into the maze. The hedges were expertly manicured to be rigidly plumb and so dense that it was markedly darker and cooler inside the maze. I could hear a gentle rustling ahead and so, as quietly as I could manage, I stalked along the narrow passages. More than once the path doubled back and Miss Reynolds passed near me separated by only a thin wall of leaves and branches. I hoped my movements were more silent to her than hers were to me. After what seemed to be an improbably long journey I found myself at a dead end, and having met no diverging paths for at least a minute I found that I had lost the sound of her dress dragging along the shrubs. I cast about for any foothold that might allow me to look above the maze but no such cheat manifested itself. I took a moment to consider the possibilities. Emily could be passing through the maze to the opposite side, or she could be progressing towards the garden at the center. For that matter, she could be making a rendezvous at any prearranged point within the maze.

Hesitant to fall any further behind in my pursuit I determined that the garden at the center was the most likely goal, and should that prove false, it was the spot from which I had the greatest chance of pursuing her further. In a moment of pique, I tried to push through the nearest barrier in hopes of passing directly through to my destination. The hedge was surprisingly impermeable. Decades of patient horticulture had nurtured a formidable barrier. So I relied upon my sense of direction and moved ever towards the center. With each silent moment that ticked by I became surer that I had bungled the entire endeavor. At last, I came to a row where sunlight trickled through and I discovered a gap that allowed a view of the central garden.

Within I saw Miss Reynolds tete a tete with a figure turned away from me. They each had their hands on the portfolio and Emily seemed reluctant to surrender it. The man was whispering something to her, to which she gave brief, perfunctory responses. At last, she let the portfolio fall away from her grasp, her body language shouting resignation. I thought that this rogue was somehow blackmailing the girl, but then he cupped her chin and kissed her. I had just laid my hand on the stock of my Webley when she drew the man in with both of her arms. I stepped back from my peephole and waited until I heard movement again. When I resumed my observation of the scene I saw the two departing from opposite sides, the stranger going away and Emily returning to the hotel. She stopped at the threshold of the maze and turned to watch the man go. He did not so much as pause. Even I could read the looming heartbreak for Miss Reynolds. I made every effort to pursue the man to the far side of the maze but he had long departed by the time I found the path through. I looked out upon the rolling hills as the sun hung low in the sky. I was ill-equipped to go out onto an unfamiliar countryside in the dark. With no small trepidation, I returned back through the maze. Perhaps having gained some understanding of its design I soon found myself at the Meadowlark again, with the warm light of the dining room beckoning.

I had crossed the lawn and was just about to step inside when I was seized from behind. My good arm was pinned behind my back and my other hand clawed helplessly at the immobile elbow crooked round my throat. As I was being dragged back into the darkness I felt my revolver dangling uselessly against my side. My heels scrabbled against the grass, failing to find any purchase. In a last fit of desperation, I threw all of my weight to one side. My assailant simply seemed to disappear from under me and I found myself on the ground. Quickly I pushed myself up on my knees and went for my gun, which was now missing completely. I heard a familiar laugh.

"I'll admit I expected a warmer welcome, Watson," Holmes said, my Webley dangling by the trigger guard from a wagging finger.

"What do you mean by attacking me from behind like that?" I said, snatching the gun back.

"I do apologize, old friend, but the moment you were seen we would have been committed to seeing the dinner through."

"We aren't going to dinner?" I said, the aromas coming from the dining room now swelling around me and causing a hollow ache in my stomach.

"No need, thankfully."

"Oh."

"As I suspected, in these kinds of bucolic hamlets, the telegraph operator, and the postman are one and the same."

"What does that have to do with roast capon and saddle of mutton?"

"A postman is better than a vicar for knowing every last tittle of information in a village. It seems there is a recent immigrant by the name of Mr. Nigel Horne, who has set up shop in the old tannery."

"Indeed?"

"The postmaster finds him to be a most remarkable specimen in that he has received no correspondance of any kind."

"Surely any number of men move out into the countryside for a bit of solitude."

"Yes, but this man was quite particular in directing the postmaster to hold all mail rather than deliver it."

"Yet he has received no mail."

"Nor ever even inquired."

"Seems a strange way to run a business."

"Hmmm. The locals are not sure what he does, but they are emphatic that he is no tanner."

"What does this Mr. Horne do then?"

"I mean to see for myself. As to the results of my telegraph, I'm afraid I owe Inspector Jones a new hat. It seems Lady Longetine reacted with some vigor when he asked for the sketch of her drawn at the Meadowlark. She expressed, in no uncertain terms, that Inspector Jones had best forget whatever I had injudiciously revealed to him, which of course was nothing but the very word that earned him a beating. That confirmed the locus of the crimes, and of course, we already suspected the means. I still expect that a judge will find the Lady's charcoal sketch most interesting."

"So Miss Reynolds' sketches are being used to create fraudulent replicas, by her accomplice who I followed out to the woods?"

"Where a mysterious Mr. Horne abides for no apparent reason."

"You are suggesting this Nigel Horne's enterprise is set up to rob the guests of this one isolated hotel? That is madness surely? How could he not be caught?"

"I suspect he thinks his counterfeits to be flawless. Besides, hotels are the perfect feeding ground for criminals. The guests come and go, they are distracted, all of their routines are disrupted, and things like jewelry can easily be lost along the way. In this case, he even provides a substitute so that any suspicion is allayed until later. Weeks in the case of Lady Longetine, perhaps forever in other cases. Remember, she suspected nothing until the forged jewels began to disintegrate. If not for some minor inconsistency in his method she would have never known."

"This is enough for Scotland Yard to make the arrest, surely."

"Lady Longetine will not register an official complaint, and I doubt any other victim will either. Their reputations are worth more to them than a given valuable, which is exactly the arbitrage Mr. Horne is counting on. In a way he allows his victims to blackmail themselves with vanity and pride.

Besides, I came to see his process and I mean to do it."

As good as his word Holmes immediate set off as I hurried to keep pace. The moonlight did little to penetrate the hedge maze and yet Holmes passed directly through as assuredly as if he had nurtured the thing into being himself.

"This horticultural puzzle was designed to deceive," Holmes said in answer to my silent ponderings. "Yet even the best gardener cannot hide the scars of decades of wanderers wearing paths into the ground. The greatest erosions and most elaborate restorations are as good as signposts."

I could hardly see the ground in the moon cast shadows myself, but there was no arguing with the way Holmes dissected the maze in minutes.

"Ha!" Holmes barked when we arrived at the rolling hills lying before the trees. "A clever man indeed. Had he always followed the same path he would have worn a tell-tale trail. Here, you see the faint traces of at least two comings and goings. More have surely been lost upon the resilient heath in the recent rains. No matter, but one trace is all I need."

Following some track that was invisible to me, we crowned the hills and passed through the trees. The stench was the first sign Holmes was on the right track. It was not that of a tannery but rather a chemical scent, almost industrial in nature. When Holmes paused for a moment and cocked his head I was sure he had discerned many of the components of Horne's concoction already. We continued until the trees ended. A distance away we saw a ramshackle building, the stonework and large timbers largely intact, but the thatch work long since collapsed. There was a faint flickering visible through warped wooden shutters. Holmes crept up to peer in. I followed on his heel with my Webley at the ready. More than once a villain had gotten the drop on us in his own lair. Holmes seemed transfixed, yet for me, there was little but dwindling fortitude and the oblique sounds of a craftsman inside at his trade. As the moon crossed overhead I slumped against the wall, and finally sat with my gun across my knee. At some point I must have dozed for Holmes was gently shaking my shoulder and gesturing that we should retreat into the woods. The pink fingers of dawn were just peeking over the canopy.

"Remarkable," Holmes whispered. "Mr. Horne is truly an artist in his own right. It is a shame he has abused his talent thusly."

"We have him dead to rights, at least," I yawned.

"I'm afraid the law is ill-equipped to understand the implications of his laboratory, and he burned the incriminating diagram upon completion of the piece. At the moment all he has upon him is a bit of costume jewelry."

"What was the meaning of our vigil then?"

"It was a master class in forgery. I've learned as much from observing Mr. Horne for a night as I might have in a year of study on my own. It is a rare pleasure for me to be a student."

"My aching bones beg to differ."

"Fear not, Watson. The criminal will be in shackles within the hour. In the meantime, let us return to the hotel."

Holmes surprised me by making his way out to the road rather than trailing Mr. Horne directly.

"We know precisely where he is going and I mean to be there first," Holmes said.

"Surely this is the longer route."

"Yet quicker nonetheless."

We stepped out of the trees to find a sour-looking man with a rifle across his lap sitting atop a sturdy haywagon.

"Constable Juno, I presume?" Holmes said.

"So you are the famous Mr. Holmes," the man spat from beneath a bristly mustache. "I don't much appreciate you stirring the pot around here. And without so much as a by-your-leave either."

"My apologies, sir. I left word for you at the earliest opportunity as soon as I knew there was a situation worthy of your attention."

The constable seemed to ponder for a moment before spitting in a great arc towards the far side of the road.

"We don't have time to waste," Holmes said. "If you do not find this morning's endeavor to be worth your while I shall gladly stand you a few rounds at the Meadowlark."

Juno made some kind of clicking sound deep within his jaw. "Get on."

Holmes instructed the country constable to park his wagon around the far side of the hotel. Quietly we slipped through the servants' entrance and had the room opposite the Whitshire sisters unlocked. All of the guests were at breakfast and so the guest rooms were completely silent and void. Holmes was peeping through the curtains he had just closed.

"There he is!" Holmes hissed.

Juno took his place at the crack in the window dressing.

"All right, Mr. Holmes. You have produced a mysterious figure in black creeping from the maze. You have my attention."

We crossed the room and put our ears to the door. There was a slow creaking upon the main stairway, and then silence for several moments. The next sound was the tumble of the lock across the way.

"He's got a key!" Juno whispered.

"A trivial matter for a criminal fabricator of his talent," Holmes said. "Give him a few moments more."

Holmes ticked off the count to three with his fingers and then we burst forth into the hallway. There, framed in the open door as pretty as a picture, was Nigel Horne with his hand in Minuet Whitshire's jewelry box. Quickly he yanked the genuine necklace out and tossed in the replacement before frantically glancing about the room. He turned and began wrenching at the window.

"Please, Mr. Horne," Holmes said. "It is a sheer three-story drop to the ground. You may not survive it and you surely won't escape that way."

Horne turned to face his captors, calm seemingly washing over him.

"This is it, then?" he asked.

"There are but few criminals who have impressed me, Mr. Horne. I count you among them."

"And yet it will be the shackles for me."

"The gallows more likely," Holmes said.

"You can spare the girl," I said.

"What girl?"

"Why, Emily Reynolds!"

Horne snorted. "Why bother."

My fists were clenched and my aspect red. "Is she not dear to you? You certainly kissed her thusly."

"I kissed her because I could. She is in my power completely."

"Was in your power," Holmes corrected. "How?"

"She is a naive idealist, blind to the ways of the world. She was so eager to help the downtrodden, particularly a fellow artist. It was easy to win her affections with my tragic story." Horne smirked at me.

"Which was?" I managed through clenched teeth.

"Mr. Horne was a jeweler or at least a jeweler's apprentice," Holmes said. "That much is clear from his craft. He enjoyed an education far beyond his means, as is evidenced by his art, his manners, and his dress. He was cast aside unfairly, and by a young woman, perhaps a fiancée, as is evidenced by his self-loathing, and his choice of enterprise."

"Simple," Horne sneered. "I thought you were meant to be clever, Mr. Holmes."

"So you compromise Miss Reynolds and then use her disgrace against her?" I said.

"Steady, Watson," Holmes said. "Mr. Horne is playing a bigger game. You involved Miss Reynolds in one of your thefts, knowingly or unknowingly on her part, and then used that to drive a wedge of control deeper and deeper."

Horne's smirk faltered a little.

"I'm guessing you told her a tale of a family heirloom, a wedding band that was both sentimentally and monetarily irreplaceable to you perhaps. Maybe that was even true?"

Horne's mouth was flat now.

"In any event, it was the perfect romantic wound for Miss Reynold's to heal, and it allowed you to impress her with your own, not inconsiderable, artistic skill. Now you were in control and you drew her further and further into illegal behavior, inch by inch, until she was fully enmeshed in your scheme. You used her good nature and independence to turn her against her own father, her own art, and her own best interests. Like a snare everything she did just allowed you to squeeze tighter."

"That's right, I've had my fun with her. Let the law take its course, and let the devil take me," Horne said to a very befuddled Constable Juno.

"I appreciate your discretion, Mr. Holmes," Emily Reynolds said. To see her now, perched upon the chaise at Baker Street, restored in effect and appearance, was to appreciate how much she had wilted in the shadow of her oppressor.

"It was a personal satisfaction to me to catch the man in the act and thus strike him where it would pain him the most, in his twisted pride. Unlike his other victims, the Whitshire sisters reveled in the infamy and were delighted to allow a case to be brought against the man. There was no need to draw you into it."

"I'm sorry to be so much trouble to everyone," Emily sipped her tea. "I feel like such a fool."

"There, there," I said. "It is a sad fact that people of conscience are always vulnerable to people without conscience."

"Who was Nigel Horne? Why did he torment me?"

"The name is an alias, of course. Some wearisome afternoon I may delve into my lumber room and tease out his particular identity from my library, but for now, it suffices that he was a man at loose ends and apparently without recourse to his specialized trade."

"Whyever not? For all of his horribleness, he was truly gifted."

"While I hesitate to guess, I do find his cruelty towards wealthy young women to be suggestive, but not definitive. I suspect that you were caught in a reenactment of sorts, though perhaps with the roles reversed. Mr. Horne was a man fixated on the past. My polar opposite in a way and that was my blind spot."

"How do you mean, Holmes?" I asked.

"After observing him at work I now believe that his original vocation was, in fact, art restoration. What I took to be a new technique was, in fact, a very old one. It seems he took the art of Roman dichroic glass and applied it to paste."

"I'm afraid I don't follow, Mr. Holmes," Emily said.

"Nor I," I said.

"Another test for paste is to examine the reflections within a jewel," Holmes explained. "A natural gemstone, once cut, will reflect like a kaleidoscope, each face in a different direction. Paste, even when cut, does not share this property. All the reflections will be aligned."

"Remarkable!" Emily said.

"And useful in detection for those times you can't handle an item directly. However, the ancient Romans discovered that integrating gold powder into glass restores the kaleidoscopic effect. As you know I spent a few years knocking about the British Museum before I found my calling. That collection holds several remarkable examples. Horne must have learned this old trick during his apprenticeship and then hit upon the idea to apply it to paste. Impurities in the gold dust he scavenged interacted poorly with the lead oxide and potassium carbonate in the paste, causing a visible separation."

"Too clever for his own good," I said.

"At every step," Holmes nodded.

"What have you told my father?" she hesitated.

"Nothing at all. I was quite clear that I would only give him such information as was needed to secure your safety."

"Without calling upon him to pay you, which would betray my secret, I'm afraid I can only give you what little Nigel left of my earnings," she produced a small purse.

"I'm sure you will meet people during your artistic rambles through the city that need that more than I," Holmes said. "Another client will be padding my coffer presently."

"Perhaps I might offer you a drawing then?"

"There are quite enough portraits of me in The Strand."

"What of your beloved Baker Street?"

I was surprised to see Holmes retreat wistfully into himself for a moment. "I would be glad to see it."

As I escorted Miss Reynolds out I warned her, "Mr. Holmes is most particular about details. Most particular."

When I closed the door I notice the post had arrived. As had become usual there were two perfumed envelopes, one ivory, another a deep speckled grey. Each was perfumed and each was written in an eccentric yet undeniably feminine hand. It seemed both Arietta and Minuet Whitshire remained quite charmed with Holmes, even after his ruse had been revealed. If anything, discovering the famous detective's true identity only whet their appetites.

"Are you quite sure neither of them has the slightest interest in your biographer? I am a war hero, you know, and a bit of a sensation in the literary world."

"Take them both as far as I'm concerned," Holmes embraced his violin and began sawing aimlessly. "As for me, I've been thinking of a continental retreat. Do you believe two or three years would be long enough to throw them off my scent?"

The Adventure of the Pharoah's Tablet

Left to his own devices my friend Sherlock Holmes would hardly set foot outside of Baker Street, preferring that the cases which provide his livelihood be brought before him, rather than requiring him to venture out. His sustenance would come from Mrs. Hudson, his chemical supplies brokered by telegram, his tobacco, and newspapers delivered by standing arrangement. Indeed I daresay it was providential for Holmes that Stamford found himself in a position to arrange our meeting. My stories brought Holmes a certain fame, and with that fame came cases too outre to be solved second hand, and clients too demanding to allow Holmes to remain seated in his club chair by the hearth of 221B Baker Street. Then again, on a dull day such as this in the dreadful month of September, I could at least serve as the great detective's personal secretary, for as of late his post would accumulate unopened in the nooks and crannies of the flat. Holmes had come to feel that cases of sufficient import and intrigue should be pleaded in person, or at the very least by telegram.

So it was that I sat at the table with a letter opener in hand, gutting envelopes like fish. Most of the queries were trite and banal as Holmes feared, but those few that seemed to me to hold some interest I would read aloud. Holmes' response was often no response at all, although a few elicited a weary sigh, and others were plucked from my hand and fed to the fire. Such was the case for the card currently pinched tightly between my fingers. Holmes was grasping the other end and we were in a tug-of-war.

"We've nothing else on," I said.

"You've struck upon a combination of the two least interesting topics in the world. First, ancient history, that dreary subject wherein there is nothing left to happen and every aspect has been exhausted. Second, mumbo jumbo, or parlor tricks for the simple-minded, who, by the way, never appreciate it when I pierce the veil of their intellect with the blade of rational inquiry."

"Professor Morgan's salons are quite exclusive, Holmes. To be honest I'm surprised even you were invited. Thus far they have been the purview of royalty and captains of industry and government."

"Dull company, indeed."

"If you suppose the Professor a charlatan then take this as a challenge to expose him."

"I am being invited to play his game by his rules. My attendance would be an implied endorsement, and should the illusion prove insoluable to me at the moment, a validation of the professor's absurd claims."

"Ah, you fear the man is your mental superior."

"I can't count my peers on one hand and Professor Morgan is most certainly not among them."

"I shall send the RSVP, then."

"If at the same time, you make a reservation for a late supper at Simpson's then I suppose the evening will not be a total waste."

After I had dispatched the message I spent the rest of the afternoon infused with a great sense of satisfaction. I had managed to pry Holmes loose from his chemical bench for at least one night. I also looked forward to seeing the Professor's metamorphic tablet myself. No doubt Holmes was right and it was a simple parlor trick, but the thing had a certain notoriety and cachet this season in London, and it would be a coup to be among the select few to have seen the thing. The thought of capping it all with some roast beef and Yorkshire pudding didn't go amiss. I warmed my stomach with some brandy in anticipation and pondered what question I might ask the all-knowing tablet. Before I knew it I was roused from my daydreams by the chiming of the clock. I quickly shaved and slipped into my evening suit, which hung ever pressed and ready but rarely used in my bureau.

Holmes had made no concessions to the refinement of the event or the illustrious company which we were about to join, remaining in the same clothes he had worn for days. Thankfully when he exchanged his housecoat for a jacket and combed his wild hair the effect was not wholly unsuitable. As a bit of a celebrity known for his Bohemian habits, Holmes was allowed a certain degree of latitude, much like a painter or a musician. Mrs. Hudson straightened my tie and simply tsked at Holmes as we stepped out into the fine London evening. At this time of day, cabs were easily hailed and soon we were clopping towards Hightown Manor, London home of Lord and Lady Grantlee. When we arrived I saw the place had been strung with paper lanterns, giving an Oriental impression to the proceedings. We were received at the door by a fatigued butler. These seasonal homes were easy postings for much of the year, but the staff was forced to severely muster when the Grantlees came to town.

"You are the first to arrive, Mr. Holmes and companion," he intoned. "Please, repair to the sitting room and I shall pour a drink for you."

"Nothing for me," Holmes said. "My faculties shall remain sharp."

"Very good, sir."

"As one of naturally dull faculties I may safely take you up on your offer," I said.

The man bowed slightly and we were left alone in the sitting room. The walls were papered in pink with a trefoil motif, and the furniture was rosewood polished to a high sheen. Everything that might reasonably be gilded was, and a few other things besides. On one wall was a hunting scene, the autumn trees painted in warm colors. On the opposite side, a painting of a ruddy-cheeked woman gazed benevolently down, pearls trickling down from her ears, around her neck and down onto her bodice. Her puffed sleeves alluded to an older era, but something in her countenance belied a modern understanding of the world, and I suspected this depiction was of the current Lady Grantlee.

The warmth of my sherry had just begun to spread across my cheeks when the next guests arrived. He was a man of receding hairline and sagging countenance, his suit was of fine material, but a conservative grey and well worn. She, on the other hand, wore a dress of a violent purple hue cut in what I understand to be the latest fashion, and yet the material and construction were cheap, even to my eye. Holmes had no doubt observed all of this and no doubt more by the mere reflection of the window, before turning around and offering his hand to the man in a supercilious fashion.

"Deputy Mayor Umberton, I don't believe we have had the pleasure," Holmes said.

Umberton sputtered as he shook Holmes' hand, unaccustomed to being recognized. "And you, sir?"

"Mr. Sherlock Holmes, consulting detective."

"And you must be Dr. Watson," the man nodded to me. "Obviously I know who you are, but how do you know me?"

"It surely isn't because he has done anything of interest to a detective," the woman said, sidling up to Holmes.

"My wife, Mrs. Umberton," Umberton sighed.

"My friends call me Dolly."

"Indeed, Mrs. Umberton? As you say, the Deputy Mayor's career has been beyond reproach. An unimaginative drone plugging away for the good of the hive."

"Why see here…"

"Your suit is bespoke, Saville Row, Harrington and Son if I am not mistaken. The habiliment of the powerful, and yet I daresay you own but...three...suits and they are pressed into constant service. By contrast, most men who own such a suit easily own a dozen more and wear them only a few times a season, tossing them well before they develop shiny elbows and frayed cuffs. You have the poor eyesight of a man who squints at documents all day but not the calusses of a man who writes not the sleeves of a man who types. A solicitor perhaps, but then a solicitor would have never ceded control of this conversation so easily. A scholar would never forsake his spectacles nor have spent a tenth as much at the tailor. A politician then, but not one who shakes many hands, not a senior functionary. Cross-referencing the known facts in my mental index I arrive at you, Deputy Mayor."

"Astounding!"

"Deduce me, next!" Mrs. Umberton cooed.

"I hardly think it will be the attention you desire, dear lady."

"My friends will be positively envious that the famous Sherlock Holmes applied his deductive reasoning on me."

"Unlike your husband's suit, your raiment is a cheap imitation, perhaps passing muster at a distance but up close surely any person who cares about such things must see right through the deception. So, you do not spend much time in direct proximity with the elite to whom you aspire, but if seen in passing, through a carriage window perhaps, you wish to appear current and en vogue. A woman's wedding ring is telling in many ways, amongst them that it is the best piece the groom could afford at the time of the happy nuptials. Yours, a modest but precious band, is in line with your husband's place in the world, as is your necklace, your earrings, your brooch, your hairpin, all just as we would expect them to be for a man of a middling government career's means. And yet this perfume..." Mrs. Umberton flushed now, "ambergris and civet, rare floral extracts from the sub-continent, that cost a pretty pound."

"You are mistaken, Mr. Holmes," she said, now shying away.

Holmes pursued, "I assure you I am not. I have quite the developed olfactory sense and I am developing a treatise on the topic. Perfume, being always artificially introduced to an environment, is an invaluable detection tool. It can linger for hours after its wearer has departed, and a custom scent like this is as singular as a fingerprint."

"I assure you, Mr. Holmes, this is but a common scent from a bottle presented to me by my loving husband."

"Perhaps," said Holmes, smiling to himself.

"Let the lady be," came a booming voice from the doorway. "Perfumes and cosmetics are no fit subject for a man to know of in any event. Let the ladies have their feminine mysteries, we've worlds to conquer."

This new speaker was an aged man in elaborate military dress. I, of course, immediately recognized the eccentric plumage of a veteran of the Crimean War. His white whiskers were carved into an elaborate design upon his face. His skin remained a dark chestnut against his white hair as if the sun he had absorbed almost four decades prior continued to roast him. His watery eyes were nearly lost in a web of wrinkles. At his elbow hung a striking young woman, her skin an exotic bronze, her amber eyes upturned ever so slightly. A high necked dress of emerald and gold held close about her. I felt my bile stir as my first thought was that the man, this ancient Colonel, had somehow absconded with a child bride after developing a taste for the exotic during his time in the collapsing Ottoman Empire.

"My granddaughter, Elizabeth," he said directly to me, as if reading my mind, soldier to soldier. "She goes in for all of this spiritual rot, as did her mother. Too much savage blood still in her."

"And you, Colonel?" I said icily, putting a stop to any further insulting comments.

"John Mathers, 1st Brigade of the Light Division, marched on Sevastopol. I've seen what happens when magic meets lead and I'll tell you which one wins out every time."

"Excellent, our little party is now complete," said the man now entering. It was easy to recognize the Professor, who, as the man of the moment, had been depicted in every newspaper and upon dozens of posters and flyers. Immediately behind him was the living incarnation of the painting upon the wall. As depicted, Lady Grantlee had a mischievous twinkle in her eye as she came in and graciously welcomed everyone.

"Let us get down to business, shall we?" the Professor said. "I have invited tonight some of the greatest skeptics in London, for it is a trifle to amaze the uncritical, but an achievement to convince those such as yourselves. I am confident that when you have witnessed the metamorphic tablet of Ra-Atet you shall be my greatest disciples."

"Ha!" scoffed the Colonel. "Have at it then, I mean to be at the cribbage table at the Officer's Club before the hour has elapsed."

"Grandfather!" chided the beautiful Elizabeth.

"Think nothing of it, my child," said the Professor, "I understand that men such as yourselves do not stand on ceremony, and have no need for pomp and circumstance. Therefore I shall ask Lady Grantlee to retrieve the tablet in the most expeditious manner."

The Lady nodded to the Professor and produced a key from her bosom. With measured steps, she paced the room and unlocked a great cabinet. Inside was a velvet wrapped parcel, a large glass bowl, and a variety of phials and beakers, each labeled with hieroglyphics.

As the Lady began to transfer the things from the cabinet to the table Holmes spoke. "May I inquire as to why Lord Grantlee is not present?"

"I hesitate to say," Mrs. Grantlee responded. "But I suppose we are among trusted company and so I may reveal a little. My husband and I have become convinced of the authenticity of the fortunes predicted by the tablet. The transcendent pharaoh Ra-Atet has given my husband business advice upon which he currently acts. I'm afraid it has taken him abroad, but when he returns our family's wealth will be secure for generations."

"And now you host these salons for others?" Holmes asked.

"The Pharaoh asked it of us, and it is so little in return for the boon he has bequeathed."

"And you, Professor, why does the Pharaoh not favor you with a fortune?"

"As an academic, I do not seek material wealth, but this rediscovery will etch my name in the annals of history. Please, Mr. Holmes, everyone, come see for yourselves."

We pressed around the table, peering at the blank slate before us. I was hard-pressed to decide if the rock could look ancient, but I supposed at the very least it did not appear to be freshly chiseled. Holmes reached for it, but the Professor stayed him.

"I'm sorry, Mr. Holmes, without knowing how the spell works, I hesitate to do anything to break it. Only I may touch the tablet."

"I see. Perhaps I could handle it through the velvet, as Lady Grantlee did."

"Perhaps, after my demonstration."

"Ooh, ancient mummy magic, I can feel it radiating through my whole body!" Mrs. Umberton said.

I looked to Elizabeth who said nothing but was transfixed by the stone. Her grandfather was chomping his cigar in impatience. The Deputy Mayor was tugging at his collar and remained a step back from the table's edge.

"One of you may ask a question of the tablet."

"Oh, let me do it!" Mrs. Umberton declared.

"My granddaughter is the youngest and should have the first crack at your little game. It would do her good to see it for the fraud it is."

"To be honest," said the Professor. "There is one of you I was hoping to impress most of all. I would like to give this honor to Mr. Holmes."

"I should like to decline."

"Really, Mr. Holmes? Surely no one is better placed to put the tablet to the test."

"I share the Colonel's opinion that this is a charade, and you have now tipped your hand that tonight's demonstration was planned specifically to fool me. I say let the Deputy Mayor ask a question. He wants nothing to do with this business and thus is the closest thing we have to a neutral observer."

"What a waste!" said Mrs. Umberton. "To throw away a mystical consultation on the most boring man in the room. You'd do as well to have the chair ask a question."

72

The Deputy Mayor's jaw clenched and he stepped forward. "Very well, Great Ra-Atet, I have a question for you. Will I ever again know a moment of happiness?"

It was the Professor's turn now to take measured steps around the room to the cabinet, from which he placed the bowl and retrieved one of the beakers. "The healing waters of the Nile. Ra-Atet draws his strength from this precious fluid, the mother's milk of the world."

"How did you select among the many bottles?" Holmes asked.

"The particular bottle is trivial. Each is but a sip from that life-giving confluence, packed out discretely. The Egyptians guard the water most jealously."

"Even so, why keep the water in separate jars?"

"Why do you isolate the specimens in your scientific studies, Mr. Holmes? To prevent cross-contamination for one. To minimize the chance of losing everything to a careless breakage for another. Further, the water has a spiritual integrity, and to jumble it all up would be to lose all of that."

Holmes curled his lip with contempt but said nothing. The Professor now uttered a Coptic prayer while gently pouring the contents of the beaker into the bowl. When it was full he reverently lifted the tablet and laid it down in the water. After a few moments, the water became hazy and then opaque. Holmes leaned over the bowl, intently gazing down. The liquid bubbled and fizzed, releasing an eerie, dense vapor that crawled over the edge of the bowl and across the table. When finally the fluid was at rest again the Professor reached down, probing for a moment before pulling forth the tablet, now inscribed in an unsettling, willowy script. At first, I thought it to be more hieroglyphics or some ancient cuneiform, but at last, I saw it to be English, merely inscribed with strange spacing and overlapping letters.

"What does it say?" Mrs. Umberton cried.

"The House of Umberton knows relief already, before truth, and an end to ruination."

There were gasps heard round the room.

"That didn't really answer the question, did it?" Holmes said.

"It says Umberton, clear as day!" said the Deputy Mayor.

"The great Pharaoh Ra-Atet knows our name!" Mrs. Umberton cheered.

"I'll inspect that table for myself if you don't mind!" said the Colonel.

"I'm afraid the tablet is in a delicate state after transmogrification."

"I'll just bet it is," the Colonel said.

"Grandfather!" Elizabeth tugged at the man's sleeve with her delicate fingers.

"You had said I might examine it?" Holmes said.

"If you come back in the morning something can be arranged," the Professor replied. In the meantime, I shall provide you with a rubbing. And you as well, Mayor Umberton, of course."

Lady Grantlee produced sheaves of paper and a thick charcoal, with which the Professor transferred the image on the stone.

"You must send word of the accuracy of Ra-Atet's prediction," The Professor said. "Promise us!"

"Perhaps we could tell you in person, at your next salon?" Mrs. Umberton said. "I expect there will be more famous people there?"

"Delighted to have you, my dear lady. Now, the spirit of the Pharaoh is exhausted. Let us all retire for the evening and wait to hear the Deputy Mayor's happy report!"

Holmes and Elizabeth took this last opportunity to peer down into the dark water, a reflection of Holmes' suspicion and the girl's wonder peering back up at them. The Professor had encircled Holmes with a convivial arm to lead him away and Lady Grantlee was pressing the rubbing into my hands. Of a sudden, we were back on the street. The Umbertons were already climbing into their carriage.

"It was simply divine," said Mrs. Umberton, "and did you hear, we can come back again! I must send a letter to absolutely everyone."

The Deputy Mayor himself looked ill as he sunk back in his seat.

The Colonel stepped in front of us. "Mr. Holmes, as a modern man of reason you know as well as I do that what we just witnessed was poppycock. And the way we were hustled out of there afterward, that seals it. You can prove the man is a fraud, can't you?"

"Not yet, but a fraud he must be, and so the evidence must be as well. I mean to take the professor up on his offer and inspect the thing tomorrow."

"I'll stand you three gold sovereigns and an evening at the Lion and Sabre if you can prove it."

"The satisfaction of proving the truth of the matter shall be enough."

"Mr. Holmes shall graciously accept the prize as well," I hastened to add. Our income was fickle but our expenses were not. Mrs. Hudson would have my head if I let a year's rent trickle through our fingers.

"Make sure you are truly seeking the truth," Elizabeth said. "The answer you seek may not be the answer you want."

"Perhaps we could consult with you further on this matter, Miss?" I interjected.

"Get in the carriage, Elizabeth," the Colonel said. "You don't need to be wasting Mr. Holmes' time, and no one needs to be wasting any of yours." He eyed me as he pulled himself up into his seat and they clattered away into the night.

The next morning we received word of the success of the tablet's prediction, but not from Deputy Mayor Umberton but rather from our old acquaintance Inspector Althelney Jones.

"A proper hash you've made of this, Mr. Holmes," Jones said as he removed his hat.

"I beg your pardon?"

"The Deputy Mayor's home robbed, right out from under your nose."

"I have never had the misfortune of attending Mr. Umberton in his abode."

"Maybe not, but you knew it was going to happen."

"How could I?"

"You heard the Sphinx's riddle, the Deputy Mayor told us so himself. 'The House of Umberton knows relief already, before truth, and an end to ruination.' While I think you take all too much credit for the luck and happenstance which places criminals in your lap, even I will admit you have a knack for little puzzles. Even Mr. Umberton himself easily cracked the code once he came home to a burgled house. If he can do it, Mr. Sherlock Holmes would have known the answer to the riddle right off the top."

"Yes, well, the Sphinx is a Pharaoh and the riddle is a fortune and it is a trivial matter to see the solution to any puzzle that has already been pieced together. You yourself excel in the field, Inspector."

"Ta, Mr. Holmes, but that still doesn't explain why you allowed the burglary."

"I allowed nothing."

"That's not the way it looks, Mr. Holmes."

"I have an appointment with Professor Morgan to view the tablet this morning. Why don't you come along? It may clear a few things up."

The three of us climbed into Jones' carriage and were soon back at the Grantlee Manor. Lady Grantlee herself soon attended us in the familiar parlor.

"I had expected to speak with the Professor," Holmes said.

"He has been summoned by half of London to provide assurances after last night."

"Last night?"

"Well, Mr. Holmes, I struggle to put it delicately but the events of last night showed that the deductions of a famous detective do not hold a candle to the predictions of the Pharaoh Ra-Atet."

"Is that what was shown?"

"Did the Pharaoh not predict exactly what was to occur? Even with that prediction in hand, did you not fail to prevent the robbery?"

"I believe I have the Professor's permission to examine the tablet?"

"I suppose he did say he would allow it yesterday evening." Lady Grantlee carefully stepped around the room in a now-familiar pattern. She extracted the tablet from the locked cabinet and carefully laid it upon the table.

Holmes set upon it with his magnifying glass. Gently he lifted a corner of the tablet from beneath the velvet and let it drop to the table again.

"Please be careful, Mr. Holmes. This is already an unprecedented liberty you are being allowed."

"What of the Nile water, might I inspect that?"

Lady Grantlee moved to block Holmes. "Even I do not handle the water, Mr. Holmes. Further, that was not part of the agreement you had with the professor."

"Alas, I suppose you are right. One last thing before we leave, Lady Grantlee. My partner Dr. Watson has misplaced his pocket watch and I suspect he may have left it here by accident. The clasp is loose you see, and comes easily undone."

I wasn't sure what Holmes was up to but I casually moved my hand to my vest pocket to obscure my watch. I was much surprised when my thumb met the vacant lining of my vest. There was a twinkle in Holmes' eye as he patted his own pocket.

"I am not aware of any pocket watch being discovered."

"I'm afraid I really must insist. It is a plain watch of little monetary value but it has passed from his father to his brother and now ultimately to Watson himself. I know it to be of great sentimental value. I imagine a reward would not be out of order should one of your staff have discovered it."

"Ah, yes indeed," I said to Holmes. "There will certainly be a just reward when my watch is returned."

"Fine, but then I really must ask you to conclude our visit. The Professor will no doubt gladly receive you at a more convenient time." She moved to the doorway and called back into the house, "Charlotte, Petunia, come here!"

While her back was turned Holmes seized a beaker from the cabinet and, uncorking it, poured the contents over the tablet which then hissed and fumed.

"Mr. Holmes!" Lady Grantlee gasped. "This is outrageous! You will leave at once and you are not welcome to return!"

"Wait!" said the Inspector. "The tablet is forming words."

They were so shallow as to be barely perceptible and contained entirely within the liquid splash, but plainly enough the tablet read: Easy lies and sneaky hands reveal the desperation of Sherlock Holmes.

"Dash it, Holmes if you have dragged me into a mummy's curse I'll have you breaking rocks for the rest of your days!" Jones said.

"Go now, you are not welcome in this house!" Lady Grantlee said.

"Take the tablet into evidence, Inspector, and the so-called water as well."

"I'm going nowhere near that thing! Besides, the only act of which it is evidence is your boorish behavior."

"Tell Professor Morgan that he can expect the three of us for his weekly salon and that the Inspector will be bringing his handcuffs," Holmes said.

"Don't you worry, I'll be telling the Professor all about this, and writing to my husband as well."

I saw Holmes' face fall for just a moment. "Until then, Lady Grantlee. I do apologize, I sometimes forget myself in the pursuit."

"I can't believe what I just saw, Mr. Holmes! The metamorphic tablet of Ra-Atet is real, and it is out to get you!" said the Inspector.

"I can't believe what I saw either," Holmes said. "Just make sure that you are back here this Saturday evening. I'm going to give you the arrest of the decade. You'll have your cuffs on the wrists of the spirit of Ra-Atet or you'll have them on the wrists of Sherlock Holmes."

Holmes would see no other callers that week, spending the days out of the flat. I was able to gather that he had commandeered the chemical lab at St. Bart's, eventually leaving with a laden satchel. For a shilling, I was able to prise from the Irregulars that Holmes had sent them running all over London with a shopping list of strange ingredients to be obtained from the most unusual vendors. Following him myself I watched him disappear into the King's College secret archives. He was out all night that time. On another night as I passed to the water closet, I saw Holmes hunched over his chemical bench, tendrils of smoke cascading down.

"You've almost cracked it, Holmes!" I said. In reply, he lobbed a pestle in my general direction without even looking up.

At long last Saturday evening had arrived. Holmes sat perfectly still in his chair, his long, slow breaths evident from the gentle billowing of his pipe. I had often seen Holmes like this, perfectly composed, perfectly at ease. It was only while waiting to spring the final trap on his prey that he achieved this state of transcendental composure. I ate my roast and his as well, knowing that he would take no food until the case was through. Inspector Jones knocked shortly after dinner and we were off. When we arrived at Grantlee Manor the Umbertons were present, as was Colonel Mathers and Elizabeth. The room was packed, in fact.

"It seems word has circulated that the Pharaoh Ra-Atet and the great detective Sherlock Holmes mean to have it out," the Professor smirked.

"I told absolutely everybody," said Mrs. Umberton.

The Colonel leaned into Holmes conspiratorially, "You've got him, old boy, I can see it in your bearing. Good hunting!"

"I have to express some surprise," said the Professor. "Ra-Atet already revealed you for the cad you are."

"I agree that a cad has been revealed by this tablet."

"Why trade barbs with me when we can hear directly from the Pharaoh?"

"Capitol suggestion."

The Professor nodded at Lady Grantlee, who began her customary procession around the room. The crowd parted easily before her. She extracted the key and turned it in the lock, the mechanism easily audible in the silent tension. The bowl was produced, and the wrapped stone. Lady Grantlee gently folded back the covering, as if she were unswaddling an infant. The silent crowd now began to murmur. She laid it down to rest in the bowl.

"You've had a week to try to outsmart Ra-Atet," said the Professor. "What question do you put forward?"

"The only possible question," Holmes said, slipping into a dramatic register. "Oh, most venerable Pharaoh Ra-Atet, I bow before your secret knowledge and testify to its ultimate truth, I beg of you to reveal that which I cannot, and demonstrate the mastery of genuine wisdom here before these assembled witnesses."

The crowd, myself and Jones among them, murmured in surprise.

"Have your bracelets at the ready," Holmes whispered.

An empty smile played across the Professor's face, but only for a moment. With a minuscule shrug, he proceeded to the vials of Nile water and plucked one forth, holding it up to the crowd as he began his Coptic incantation. He paused just as the liquid was about to leave the container and cocked his head at Holmes one last time. My friend, for his part, had folded his hands together and stooped contritely. I widened my stance and shifted back and forth on the balls of my feet. Holmes would genuinely assume that pose for no man, he was a viper lulling his prey before the strike.

The water trickled from the glass and began to sizzle upon the surface of the tablet. A malicious grin now split the Professor's face. He dumped the rest of the container out into the bowl, and it smoked and bubbled and churned. It was Holmes' turn to smile now.

"Pluck it out, reveal the truth to us all Professor."

Morgan's face had dropped, beads of sweat now bespeckled his brow. "Wait!"

"Wait? Wait for what? The Pharaoh has endured the eons to convey this message to us. Surely the least we could do is bring it into to light."

"Show us, Professor!" Mrs. Umberton cried. The crowd pressed together expectantly.

Morgan hesitantly dipped his hands into the bowl as if he were afraid to touch the water. The tablet was revealed for but a moment when the Professor shouted with rage and attempted to smash it upon the ground. Holmes seemed to have anticipated such a result, for the snatched the tablet from the air the very moment it left the man's hands.

"Colonel Mathers, would you do the honor?" Holmes presented the tablet with a flourish.

"With the greatest of pleasure," the Colonel said, before mumbling to himself as he attempted to decipher the strange writing. "My word!"

Elizabeth gasped and then looked upon Lady Grantlee with that natural sympathy that is the special domain of women.

"What is it?" Lady Grantlee demanded.

"Clear out you lot of benighted poppets," bellowed the Colonel. Some responded at once to his commanding voice, others needed to be prodded by myself and Inspector Jones. Holmes stood fast, barring the exit of Professor Morgan.

"You had best sit down, my Lady," Elizabeth said, taking Lady Grantlee by the arm and leading her to a chair.

"I don't understand," Lady Grantlee said.

"Handcuffs, Inspector Jones, and don't let the Professor out of your grasp," Holmes instructed.

81

With great sadness, the Colonel turned the tablet over to Lady Grantlee. I looked over he shoulder to see the following inscription: Morgan a fraud, Lord Grantlee murdered in Hampstead, SH."

"How can this be? I receive a letter from Lord Grantlee today."

"In fact, you received a telegram."

"Yes."

"Telling you that Lord Grantlee had set sail for Panama to settle a contract personally."

"Yes, but how…"

"Of course the ship to shore telegraphs gave the perfect excuse for short communiques, all in type. The story would allay suspicion for weeks, maybe months. At any time this fictional Lord Grantlee could be disposed of far overseas."

"Fictional?" asked Jones.

"I'm afraid the genuine Lord Grantlee lies under the lakes of West Hyde. An Inspector Caldecott made short work of that nefarious accomplice after I traced back along the lines the telegram Lady Grantlee received. That last, corruptible operator was easily convinced to reveal the sender, for he stood to lose his job or his life."

"But why would you do this?" Lady Grantlee shouted at the Professor. "We have shown you nothing but kindness and charity."

The Professor simply snarled and strained at his restraints.

"I am afraid that to a vicious mind kindness is seen as weakness. And Professor Morgan has become quite vicious thanks to his association with the last living remnants of an ancient society of assassins."

"Absurd!" cried Lady Grantlee.

"His published work reveals his long affiliation with the desert encampment of Abu Shad, and also that he was following the classic arc of going native. His phraseology borrowed more and more from ancient Oriental scrolls until he suddenly ceased publishing. That incantation he uttered over the tablet is actually from a Demotic stelae and invokes a spell of deceit and camouflage. It is essentially a cutthroat's prayer for protection."

"How could he, and you, command the tablet?" asked the Inspector.

"Aha! That is indeed ingenious, although the credit is due to some ancient alchemist and not the Professor." Holmes lifted the tablet above the bowl and began pouring the contents of other bottles upon it. "By delving into Haliburton's *Collectanea Ægyptiaca* I easily determined that the glyphs on the labels were gibberish. That, of course, identified Morgan as a fraud." There was more smoking and hissing and soon he presented to us a tablet completely crisscross with diagonal lines, a tessellation of hundreds of diamonds looking much a serpent's scales."

"What is this?" Jones bellowed. "You have completely destroyed the evidence."

"To the contrary, I have revealed the mechanism of the Professor's charade." Holmes produced two small jars from his pocket, packed with what appeared to be mud. You simply press one compound into the cracks like mortar, leaving open the spaces that form the letters you desire. You then fill those cracks with another compound. The two compounds both dry to look just like the stone of the tablet, but each is soluble in a different solution. By utilizing the right dissolver, the Professor was able to revel only the letters he wanted. For my demonstration, I utilized only the base compound meant not to be dissolved and one dissolvable compound, but I believe the Professor had developed a system for laying different messages on top of each other so that depending on the question he could reveal a particular answer."

"That is why the writing looked so strange," I said.

"Indeed, it is remarkable he was able to craft decipherable messages at all."

A haughty sneer twisted Morgan's face,

"And that is why he was so sensitive about the bottles," said Lady Grantlee.

"Yes, the tablet could be prepared in advance, but the bottles and the revelation were performed live with no room for mistake. He needed to be exactly sure of which bottle revealed which message."

"I've never seen anything like it!" Jones said.

"I don't think many have in a millennia or more. This kind of ancient spycraft is largely impractical, except for magic tricks."

"And schemes against the gullible," Mrs. Grantlee began sobbing. Elizabeth held her shoulders.

"It was a scheme hatched over millennia and forgotten again for as long," Holmes said. "I flatter myself to be a competent chemist and performer, and yet even with my encyclopedic knowledge of criminality I was stymied for a time."

"But how did the Professor predict the future, as he did on several occasions?" Jones asked.

"His predictions amount to confessions, for he committed every predicted action himself, or had them committed anyway."

"The burglary of our house?" demanded Mrs. Umberton.

"Amongst many other deplorable acts."

"Again I ask to what end?"

"Professor, do you care to lecture today?" Holmes asked. The man just barked.

"I expect that shortly you would have received telegrams inviting you to join your husband in Panama, and instructing you in the mechanics of transferring the goods and wealth of the Grantlee estate there. Once completed you would prove as disposable as your husband and the Professor could carry on his researches in comfort as a wealthy expatriate of the Crown. Money would answer any questions asked there, and your disappearance from England would be well-explained. By the time your family or friends raised a definitive alarm, Professor Shelford would be far beyond your, or even my, reach. As with so many of his ilk, his hubris was his downfall. To tweak my nose was sheer folly."

"Perhaps he meant to hang the whole affair on you, Mr. Holmes?" Jones offered.

"Or discredit me at the least. As promised inspector, one would-be Pharaoh, bound and ready to be buried."

The trial kept the Professor and Lady Grantlee in the papers through the winter. She weathered it admirably well, he much less so. The fame he so courted ensured his ultimate rendezvous with the hangman, and I for one can't say I'm sorry for it. Colonel Mathers made good on his promise to toast us and gild our palms. To this day he sends us news of strange little mysteries he believes need debunking. I cannot pry from him a single word about young Elizabeth. We saw the Umberton's but rarely, and it seemed from their reticent manner that they never quite shook the suspicion that Holmes could have prevented their burglary. Holmes himself seemed quite pleased with the outcome, and while predictably Althelney Jones received the credit, Holmes consoled himself with the collection of strange books he had liberated from the library. He would have a new assortment of tricks soon, I imagined. As for me, I was happy enough to sit by the window and supply a few more stories for the old dispatch box. I put this tale aside for a day when it will do the unfortunate Lady Grantlee no more harm.

Criminals don't keep regular hours, and neither do patients, so I was long accustomed to being roused from my repose at all hours. Yet that insistent knocking upon the door of 221B Baker Street, just as I had lost myself in Stevenson's latest novel, was nonetheless vexing. Holmes, of course, took no notice of it, so absorbed was he in pinning some rare specimens of African beetle to his felt entomological board. They were splendid beasts and yet it was impossible my friend was truly oblivious to the racket down below.

"It seems someone wishes to speak with you, Holmes."

"Mrs. Hudson will soon greet our caller."

"If she is forced to rise from bed and dress simply to open the door there will be an earful for each of us tomorrow."

"I am in the midst of a delicate maneuver," Holmes sighed. "You are certainly welcome to make the trip down the stairs and back again."

"It's just that I've had a tipple of brandy, you see," I began just as the debate became moot. Mrs. Hudson's door slammed open at the bottom of the stairs, and an icy reception was offered to the poor soul outdoors. A few moments later Inspector Gregson shuffled up the steps, stooping like a chastised pup.

"Sorry to bother you at this hour, gentlemen," Gregson began.

"Think nothing of it," Holmes replied, turning away from his workbench with a jeweler's loupe still resting in his eye. "We do not keep the same hours as dear old Mrs. Hudson."

"Or rather, she does not keep the same hours as you, Holmes," I replied.

"What brings you here on this fine autumn evening, Inspector?" Holmes asked.

"A bit of an unusual case, as you might expect," Gregson said, sitting heavily upon the loveseat. "A bit sensational. We'd like to get a handle on it before the newspapers muddy it all up."

"The press has already caught wind of it?" Holmes asked.

"Not that I know of, but this kind of thing always finds its way onto newsprint."

"If the opportunity yet remains, I should prefer to see the scene before any journalists have arrived," Holmes said. "They always insist on making such tawdry sketches of me as I conduct my investigations. Of course, the newspaper artists are well-practiced in creating scenes from whole cloth, but at least I shan't be distracted by serving as a live model. I take it you have a carriage waiting?"

"Why, yes, Mr. Holmes," Gregson said with palpable relief.

"Bundle up, Watson," Holmes said. "A cold wind blows this evening."

"You've got the Inspector with you and I'm rather in for the night already," I said.

"Tut, you've had your feet up all day, Watson. A little sport will be good for your constitution."

I cast a longing glance upon my novel as I placed it on the side table and retired to my room to bundle up. It was a night when I felt a gentleman would be well served by a muffler around his collar and a Webley in his pocket. When I returned Holmes was already at the front door calling for me to hurry along. It was a short ride to Bushy Park and a good thing too, for Gregson refused to comment on the case along the way. As we entered the park I noticed policemen standing just off the road at regular interviews.

"Is the road blocked off?" I asked.

"Not as such," Gregson said. "We don't want to draw attention to the situation. And besides there more on foot in here than in a carriage, so a barricade wouldn't do much. We decided to cast a net rather than build a wall. Anyone who wanders by is being redirected out of the area. We're telling them there are convicts on litter brigade further along."

"What is actually further along?" I asked.

"See for yourself," Gregson said as the carriage came to a halt.

We alit and the surrounding park was lost in the deep dusk. Directly ahead three lanterns were placed facing inwards, giving the patch of land in between a shadowless, otherworldly feel. Gregson gestured and Holmes moved forward, examining the ground.

"Judging by the battalion-worth of footprints this is clearly the mushroom that elicited so much interest," Holmes said.

"That is the one that started it all, yes," Gregson said.

On tiptoes, Holmes stalked closer. "Ah, yes, I see."

"Was a group of boys out here with snares and sticks. You can take a couple of rabbits easy and a pheasant or two with a little luck. It's not precisely legal, but nobody is spending any time enforcing poaching laws out here. Plenty for all."

"They didn't take it with them?" Holmes asked. "I would have when I was a boy."

"Of course not! Although I understand they did pick it up before they knew what it was."

"That is unfortunate," Holme murmured.

"The others are intact," Gregson said.

"The others!" Holmes said, practically skipping to the next mushroom. "Ah!" With the toe of his boot, he gently nudged each fungus he came across before letting out a sound of satisfaction.

"What is all of this?" I asked.

"A fairy ring," Gregson said.

"I can see that it is a fairy ring," I replied. "Common cloud funnels; I don't see what all the fuss is about."

"Walk directly to this one," Holmes instructed, indicating the first mushroom he had examined. "You can't do any more damage to the ground there than has already been done."

Somewhat irrationally I paused at the edge for a moment, fearing the curse that would fall upon anyone who broke the sanctity of a fairy circle; nursery rhyme knowledge well known to every child in Britain. I could hear Holmes snort, but I noted that Gregson made no move to cross the circle. Chiding myself I stepped in and knelt by the fungus. On the far side lay a delicate skeletonized hand, the radius, and ulna terminating sharply as if the hand had been severed with a blade.

"There is a piece of this mortal puzzle under every large growth," Holmes said.

"Someone scattered a dismembered skeleton around a fairy ring?" I asked.

"Perhaps," Holmes said. "Or perhaps the fungus colony grew up through a buried body. Was this ever a cemetery?"

"We won't have access to that kind of record until the morning," Gregson says. "But the bones look fresh. Too fresh for an ancient burial anyway."

"Watson, do you concur?"

"It is difficult to date exposed bones precisely, but I would tentatively agree that these are modern remains, and I don't think they were ever buried."

"I'd like to take a few samples if you don't mind, Gregson. I suspect the place will soon be picked clean by morbid gawkers if you don't move the remains. I'd take the mushrooms as well, just in case they contributed to this death. They should be edible but a corpse is always a cause for caution." With that Holmes gathered a morbid curio sack of phalanges, teeth, and hair. He topped it off with a couple of mushrooms and a vial of dirt.

"Clean it all up, then?" Gregson asked.

"Document it twice, then gather it all together and lock it up," Holmes advised. "And send the policemen home so no one can be sure exactly where the ring was. I'll contact you with my findings soon."

"Very good," Gregson said. "The carriage can take you back to Baker Street."

When we settled inside Holmes turned to me. "This may be more in your line than mine, Watson." Then he called up to the driver, "To St. Bart's!"

"Surely it was a gruesome flight of fancy to imagine that the body was torn asunder by villainous fungi," I said.

"I find it remarkable that such things don't happen more often," Holmes replied. "A decaying body is such rich fertilizer. In the ancient caliphates surrounding the Egyptian kingdoms, legend says that squatters would sometime be shackled to saplings and then fed and nurtured until being disjointed as the tree grew. A gruesome form of execution that would sometimes take years."

"Surely not," I objected.

"Don't give Mrs. Hudson any ideas just in case," Holmes laughed.

We soon arrived at my old hospital and Holmes led the way to the pathology lab, as sure as if he were the superintendent. The place was empty this time of night but, of course, my friend had his own keys. With his help, we made quick work of examining the specimens Holmes had collected. "A lady it would seem, a diet high in sugars and acids, drank purified water. Her flesh did not rot away, these bones were cleaned. A body snatcher perhaps?"

"It is not beyond the realm of possibility," Holmes said. "There is yet a macabre trade in human remains for the amateur physiologist."

"Or worse," I spat.

"See what you make of the mushrooms," Holme said.

"As an accomplished naturalist, you have me there, Holmes."

"Just look," Holmes said, indicating a slide he had prepared resting under a microscope.

"It is pitted," I observed.

"Only in this cross-section. Hold one up to the light and you will find it is perforated with tiny passages."

Indeed tiny pinpricks of light shown through all over the fungus.

"Bacterial mycophagy," Holmes pronounced.

"Which developed intro necrotizing fasciitis?" I scoffed. "I've never heard of such a thing."

"Rather the other way round, I imagine. The bacteria ran out of flesh and made a go of it with the meat of the mushroom." Holmes said.

"Have we been exposed then?" I didn't fancy the chemical bath that awaited me.

"We will keep an eye on this sample, but it looks to me as if the bacteria were starved to death."

"Simple misadventure then?"

"I don't see that she wore any clothes, or indeed had any belongings. Unlikely in someone with such healthy teeth, and certainly unusual in a public park, so I expect there is another party involved in some capacity. Of course, the severed hand is also suggestive."

"Where can we even begin? Our only witness is an infested mushroom."

"Perhaps," said Holmes. "Perhaps not. I know of an outre gallery we should visit."

"At this time of night?"

"My dear Watson, the dead of night is the only time this gallery is open."

It didn't make much sense to me but the clock had already struck that dreadful predawn hour when I knew the night's slumber had escaped me, and so I followed my friend back out onto the street. I had expected that we would take a carriage to the East End and so was surprised when Holmes started threading the alleys leading north. We quickly found ourselves in unfamiliar and unseemly territory, with the footfalls of unseen persons seeming to dog us and a disconcerting racket coming from every darkened door. I was just about to pull at Holmes' sleeve and demand that we return to the streets of our London when he suddenly sprinted up some steps and threw open the door of what smelled like an opium den. Only my rational desire not to be left alone on these forbidding streets alone compelled me to enter, my hand resting on the grip of my Webley.

Inside was something like a sitting room but with black lace hanging down from the ceiling over each piece of furniture like mosquito netting. Within each cocoon lulled some dope fiend nodding his or her head to the strange music being picked out on a stringed instrument I did not recognize. Around the room were paintings with images akin to tarot cards, but as if designed by the Grimm Brothers, all cragged trees and blood-red moons. Squires slaughtering strange beasts or sometimes the opposite and, of course, there were pale maidens cavorting in the moonlight. I am a worldly man but it was all a bit too French for my tastes. I wondered exactly why Holmes might be so familiar with this so-called gallery. My friend was at the stairs in a heated debate with a woman who appeared to be the madame of this establishment.

"Absolutely not," she declared, her arm barring Holmes' way.

"I must insist," Holmes said. "Show him my card. Monsieur DeValet will see me."

"It is impossible," the woman said. "He is working and not to be disturbed."

"Mademoiselle, DeValet can speak to me now or speak to the Yard in the morning."

"You have no right," she protested.

"Perhaps we should come back later, Holmes," I intervened.

Holmes sighed. "Perhaps you are right, Watson. *Bon Nuit*," he tipped his hat to the woman.

"Now you see sense," she said, taking each of us by the elbow and moving us to the door. It seemed we weren't the first visitors she had put back out on the streets.

"Perhaps we might make an appointment," I offered, and as the lady considered Holmes spun away from her like a full-back, flying up the stairs before she could yelp. It was my turn now to take her elbow while Holmes quickly raked the lock and flung the door open. The madam had pushed me away and I found myself taking two stairs at a time to try and catch her. Together we burst into the room at the top of the flight and found a man sprawled on the floor with a nearly empty bottle of absinthe in his grasp.

"Oh, Henri, no!" the woman cried, rushing to cradle the man's head in her hands.

"He should vomit before that vile liqueur does him in," Holmes observed.

I fetched a chipped washing bowl from the bureau and handed it to the woman. "Why, Henri, why?" She pulled him forward so he was slumped over the bowl which she placed in his lap. DeValet was unresponsive to her entreaties.

Holmes stepped forward and tossed a snippet of the victim's hair into the bowl. DeValet tossed the bowl away as if it had scalded him and curled up in a ball.

"Give me a name, DeValet," Holmes whispered.

"Mug Ruith," DeValet wheezed.

"The lady's name was Mug Ruith?" I asked.

"Mug Ruith was a powerful druid," the madame interjected. "DeValet has been painting the *roth rámach*."

"Irish folktales," Holmes interjected. "Mythological nonsense."

"I wish that were so, Mr. Holmes," DeValet said, seemingly recovering from his momentary terror. "I am afraid that I have angered the ancient masters with my foolishness."

"How so?" Holmes asked.

"I have painted all the great mythologies, Norse, Egyptian, Mycenaean, Roman, Greek," De Valet said.

"I am familiar with your previous handiwork," Holmes said.

"Until recently I would have agreed with you that it is all nonsense. The Pythagorean Mysteries become a fad one season and are replaced by the fire dances of the Zoroastrians and so on and so forth, and as my patrons chase the latest philosophy I provide the paintings that give the whole affair a certain dignity."

Holmes made a non-committal sound.

"But there is something to this Cycle of Kings, Mr. Holmes. Something like I have never experienced before. It is real, the visions are not just hallucinations. You hold the proof in your hands."

"I hold the remains of a woman who died playing your parlor games," Holmes said. "Supply me with a name, or I have the Yard turning this place over by breakfast."

"We were told her name was Bella," the madame interjected.

"She was not a regular of this establishment?" Holmes asked.

"She was just a model," the madame said. "Most of the young ladies are. This hocus pocus is mostly the domain of wool-headed old men and a few silly ladies. It's an excuse, you know, to obtain these boudoir images, to spend a little time with ladies dressed up like fairies or what have you. Playacting is what it is."

"Pardon me, Madame...?"

"Vivienne Corbeau," she replied. "Yes, it is a horribly false name. Unlike Henri, I have a regular life to live during the day."

"Yes, well, there are any number of establishments in London that provide, ahem, playacting. I don't quite understand this arrangement."

"That's just it, Mr...?"

"Er, Watson," I stammer. "Dr. Watson."

"Of course, who else would be at Mr. Holmes' side. I quite enjoy your stories."

I felt a flush escape my collar.

"The salon, the companionship, all of that is part of an experience that ultimately surrounds the art, and Henri's art is quite splendid. Someday he will be considered a major painter of our age, but for the moment he must toil among the throngs of grasping London artists. We have created an environment that has an element of the salacious without ever being scandalous. None of our patrons need fear being caught out here, but at the same time it is just indecorous enough that there is a thrill to it."

"May we see the paintings she modeled for?" Holmes asked.

"There was only one, and the patron was quick to pick it up. He was gone before Bella came back, even."

"Bella came back after she was painted but before her death?" I asked.

DeValet sobbed. "Cursed she was!"

"She'd taken ill all of a sudden," Corbeau said. "Deadly ill as it turns out. She'd wanted the costume she had worn."

"Costume?" Holmes asked.

"She dressed up as Tlachtga, the daughter of Mug Ruith. Wore a bull skin robe and feathers, the traditional ceremonial dress for the festival of the Hill of Ward."

"She thought the costume was the cause of her illness?" Holmes suggested. "Did you give it to her?"

"Would that I could have, the poor thing," Corbeau said. "The outfit had been provided by the patron, and he had taken it with him again."

"None of this matters," DeValet spat. "The whole thing was brand new, a more perfect bull skin I have never seen."

"And the feathers?" I asked.

"Pristine, straight from the peacock, I'd imagine. It was Mug Ruith punishing us for our sacrilege!"

"That's as may be," Holmes continued, "but I will need to speak to this patron."

DeValet and Corbeau shared a quick look.

"We don't know who he is precisely," Corbeau said. "Part of what our patrons pay for is discretion, and that takes care of itself if we don't ask too many questions. We do recognize some of them of course, but not in this case."

"DeValet, you will provide a sketch of the man," Holmes commanded.

"I never saw his true face," DeValet said.

"I can do it," Corbeau said. "I am nothing compared to DeValet, but I had some tutelage in the arts as a girl." She set about making a charcoal sketch.

"Fine, then, DeValet, you shall provide a sketch of your painting, with every detail accounted for."

"I had the ghoulish things destroyed after Bella's horrible end. Oh the agony, it was a terrible thing to see."

"I can provide the sketches as well," Corbeau interrupted. "I keep the ones DeValet discards. As I say, he will be a great name someday, and someday I will be in want of a comfortable retirement."

"Most accommodating, Madame Corbeau," Holmes said.

"Meet me down in the parlor," she replied.

"And you will be here if I have further questions, DeValet?" Holmes asked pointedly.

"If there is any mercy death will have taken me first," the artist spat back.

A few moments later Corbeau joined us in the parlor and presented us with a couple of loose sketches. The first few were rough figures crudely blocked in.

"Not much to go on, I'm afraid," she said.

"So long as he laid out all of the essential details these shall suffice," Holmes said.

Last in the bunch was a striking charcoal portrait, so remarkable that there was a spark of life to it.

"Why, Madame Corbeau is this your work?" I asked. "If you ask me this is the superior of DeValet."

"Henri is a genius," she replied. "I am but a dilettante."

"You should be making your own fortune, if you ask me," I added.

"Good evening, gentlemen," she ushered us back out.

"Was I mistaken, Holmes, or did that drunken boor just admit to being present at this young woman's death. I'd have put bracelets on him right then."

"Madame Corbeau was being so helpful, and I didn't want to interfere with her. We shall visit Gregson on the way home and advise DeValet's arrest. That will serve the twofold purpose of giving the artist a place to sober up and keep the good Inspector out of our way for a while longer."

As always, behind a thin veneer of bullishness Gregson was quite happy to receive any intelligence Holmes could provide. Because the street addresses in the warren we had just left were casual, to say the least, Holmes put a pin in the station's map to demonstrate DeValet's location.

"You are certain he killed the girl?" Gregson asked.

"I am certain he was present at the event, and he clearly feels much remorse," Holmes said. "DeValet is easily a party to the lady's death, but exactly what part he played I leave to you to discover."

"You've done well on this one, Holmes. If this pans out I'll stand a round tonight, gents. Even you are invited, Lestrade," he called over his shoulder to his rival and our sometimes collaborator. Lestrade responded with a knowing smirk. Each of the policemen could see Holmes' games when they were being played upon the other. I tipped my hat to the other Inspector as we left.

I fell straight into bed when we, at last, surmounted the stairs of Baker Street, without so much as removing my shoes. When I awoke the white tendrils of dawn had been replaced by the red cheeriness of afternoon. I entered the parlor to find Holmes barricaded behind stacks of books. Dream analysis and pagan rituals and all sorts Holmes didn't usually go in for. I idly looked about on the shelves to discover what dusty corner of his collection these tomes might hail from, without success.

"Ah, Doctor Watson," came Mrs. Hudson's chiding voice. "I was a bit disappointed that you left it to me to open the door to every strangler and masher in London last night. Then again, you look as if you have joined their ranks."

Unthinkingly I felt the stubble at my jawline and looked sheepishly down at the clothes I had slept in.

"I was just getting up to answer the knock when you beat me to it," I replied. "In a contest of the spriest, I do not fancy my chances against you."

She clucked but lay the tray she was carrying down upon the table. Removing the cloiche revealed a desultory meat sandwich and some cold tea.

"Ta," I sighed.

"The first time I brought this tray up it was a feast. You slept through that and the next two as well. I may provide a light board but I'm not your cook." With that, she spun on her heel and exited.

"Back at it already, Holmes?" I asked as I poked at the rainbow sheen on the meat.

"Steady on since last night," he replied.

"You need to sleep, Holmes."

"In this case, a little deprivation may serve us well," Holmes said. "What little we know about the patron is encoded in these sketches. Symbols and archetypes, that sort of thing."

"And the excellent portrait Madame Corbeau rendered."

"The lady is a true talent, but this city is home to millions. Even our friends at the Yard don't just wander around with a sketch in hand hoping someone recognizes it."

"Attempting to identify someone with a few token scraps from their unconscious seems just as hopeless."

"Perhaps. The subject of Tlachtga itself is suggestive. She was ill-used by the three sons of Simon Magus and died from grief after giving birth to three boys, one by each of her assailants."

"Ghastly!" I cried.

"The followers of Simon Magus held a different, distinctly unmodern ethos. So, was the patron perhaps casting Miss Bella in the role of mother, perhaps even unwilling mother?"

"Why go through the rigamarole of DeValet's studio?"

"Because the mythology is important to him. He wants to embody that archetype. For the moment I am also presuming he is Irish."

"Pre-Celtic religion just happens to be DeValet's current subject. That may not mean anything."

"The patron came ready with his own costume. With his own costumes if I don't miss my guess. An immaculate bull skin as described is likely a specialty item. That is one place to begin. All the better if one could purchase a peacock mask at the same establishment."

"I'm surprised you didn't leave that plodding work for Gregson," I said.

"Normally I would but in this instance, I think a little more diplomacy is required than the Inspector finds natural."

"What of the other symbols?" I asked.

"The orientation of this wagon wheel indicates a particular time in association with the equinoxes and solstices. It is difficult to know how precise this sketch is, but based upon the ancient constellations depicted above, it suggests a mid-century date. The white flowers wound through it suggest a wedding."

"A wedding sometime in the last fifty years?"

"Or about four thousand years ago or four thousand years in the future. Within the last few decades seems most likely. It reinforces the theme if nothing else."

"That makes the bull skin look more appealing," I said.

"The rest is worse, crows and hearts within trees, triskele, all treacle that could mean anything. We can only hope the combination proves telling as we proceed."

Alongside his more esoteric researches, Holmes had also drafted a list of fine leathercrafters around town. We paid a call on them one by one, beginning with those who might also supply the peacock mask. At each Holmes posed as a customer, asking after an authentic buffalo robe so as not to tip his hand. By the end of the day we had three of the things to cart around, and a bearskin that had been presented to us under false pretense besides. None who produced anything of quality dealt in whole bull skins and none who dealt in bull skins showed signs of artistic quality.

"We are going about this business the wrong way," Holmes sighed. "We need a proprietor who can do top-flight work but we must also account for the parasites."

"Perhaps he works in the theater?" I offered. "That would be in keeping with the patron's apparent affinity for high culture in low places."

"He certainly seems to have a flair for the dramatic," Holmes conceded. "Let us consider for a moment the idea that the patron brought the parasite to the robe, rather than vice versa."

"It is also strange that this well-bred woman has yet to be reported as missing," I mused.

"There are thousands of governesses and lady's maids and other genteel servants in London who might be little missed by the outside world in such a short time. No, let's follow the line of the parasite for a moment. Strange illness, exotic interests, money to spend on garishly eccentric pursuits. Let us exchange our bull skins for dinner jackets," Holmes said.

"What do you have in mind, Holmes?"

"I have long had a standing invitation at the Royal Geographical Society. I'd say it is past time to accept it."

We returned to Baker Street where I am afraid I met a wardrobe of slim choices. I would never pass for one of the peerages but at last, I cobbled together a suit which I felt was presentable. When I returned to the study I found Holmes gazing idly out of the window in an exquisite suit of deep emerald wool woven so fine and smooth I had initially mistaken it for velvet.

"Holmes, where did you ever get such a thing?"

"Dreadful, isn't it? After that Savile Row business, Morton sent it over. You know how our more illustrious clients like their little mementos."

"What Savile Row business?" I asked. "Who is Morton?"

"Last Boxing Day, don't you remember?"

"I remember waiting outside the opera half the evening for you to arrive with the tickets and nearly catching my death of pneumonia."

"Yes, that's right. I was briefly delayed by the Morton case. I'm sure you wrote about it, The Adventure of the Double-Breasted Double-Cross or somesuch."

"This is the first I've heard of any of this. You told me your carriage threw an axle."

"It did," Holmes says. "In any event, Morton sized the suit from memory. Even I would be hard-pressed to do better. Shall we?"

The Society met in Lowther Lodge, a whimsical red brick building of gable pitches and ornate chimneys. Legend had it there were vaults below filled with literal treasure troves of arcane artifacts from around the globe. As we approached, the man at the entrance stiffened for a moment before bowing and sweeping the door open for Holmes. In contrast, I found a white glove pressing against my midriff.

"Is this, er, gentleman with you, Mr. Holmes?" the doorman asked.

"I'm afraid so," Holmes said. "He is most indispensable to me."

"The invitation was really just for you, Mr. Holmes. If we allowed our guests to invite guests and so on and so forth you can see how things would quickly get out of hand."

"Perhaps we should ask Lord Markham?" Holmes pressed. "I am sure he won't object."

"Just let the man in, Stilson!" came a boisterous voice from inside.

Stilson sighed heavily. "Very good."

Inside the Society looked much like any other posh social club I'd ever been in, which was a bit of a disappointment. That feeling only lasted a moment, however, when we came face to face with the figure Madame Corbeau had sketched.

"Mr. Sherlock Holmes, the famous detective," the man bellowed. "What brings you here? If you take it into your head to start exploring the empty spots on the map there will be naught for the rest of us to do, and London will be the worse for it besides."

"Worry not, Professor Flynn, I am here in my traditional capacity."

"You know my name, do you? You are a clever sort."

"I must admit I did not immediately place you, but now that I see the Ordú a Cláirseach órga around your neck, along with your accent and the characteristic discoloration of your fingernails, ears, and nose…"

"Occupational hazard of the professional mycologist, I'm afraid," Flynn said.

"Indeed, I endure a few occupational hazards myself," Holmes said. "Your treatise on the trans-Pacific diaspora of the *amanita muscaria* was most insightful."

"Ha! Men in my line of work have very few admirers," Flynn said. "Let me get you a drink." He whistled through his fingers and a tray of whiskey glasses soon appeared. "Only the finest *uisce beatha*, of course."

We toasted to good health and then I unadvisedly downed the amber liquid. It tasted of wood polish and felt worse as it slowly trickled down my esophagus. I noticed too late that Holmes left his dram swirling in his glass.

Flynn pounded me on the back. "There's a good man. It's my family's private reserve. Comes from sacred peat that was trodden by St. Patrick himself."

I could only wheeze in response. Thankfully Holmes intervened.

"Where have your travels taken you recently?" my friend asked.

"I'm on expedition right here in London if you can believe it," Flynn said. He leaned in close. "I caught wind of an ancient Celtic cairn that has recently been upturned right here in the city. The fool who discovered it thinks it is cursed, so he relinquished his claim to me in exchange for the promise that I would exorcise the place." Flynn laughed cruelly.

"Why did he turn to a mycologist for an exorcism?" I asked.

"I actually went to him. Recognized some unusual specimens in some sketches he had done for me in advance of a painting I had commissioned. Investigating the site I discovered the cairn underneath. A cache of pre-Celtic treasures, and a colony of unknown fungi worth more than the rest. My findings are already in press and the colony removed to a secure location. My fortune is made, gentlemen."

"Might I see the cairn?" Holmes asked. "I have a professional interest in how bodies might be hidden and rediscovered."

"I don't know," Flynn said. "I think it might be wiser to keep my secrets until my findings are published."

"I suppose you are right," Holmes sighed. "I'm afraid the cut-throats of the West End have nothing on those in academia." With that, he raised his glass to Flynn and downed it. "I can never hope for a whiskey this fine again. Might I have another taste?"

"That's the spirit, Mr. Holmes!"

To my surprise Holmes spent the next hour going drink for drink against a man three stone his superior, keeping up a patter of jokes and off-color stories to distract Flynn. Finally, the boisterous scientist was unable to even lift a glass, so Holmes offered to see him home. My friend's eyes were glassy and there was an unusual sway to his step, but he seemed to have held the liquor much better than his rival. When he called for our coats he also slipped a note to the waiter who returned with a concoction that looked and smelled of the liquid refuse of a fish cannery. Holmes downed the loathsome mixture in one gulp and by the time we were on the street he seemed much recovered, apart from the fact that he had donned Flynn's coat and put the somnambulant man in his own.

"I wonder where we shall hail a carriage at this hour, old chums?" he declared loudly to no one in particular. It was only then I realized that Flynn likely had a valet waiting for him and Holmes was trying to throw the man off their scent. It must have worked for no one intervened as we hoisted Flynn to the corner and loaded him into a passing hack.

"Take him to Bushy Park and wait for me, Watson," Holmes said.

"What am I to do if he awakens?" I asked.

"I doubt that will be an issue, but should he rouse do your best to keep him in the park. Lead him towards the fairy circle if you can."

With that Holmes slapped the side of the carriage and it clattered away with myself and Flynn on board. I just had time to see Holmes hail a dogcart before we were around the corner and gone. When we arrived at the locked gates of Bushy Park the cabman took little notice of me dragging an unconscious man out of the vehicle and depositing him on the ground. I supposed those who drive in the lonely hours of the night must be used to all manner of things. Just in case, I pressed a few more coins into his palm before he departed. I waited next to the snoring Irishman for what seemed like an eternity but which my watch only read as slightly less than an hour. Holmes then came stalking down the road with a buffalo skin over one shoulder and a lantern dangling from the opposite hand. He simply nodded to me as he let his burdens settle to the ground and made quick work of the lock on the gate. We spread the buffalo skin out and used it as a liter to carry Flynn to the fairy circle at the heart of Bushy Park. The man slept on, oblivious to the whole affair.

When we, at last, arrived Holmes began stomping around the fairy circle until he found a soft spot in the dirt. We turned the lantern upon it and dug with spades Holmes had secreted in his pockets. The freshly turned dirt soon gave way to a large stone. When Holmes had pried that away there was a black hollow beneath us. Holmes took the lantern and revealed a small chamber within. He slid inside and I watched the light dance around as he made his inspection.

"All right, let's lower him in," Holmes said from below.

"You mean to bury him alive?" I protested.

"Only symbolically," Holmes assured me.

"But we are putting him in a hole in the ground?"

Holmes gestured impatiently so I dragged Flynn by his heels and fed him through the opening to a waiting Holmes, who laid him out as if for his final repose.

"Now, the buffalo skin," Holme said.

I passed that through as well. Holmes wrapped himself in it and produced a feathered mask from the inside of his coat. Then he knelt down and wafted smelling salts beneath Flynn's nostrils. The repugnant mycologist shot bolt upright and regarded the strange figure above him for a moment before screaming.

"Please, Tlachtga, I didn't know this was real," Flynn begged. "I thought it was all a laugh."

Holmes stepped forward and lifted Flynn by his lapels, pressing him into the crumbling dirt above.

"We were modeling for DeValet when the girl lost her breath. Just the spoors, I thought, so we left. She was better once we were away. I paid her the full fee and that was the end of it as far as I was concerned. Then a few days later I hear she is looking for me because she has developed a sickness and she blames me for it. Well, as you can plainly see I developed a sickness too and I blame her for it. These artistic types, beautiful on the outside, rotten on the inside."

Holmes tossed the man to the ground. "You never meant the girl any harm?" he asked in an eerie falsetto.

"I swear to you, Tlachtga, I don't know a thing about her save she said her name was Bella and she wanted me to pay her directly. I had already paid the fee to DeValet's woman, but Bella demanded it all over again. I paid her just to be done with it. Had I known whatever foul taint she carried would eat away at my face like this I can assure you I would have handled the situation much differently. Thank providence I had just had that portrait made. I've had it photographed to be used for publicity. As it is I can only give lectures to darkened halls. I can blame it on the mushrooms, but I shan't see a tenth of the revenue that I might have garnered had not she blighted me."

"That is why you struck her down?" Holmes asked.

"I never saw her again after she demanded her ransom."

"And the robe?"

"Yes, she went on about the robe but I only had it the day of the portrait sitting."

"Where did you get it from?"

"DeValet's woman gave it to me. I understand that the costumes come as part of the service."

Holmes shrugged off the buffalo skin and mask. "Well, this is a merry chase we have been led upon, Watson."

"Holmes?" Flynn gasped. "What is this?"

"My apologies, sir," Holmes said. "We had been led to believe that you had murdered the woman who modeled for your pictures. I'm afraid my predilection for the sensational led me down the wrong path. What we have here is a very trite domestic issue dressed up as a mythological tragedy. Help Lord Flynn up, Watson."

I reached down into the hole and pulled the man out. He yet smelled like a bar rag and I suspected most of this would be but a hazy impression in the morning. Holmes sprung out behind and let out a sharp whistle. Gregson and his men appeared from the trees.

"I heard it all, Mr. Holmes, but I don't know what it means," Gregson said. "Is this our man or isn't he?"

"Well, he has stolen a bit of Britain's history from the heath of this Royal Park, an ancient trespass punishable by death," Holmes said. "However, should those artifacts find their way to the Royal Museum as a donation I don't think there is any need to be draconian about it."

"And my fungal colony?" Flynn asked.

"I think it would be an unconscionable waste to leave that in the hands of anyone other than the top mycologist in Europe. I look forward to reading your paper, sir. Good evening."

An understandably befuddled Professor Flynn wandered off into the Park.

"I say, Mr. Holmes, it will mean my job if I come back empty-handed."

"Let us pray we are not yet too late," Holmes said. "We need to get to DeValet's studio as quickly as we can."

"We still have the man in custody."

"I'm afraid it is Madame Corbeau we need to account for now."

As we galloped across London in the lumbering paddy wagon Holmes explained.

"I must say, it seems like a lot of pomp and tomfoolery to me," Gregson replied.

"That is precisely why I maintain that there is hope for you yet," Holmes said.

The patrolmen quickly turned the studio over but it was Corbeau had absconded.

"If only I were as clever as your stories make me out to be," Holmes said. "She has a day's jump on us and could be anywhere. What are the nearest banks? Cander and Son? No, she'd be conspicuous there. Scottish Widows? Perhaps. Blount's? Yes, part of the Societe Generale, a consortium of banks centered in France. Gregson, see if Madame Corbeau, or any woman of her description, has a vault lease there. I must send a telegram to our friends at the Sûreté."

A sober DeValet was able to fill in many of the gaps for us. It seemed that he had been most beguiled by Bella, falling in love with her instantly, as only a gin-soaked artist can. Madame Corbeau called the girl an unnecessary distraction who caused the painter's work to suffer when she was the subject. In fact, DeValet felt he did his best work when Bella was around.

"So she was not unknown to you," I asked.

"Not at all. I had known her for two blissful years, though I hardly think she took notice of me. Many of these models hope to catch the fancy of a rich husband. The artist is invisible to them. I saw her only infrequently because Madame Corbeau refused to book her. It was only on those rare occasions when she was out and I made the arrangements myself that I could bring my beautiful Bella in on a job."

"Why did you not tell us this before?" Holmes said. "We might have saved some time."

"I was not in my right mind, for one. The most recent crate of absinthe which Madame Corbeau brought back from France seems unusually potent. Besides, I do not believe Bella's family are aware of her exertions. They have lost their daughter once already. To find out she lived a secret life of scandal would be too much to bear I should think."

"Has it ever occurred to you that Madame Corbeau herself might be the villain in all of this?" I asked.

"To what end?" DeValet asked.

"It is my surmise that she loved you," Holmes said. "In her own villainous way. At the same time, she hated you, jealous of the attention you received when she was the superior artist."

"Madame Corbeau an artist? I think not," DeValet said.

"And that oversight cost Bella her life," I said. "Unable to disentangle you from the girl, Madame Corbeau decided to murder her and ruin you in one swoop."

"Impossible!" DeValet said.

"We have caught her in a number of lies already, including framing an innocent man. Worse, she has long been stockpiling your art as a nest egg, and the moment we arrived she put her plan to escape into action."

"But for a murder, it was so poorly done," DeValet said.

"Poisons are a tricky business, and outre poisons even more so. Had Miss Bella not had an allergic reaction to the mushroom spoors she would likely have died on the spot, along with Professor Flynn and perhaps even yourself. As the wearer of the tainted bull skin, Bella was exposed to certain parasites to an extent that eventually proved lethal. Professor Flynn received only an incidental exposure, and I believe even that was mitigated by the mushroom colony he saw fit to steal. The parasites seem to be as attracted to that as to human flesh. Nonetheless, he will be scarred for life."

"As will we all."

"When Miss Bella returned demanding satisfaction Madame Corbeau took the opportunity to finish the job, returning the stricken girl to the place of her fatal allergy creating her own morbid tableau. Little did she realize the symbiotic relationship between the parasites and the mushrooms would quickly create a more gruesome scene than she could have dreamt of. Have you any paintings of a dismembered woman lying within a circle? Or worse, sketches of a design yet unpainted?"

"That could describe dozens of paintings I have made," DeValet said. "The general composition is reminiscent of The World card in the Tarot, but women represent fertility, the cycles of nature, motherhood and more. And circles are just as multifaceted."

"Did Bella ever pose for such a painting previous to this?" Holmes asked.

DeValet's face fell.

"Where is that painting?"

"Madame Corbeau manages the practicalities," DeValet said.

"It will soon be discovered," Holmes said. "It is the smoking gun meant to convict you if her frame-up of Professor Flynn did not take."

"This is beyond belief, Mr. Holmes!" Gregson objected.

"And yet, listen to the newsboy," Holmes replied.

Indeed, through the window, we heard the whelp's pitch. "Madman artist paints his murders before committing them! Every shocking detail for twopence!"

Gregson yelled out the window for the boy to hand a newspaper over. He was refused until he had coughed up the 2p.

"Well, I'll be, the blaggards!" Gregson said, crumpling the paper and throwing it at the floor.

I picked it up and smoothed it out. "*The Globe* has made a breakthrough in the faltering investigation of the Bushy Park Witch Slaying," I read. "A salacious painting had been delivered to our offices proving that eccentric artist Henri

DeValet has long held murderous designs upon the woman, known only as Bella, found in Bushy Park. It is impossible to ignore the occult aspects of the bloody murder and we can only lament that the poor girl had lost her soul to Satan afore she lost her life to DeValet. It goes on like that. They have all but strung DeValet by his neck, and the depiction of the Yard is… unflattering."

"I'll show them who is a woolly-headed plodder!" Gregson bellowed.

"I'm certain you will, Inspector," Holmes said. "Nonetheless, you must now protect Monsieur DeValet until this furor has died down."

"It would be no small help if we could put the cuffs on this Madame Corbeau," Gregson puffed.

"I regret that I allowed her to slip away," Holmes said. "That pleasure will be had by our Gallic friends across the Channel."

Suffice it to say Gregson was not well pleased. When the notice of Madame Corbeau's arrest came across the wire Holmes tasked half a dozen patrolmen with peddling copies to all the major newsdesks of London.

"The morning editions were DeValet's execution order, the afternoon editions shall be his reprieve," Holmes said.

"This says they arrested her in the remote hamlet of Bois d'Coeur," I observed. "How did you know to look for her there?"

"Upon further examination, I realized the elements in DeValet's sketches which we were unable to place came from another hand. As you rightly observed there was another artist involved. Madame Corbeau seems to have assisted DeValet in his compositions as well as his receipts. While the crow and the triskele and the heart within a tree were so much noise within Celtic iconography, they were much easier to place within ancient Galli culture. Corbeau was signing her work, such as it was. I imagine she even expected to be the subject of this portrait."

"And when DeValet put Bella in her place…" I offered.

"An insult Corbeau no doubt felt on both a practical and emotional level. It drove her to murder."

"Where did she get the flesh-eating bacteria?" Gregson wondered.

"Bois d'Coeur is in the dairy-rich grassland that flows onwards to Switzerland. Each family has their own secret for making the rich, pungent cheeses the region is known for. The French police will have no trouble identifying the family that risks death in pursuit of *belle fromage*. The locals surely know already. Gourmands take a perverse pride in conflating danger and luxury."

A month later a crate of soft cheese wheels arrived from France.

"Ah, Watson! You've spoiled your Christmas present," Holmes lamented.

"Surely this is not the poisoned cheese from the DeValet affair," I protested.

"Don't be foolish," Holmes replied. "The cheese isn't poisoned. It never was. The bacteria used in the fermentation simply devour human flesh." Holmes had pried the crate open and sliced a sliver of cheese with his penknife. "It is perfectly safe, and delicious."

"Get this dreadful stuff out of here!" I demanded.

"Just a few weeks in the larder and then I'll have Wiggins set about delivering them."

"Don't draw a helpless child into this," I said. "If so much as one person dies we'll all hang."

"By this stage, all the bacteria have perished, Watson. You know this better than I. This is nothing more than a piquant *amuse-bouche* with a compelling anecdote behind it."

The Two Patricks

Winter was turning to Spring and a light rain traced the windows of 221B Baker Street. Holmes was tending to his little garden box, gently watering and pruning his poisoner's collection of monkshood, foxglove, cuckoo pint, nightshade and, of course, hemlock. I had objected to having such a deadly collection in the flat but Holmes assured me that someday I would be glad of it. Mrs. Hudson had no idea of the nature of the garden and was quite taken aback when I slapped her hands away from an alluring purple blossom and forbade her ever to touch the flower box again.

For my part I was nestled in my reliable club chair, lingering over a fine cigar and flipping slowly through *The Times*, and listening to the gentle patter of the rain. The front page was, of course, all about the incredible return of lost scion Patrick Blackhouse to his parents after 16 years of captivity. As a child young Patrick had been kidnapped right off the grounds of the Blackhouse estate. According to the newspaper he had been taken by a traveling show troupe. Sylvester Love was a master of the sword arts, including swallowing. His wife, Naomi, performed a snake act portraying the Seduction of Eve. Their own son had disappeared into the crowd at Newcastle the year before, never to be seen again. Insane with grief Naomi had taken Patrick and raised him as her own. It was quite a story, to say the least.

"That it appears in a newspaper is no guarantee that you are looking at one rather than the other," Holmes said.

His sudden intrusion startled me. "What's that?"

"You were just thinking that sometimes the truth is more fantastical than fiction. I suggest to you that appearing in a newspaper is no guarantee of truth and no proof against fiction."

"I'm not as simple as all that." I lifted the paper up before my face to create a barrier between myself and the Great Detective.

"She'll quite like that."

"Damnation, Holmes! You can't hold half a conversation with a fellow that doesn't even know it is happening. What are you on about now?"

"I daresay Mrs. Watson will enjoy your day at the Royal Jubilee Exhibition. I hear the fountain at the center of the hall is breathtaking."

"Aha! I've got you now, Holmes! I was thinking of no such thing!"

"Your mind was stirred by the wedding announcements in the paper, reminding you of your own anniversary. You quickly dismissed an advertisement for ladies' boots, wisely deciding the issues of both size and style were unduly fraught. You lingered upon an advert for an electro-magnetic hairbrush, rather too long for a professed man of medicine, before coming to rest on the article describing the Jubilee Exhibition Hall recently built by Maxwell and Tuke. You then absently felt for the train schedule book in your breast pocket, showing that you had moved from abstract thoughts to planning the practicalities of the trip. I cannot be blamed if I can follow your thoughts better than you can yourself."

"Humpf. Just mind your plants, Holmes."

The bell at the front door rang. A minute later Mrs. Hudson appeared in the doorway to the study. "Mr. Holmes, a lady to see you. A rather dignified one at that, unlike the types you usually consort with."

"Yes, very good, Mrs. Hudson. Please show her in."

Mrs. Hudson went back down the stairs and in her place appeared a woman regal in appearance. She wore a fine blue velvet coat over a striking satin dress, pristine even in this rainy weather. Lace ran to her wrists and throat and upon her head, she wore a tall hat tied with a sharp bow. She looked appraisingly at myself and Holmes. There was a great pause and then to my surprise, Holmes put down his gardening implements and stepped towards our visitor with his hand outstretched.

"Lady Blackhouse, I presume?" She gave a small start and then a stiff smile.

"Mr. Holmes? It appears your reputation is well-founded."

"Simple observation, madam. Your clothes are new and expensive, but not needlessly showy. You are comfortable wearing luxury items so your new wardrobe does not suggest a change in station. The colors are unfashionably dark for spring, but rather less dark than the mourning black I suspect you have become accustomed to wearing in recent years. Your lack of ostentation in jewelry suggests old money and yet you are unfamiliar to me. A member of the social elite who has shunned high society. You are disturbed enough to seek out the aid of a consulting detective yet clearly not distraught. From this I surmise that you are a wealthy woman who has spent many years suffering and only recently have events turned for the better, and yet this has not brought you the happiness you anticipated. Further, you believe something to be amiss in your good fortune. London is abuzz with the news of a well-to-do family that has recently experienced a mixed blessing in the form of the return of a lost child under unclear circumstances. Exactly the type of situation beyond the scope of police assistance."

"You know so much at a glance it almost feels as if it might be redundant to tell you the rest."

"Not at all. Please, sit and tell me what the newspapers do not know."

"You see, Mr. Holmes, there have been threats upon the life of my Patrick."

"Threats?" I bellowed. "Against a child just reunited with his family? Unbelievable!"

"Nonetheless the threats are real. The papers still talk about Patrick like he is a child but he is a full-grown man. He has lived a full life while he has been away. A life that we know nothing about."

"A life that may have followed him back home?" Holmes asked.

"That's what we are afraid of, but Patrick won't talk about his past."

"What form have these threats taken?"

"Initially there were just shouts in the street wherever we went, then the letters started, and finally someone hurled bricks through our windows."

"The police will not take action?"

"They have patrolmen walking the Blackhouse grounds but that has done little to stop the abuse."

"And these letters, do you have them?"

"No. Patrick destroys them all upon reading them."

"Have you read them?"

"Never. Patrick has not stepped outside since he returned home, so he is always there when the mail is brought in. The letters upset him so we have tried to learn the contents but he is very secretive."

"What about these bricks? Anything special about them?"

"Each had the word 'liar' inscribed in capital letters. Scratched in, as with a knife."

"I see. And have those bricks been destroyed as well?"

"Patrick smashes them with a hammer and then throws the remains out in the woodlands behind the house."

"Do you not find Patrick's behavior suspicious?"

"He is so angry and so strange it is hard to gauge his behavior by normal standards. Lord Blackhouse advises patience, predicting that things will return to normal when Patrick has recovered from his ordeal. But I just don't know, Mr. Holmes. He lived with his kidnappers far longer than he lived with us. In many ways that is his normal life and this the interruption. I wonder if he now regrets returning to us."

"Has he had contact with his kidnappers since returning?"

"Not that we know of. Not unless that is what these letters are about. I do not believe he has made any attempt at outbound communication. Quite the opposite, he seems to retreat further and further into himself. I fear this harassment may just be one trauma too many."

"We shall be happy to look into this matter, Lady Blackhouse. I would like to come and examine the property at your earliest convenience."

"Of course, Mr. Holmes. I wonder if it would be convenient for you to visit during the day tomorrow?"

"When Lord Blackhouse is otherwise occupied?"

"How did you…?"

"Ladies of your station either seek justice through their husbands or despite them."

"Yes, well…"

"It is quite alright by me, Lady Blackhouse. I daresay the fewer parties involved the more efficient the investigation will be. Do you expect Patrick to be around?"

"Patrick is always around, Mr. Holmes. However, I expect he will avoid you as he does any stranger."

"Very good. Dr. Watson and I shall call on you mid-morning tomorrow."

The next day Holmes and I found ourselves walking up the driveway to stately Blackhouse Manor. Despite the family name, the home was actually hewn from a pleasant pink stone with earth-colored accents around the windows and doors. I noticed that several of the windows were boarded up.

"Perhaps the local glazier did it," I offered. I noticed that Holmes had yet to look up at the building. His eyes were intently fixed upon the soggy ground. When we reached the front door we were received by a maid. Lady Blackhouse appeared shortly from up the grand staircase before us, and as she reached the bottom I noticed a strange figure had crept to the banister to look down at us from above.

"Mr. Holmes and Dr. Watson, how good of you to come."

"Not at all, Lady Blackhouse. Tell me, were there any more incidents yesterday?"

"Another brick, I'm afraid."

"May I see where it landed?"

Lady Blackhouse escorted us two rooms over into what appeared to be some sort of office. There was a massive desk in the center of the room with a large blotter, a small globe, and various other practical knickknacks. Against one wall was a secretary's roll top desk and along the rest were shelves of ledgers, logbooks, and other impersonal paraphernalia.

"What is this room?"

"Lord Blackhouse's office. He still personally oversees the many diverse enterprises under the Blackhouse name, though in truth his man Ronald Weiss does most of the actual work."

"Do you attach any significance to this room being attacked?"

"None, I presume the vandal is choosing rooms at random from the outside and this was just the next unbroken window."

"So the windows have been broken in order?"

"Not exactly. The first brick was through our parlor window while we all sat around the piano after dinner. The next through the dining room window while we were seated. That one knocked the serving bowl of soup right off the table. The third came through the window of the library where Lord Blackhouse and Patrick were reading. Then this."

"Lord Blackwell was working in this room when the attack occurred?"

"No, the room was unoccupied when the attack happened."

"How quickly was the room examined after the incident?"

"That is unclear, Mr. Holmes. I had gone into London for the day to update my summer wardrobe. As you correctly surmised I have worn black for the last 16 years. It is appropriate that my appearance reflect my joy in having my son returned to me." I couldn't help but notice that her demeanor did not match her words. "Only the maid was here at the time, and Patrick, of course. She heard the crash of the window breaking and locked herself in her room, poor thing. Patrick claims not to have heard it at all, but I think that a lie. Patrick is always around and he hears everything." She wrapped her arms around herself as if warding off a chill. "Lord Blackhouse discovered the broken window much the same time as I was knocking at the maid's door to inquire as to why the house was not prepared for dinner."

Holmes began to walk around the office, scrutinizing every aspect. He took a special interest in the window, now boarded up, and the floor before it. "Who cleaned the room?"

"The maid, after the police had been here."

"And the window?"

"There's a local man named Gerry Springs who manages the grounds and does basic repair work like this. We don't employ him exclusively. He works for many of the families in this area."

"I should like to speak to the maid."

"I shall retrieve her at once." Lady Blackhouse stepped out into the hallway and shrieked. "For Heaven's sake, Patrick. Skulking around out here in the dark!" We heard the lady proceed down the hall one way and Patrick clomp away in the other.

"I say, Holmes, she seems unenthusiastic about her returned son."

"Indeed. It is too early to be sure, but keep that lack of maternal affection in mind. I think that Lady Blackhouse knows more than she is telling. Remember, she nominally asked us to investigate who is attacking her house and family, but in the same breath all but charged us with investigating Patrick himself."

"What could it mean, Holmes?"

"Let us begin with the small crime before us."

"Taken on its own it is pure vandalism."

"I don't think that it is."

"You don't think this is vandalism?"

"I think the previous acts of vandalism presented an opportunity to someone. Step here."

I stepped on the corner of the rug that Holmes indicated. It felt strangely gritty underneath my feet.

"The rug retains the minuscule fragments of broken glass. Someone stepped there, on top of both the glass and the rug grinding in the shards. Assuming that they started at the window…"

"You think someone broke in?"

"We saw the other broken windows on the way in. They all shared the characteristic jagged puncture of glass that had been shattered by a thrown object. This window, on the other hand, has been cleared to the bottom frame, with the glass collecting just below the window instead of being expelled across the room. Someone attacked this window brick in hand and knocked out all of the lower glass before climbing in. The crushed glass in the rug tells us he went to this side of the room." Holmes now writhed back and forth like a cobra about to strike before the file boxes shelved on the wall. "Here, Watson!"

"What is it, Holmes?"

"Do you see the scuffs on this shelf here?"

"By Jove! You're right, Holmes! This file box has been stolen!"

"Not quite."

"But you just pointed at the evidence yourself!"

"This file box is not in its proper spot but I suspect it is still on these very shelves. This is it. You'll notice that the cleaning in here is perfunctory. I suspect Lord Blackhouse doesn't like his business papers being touched. Likely the maid must clean while he is in the office watching her. In any event, these older file boxes are topped with years of dust, but this current file box, pulled from the very end of the shelving, is completely dust-free. Quickly, let's take a look in the surrounding boxes before Lady Blackhouse returns. I see, personal correspondence, and the missing box appears to be from about 23 years ago. Very interesting. Someone has taken the box for 1864 and Lord Blackhouse has attempted to disguise that fact. It's blackmail, Watson. We must speak to Lord Blackhouse in private." Lady

Blackhouse returned with the maid. She curtseyed holding her apron out but did not meet Holmes' gaze.

"When you entered the room after Lord and Lady Blackhouse came home how do you find it?"

"How do you mean, sir?"

"Describe the condition of the room."

"There was glass everywhere. I picked up as much as I could before Lord Blackhouse lost his patience and ordered me away."

"I see. And what was Lord Blackhouse doing when you entered?"

"I don't rightly know. There was a great commotion as we approached the room but when we entered he was leaned up against those shelves there."

"And he stayed there until you were done cleaning?"

"Yes, sir. I suppose he was trying to stay out of the way."

"Very good. And what did you do with the brick?"

"What brick?"

"Thank you very much, miss. This has been most informative."

"Ta, sir, but I don't think I understand."

"That is quite alright, Lucinda," Lady Blackhouse said ushering her out of the room. "Please have lunch ready for our guests."

"Quite unnecessary," said Holmes.

"I insist."

"We really must be on our way."

"Lady Blackhouse insists, Holmes," I said holding my empty stomach. I knew that once Holmes caught the scent there would be no stopping for mere sustenance.

"I regret, Lady Blackhouse, that pressing business calls us elsewhere. I hope to send word shortly that this unfortunate situation has been resolved."

Back on the street Holmes walked to the second cab available and asked for the St. John's Club. "Are you a member there, now?" I asked, wistfully thinking of the lunch that had almost been.

"Of course not, but we know of someone who is. Lord Blackhouse had no fewer than three visible pieces of paper with St. John's Club letterhead visible in his office. I surmise that he is not only a member but a regular who incurs ongoing tabs." We arrived at the understated building and Holmes rapped at the modest white door. A nonplussed older man wearing a frayed tuxedo opened it.

"This is a private club, gentlemen."

"We are here to see Lord Blackhouse."

"I cannot confirm the presence of any member, nor indeed the membership of any person."

Holmes retrieved a calling card from his coat. "Should there be a Lord Blackhouse inside please pass along my card and inform him that I specialize in just the kind of shelving problems he is currently experiencing."

A few minutes later we found ourselves in a quiet corner of the club meeting with Lord Blackhouse himself. He was a giant of a man, balding in that way that suggested excess virility and chomping at a cigar. "What do you know of this business?"

"I know that a box of personal correspondence from 1864 was recently burgled from your office under cover of a false act of vandalism. I know that this burglary was committed by someone other than the person throwing bricks inscribed 'liar' through your windows. I know your wife believes those bricks to be intended for Patrick, but we two know those bricks are intended for you."

"How dare you come in here are besmirch my character." He rose from his chair and began pacing at the window.

"While I detest coincidences the proximity of the return of your son with this burglary demands examination. I note that the year in question is not the year the boy was kidnapped but the year he was born."

"What business of yours is this... Mr. Sherlock Holmes?" he asked, brandishing my friend's calling card.

"Your wife has engaged my services to investigate the vandalism and also Patrick's past. By that, she, of course, means the time between his kidnapping and return. However, it is now apparent that the intrigues surrounding this young man began much earlier."

"Have my family not suffered enough without your meddling?"

"You misunderstand me, sir. I assure you that if I look into your blackmailing and your missing correspondence I will come to the whole truth. However, that is not my charge at present and should you provide me with the name of your blackmailer I shall have no need at the moment to inquire any further on this particular topic."

"And if I throw you out of here right now and forbid my wife to ever speak to you again?"

"You will have made your wife rightfully suspicious and she will no doubt reach out to the police or others. You will be forever beholden to your blackmailer and believe me when I say blackmailers never let someone out of their grasping claws voluntarily. Patrick and your home will continue to be under siege from the original assailant. And, most importantly, I will still be on the case without feeling beholden to protect you in any way whatsoever."

The man's face was a deep red but as he mulled over his options it slowly returned to normal and finally, his shoulders slumped. "Sylvester Love."

"Sylvester Love the gypsy who kidnapped Patrick? How could he possibly blackmail you?"

"Suffice it to say that there is a complicated relationship and Lady Blackhouse and I do not wish to reveal the exact nature to the public, and more importantly, to Patrick. I certainly do not want to reveal it to you. I assure you that no peace can be brokered with Sylvester Love, but if you can steal the documents away from him I shall pay you a princely sum."

"I am not a sneak thief and I do not accept blind commissions. I shall pursue the goal of stopping the attacks against your property and determining the nature of the danger to Patrick. Whether the results of this investigation are to your benefit or detriment is of no concern to me. Good day, Lord Blackhouse."

Holmes did not so much as pause as we exited back onto the London street.

"Hold up, where are we going now?"

"We are looking for gypsies recently arrived in London. Where would you hide, Watson?"

"In a city like London, anywhere."

"Not anywhere. Even in this modern age, prejudice against gypsies would narrow their options considerably."

"Maybe they are in disguise then?"

"Maybe. Avenging these wrongs might drive them to such ends. Consider this, in a country household where there is a shared housekeeper, a naive maid, a disturbed shut-in, and no doubt any number of delivery boys from the greengrocer and the butcher and so forth, surely there had to be opportunities to simply stroll into the house to steal the file box of correspondence. Instead, the thief approaches a near-empty house and smashes a window with a brick he found at hand. What does that suggest to you?"

"A spontaneous crime of passion?"

"Against an empty house? No, but I do believe it was a crime of opportunity. Someone approached the house and when given the opportunity to act unimpeded chose to smash their way in with the crude implements available. That shows a lack of planning, a lack of self-control and an unfamiliarity with country estates in general. And yet this thief had some familiarity with this house in particular, for he went straight to the office window and then straight to the boxes of correspondence."

"So an amateur thief who was casing the house and acted before he had a fully formed plan."

"Perhaps, although I suspect it was someone who had been to the property before, working up the courage to confront Lord

Blackhouse. Set on a fight, finesse did not cross his mind when his plans changed from attack to blackmail. In any event, I do not believe we are dealing with a master criminal who has put a lot of forethought into this. I think we are looking at an aggrieved father who is wholly unfamiliar with the ways of polite society. I believe Sylvester Love is very much still a gypsy in appearance and behavior. An angry gypsie not given to subtlety, he would surely draw attention to himself throughout most of London. Where is one place a man like this would not draw attention?"

"You've got me there, Holmes."

"We are arriving as we speak."

Looking up I saw the fabulous Jubilee Fairgrounds Pavilion, with its delicate ironwork filigree supporting a fantastical glassed building. "Remarkable, Holmes! But I really hoped to see this with Mary. Besides, I doubt the Royal family is any more likely to associate with vagabonds than anyone else in London."

"In an official capacity to be sure, but you can see for yourself the ramshackle tent town that has sprung up around the hall proper. Hundreds of unlicensed vendors and performers and craftsmen doubling or more the number of attractions at the Jubilee."

"Whyever don't the officials clear them out?"

"I'm sure they are all rousted at least once a day, maybe more. Still, these unsavory hangers-on only serve to add to the allure of the fair." Holmes asked around for Sylvester Love. At first, we met harsh glares and silence from the traveling itinerants until Holmes let on that he'd come back to purchase a magic oriental sword from Sylvester. Holmes affected just the right amount of guilelessness to seem a genuine victim of fraud. A man who read fortunes in corn husks offered to escort us to Sylvester Love for a shilling. He had talked Holmes out of two more by the time we arrived outside Sylvester's tent. I found myself subconsciously guarding my coin purse as he left.

Holmes announced himself at the flap. At first there was no response but finally, a woman's voice replied.

"What do you want?"

"We are looking for Sylvester Love."

"There is no one here by that name."

"Is he out spying on the Blackhouse Manor again? Looking for a chance to rescue his son?"

"Who are you?" A woman head, wrapped in a fanciful silk scarf, emerged from the tent.

"I am Sherlock Holmes, a consulting detective and this is my partner Dr. Watson."

"How do you do, madam?" I tipped my hat to her.

"What business is this of yours?"

"Lady Blackhouse engaged me to find the cause of the attacks on her son and put a stop to them."

"Patrick is more our son than theirs!"

"A decision for Patrick to make now that he is a man, I think."

"We just want to speak to him! Is that a crime?"

"No, but breaking and entering and stealing Lord Blackhouse's personal correspondence is."

"What are you talking about?"

"Your husband did just that yesterday afternoon."

"Lies! We simply wait out in the trees, whistling the call of our family to him. I know he hears us because he always turns away. I just want to hold him in my arms and explain."

"Explain what?"

"You would not understand. The situation is very complicated."

"Does your husband understand?"

"Yes, of course! He was going to confront Lord Blackhouse for buying our baby so many years ago."

"Instead he has stolen Lord Blackhouse's correspondence from the year Patrick was born."

"I know nothing about this! Sylvester has not been home since yesterday."

"Is that strange?"

"Not necessarily."

"Does your husband know the whole story? The one that you and Lord Blackhouse and Patrick know?"

"Take your gorger lies and leave!"

"I only ask because if he has already looked at the correspondence in the box he stole…"

"No!"

"Is it possible there are letters that detail the situation?"

"That and more! It is the end of me if Sylvester reads those letters. I thought I was in love! I thought the baby meant Blackhouse and I were meant to be together!"

"What happened to that baby, Mrs. Love?"

"Lord Blackhouse took it from me and has secreted him away! I could not tell Sylvester why, of course, but others had seen Blackhouse drag our baby out of my arms. They told Sylvester who did it. I could not tell him why so I lied. I claimed that Rasputin, our clan leader, had lost the baby gambling. Blind with rage Sylvester had beaten the man to death before I could change my story. He spent five years in prison, and when he got out he immediately went to England and rescued who he thought was his son, the Blackhouse's own child, Patrick. I never told him the truth. He has lived these last sixteen years believing he was reunited with his son. Patrick, as you have seen, does not resemble Sylvester at all. Sylvester is too blind to see it but others talked. Patrick was lobbying to join the kris, or governing body of our clan. The whispers from his detractors only got louder. Finally, I felt I must tell Patrick the truth before it came out in some other, more destructive way. Patrick fled back to England and Sylvester does not understand why."

"So, if he read the contents of those letters, he has lost two sons, and his faith in his wife all in one blow. Hurry, Watson! We must get back to the Manor!"

We were up in a hansom rattling through London at top speed before I got the chance to ask Holmes the question that had been nagging at me.

"What did you mean that Love had lost two sons?"

"The first, obviously, is Patrick, who has abandoned the family that raised him. The second is the baby of Mrs. Love and Lord Blackhouse, the first baby Sylvester Love thought was his. Lord Blackwell has hidden that child away. Made a fool twice and now without a son to carry on his family line, I suspect Mr. Love will be exacting his revenge on Lord Blackhouse in short order."

We galloped back to the Manor and found the house in commotion. I feared we were too late to save Lord Blackwell and was surprised when I heard a man bellowing out in the garden. My physician instincts kicked in and I ran around to the back of the house. There was a large rough man, skin tanned to leather, cradling a smaller man laying limp on the ground. The maid Lucinda looking on from just outside the door, gasped as we exited.

"Poor young Mr. Springs. Poor old Mr. Springs. Poor Patrick. What a terrible situation for everyone!"

"What happened here?" Holmes shook her by the arms.

"Patrick, whose mum, er, other mum, false mum…"

"Get on with it."

"Patrick, who grew up handling snakes, was just showing young Mr. Springs, the groundskeeper Gerry's boy, how to safely move the adder that had nested in the garden. All of a sudden the snake bit young Mr. Springs.

"Did you actually see this happen?"

"No, that's what Patrick told old Mr. Springs when he came running over."

"Patrick… Patrick…" old Mr. Springs wept.

"Strange. Why do you suppose he calls Patrick's name?" I pondered.

"That boy's name is Patrick, too."

"That's the second Patrick?" I asked, catching Holmes' eye.

"The first Patrick if you ask me," the maid said. "As he has been here longer, but I suppose it is all a matter of perspective."

"Ah," said Holmes.

"What is it?" I said.

"In casting this snake out of the garden young Patrick has revealed to me the fruit of knowledge, and it is bittersweet."

"That is strangely poetic of you, Holmes." I hurried to the side of the young man. Blood soaked one shoulder of his shirt. Using my pocket knife I tore his clothing away. I called for the maid to bring water and washed the wounded area. Patrick Springs jerked back into consciousness with a scream. "Hold steady. Hmm. The wound is red and the skin is blistering. You have definitely been bitten by an adder."

"Can you save him, Doctor?" Gerry cried.

"An intravenous application of ammonia and strychnine is indicated, but to be honest even if we had the means I would advise against it. Your son has a fifty-fifty chance of surviving the adder bite without it. However, if he survives he will recover fully. The counter venom solution increases the odds of survival only slightly with many deleterious and permanent side effects. Let him rest here and leave it to Providence."

"I just don't know…"

"The Doctor is right, Gerry." Lord Blackhouse had appeared from the house. He kneeled down in the dirt next to the poisoned man and hesitantly took his hand.

"But, sir…"

"I have seen this before, in India. The best action we can take is no action, and pray for the best."

"Nigel, in this affair you are not the master." Lady Blackhouse was huddled in the doorway now with the maid, drawing a shawl around herself. "Let his father decide." Lord Blackhouse and Gerry Springs looked at each other.

Patrick Blackhouse sprang from around the corner of the house. "Yes, let his father decide."

"Patrick! I thought you had ridden into town to fetch an ambulance! This boy is dying!"

"There will be no ambulance, mother. Now, father, decide the fate of your bastard son."

"Whatever are you talking about, Patrick?" Lady Blackhouse demanded.

Lord Blackhouse slumped his shoulders and sighed. "It is true, my wife. This young man is my son by a gypsy woman I spent time with before we were engaged."

"Bastard!" A shot rang out from the trees. A very drunk Sylvester Love staggered out, shotgun waving precariously about. "You defiled my wife, you stole my child, your lies had me raise another in his place and then you took him away from me too! Now you will pay!" He cocked and raised the gun again. Everyone braced for a new round of shot but thankfully the gun jammed. As Sylvester attempted to fix the gun through a haze of heavy inebriation Holmes sprung into action and deftly plucked the weapon from his grasp before pushing him down to the ground.

"Stay there, sir, and do not force me to take further action. You are the one innocent party in this sordid affair and thus far you maintain my sympathies. One more move to cause injury will change that, however."

"Innocent!" Lord Blackhouse exclaimed. "He kidnapped my son and held him captive for 16 years!"

"He rescued who he believed to be his own son. His blind faith in his wife allowed him to accept a ludicrous story. I prefer a sharp mind but that action smacks of the good heart my partner Watson is so apt to admire when we find one. Patrick's clear distress over choosing between a life as the Blackhouse heir, a life he wants so bad he attempted murder to secure it or returning to the loving family he has always known, serves as proof Sylvester provided an excellent childhood for the boy, despite his relatively low circumstances."

"He is still a kidnapper in the eyes of the law!" Lord Blackhouse bellowed.

"As are you," Holmes observed.

"What do you mean by attempted murder, Mr. Holmes?" Lady Blackhouse asked.

"As Dr. Watson here can attest, I have had several opportunities to encounter poisonous snakes in my work and I have thus made myself quite knowledgeable about their characteristics. The English adder, while quite deadly, is also quite passive. One has to literally step on it before it will strike. More so, it certainly has no propensity for leaping from the ground to strike the upper body."

"He didn't know how to handle the snake and when I tried to take it from the boy it struck out. It was an honest mistake." Patrick Blackhouse insisted.

"Ohhhhhh, Patrick." Sylvester moaned. "It was murder then."

"What do you mean?" Gerry asked.

"I've handled a thousand adders a thousand times in my day as part of my wife's act. They strike close. They would strike the hand holding them, not leap for another person. To get an adder to bite someone in the chest you would have to press the poor beast there, or dump it down their shirt."

"I suspect that would result in a bite on the stomach, not the shoulder. No, Young Mr. Blackhouse here wielded the serpent-like a poisoned knife."

Seeing even his own gypsy father turn against him Patrick Blackhouse panicked and began to run off into the darkness. With surprising speed, Gerry brought him to the ground. "You'll pay for what you did, boy. If he lives the police will do for you, if he dies you'll have your reckoning with me."

Holmes then sent me back into town to fetch the police with the admonition that they had best bring a wagon and a few extra men to handle everything that was happening at once on the Blackhouse estate.

Having committed similar crimes the deplorable Lord Blackhouse and the unfortunate Sylvester Love found themselves serving similar sentences. Unable to escape his past crimes, Lord Blackhouse used all of his influence to ensure he would be sent to a reformatory up north where he would spend his sentence in bucolic retirement while Sylvester Love would be trapped in the county jail performing hard labor. Holmes used all of his influence, more than a few judges and corrections officers owed him a debt of gratitude, to ensure that there would be a confusion in the paperwork which caused their ultimate destinations to be switched.

Patrick Blackhouse benefited from the sympathy of the public and testimony from experts in the burgeoning field of psychology. He was given the benefit of the doubt that his strange and murderous behavior was the result of mental stress from his many ordeals as a child and he was remanded to care in a lunatic asylum. Patrick Springs lived through one night and then another, his convalescence taking place within Blackhouse Manor where he was nursed back to health by the ministrations of Lady Blackhouse. Gerry Springs had stayed by his adopted son's bedside day and night during the crisis and I hear he and Patrick continue to reside there with Lady Blackhouse to this day in an arrangement described by onlookers as most congenial for all parties. Holmes also found a companion in all this. The adder that brought the whole event to a head now lived in a vivarium above Holmes work area. I found the proximity of Holmes' beautiful but poisonous flowers and his venomous but innocent snake to be amusing. On more than one occasion I visited 221B Baker Street unannounced to find Holmes chatting with the small beast. Mrs. Hudson for her part refused to enter the flat while the snake was in residence. I believe Holmes found this convivial as well.

"How did you get all of this anyway? It must have cost a fortune."

"Monsieur Dubugue meant to dispose of this like any other perishable evidence. I offered to accept it in lieu of a monetary award. He seemed to be as eager to be rid of it as you."

The Adventure of the Gnarled Beeches

My friend Sherlock Holmes never expressed a particular reason for his retirement. I have often wondered if it crept up on the great detective, as it did for myself, or if there was a moment in time when he decided that his work was complete. For me, the first inkling came as 221B began to coalesce into a kind of order. I never saw Holmes lift a finger and yet the sheer bulk of his haphazard collection seemed to slowly evaporate, and what remained became neatly organized and tidied. As for the man himself, he was as industrious as ever, but his efforts were focused between the pages of his natural science books, which had always been present but now took pride of place upon the shelves of our flat. Our friends at Scotland Yard rarely came around, and when they did Holmes would decline to join them in their cases, preferring to offer what observations he could from his armchair and then sending them upon their way. He had suffered from spells of listlessness before, and so I fear I underestimated the situation. Unaware that I was enjoying the last few months of the happiest period of my life, I found myself at loose ends, aimlessly puttering around the drawing-room while Holmes sat reconciling the figures in a number of almanacs. At the top of the stairs was a cardboard box where Mrs. Hudson abandoned Holmes' ever-growing pile of unread mail. Idly I would poke through it. Holmes had a variety of interesting correspondents from every corner of the globe. At the very least, gazing upon the postage stamps and deciphering the unusual addresses would while away a few minutes of the day.

On this day, however, it was an unassuming letter from Walsall that caught my eye. Unlike much of Holmes' correspondence, this envelope was completely unremarkable in every way, save one. The return address sent a shock through me, recalling one of the most horrible cases we had ever investigated.

"Holmes!" I cried. "Have you seen this letter?"

Holmes waved dismissively without looking up from his books, so I planted the envelope on top of the ledger directly under his nose. Without so much as a blink, Holmes simply moved the letter off the table and dropped it on the floor, continuing his tabulations unhindered.

"Didn't you see, Holmes? The letter came from Miss Violet Hunter. Aren't you curious to know what she has written about, all these years later?"

"An unseemly element of my vocation, which has become more prevalent over the years, is the emotional attachment that my clients form, which is expressly not reciprocal. To them I am a savior, to me, they are a set of facts which provide a temporary distraction."

"Has Miss Hunter been writing to you all this time?" When the young governess had been our client I had thought her a good match for Holmes.

"Not a jot, until today."

"That doesn't seem like much of an emotional attachment to me."

"She'll have named her child Sherlock and want me to attend the christening, or she will have found some old memento in the attic that reminded her of me or some other romantic poppycock. Did they just republish one of your stories again? That does it often as not."

"You can take a moment to look at the letter or I can pester you all afternoon."

With a deep sigh, Holmes retrieved the envelope from the floor and made to gut it with a Chinese throwing knife that he kept on his table for any number of purposes. Suddenly he cocked his head and turned the envelope over, peering at the address.

"Remember her now, do you?" I beamed. "A striking girl and clever too. I had rather hoped…"

"Look at this envelope, Watson."

"I did. I am the one who brought it to your attention."

"What do you see?"

"It's a plain enough envelope, the meticulous handwriting of a teacher, regular postage, canceled in Walsall."

"That's it?"

"Come now, Holmes, the only remarkable thing about that envelope is how utterly unremarkable it looks."

"Hmm," Holmes said, before holding a magnifying glass up in front of it. "Nothing about the stamp strikes you?"

"No, not at all. We have a book of them ourselves in that drawer over there."

"The envelope got wet and the ink of the address spread."

"Ever so slightly, it has rained every day for a week."

"Yes, but the stamp is pristine. The stain runs under it."

"So it got wet on the way to the post office."

"And then dried out completely before the stamp was affixed? No, this letter lay about for some time before it was posted. It was prepared in advance but then handled carelessly."

"You think someone other than Miss Hunter mailed this letter?"

"And held it until some condition was met."

"Dash it, Holmes, open it already."

Holmes expertly slashed through the envelope and scanned the contents.

"We must get to Euston Station as quickly as possible. History is repeating itself - Miss Hunter has sent a letter and we may already be too late."

Holmes surprised me by plucking down a copy of *The Adventures* from the shelf.

"The matter was a personal affair until you published your account, which remains the fullest and best."

It was just like Holmes to intermingle a criticism and a compliment, particularly in regard to my writing. I remain to this day unsure of his final opinion of my work.

Once we were secure within a private car Holmes disclosed the contents of the letter to me.

"It seems Miss Hunter believed she was being watched by Edward Rucastle."

"Still Miss, then?"

Holmes went on as if I hadn't said anything. "It appears young Edward so resembles his father that she dismissed the first sighting as a figment of her imagination. At the time of this letter she had seen him several more times, and each time he was becoming more brazen, yet she had not been able to confront him directly."

"I should hope not. No wonder she wrote to you."

"As I expected, she left this letter in the care of another, only to be sent as a contingency."

"Under what circumstances?"

"Miss Hunter's disappearance." Holmes puffed at a cigarette.

"Or death?" I managed.

"In the event of her death, the local police would surely be involved. Besides, I have not seen any such mention in the papers."

"Some hope then?"

"This letter was postmarked days ago. If you had not been rummaging I might never have seen it."

"You are as entitled to a holiday as anyone, Holmes."

"I'm afraid deduction is an all or nothing business," Holmes said. After that, I was unable to pry another word from him until we arrived at New Street Station. High Street, the heart of the town, was built upon a hill, and despite the remarkable breadth of the road, the uniform buildings upon each side created a brick canyon that was most claustrophobic. Where London has an organic chaos, Walsall felt as if every brick had been plotted a decade before it was laid. The looming commercial buildings gave way to street after street of identical houses. At last, we came to the Woodhill School, nearly indistinguishable from the buildings around it save for the small plot of grass given for the children to play in. Without hesitation, Holmes walked right inside. Immediately to the left of the entrance was an administrative office.

"May I help you, sir?" Said a much-inconvenienced woman behind a small desk.

"I must speak with Mistress Hunter immediately," Holmes said, with no small amount of ingratiating charm.

"Mistress Hunter is not available," the woman puffed. "School is in session."

"I'm afraid I must insist."

"May I inquire as to what this is about?"

"Personal business," Holmes said, taking the letter from his pocket and waving it in front of the woman.

"Perhaps I could help you," the woman made a hesitant snatch at the letter.

"I think not," said Holmes, suddenly lunging past her and throwing open the door in the back wall. "Not here, I see. Shall I poke my head in each and every classroom? The matter is quite urgent."

In a hissing whisper, the woman replied, "Please, sir. The children don't know."

"That Mistress Hunter is missing."

"Yes, sir."

"For how long?"

"Days now."

"Is that unusual?"

"Unprecedented, sir. She keeps her other affairs quite separate from her duties here."

"Other affairs?"

"Who did you say you were?"

"Does Mistress Hunter have a special confidante?"

"Why, me, sir?"

"No, I don't think so. You are far too interested in getting a look at this letter I'm holding. The person I am looking for already knows what it says."

"The impertinence! You barged into a school, knocking down doors and making demands to see an unmarried woman who has gone missing. For all I know you have snatched her up. They say that criminals always return to the scene of the crime."

"If I had taken her I wouldn't be here demanding to see her."

"I've half a mind to call for Inspector Ralling anyway."

"By all means, perhaps this inspector can shed some light on these matters."

"Just leave, the both of you, before the children see you."

As we returned to High Street, Holmes barked, "Missing for days and the fools are keeping it a secret. Chances are we are wasting our time, Watson. Probably suggests that the girl is already done for."

"We have to know for sure, Holmes!"

"Yes, well, let us step beneath these blue lamps and see what we discover."

Holmes had led us unerringly to the police station. Inside Holmes asked after Inspector Ralling. A man soon appeared, standing with the ramrod posture I had long since lost. His suit was pressed, his mustache was waxed and his sandy hairs combed so neatly I wouldn't be surprised if every strand was individually accounted for.

"Gentlemen," he nodded. "May I be of assistance?"

"I understand you are the person to speak to about Violet Hunter?"

The policeman blanched. "Please, let us speak in private."

He led us back to a small interview room.

"What do you know?" he asked.

"We know that Miss Hunter has been missing for several days. What we do not know is why that is a poorly kept secret."

"May I ask how you come to be involved in this?"

Holmes produced the letter again, but this time he allowed it to be taken, and read.

"The famous detective," Ralling sat back in his chair. "Are you as good as they say?"

"Better in some ways," Holmes lit a cigarette. "I keep my best tricks to myself. I will grant that my friend Dr. Watson does romanticize some elements, for literary effect."

"If I wrote the stories the way you wanted I'd never sell a page," I said.

"Pity," Holmes puffed. "I'll write my own accounts someday, and then we'll see."

"What of 'The Copper Beeches'?" Ralling asked. "Was that romanticized?"

"Quite the opposite, I'm afraid," I said. "I have found that while readers think they have an appetite for blood, the truth can be too grim to stomach."

"You've read it?"

"Of course. Miss Hunter was a celebrity for a moment when the story was published."

"How did she like that?" I asked.

"Not at all. I understand she burned every copy found on school grounds and even prohibited the very words from being spoken among her students."

"But that fascination passed," Holmes said. "Because of her other affairs."

The inspector screwed his face uptight.

"What do you know of that?"

"Nothing beyond the fact that these other affairs are the reason her disappearance is being kept a secret. I hardly need to tell you that a woman missing for this long has likely met her misfortune."

"As a rule."

"But in this case?"

"Miss Hunter is… capable."

"Capable?"

"You saw for yourself, back then, that she was independent and brave."

"Fine words for a headstone."

"Those things that happened back then gave her a purpose. She didn't want to be at anyone's mercy ever again."

"So you trained her?"

At this Ralling jumped in his seat. "Fine, Mr. Holmes, you've got me, and I'm relying on your gentlemanly discretion.

She was teaching herself to shoot, but she was doing it out of books, in secret. She learned just enough to be a danger to herself."

"How do you rate her?" Holmes asked.

"She's a crack shot with a pistol," the constable said. "Shoots better than half the force, particularly in the heat of the moment."

"She is in the habit of being armed then?"

"Yes, sir. I don't know where she keeps it but I've seen her produce her Colt hammerless when the need arises. She learned on an old Enfield, so I suppose that must still be around somewhere too."

"And you allow this?" I asked.

"Nothing illegal about it. Besides, I hate to admit it but the law has certain limitations in regards to domestic welfare."

"You mean the law turns a blind eye when convenient in matters of household discipline."

"I'm agreeing with you, Mr. Holmes. As much as I can while keeping my job. You can save your disapproving look, sir. Good men stay on the force by getting along sometimes."

"Miss Hunter supplied these deficiencies?"

"Much as you do, sir. In her own way."

"Are you saying Miss Hunter was some kind of vigilante?" I asked.

"I'm saying she would not turn a blind eye, and she was set for disaster. So I and a few other sympathetic souls helped her along."

"Trained her?" Holmes asked.

Ralling nodded.

"Anything else?"

He shrugged. "We help where we can."

"How are you helping her now?" I asked.

"I've had nothing to go on, until this letter."

"Miss Hunter did not inform you of her suspicions about Edward Rucastle?"

"As I have indicated, she is fiercely independent. These days I do little more for her than smooth over any little issues of legality that may arise. Often as not against her wishes."

"Before you read this letter what was your best theory?" Holmes asked.

"That's just the thing that baffled me," the constable said. "She hasn't been up to much as of late."

"Why not?"

"Over the years she has run off the worst offenders; made a bit of a mark on the city."

"I've dealt with a thousand criminals, and while I think London is better for it, there are always more miscreants festering in the shadows. No lone crusader can cure a city of crime."

"With all due respect, sir, this isn't London, and Miss Hunter focuses purely on abused woman. More than that, she inspires them. It's true to say that she could not intervene in every case, but thanks to her we've seen fewer battered wives. Fewer girls shrinking and cowering and skulking around the dark corners of their own homes. It's not a panacea, but every cop on the force has noticed it."

"Not everyone would be happy about such a change in the status quo," Holmes observed.

"Surely not. I could give you a list of right bastards who would be at the top of my list of suspects, but most of them would be crowing about it themselves. And as I said, there has been no precipitating incident as of late."

"That you are aware of."

"Yes, Mr. Holmes. You can be sure every peeler will be looking for this Edward Rucastle."

"Even if Rucastle was here he surely disappeared at the same time as Miss Hunter."

"It is the only lead I have to go on, unless you can suggest a better one."

"Her assistant at the school spoke as if Miss Hunter was still active in her avocation. I would look to your blotter for

140

suspicious events and put the word out to local physicians as well. Any lout who was pushed to kidnapping or worse probably had a non-trivial altercation with her."

"And you, Mr. Holmes?" The constable said.

"Every trail here is cold and it pains me to say I have only myself to blame. With Miss Hunter's very life on the line, I'm afraid I am left with little recourse but to make an inductive step of logic."

"You are going to guess?" I gasped.

"It hardly even qualifies as so much as that. If we cannot find Miss Hunter perhaps we can find Edward Rucastle, and I only know of one place he has definitely been. If we catch the next train we may yet be there by nightfall."

Aboard the train Holmes disappeared into himself, pressing his face against the window to avoid conversation. I was left to my own devices, trying to imagine the governess we had met as a gun-slinging arbiter of justice. So often had I tied a tidy bow upon the end of Holmes' cases, I thought, but not all his cases ended so neatly. The victims, indeed, even the perpetrators, live out their days beyond the edges of my manuscripts. Perhaps it would be worthwhile to revisit them, I mused. At the Winchester station, we hired a cab to take us out to the Copper Beeches. The driver warned us that there was nothing of interest to see at the old house, so famous in fiction, but that he could take us on a tour of the grisliest murders in Winchester, some which hadn't even made it into the papers. Holmes pressed a coin into the man's hand to take us to the Copper Beeches in silence and keep his macabre malarky to himself. The driver was taken aback, but the coin still slipped into his pocket, and the carriage still rolled forward. I noted the site of the old Black Swan Hotel where we had previously met with Miss Hunter. It appeared to have been torn down and replaced by an accountancy firm.

"So much of our history exists only in your stories now, Watson," Holmes sighed. While Holmes was prone to melancholia, never had I seen it take hold in the midst of a case, on the very cusp of capturing a villain.

"Take heart, Holmes," I said. "Even now we trundle over Thor Bridge. Do you remember that vengeful Brazilian? Now that was a fine piece of deduction."

Holmes merely shrugged in reply. Soon we were looking up the hill at the old house I remembered so well. Above the sky had reddened as the sun began to dip beneath the horizon.

"There it is," the driver said. "I tried to tell you there wasn't much to see."

"Does anyone still live there?" I asked.

"The crazy old man from the story and his son still live up there but they are hardly ever seen. Every once in awhile there's a rifle shot or two, and the whimpering of their mutts. There's a stench off the house, too, when the winds blow towards you. It'll probably be easier to burn the place down when they go."

"What of the wife?" Holmes asked.

"She left shortly after Mr. Rucastle's convalescence. I didn't see her firsthand, mind you, but I heard she staggered into the train station one morning gaunt and pale as a ghost, her dress faded and tattered and not a thing to her name, save the purse she emptied on the ticket counter. While she waited for her train a constable was sent for, and at the sight of him she ran, and hasn't been seen since."

The cabby was anxious to leave but another pound from Holmes' purse convinced him to stay until dusk.

"No longer," he warned. "I'm no coward but I'm no fool either."

"Quite wise," Holmes replied. "I said as much when we were here last. The open country is a horrible, hellish place."

I had forgotten about my friend's aversion to these bucolic hills. He happily camped out upon deadly moors and sauntered through the lonely Alps yet the quaint homesteads of Hampshire filled him with horror. I wondered for the thousandth time about Holmes' childhood. He had once mentioned being the descendant of country squires. Had he grown up in a place like this, and if so what tragedy befell him to send him burrowing into the festering underbelly of London for safety? This would have been an opportune time to press the question and now, of course, when the time for such questions has passed, I regret having held my tongue.

Holmes tromped directly up the hill and I nearly had to run to keep up.

"Perhaps we should have a quiet look around the grounds, first?" I offered.

"If the Rucastles are home, they have likely already heard our arrival. Besides, what if their hound is loose?"

"I shouldn't think the elder Rucastle would want any dogs around after having his throat ripped out by the one we put down."

We passed under the stand of trees that had given the house its moniker. No longer copper, the branched stood bare and gnarled.

"My mistake last time was failing to interpret the father's character from the son's behavior."

"Like father, like son."

"People don't change their ways, and neither do families. Edward Rucastle is Jephro's son, and that means dogs. Vicious dogs that resonate with their vicious philosophy."

I found my Webley was in my hand and my heart was pounding furiously. After what seemed an eternity we were at the front door. There was a distinct odor of decay about the place, and the siding and frames seemed to have swollen and puckered. The door itself no longer fitted the jamb and was merely lain against it. Rather than knock Holmes gently levered it open and slipped inside. His movements conveyed no sign of fear but I noticed his favored riding crop now resting in his hand. Holmes was prepared for a fight.

It was difficult to believe that anyone was living here. The place was filthy in the way of abandoned buildings. There was a thick layer of grit upon the floor, the furnishings were toppled and broken, and the paper peeled from the walls. Holmes paused for a moment to observe the entry. I could hear only my own ragged breathing in the eerie silence and then there was a tortured creaking from the far side of the house.

"Holmes!" I hissed.

"Steady, Watson. It is a wonder this house stands at all. That is just as likely to be a note in the inexorable dissolution of this place as it is a murderer hiding in the dark. Besides, a silent house would not bode well for finding Miss Hunter alive."

The waning sunlight barely penetrated the filthy windows and so I wrenched a taper from the fixture at the bottom of the stairs and struck it with a lucifer from my pocket.

"I wonder if the cabman has a lantern," I muttered.

"Certainly not one that he would relinquish," Holmes said.

He momentarily stepped into what must have been a parlor at one time. That must have been the very window where Miss Hunter was sat to fool Alice Rucastle's fiancee, I mused.

"I dare say there has not been much entertaining in this place for some time," Holmes said.

Carefully we made our way up the stairs. Holmes gestured at the floorboards. Here, at last, were signs of occupation. Muddy prints pointed the way to two of the doors on this floor. One of the doors was secured with a prodigious Bramah lock.

"It has been rebuilt, like a fortress!" I exclaimed. "That must be where Edward Rucastle is keeping Miss Hunter."

"We've seen no sign of either of them yet, Watson."

Holmes made his way towards the other suspicious door.

"Surely, Holmes, that is what we came for!" I gestured back at the bolted door.

"Tut, Watson. It will be no small feat to spring that lock, even for me. In the meantime, our attention would be turned from this room."

This door opened easily upon a room darkened by drawn shades. With my pistol in one fist and the candle in the other I cautiously made my way in. It was a bedroom, and unlike much of the rest of the house, it seemed to be in habitable condition.

With Holmes at my back, I made my way across and threw aside the drapes to allow long fingers of the evening sun in. I turned to survey the room again now that it was lit and stifled a scream when I saw a figure behind Holmes. My friend followed my gaze and turned on his heel, lashing out with the crop like a striking viper. The figure was unmoved, in fact, was immobile, resting in a rocking chair opposite us.

"Jephro Rucastle," Holmes observed.

The man seemed to stir, slightly. His eyes were unfocused and distant.

Still, with my Webley at the ready, I chanced to move a few steps closer, holding the candle close to Jephro's face to observe him. "Do you see these black tendrils spreading out from his bite wounds? Internal chemical burns. He was treated with lunar caustic."

Holmes sneered. "That dog had many problems, but he was hardly rabid."

"An overabundance of caution?" I wondered.

"Or a bit of justice for young Alice? Silver nitrate poisoning would have produced much the same symptoms as her brain fever."

"No doctor would conscience such an act. It is tantamount to torture. Besides, someone cares for him. He certainly isn't caring for himself in this state."

"It remains to be seen what that state is." Holmes began rummaging in the dresser. He produced a pair of stockings and tied Jephro's wrists to the arms of his chair.

"Is that really necessary?" I protested. "I don't think the man even knows where he is."

"Look at his boots, Watson. That fresh mud means he is not as much an invalid as he seems." Holmes began prying at the lower drawer. "This is the very place where Miss Hunter discovered Alice Rucastle's lock of hair. If Edward has brought her here I'll bet we find a fresh braid in this very drawer."

The lock popped beneath holmes nimble finger and he slid the drawer open.

This time I was unable to stifle a shout of horror. The drawer was filled with chestnut braids. "How many?" I gasped.

"A dozen," Holmes said. "I imagine this is Miss Hunter's." The braid was as long as Holmes' arm. "It yet smells of soap and the ends are freshly cut."

"And the others?"

"I'd like to get them under a microscope, but my first impression is that each is unique."

"Meaning each is a new victim."

"Let us wait for the facts, Watson. Perhaps there are a dozen women in Winchester who consider themselves well paid for a hair cutting."

"You can't be serious, Holmes."

"Let us find Miss Hunter. The rest can wait."

Rusty hinges creaked on the periphery of my hearing. Holmes paused for a moment to listen and then gestured that we should return to the landing. Behind us, he pulled the door shut.

"If this door opens again, be ready to take decisive action," Holmes said.

He approached the vaulted door across the way and produced his lock picking kit from his coat pocket. He depressed a spring-loaded post in the middle and the began poking around the edges of the cylindrical tumbler. There was a distinct cough downstairs.

"That is no house noise," I whispered. "Hurry up!"

"The Bramah is built upon redundancy," Holmes said. "Each arm is no more complicated than a remedial padlock, but there are seven arms, and I have to keep them under tension the whole time. With a steady hand, it is easier to pick than even a basic Chubb, but it does take a moment.

Jephro began moaning in the bedroom, but I feared to point my revolver away from the darkened staircase. Night was falling and I expected to hear the cab retreating at any moment. At last the lock turned and Holmes pushed the door in. The muddy prints continued to all three doors in this hallway. The first door opened into a bedchamber, a spartan mattress in the center and a family portrait of the Rucastles on the wall, Edward and Alice still children. The next door was made of thick hardwood and had two sliding openings, at eye-level and at the bottom. An iron bar secured it. Throwing it open I was surprised to discover that, with the exception of the boarded-up windows, the furnishings could almost be described as luxurious. This was where Alice had been kept during her convalescence, I realized. It had been meticulously maintained, like a shrine. The girls that Edward took were just another element of this diorama, I realized. A perfect moment, at least in Edward's mind, frozen in time.

Holmes pulled at the window. "Sealed shut. I suppose he doesn't want his Alices escaping."

"Shouldn't Miss Hunter be here?"

Holmes drew a finger across the rosewood writing desk, leaving a line in the dust. "I don't think anyone has been here for a few months."

"But her hair was in the drawer."

"It would seem she is a special case. Perhaps all of this proved unsatisfactory, and Edward has moved on to a new game. Let us see what the next door reveals."

In this room, hanging from pegs on the wall, were dresses, and beneath them boots and other knick-knacks.

"What is this, Holmes? It is like the wardrobe closet of a theatre."

"The locks of hair were for Jephro. These are for Edward. I fear you are right, Watson. Edward Rucastle is a murderer, and his victims never escaped this place."

"Where are they?" The hollow clothes were heartbreaking, so small and fragile.

"I recall that there is a basement," Holmes said.

"Just as clever as your stories," came a voice from behind us. "And just as stupid."

I turned to find a man holding a rifle on us. His face was twisted by a cruel sneer but there was no mistaking that this was Jephro's son.

"Is that the gun that shot Carlo?" he asked.

"Who is Carlo?" I replied.

"The dog," said Holmes.

"I had no choice, your father was being killed. I saved his life!"

Edward laughed. "I suppose I should thank you. I doubt father would do as much if he understood what has happened to him. If he had died who knows what would have become of me? With Alice gone all of this would have been lost," he gestured at the house.

"Instead you were allowed to fester in your own trauma and delusions," I said. "It made a monster out of you. I made a monster out of you."

"You give yourself too much credit. I am my father's son. He killed my mother, then he killed my sister. I learned cruelty at his knee, or rather from his boot."

"Don't you know that your sister escaped with her fiance? She is likely still out there, somewhere."

"That's a lie fed to me as a child. Alice would never have left me here, with my father."

"Perhaps she sent for you and your father interfered," Holmes said. "Sometimes the law can be used for ill as well as for good."

"I have known scant few moments of kindness, gentlemen, and the last was in her sickbed. I would bring her food and she would sing to me, and pet my hair. She needed me, and I liked it. I cared for her. I tried to, anyway, but father worried her until she died. He knew it was going to happen."

"What makes you think that?" I asked.

"He brought me a new one," Edward said. "Cut her hair and dressed her up just like I liked. But you took her away." He pointed the rifle at Holmes and his finger twitched on the trigger.

148

"Wait!" I said, stepping between them.

"And you killed Carlo," I read murder in his eyes, "And then I had nothing left but father."

"So you crippled him with poison, so you could be in control," Holmes said.

"We were pariahs up here on the hill. The villagers shunned me, and so I had to find my own amusements. The loneliness was crushing until one day I saw Alice on the road. Not the real Alice, of course, but an Alice, and she was kind to me. So I took her and I showed her where her place was. Made her my Alice, the one I wanted. She didn't understand. They never understand. But I trained her, like a dog. Starved her until she recognized her master, gave her the boot when I needed to, and she was good. For a while."

"And then?" I asked.

"She tried to run," Edward said. "They all try to run, eventually."

"Where is Miss Hunter?" I demanded.

His sneer now almost touched his ears. "She was willful. That was father's mistake. She was willful from the moment he met her. He wasn't prepared to break her."

"He wasn't trying to break her," I bellowed. "It was just a dodge, to get rid of Alice's fiancee. Jephro Rucastle had a lot to answer for, but he wasn't a monster."

"You don't know my father."

"We know his handiwork anyway," Holmes said. "He drove his second wife to madness."

"She was smart, kept quiet, stayed obedient until the end. Mother and Alice defied him, so he had to kill them."

"Have you killed Miss Hunter for defying you?" I asked.

"If all I wanted was to kill her I could have done that in Walsall."

"Ah," said Holmes. "Now I see. We are perfectly safe, Watson."

"We are?"

"Young Edward here has proven himself his father's superior in every way but one. You made Jephro Rucastle infamous."

"You mean that Edward wants me to publish his story?"

"I fear that we are creating the very malignance that we mean to combat. New generations rise to the challenge of being worthy of my brain and your pen."

"You can't be serious, Holmes!"

Edward's rifle drifted towards the floor. "We have an understanding then?"

"Understanding is not agreement," Holmes said.

The rifle started to rise again, but my Webley was already pointed at Edward's lapel.

"Drop the gun," I said.

Edward cocked his head but set the weapon down with a shrug.

"Back away," I said. "Into Alice's room."

He acquiesced with surprising ease, making no move to interfere as Holmes slammed the door shut and threw the crossbar into place.

"The game has changed," Holmes said.

"Perhaps now that he thinks I will make him famous he simply wants to live to see it. These repeat killers like to gloat, don't they? I can already envision his cell covered in his own newspaper clippings."

"No, Edward thinks he has the advantage, somehow."

My sense of victory was indeed short-lived for the moment we were back on the landing I saw that the other door was ajar. Holmes rushed ahead into the bedroom but before I could even protest he had returned.

"The brute pulled the chair apart to escape."

"Without us hearing him?"

"The locked wing must be insulated to keep any sounds in… and in this case, out."

"We can't leave without finding Miss Hunter," I said.

150

"Edward all but admitted he buries his kills in the basement."

"Surely there is still hope for Miss Hunter."

"Let us know the facts before we resign ourselves to hope," Holmes said.

Fearlessly he dashed down the stairs into the darkness. I hurried after, both so that I might aid him with my pistol and so that I would not be left alone in this horrible house. As we passed the front door, still hanging open, I despaired to see that the driver had made good on his promise to depart at nightfall. At least he knew we were here. I hoped he might send the police.

In near darkness Holmes pressed through the house, finding the basement door at the rear of the kitchen. Here, too, a Bramah lock had been installed. To my surprise, Holmes turned not to his lockpick but rather to the poker that rested near the long cold oven. He lunged forward and plunged it into the far side of the door. He then seized the implement with both hands, stepping into it and wrenching it around and up. The iron poker flexed, and just when it seemed it might bend the door whined, and then shuddered. Holmes leveraged the poker against the wall and the door splintered away from its hinges.

"So much for a new lock on an old door," Holmes said.

He took the candle from my hand and began down the steps. I did my best to stay within the flickering halo of light. Like many old country houses, the basement was hewn directly from the earth. My gaze was frantically pinwheeling around, my brain trying to make sense of the shadows and the darkness. My heel slipped and I found myself ankle-deep in loose dirt. I had stepped upon a grave, I realized, and I recoiled with an instinctive horror. A body lay just below, perhaps it was the bony remains of a life long extinguished, or perhaps it was Miss Hunter, still warm to the touch. In my mind, a putrid horror stirred from its slumber at my ill-placed step. Holmes had continued unabated, surely untroubled by any morbid fantasies, and I was now stranded in the dark. I could move towards the candlelight, but what other peril was invisible to me? An open grave seemed a real threat, and who knew what other malicious games Edward was up to. Mere steps behind me were the stairs to the kitchen. Or had I turned when I recoiled? All of a sudden the ground felt as if it had bucked under my feet and I felt complete disorientation, unsure even if I were standing upright or cocked at an unnatural angle.

I decided to make my way to the wall and follow that around and so began carefully inching forward, probing the dirt with my toes and helplessly swiping at the empty space in front of me. At last, I felt the cool grit of basement wall on my fingertips. I breathed a deep sigh of relief and felt a laugh rising in my chest. Before it escaped my lips my throat was cinched tight. I dropped my Webley and pried at my neck with my fingers, but I was unable to get any purchase on the smooth band that was suffocating me. I felt along it and discovered it was a slender material drawn tight. Stockings, I realized. Jephro had lain in wait for us. I tried to shout a warning to Holmes but couldn't manage so much as a wheeze. Where a deep blackness had enveloped me before now points of light swam like a school of fish, around and around. If I hadn't dropped my gun I could have shot the fiend, but instead, I dangled helplessly before him, the strength in my limbs ebbing.

Knowing I had but moments left to act in this world I levered myself against the garrotte and took three quick steps up the wall. At the apex I pushed with both feet and, as I had hoped, threw Jephro off balance. He toppled backward and landed with a sickening snap. His arms went limp and I whipped the silk stocking off from around my neck, which felt like it was being pricked with a thousand hot needles as my circulation returned. At that very moment, moonlight washed over the scene and I saw Holmes silhouetted on the far side of the basement. Between us were the graves we feared we would find, and at my feet was Jephro, his head lolling over the edge of the fresh grave I had disturbed earlier. There was no question that his neck had broken when he fell as straight and unguarded as an overgrown tree, his powerful arms strangling me rather than breaking his fall. Each gasp of cold air I sucked in pummeled my lungs like fists.

"Stop dithering, Watson!" Holmes called. "Edward has beaten us to the kennel. Have your bullpup ready to bark back at whatever hellhound he is about to unleash."

I regained my Webley and put it through its paces to ensure it wasn't jammed with dirt. Carefully I picked my way through the Rucastles' sordid catacomb. When I reached the outer steps Holmes gave me a brief appraising look and then bounded over the top.

Across a small pitch, Edward leaned against the kennel with his insufferable smirk.

"Your father is dead," I said, peevishly, hoping to put Edward off his game.

"If a lunatic dies in a basement and nobody ever hears of it, does it even matter?" Edward laughed.

The killer was in my sight then, with my finger quivering on the trigger. "I could shoot with a clean conscience."

"Then you would have done it already," Edward said. "The two of you and your nobility. You walked away from the Copper Beeches years ago with the job half done and called it justice. Does this look like justice to you?" He gestured expansively.

"A mistake I will not make again, I assure you," Holmes said, approaching Edward in a grappling pose.

The villain unlatched the door behind his back. "You lack the animal honesty for true justice. In nature the question is not 'may I' but 'can I' and the answer is decided in blood. They just live and the rest perish." He threw open the kennel door and inside was a rattling of chains.

"I accept your terms," Holmes replied.

"What?" Edward was taken aback.

"We will forsake the niceties of society and put the question to a test of mettle." Holmes was stripping down to his undershirt.

"You can't be serious!" I gasped.

"Why not?" Holmes said. "We have learned at great cost that there can be no half-measures with the Rucastles."

"To the death?" Edward salivated.

Holmes simply nodded.

"This is madness!" I cried.

"You are not to interfere, Watson. This business must reach its ultimate conclusion."

Edward slipped free of his filthy coat as well. There, in the moonlight, beneath the gnarled beeches, the two men circled each other. Edward lunged forward and Holmes slapped him away, bouncing on the balls of his feet like a prizefighter. Edward roared with rage and rushed in. This time Holmes wrapped his arm around Edward's neck and forced him to the ground. In return Edward sent a pounding elbow into Holmes' ribs over and over, breaking Holmes' grip. They staggered around each other again. I had feared that Edward's relative youth, and reckless insanity, would be decisive, but Holmes' dispassionate calculation and long expertise in bartitsu evened the contest. They locked arms and grappled now, Holmes grinding his thumbs into Edward's shoulders, and Rucastle trying to force Holmes to stumble backward. All of a sudden Holmes rolled in the direction Rucastle was pushing, using the force Edward was exerting to flip the man over. Rucastle landed hard on his back and wheezed. Holmes pressed his foot down on Edward's back and locked the lunatic's ankles in a vice-like armlock, keeping him pinioned by his own weight.

Edward rocked back and forth on the ground until he got out from under Holmes' boot. He rolled away and got back on his feet. Both men were winded now, and I doubted whether either had the wherewithal to finish the other off. Holmes moved in for a feint and Edward slapped him in the face with a handful of dirt. For just a moment Holmes was staggered while wiping his eyes but it was all the opportunity that Edward needed. He drove a punishing fist into Holmes' solar plexus and the clubbed the back of Holmes' head with two fists intertwined when he was bent over. Holmes was on all fours now, seemingly struggling to regain his composure. Edward slipped a knife from his boot and now raised it over Holmes. The whole terrible tableau was frozen for a moment and then red flowers bloomed across Edward's chest. The maniac toppled backward. I ran to Holmes.

"Watson, I told you not to interfere."

"I'm ashamed to say that I did not," I showed him the unfired Webley. "The moment got the better of me."

"Then who...?"

The chains began to rattle inside the kennel again. I moved in front of Holmes and aimed the Webley. Out of the dark lurched a dark shape. As it moved into the moonlight it reared up and I gasped.

Violet Hunter stood before me, smoking pistol in hand. One side of her face was swollen and black and her hair was roughly chopped. What was most remarkable, however, was the metal collar resting above her tattered dress.

"But how...?" I stammered.

"Edward Rucastle remained trapped in the moment when he believed his sister died and he lost everything he cared about," Violet said. "For all of his vileness, he was a boy trapped in a man's body."

"I don't understand," I said.

Violet smiled at me. "Feminine modesty can be a sword and a shield, Doctor Watson. A woman, even an eccentric like myself, can't walk around with a gun belt on. So I improvised." She patted her thigh. "Even a governess wears enough layers to keep a few secrets, and a holster doesn't know the difference between braces and hose supporters."

"And Edward never developed an interest in what might be under a woman's skirt?" Holmes said.

"He wanted a sister. It was part of his very limited view of women. Something you two might reflect upon."

"If you were armed why did you not act sooner?" I asked.

"Edward must have drugged me. I awoke here, already in chains. Alone I would have simply perished from starvation. I needed someone about who could release me." She put a meaningful weight on her last words.

"Ah, yes," I said, before fumbling through Edward's pockets. I found a ring holding keys both remarkably new and remarkably old. Carefully I released Miss Hunter, well aware that her finger yet rested upon the trigger of her weapon, and that her hand still trembled from heightened excitement. When I stepped away I was surprised to see Holmes ruminating upon Rucastle's corpse. Of course, he often was prey to morbid fixations, but this was no scientific examination. My friend was deep in a solemn reverie. At last, he seemed to feel our eyes upon him and he snapped back to attention.

"It seems I again failed you due to a lack of imagination, Miss Hunter."

"To the contrary, Mr. Holmes. No sane man could have anticipated this, and you have come when I have needed you and taken action at the crucial moments."

"You are too generous, Miss Hunter. For all his madness Edward Rucastle has given a bit of clarity to my thinking. As my friend Watson has so aptly shown, Sherlock Holmes is a gentleman detective. That is not what the new century calls for."

"Steady on, Holmes. Let's go back to Baker Street. A cup of Mrs. Hudson's tea and a fresh collar will set you right, and then on to Simpson's. Tomorrow will be a new day."

Holmes laughed. "Good old Watson! Our business is not quite finished. Go fetch the police, will you? Miss Hunter and I shall endeavor to make ourselves presentable."

The story of the horrors at the Copper Beeches was quite a sensation at the time, and Miss Hunter was once again a celebrity, despite her best efforts to escape London and the yellow press. She only commented upon the matter once, giving an impassioned speech to the House of Commons in support of legal reforms to protect and enfranchise women.

Every publisher across two continents hounded me to give my firsthand account, but I only relented when Miss Hunter asked me to so that the public might have some answers and she might have some peace. I donated my fee to her school, where I hope it has done some good. Holmes and I did have that dinner at Simpson's, our final visit to that fine establishment as I recall. It was perhaps the only occasion on which I could describe Holmes as nostalgic. It was not the famous cases that he recalled most fondly, but the miscellanea. I was happy to see his spirits so quickly restored. While the memory of that dinner is bittersweet to me now I am glad that Holmes had that moment of glad resolution, for no man deserved it more.

There had been little demand for Holmes' unique services in the last few weeks and he was prowling the sitting room of 221B Baker Street like a caged tiger. He was also scratching at his elbows and Watson had no trouble in deducing the import of that gesture. When Holmes could not find stimulation in a case he would eventually turn to an injectable solution of cocaine. As a doctor Watson was well aware of the adverse long term effects cocaine would have on Holmes' body. As a longtime friend, he was acutely aware of the effect it would have upon Holmes' spirits. A brief euphoria would be followed by a sharp swing into misanthropy from which only Holmes himself could effect an escape. Watson feared that it would be one of these cocaine-shaped pits that would eventually claim the life of the Great Detective, rather than a bullet or a blade. Thankfully a distraction had presented itself.

"I say, Holmes! Look at this!" Watson proffered the evening newspaper he had been reading. Holmes glanced at it from across the room. On the page showing there was an advertisement for the Continental Circus and Variety Revue.

"Vulgar entertainments for idlers and the weak-minded," Holmes spat.

"Well, you're the one and I'm the other. Let us exhume ourselves from the confines of this flat and see what the Continental Circus has to offer." Holmes threw a searching glance across the room, looking for any other form of engagement in vain.

"I suppose when a problem refuses to present itself to us, we must make do with presenting ourselves and hoping for the worst."

"That's the spirit, old man!" They donned their coats and hats and with a brief shout up the stairs to Mrs. Hudson were off to take in the evening's festivities. Even had the two not been familiar with the fairground, where they had indeed had reason to make professional calls before, it would have been no great challenge to find it. In every street droves of people were all milling in the same direction. Following the flow of traffic quickly brought them within sight of various tents and merchant stands. Acrobats and clowns and sword swallowers and fire eaters all beckoned visitors into the makeshift compound. The smell of charred meat, stale beer, and cheap tobacco filled the air. Having resigned themselves to being part of the herd tonight, the two allowed the crowd to escort them into the main tent, paying a shilling each at the entrance. Inside they took their places on the wooden bleachers. The show began with a parade of animals around the center ring. The crowd cheered but Holmes simply fidgeted and sighed. Next came a clown troupe that ran through a number of slapstick routines. Watson quite enjoyed one where a clown removed his top hat to reveal a small money holding a cream pie. The monkey then threw the pie in the face of a pretend constable who had been trying to escort the clowns from the ring. Holmes was scratching at his elbow again. Just as Watson was trying to devise some new entertainment a ladder was erected at center ring. Then a beautiful woman in a diaphanous gown followed by a coterie made a grand sweep of the ring, waving to the audience. Watson was transfixed, certain that she had blown a kiss just to him, and thus Sherlock alone watched as a child carried a large bucket of water, almost a watering trough, out to the center of the ring and gratefully let it fall to the ground. There was a quick slosh of water. With the help of her assistants, the woman at the center of the ring began to disrobe, revealing a bathing costume underneath her gown. Watson nearly fell from the bench he had just been perched on the edge of. The woman gave one last series of waves and then ascended the ladder. At the top, she steeled herself momentarily, which also had the effect of building the tension inside the tent. Then she suddenly leaped from the top of the ladder. The audience gasped! With perfect diver's form, she slid right into the water trough making less of a splash than the boy did when he delivered the receptacle. Nothing happened for a moment and the crowd began to murmur. The basin had been too shallow to accommodate a person falling into it at that angle from that high up. Surely the woman must have broken her neck and died upon impact. But where was the body, they wondered? Suddenly the woman sprung up from the trough, glistening water streaming from her as she accepted the crowd's raucous applause. Watson was on his feet yelling brava! Holmes remained seated and his hands remained still, but there was now a gleam in his hawk-like eyes as he attempted to derive the secret of the stunt from afar.

"Watson, we shall have to endeavor to have a closer look at that basin after the crowd has dispersed,"

"Oh, yes, Holmes! I agree wholeheartedly!" Watson effused, ears closed and eyes locked on the comely diver as she was escorted from the ring. She made one last backward glance and Watson was certain her gaze had rested upon him. "I say, Holmes! I've got a bit of dust caught in my throat. I do believe I will go see one of these concessionaires about a little something to wash it down!" Watson ambled off precisely in the direction that the bewitching woman had just left. Holmes smiled to himself and settled in for the next act. The ringmaster announced Hugh Montgomery, sharpshooter, and bursting out from the performer's entrance to the tent came a frothing steed mounted by a burly man dressed in the canvas togs and distinctive bent brim hat of an Australian outdoorsman. As the horse spun in a frantic circle he calmly shot out a dozen mirrors that had been suspended from the rigging of the tent. The crowd rose to their feet with applause. Four more mounted riders dressed in native garb rode into the ring, each brandishing wooden aboriginal masks on poles. Montgomery shot each mask in turn, turning his horse opposite the direction of the circling riders. Again the crowd cheered and fought for the wooden mask fragments that had fallen into the audience. The extra riders disappeared back out of the tent and Montgomery brought his own horse down to a trot.

"Good people of London! You've seen what a cavalryman of the Light Horse Regiment can do. I can shoot better on a moving horse than a British man can standing still!" Booes from the crowd. "You've seen me shoot a stationary target. You've seen me shoot a moving target. If I could do but that I'd be an adequate circus performer for the likes of you!" More booing. "But I'm a world-class sharpshooter, maybe the best! When I fought on the northern frontier the enemy didn't give us mirrors or masks or other contrivances to shoot at. You developed a sharper eye or you ended up dead. I'll challenge any man here to a duel of pistols, live loads. I'll give you ten to one odds that I can shoot the pistol out of any man's hands before he can put a bullet in me!" The crowd gasped and murmured. "No takers? How about this?" A strange device looking almost like a sarcophagus was wheeled into the ring by a team of workmen. "Any man brave enough can shoot at me from behind the cover of this lead shield. The only risk is to your pride and your pocketbook while I put my very mortality on the line. I have this note of guarantee from your Bank of England itself. If I lose, and I won't, you will get paid what is owed you! Now, who is man enough?" From a rowdy contingent near ringside came a knotty stump of a man with a shaved head and leathery countenance.

"I'll not have you denigrating Her Majesty's Royal Army!" came the drunken slur. "I've served twice as long as you've been alive and killed twice as many! Give me a gun and I plant you in the green English countryside!" A workman hurried into the ring with a pistol and a sack of bullets.

"Here we have England's defender ladies and gentlemen. Let us give him a round of applause!" The crowd cheered. "Now, satisfy yourself that the weapon is real and in working condition." The man took aim at one of the fallen masks and put three more bullets in it.

"Aye, it works."

"Take your place behind the shield, then!" The man hunkered close up behind the shield with only his shooting arm unencumbered. He peeped through eyeholes in the shield, Montgomery paced off thirty steps and turned square to the edifice. "Ready! Steady! Draw!" Shots rang out. The drunken soldier cursed and shook his suddenly empty hand. Montgomery smirked and blew the gun smoke from the barrel of his pistol. Holmes, like everyone fixated on the duel, was surprised to hear screaming from the crowd on the opposite side of the ring. "Right through the head, they shot him dead!" someone cried. Had one of the combatant's bullets gone astray or had somebody with uncanny timing used the cover of the performance to commit a murder? Holmes racked his memory. Had he heard two shots or three? He was already pushing through the crowd to get to the body. He must see whatever evidence was available before the crowd trampled it all away.

Meanwhile, Watson was still a dozen paces behind the lady diver as she entered her wagon and then screamed. Watson hustled forward and yelled up into the open door. "Miss! Is everything all right? I am a doctor and an associate of Mr. Sherlock Holmes beside and I'll have it sorted in a tick!" The lady leaned back out of the wagon.

"I have no need of a doctor but I would not turn away a detective." She regarded Watson for a moment and then leaned back into the wagon without closing the door. Watson removed his hat and sidled right up to the opening.

"Might I first say that I greatly enjoyed your performance, miss..."

"Vivian Westing. I caught the name of Mr. Sherlock Holmes but I did not quite catch yours."

"Ah. Dr. John Watson, Army retired, at your service, miss. What seems to be the trouble? I heard you scream a moment ago."

"I'm a bit embarrassed, Doctor."

"Not at all, not at all."

"My scream was one of frustration. Someone has been stealing from me. Every time I return from a performance another item has gone missing."

"Most unusual! Are these items valuable?"

"Certainly not. Traveling performers such as myself know better than to take valuables on the road. It is simply inconvenient to be constantly at a loss for hairbrushes and thread and the like and unnerving to know someone is in here taking liberties with my personal effects."

"Quite so, quite so! You may consider me on the case, my fair lady! I know a bit about detection and will have the culprit in hand in no time!"

"Thank you, Doctor! That will be such a relief! Now, if you don't mind, I must change out of this wet costume. It is clinging to me everywhere." At that Watson stammered and dropped his hat. The door closed. Watson stooped down to retrieve his hat and decided to begin his investigation thusly. He had often seen Holmes inspect the ground at a crime scene. Unfortunately, the performers' encampment was bustling with activity and there were a hundred different footprints going in every direction. The Great Detective himself couldn't do much with that, Watson consoled himself. He paced the perimeter of the wagon, prodding the vehicle for any weaknesses. There was the door in the rear and a small window on each of the three other sides, but not even a child could fit through. Watson supposed someone could reach an arm through to grab something the size of a hairbrush, but he couldn't be sure until, if, he corrected himself, he was welcomed inside. As he felt a certain warmth escape his collar a gunshot rang out back in the performance area and the audience began screaming. Vivian Westing lept from the wagon and together with Watson and the others milling around ran towards the entrance to the large tent. Watson saw that the commotion was just above and to the right of him, and he saw Holmes fighting his way through the crowd. Watson lept up the steps and was at the scene of the crime in a moment. A man's body lay sprawled across three rows, shot through the head and gazing vacantly into the rigging above. Watson did not bother with a pulse.

"I say, Holmes! What's all this?"

"The very same crowd who were cheering for one murder a moment ago now seem to be quite inconsolable about another."

"I'm must admit to being a bit confused."

"I imagine so. While you were off quenching your thirst," Holmes cast a sidelong glance at Miss Westing, "Hugh Montgomery the Australian sharpshooter challenged any person in the crowd to a duel."

"And it was this poor sod who answered the challenge? Poor form shooting into a crowd. There are women of the fairer sex to consider!" Watson placed a protective arm around Miss Westing.

"And children as well. Some might also be of the opinion that a man should not be shot simply for attending the circus. However, it seems that even an Australian won't fire blindly into a crowd of innocent people. You'll see his opponent over at ringside steadying his nerves with a restorative." Indeed, Watson observed a group of soldiers huddled together around a bottle of whiskey.

"I don't know what passes for marksmanship down under but in my day any soldier missing the mark by that much would not be called a sharpshooter."

"To the contrary, I personally witnessed Mr. Montgomery shoot the pistol right out of his opponent's' hand. A neat trick if I do say so myself. This bullet came from another gun, one that must have been fired simultaneously to the duel."

"Surely this other shooter was seen. There must be a thousand people in this tent!"

"Indeed. In most public shootings you expect to see the crowd part in two places, around the victim, and around the assailant. Here the only reaction was around the victim."

"How can that be?"

"I wonder," said Holmes, peering up into the canopy. He turned to Miss Westing. "What is it like up there? Are there hidden spots an assailant might hide?"

"No, Mr. Holmes! Down here beneath the lights, the upper reaches of the tent appear obscured but up above the lights it is quite easy to see the whole space."

"Perhaps the assailant chose a time during the show when no performers were in the canopy. He might have gone up the outside of the tent and crawled through a flap…"

"There are always eyes up in the canopy."

"Is that so?"

"Yes. There are always apprentices about, acrobats and jugglers and clowns. In addition to the performers, there are the roustabouts. All of these people often watch the show from the canopy. It gives them the best view in the house and hides them from their various taskmasters."

"Indeed, it must be marvelous to see the circus from up high!" Watson observed.

"Trust me, Dr. Watson. The charm of the circus wears off after a while, but the charms of a woman never do, especially for boys of apprenticeship age."

"Whatever are you referring to, Miss Westing?"

"Let us just say that in close quarters lady performers often find it impossible to be completely discreet all of the time, especially when there are often neither walls nor roof. As someone with more than one costume change, let me assure you there are always eyes above us."

Watson sputtered and chomped on his cigar. "I say, the cads! I'll give them what for!"

"I appreciate your chivalrous inclinations, Dr. Watson, but the circus is simply not a genteel environment for a woman."

"Take heart, Watson. We know firsthand what an excellent resource impudent scamps can be. I can only assume we are being overheard at this very moment. I've got a penny for every set of eyes in the air that cares to come forward." There was a great jostling of the tent. Suddenly a pack of small rough figures descended upon Holmes.

"I were up there the whole time and weren't no strangers with guns up there, I'll tell you that much." Holmes flipped the boy a coin.

"What about familiar faces? Anyone up there who is unaccounted for?"

"No, sir, ain't nobody missing. It's easy money to be here tonight, innit? Whilst all this is going on nobody's calling for this to be moved or that to be hoisted. But they've still got to pay us at the end of the night."

"You're certain?"

"Yes, sir."

"Very good." Holmes tossed the girl a coin.

"Who carries a pistol around here normally?"

"Besides the sharpshooter? A couple of animal trainers, Mr. Buccoli and his guards." Holmes flipped a coin.

"Who is Mr. Buccoli?"

"Owner of the circus."

"Where is he now?"

"Probably up in some hotel suite with some aspiring local starlet" Miss Westing snorted.

"Oh?" said Holmes.

"As I said, the appeal of the circus wears off. Mr. Buccoli is rarely in attendance. Other than taking the proceeds to the bank and auditioning new talent he has very little to do with the actual show."

"I see. We may have to verify his whereabouts but it rather seems this Mr. Buccoli would hesitate to kill his golden goose in this manner. Have there been any other unusual events of late?"

"I say, Holmes!" Watson interjected. "Just before the crowd began screaming I had just begun my own investigation for Miss Westing."

"How very enterprising of you Watson."

"I rather thought so. It seems someone has been pilfering personal belongings from Miss Westing's trailer."

"Valuables?"

"No, knickknacks and baubles."

166

"Of what sort?" Holmes asked Miss Westing.

"Hairbrushes, perfume, costume jewelry of no value."

"Clothing?"

"No."

"Underclothes?"

"I should say not, Mr. Holmes!" Miss Westing blushed.

"Now see here, Holmes! I'll not hear any more vulgar speech in front of a lady!"

"No clothing, so not a lover or other personal connection. No undergarments so not a fetishist."

"Any more of that talk and we'll come to blows!"

"I should like to see your trailer, Miss Westing."

"Nothing to be gained" Watson offered as the group made their way back to the trailer. "I inspected it myself. No useful footprints, no signs of criminal mischief."

"Hmm," Holmes said as he made a quick inspection of the scene. "Do you often eat pie with your hands, Miss Westing."

"Do I what? I never! Firstly I have to maintain my figure for professional purposes."

"I can attest to that!" Watson declared.

"Secondly, I can't afford pie on what little Mr. Buccoli pays us and I'm never in one place long enough to gain the kind of suitor who would take a girl to a pie shop."

"A great tragedy!" Watson bemoaned. "If I might be so bold as to rectify that particular situation?"

"What of that window?" Holmes asked. "Do you spend a lot of time looking out of it."

"It is generous of you to refer to that hole in the wall as a window. As you can see I would have to lean over the table and crane my neck around. That's just for fresh air if any circus air can be called fresh. I go outside when I want a view."

"Quite right. I believe we should speak to the animal trainers now." Miss Westing and Holmes and Watson exited the trailer, which groaned with relief. There was no need to ask where the trainers were. The animal sounds and smells left no doubt. The party walked through the circus' private encampment to the far side. Here the horses were stabled and the lions were caged. There was even an elephant shackled to the ground slowing crushing some hay in its massive maw. Nearby was one man throwing food out to the trained dogs while also calling out tricks. The dogs yipped and barked with joy and ran in circles leaping at each other. Back in the shadows at the very outskirts of the encampment sat another man, drawn in upon himself and unremarkable in every way save for the monkey sitting on his shoulder. "Sometimes judging a book by its cover can be expedient," said Holmes, carefully picking his way through the animal debris and giving the elephant a wide berth. Watson offered a steadying hand to Miss Westing but she had grabbed her robes in both hands and yanked them up to her knees and was already off across the field after Holmes. Watson sighed and began his solitary trudge. As the group got closer the nondescript man, who had been seemingly staring vacantly into the distance, suddenly became very agitated and began rearranging the small cages and boxes around him. "Might we have a word, Mister....?" Holmes inquired.

"I am quite busy at the moment. The animals all have to be settled. Mr. Buccoli won't do with no more noise complaints, and I won't be allowed a wink of sleep until my task is completed." He hadn't even turned to acknowledge Holmes.

"What an interesting companion you have," Holmes pointed his walking stick toward the monkey. The wiry creature screeched and bared its tiny fangs.

"He don't like people. Rescued him I did, from an organ grinder what used to beat him. He ain't got much use for people since then and I don't blame him."

"To the contrary, I think he has taken quite the liking for one person, and the same can be said of yourself."

"I don't know what you're on about but I have work to do so if you don't mind I'll get back to it."

Watson finally caught up with the group and leaned up against a stack of boxes huffing and puffing. The reaction from the monkey was immediate. It leaped from the shoulders of the man onto the top of the boxes and began beating Watson about the head and face.

"Now see here, fellow! It is dirty dealing to attack a winded man unawares, even for a blasted monkey!" This rebuke was met with further screeching and slapping. Watson's hat fell into the foul mud. "If it is a fight you want it is a fight you will have. Let us at least agree to abide by the Queensberry Rules." At this, the monkey leaped from the boxes and latched himself onto Watson's head. "This is most irregular!" Watson declared as he fell to the ground.

"My dear Watson, what you have interpreted as a sporting endeavor by your simian friend there is, in fact, an effort to protect that which he holds most dear in the world."

"How's that then?" said Watson, now holding the irate monkey out at arm's length. With one last hiss of contempt, the monkey scampered off. Holmes moved toward the stack of boxes. The taciturn trainer grabbed Holmes arm. In one swift move, the trainer was on the ground clutching his head. Holmes was already turning the clasps on the box. Suddenly an audible and distinct click of a gun being cocked was heard. Miss Westing turned and gasped. The trainer gave a low mean chuckle from the ground, Watson puffed in disbelief. Holmes turned.

"We meet our true sharpshooter at last." The monkey stood on the rump of a horse, having pulled one of Hugh Montgomery's pistols from the saddle holster. The barrel was aimed unwaveringly at Holmes.

"I think it is best you leave and don't come back!" sneered the trainer.

"Even Miss Westing? You finally have her attention." Holmes observed.

"What? I...never..." The trainer attempted to get up out of the mud and flee in shame, but he slipped again and landed face first in the muck. The monkey watched the trainer and Holmes watched the monkey. The moment its focus had shifted he struck out with his cane and rapped the small furry hand holding the weapon. It fell to the ground. The monkey screamed with rage.

"What is going on here? I don't understand!" said Miss Westing.

"Animals and their trainers often develop a special sympathy," Holmes explained. "In this case, this little fellow picked up on the tender feeling that the trainer had developed for you, Miss Westing!"

"Whatever do you mean?" she protested.

"Damn you!" cried the trainer.

"What you see before you writhing around on the ground is what as known as a secret admirer."

"The cheek!" Watson cried.

"I don't understand. I've never spoken two words with this man."

"You certainly had more than two words for every Jim Dandy in every rat hole this miserable circus stops in. I hear you crying about being treated like nothing because you are just a circus girl. I would have treated you like a queen, but you never even looked my way."

"So this is who has been stealing my belongings?"

"Lies! I would never have stolen a thing! I wanted to take care of you!"

"Likely story from a nutter who works with beasts all day." Watson snorted.

"In fact, I do find it likely," Holmes said. "He saw in Miss Westing an ideal of womanhood for which to pine. Purely abstract and theoretical. I have no doubt that if we searched we would find a journal of ghastly poetry or somesuch, but this man would not sully this imaginary relationship with theft."

"I don't understand, Mr. Holmes. Then who..." Miss Westing despaired.

"Animals, much to their credit, and incapable of such flights of fancy. Unrestrained by lofty ideals, this little wretch began building a primitive love nest." Holmes pointed at the monkey and everyone gasped. "He would steal into your trailer through those tiny windows whenever there was no one around. Often during performances, I suspect. After throwing his tiny pie in the face of the pantomime constable he recently made a clandestine visit leaving behind the confectionary evidence we earlier observed."

"But a monkey in love with a woman? Surely you jest, Holmes!"

"This man was in love with a woman, in his own way." Holmes pointed towards the still prostrate trainer. "The monkey simply followed the lead of whom it perceived to be it's superior."

"Most singular! But where is this love nest?"

"As Miss Westing has informed us, the life of a circus performer is a transient one. A true nest would have been impossible, but I suspect it found a cozy box somewhere to make their own." Holmes pushed at the top box he had unlatched with his cane and it toppled over spilling forth a variety of female errata.

"But how has this monkey managed such a thing? Loading and unloading the box, moving from town to town, with no one noticing."

"Out trainer friend here noticed. He must have. Whilst he was above stealing he was clearly not above sharing in the spoils."

"I was going to return these things to her at the first opportunity!"

"Good show, Holmes! I dare say you have solved the burglaries but what of the murder?"

"I believe the same culprit stands accused."

The trainer gasped, Watson dropped his cigar, declining to retrieve it from the muck, and Miss Westing experience a minor swoon.

"The monkey! A murderer! But why? And How?"

"Am I right in thinking Mr. Montgomery has come courting as of late?" Miss Westing blushed.

"Mr. Holmes, what has that to do with anything?"

"And may I further surmise that on at least one occasion his amorous advances were at least partially successful?"

"I never!" As Holmes recovered from the quick slap he received from Miss Westing he received another from Watson.

"I've warned you, Holmes, I will not hear a lady disrespected!"

"No disrespect intended, of course. My apologies. I merely deduce that on one of his pilfering pilgrimages this monkey retrieved quite the prize - a loaded gun! A gun left in the trailer by Mr. Montgomery. Surely a man who makes his living by shooting is not careless with his tools, so the gun was not left casually. Had he presented it as a gift to Miss Westing, as a memento or as a means of protection, she would have hidden it away or kept it on her person, like any other valuable. What makes a gunman forget his gun? Perhaps the aftereffects of amorous exertion in a confined space. The gun fell from his holster and he never noticed. The monkey, unwittingly, stole the weapon and carried it up into the canopy in order to make its way back to its own stash. Juggling the gun whilst navigating the ropes the trigger was accidentally depressed."

"Right through the head of the poor victim? That's quite a shot!"

"Find the highest point you can overlooking a crowd and look down. It's all heads."

"Remarkable Holmes! Whatever will happen now? Will the police arrest the trainer?"

"I think not, at least not for murder. I would wager his circus days are over, however."

"What then, arrest the monkey?"

"I would not put it past Lestrade, but it is a simple beast with no understanding of what it did."

"So the murder goes unpunished?"

"Mr. Buccoli will probably have to pay a cash settlement, the worst punishment he can imagine. The trainer will be separated from his charges and from Miss Westing. No jail time but a lifetime of misery nonetheless. The only person who comes out ahead is Miss Westing."

"How do you figure that Mr. Holmes?"

"She can rightfully claim that her beauty has driven men to ruin and beasts to murder, She is the Helen of Troy of the continental circus industry. I suspect that will make for a pretty payday or two when news of this hits the papers."

Holmes sat at the window, watching this strangely American street, wide and smooth, running straight through from horizon to horizon below. It was so unlike his beloved London, with its dark alleys and twisted passageways, fog-shrouded and steeped in intrigue. That place, so familiar, was lost to him now. For the greater good Holmes had made the penultimate sacrifice and relinquished every aspect of his life beyond his animal existence. London thought it had lost Sherlock Holmes over the edge of Reichenbach falls that fateful day, but Holmes believed rather the opposite was true. His musing was interrupted when there came a quiet knocking at the door. The sigh that escaped from his lips was carried away on the smoke from his cigarette. He feared a pipe might betray him, even one of those wretched corn cobs they favored down South. The tobacco here was too sweet but fresh and plentiful. He opened the door and saw a man in a dark suit, wringing his hat almost as if in contrition.

"Mr. Baker, I presume?"

"Detective Shea, I perceive." Holmes gestured for the man to enter.

"You can call me Gus," Shea offered his hand.

Holmes took it briskly, but rather than shaking it he led the man further into the room and deposited him in front of a chair. He then closed the door and returned to his place by the window. Holmes knew that by sitting thus he was now obscured by the light outside while his visitor was fully illuminated so that his every minuscule tic was observable. Finally, Shea sat down.

"I sure am glad to meet you, Mr. Baker. Detective Hargrave in New York spoke most highly of you. It is irregular from the police to consult civilian detectives, you understand."

"I am most familiar with things irregular. About what, exactly, would you like to consult me?"

"I assume you read the papers and that you know about this business with Lisa Billings?"

"The young woman who took an axe to her parents? Nasty business, but concluded, or so I thought."

"She awaits her execution, and I am the one who conducted the investigation that led to her conviction."

"Congratulations, I am sure it has made your career. I fail to apprehend the intention of this interview."

"It's just that, well, the whole thing doesn't sit right with me. I've got this lump of ice in my chest that bothers me something awful in the quiet hours of the night. I think she might be innocent, Mr. Baker."

"What evidence leads you to believe that?"

"None of it, to be honest. The case against her is one of the best I've ever seen. She has the motive, what with her father so quickly replacing her deceased mother with a grasping step-mother with whom she often quarreled, and the family fortune being bled away by all those relations. Her being caught in the act of destroying evidence, burning those clothes in the furnace, I see that to be as damning as anyone does. Her lack of alibi, her strange behavior, her inconsistencies in interrogations; it all adds up."

"And yet you find yourself uneasy?"

"Terribly uneasy, Mr. Baker."

"It is a hard thing to commit a person to death, even more so a pretty child. Your reservations are natural, even commendable, but I am familiar with this case, Detective Shea. I have friends of every station on every side of the law, and I can assure you my interest has been active and thorough. You are an apt policeman, and that is a rare thing. Console yourself that justice has been served as well as man might serve it."

"Please, Mr. Baker. I fear I'll carry this guilt for the rest of my days. Hargrave told me there is no finer investigative mind in the world."

Holmes steepled his fingers and peered deeply into his own mind for a few moments. "You give me no new clues, no leads, no specific problem to solve. Where would you propose I begin?"

"The heads, Mr. Baker. We never found the heads. Even with the most suspicious interpretation of her story, the girl had but half an hour where she could have disposed of the heads and she never left the property, which has since been searched up and down a dozen times over."

Holmes snubbed the last bit of his cigarette out and then lit another. He paced the room, turned back towards Shea, and blew a ring of smoke up towards the ceiling. "If I had known in New York that this was the case I had been summoned to examine I would never have come. As gruesome as the particulars are, those missing heads are but trivialities. However, since I am already here in Massachusetts I shall discover your missing heads, and put your fears to rest."

"Oh, thank you, Mr. Baker! Thank you! I just can't go on without knowing for certain."

"When is this young lady's execution?"

"In one week."

"Ample time. Good day, Detective Shea."

After the detective had left, Holmes pulled on his coat and pinched homburg. It was a short walk down to the offices of the Herald News. Holmes had talked his way into more than one newspaper morgue by posing as a fellow journalist on international assignment here in the States. In this case, it was unnecessary, as pressmen from every corner of the civilized world had descended upon Fall River to cover Lisa Billings' impending execution. As a professional courtesy, the Herald News staff had displayed all of the relevant materials in their reading room. Holmes truly had followed the sensational case closely, but his files were back in New York. He skimmed the articles with an eye towards identifying any new suspects, or witnesses. The household had been small, at least by British standards, with only Lisa Billings, her father, his new wife, and a maid by the name of Bette Salz in residence. The week of the murders Lisa's uncle on her mother's side, John Moore, had also been present. The papers noted that Moore had since taken Salz into his service at the Moore family homestead, which

Holmes understood to be the Americanism for manor. Outside was a bevy of cabmen, jockeying for the business of the visiting journalists. The one that cornered Holmes knew exactly where the Moore homestead was but opined that there was nothing to that part of the story and that he hadn't taken anyone out there since the beginning of the investigation months ago. Nonetheless, Holmes' money was persuasive and soon he was standing before the wooden building. While the ancient stone manor homes of England seemed part of the landscape, as if they had emerged from the earth, these American houses felt as if they were tossed lightly upon the land and, subject to a breeze, might blow away at any moment. The boards of the oddly-named porch creaked hollowly beneath his feet as he approached the door and knocked. A girl he assumed to be Salz answered, blinking at him as if she had been living her life in a dark cave.

"Miss, I should like to speak to Mr. John Moore."

"May I ask who is calling?" she said with a tremble in her voice.

"Mr. Samuel Baker, a private investigator looking into the deaths of his former brother-in-law and Mr. Billings' new wife."

"I thought that was all settled, Miss Billings being convicted and all."

"There remain some small points of obscurity. If you would please present my calling card to Mr. Moore?"

The girl blinked at the pseudonymous card Holmes proffered, before finally taking it in her hands as if she feared it might be scaldingly hot. Just as Holmes shifted his weight to step inside she closed the door on him. These Americans, he thought, why were the British ever so hesitant to let them go? A minute later the girl opened the door again. She stood up straight now, and her face was bright with forced cheer. Holmes noted her blouse was now open about the neck, revealing a delicate collar bone. He found the distraction interesting. Not in itself, the fragile line of a woman's neck trickling down across her smooth skin and disappearing into the warmth of her blouse stirred nothing in Holmes, but the misdirection, and the fact that Moore's first instinct was to use his maid in this way, those observations did resonate in the mind of the great detective.

"Mr. Moore will see you. This way, please."

She led Holmes into a study adorned with animal skins the way an Englishman would only decorate a hunting lodge in some foreign territory. Moore was propped up against the mantle as if he were examining the moose head hung above. He wore a green and grey checked flannel suit, and upon his feet were boots of fine leather, but splattered with dried mud. Holmes suspected that he was that unique brand of man who fancied himself an outdoorsman but who never strayed far from the sight of his own house. In and out all day, poor Miss Sanz probably spent her life in a constant struggle against indoor tracks.

"Ah, Mr. Baker, I was just about to pour myself a drink. Would you care to join me?"

In the bright afternoon light, it was easy to see that the glasses and decanters were clothed in a fine layer of dust. Moore's swollen features and varicose veins revealed he was no stranger to alcohol, but what was on display here was just set dressing. He probably relished the times he needed to show off, the liquor in these bottles was no doubt a great improvement over whatever he imbibed in private.

"I mustn't partake while on the job, I'm afraid."

"Suit yourself." Moore filled his glass nearly to the rim. Holmes knew Americans were fond of their so-called doubles, but this was nearer a quadruple. "You have some question's about Andrew's murder?"

"In point of fact, I am wondering why you do not have more questions. His more recent sisters-in-law are gobbling up his estate, which is largely made up of your sister's former possessions. This when he so quickly replaced your sister after her untimely death. Surely that must rankle you."

"Of course it does. I spent a year and a half suing the bastard. He'd been carrying on with that Abigail well before Sarah died. Maybe even before her illness."

"You have proof of this?"

"No," Moore sighed theatrically. "Only suspicions. What with her living in the same house it is hard to come up with any evidence that she couldn't explain away."

"You contend that Mrs. Billings' mistress was living in the same house as his wife and daughter?"

"Of course, she was their live-in maid."

"I thought Miss Salz was their maid."

"Sure, after they got married Abigail wasn't a maid anymore and she never let anyone forget it, least of all my Bette."

"So Mr. Billings was having an affair with Abigail when she was his maid?"

"Practically inevitable. I don't know what people are thinking of bringing young, unattached women into happy households. The proximity, the domestic chores, it has to foster a sense of intimacy, doesn't it? And where does intimacy of feeling between a man and a woman inevitably lead? To ruin, that's where."

"Yet you employ a young woman as a maid. Are you exempt from these inevitabilities?"

Salz blushed furiously. "My personal affairs are just that; personal. I'm not breaking up any families."

"So you were suing Mr. Billings - on what grounds?"

"Infidelity would have voided the presumption of his inheritance."

"Yet you are no longer suing?"

"He's dead, now, they both are."

"And yet your family's assets, properties, and finances are all being divided amongst Abigail's relative. While you wither away in relative poverty."

"I most certainly do not!"

"Your best shoes, perhaps your only shoes, are sporting boots covered in mud. You wear a winter suit in the summer.

Your study sits unused save for those scant occasions when you must receive a visitor. You maid is dressed better than you, and I suspect you spend your whole allowance on keeping her, both for appearance's sake and for companionship. Firstly I conclude that means you can afford a maid but not a wife, at least not one of your supposed station. Secondly, I fear she may, in fact, be blackmailing you. Is that true, Miss Salz?"

The girl sputtered and backed away.

"Whatever would she be blackmailing me for?"

"She was there, that night, still in the service of Mr. and Mrs. Billings. Besides Lisa Billings herself, Miss Salz is the only witness. Becoming the lady of this household, in practice if not in name, would be quite the incentive for staying quiet."

"I am no murderer!"

"No? You have given me a thorough statement of your motive. You were at the right time and place. In fact, you were there at only the right time, unlike Lisa Billings, who had years of opportunity to commit the murders."

"Get out, Mr. Baker! Get out!"

"The courts will look kindly upon you, even now, Miss Salz. Wrongfully, the legal system does not consider women to be truly criminally capable or culpable. Confess and move on with your life. He'll resent you always and dispose of you at the first chance, that's no life for a clever woman."

Moore had forced Holmes back out the front door. "Do not come back."

The seed had been planted, Holmes thought with a wry smile. Only time will tell if it bears fruit. An interview with Lisa Billings herself was now in order. She was being held in Taunton Jail, a multi-story brick edifice. Holmes knew that, due to the low pay and unusual hours, many jail guards were bachelors, and more important, most bachelors do not do their own laundry. Holmes walked past the jail a block and began asking about local charwomen, particularly ones known for being discreet. The first lady he found worked from the back of her home, which was generally clean and well-maintained, despite the pack of children running through and around it. Holmes demurred. The next lady wore no fewer than three crucifixes and had rosary beads wrapped around both hands. Holmes simply back away and kept inquiring until he was pointed to a third lady. She worked from a back alley that smelled of lye. Clothes in various states of disrepair hung from a hundred lines strung every which way between the buildings. As Holmes came quietly around the corner the woman had been gleefully turning out all the pockets on the line before her, cackling when she came across a coin. Holmes smiled to himself and liberated the bills in his wallet before carefully stashing it deep within his inner vest pocket.

"My good lady, I hear you are known for your discretion."

"More so for my perception. What do you want?"

Holmes unfolded one of the dollars. "I'm attending a fancy dress party and I should very much like to attend dressed in an authentic guard's uniform."

"Sounds like a masquerade, more like. It would be an unconscionable breach of my professional ethics to just go handing out official uniforms."

Holmes unfolded another dollar. "Would it really be unconscionable? It really just a merry lark, and of course I would show my appreciation for your indulgence of my whimsy. And have the uniform back in a few hours with none the wiser."

"I appreciate whimsy as much as the next person, but I still feel anyone with a conscience could not abide such a transaction. Two dollars is such a cheap price for which to sell one's conscience."

Holmes heaved his shoulders in a deep sigh and made a great show of unfolding a third, and last, dollar.

"Cheap to you but dear to me. Not too dear, I hope."

The charwoman snatched the bills from Holmes' hand. "Age has left me blind and deaf. I suppose if someone were to abscond with that parcel over there while my back was turned I'd be none the wiser. And if it were to return before the owner calls for it, no one need know." She plodded heavily to the far end of the alley and began singing loudly to herself. Holmes grabbed the parcel, peeking quickly inside to verify the contents, and then disappeared back out onto the main thoroughfare.

Holmes paid a nickel to enter a public bathhouse and, in the changing room, quickly exchanged his own clothes for the uniform. The rightful owner was shorter and stouter than Holmes. It is a shame Watson is not here, he thought, the smile on his lips almost immediately weighed down by the lump in his throat. In front of a mirror, he practiced a stooped hunch that made the poor fit of the clothes slightly less obvious. He turned on his heel and, with the strolling swagger common to louts on two continents, exited to the lobby. There he paid another nickel to store the bundle of his own clothes behind the reception desk. Then he was back out on the street jutting out his jaw and giving a hard eye to everyone he passed. He knew his performance as a petulant bully was complete when the crowds on the sidewalks began to part before him. He carried this momentum straight through the front doors of the jailhouse.

Holmes had no idea where he was going but in these situations, it was always best to convey unshakable assurance, and so he strutted through the door to the left as if he had done so a thousand times before. The prison staff hardly gave him a second look. Inside the prison wing was three stories of cells on each side of the space. From the banging and hollering, Holmes knew that most of the prisoners were male. Was the other side the women's wing? Were there enough female prisoners to justify that? As the passed a man dozing at a desk, who must pass as a supervisor, Holmes deftly liberated a logbook. Without losing a stride he continued on to a staircase, where halfway up was a landing out of sight of the prisoners and the head guard. Holmes opened the logbook and found an index of prisoners, cross-tabulated with their cell numbers. Lisa Billings was a late entry and an unusual one at that. Most cells were identified with a three-digit number and a letter. Billings' cell was simply listed as 'restricted.' As Holmes pondered that meaning of the phrase, heavy footfalls approached down the stairs. Holmes tucked the book under his arm and turned just to run right into the descending guard.

"Damned fool." The guard shoved Holmes into the wall and kept walking down the stairs. Holmes carefully wrapped his hand around the keys he had just purloined so they would not jangle and then climbed the rest of the steps. He looked over the railing of this elevated floor, seeing dozens of criminals pacing their cells across the way, with two guards on different levels doing their rounds. Then, recessed behind the stairs opposite he saw a red door, and stenciled upon it in white the word 'Restricted.'" Holmes resumed his belligerent saunter across the rest of the level, in case the guards opposite him were observing. Then he scampered down the stairway at the far end of the wing, crossed over to the other side and, to the jeers and whistles of the prisoners, proceeded to that red door. Quickly he cycled through the keys on the stolen keyring until with a satisfying click the red metal door drifted open.

The air inside was cold and musty. As Holmes stepped in he discovered steps leading down to a subterranean floor. He pulled the red door shut behind him and turned the lock from the inside. He struck one of the lamps hanging from the wall and carefully stepped down into the darkness. Unlike the cells above, down here were simple cages of wrought iron. In the distance, there was a rustling sound. When Holmes held the lantern in that direction he saw a girl, haggard and wan, pressed up against the bars of her cage.

"Water, please," she called. "I am so thirsty."

"I'm afraid I did not bring anything..."

"There is a faucet, over there," she pointed into the dark corner. Holmes moved in that direction and found something that was not a faucet, but more of a release valve in the plumbing. Beneath it was a table containing dented, rusty metal cups and plates. He took one of the cups and opened the valve. The fluid that issued forth had a strange sheen and it smelled fetid.

"I do not believe this is suitable for consumption."

"It is all they give me to drink. The stomach pains and the headaches are awful, but I must drink, musn't I?" Her arm was straining through the bars greedily. Reluctantly, Holmes surrendered the cup to her, and she sucked the fluid down carefully but with great alacrity.

"You are Lisa Billings?"

"Do you see anyone else down here?"

"They keep you like this, in the darkness, in a moldering basement?"

"It is awful, a nightmare, but perhaps better than above."

"How so?"

"You do not want to be a celebrity inside a jail. Even less so if you are a woman."

"Are you alleging that you are molested?"

"I'm alleging that I would be, up there. The warden and the guards, they let the prisoners police themselves for the most part. Unless someone is trying to escape, or there is an inspection coming, they mostly stay out of the way. But you should know that." She eyed Holmes' uniform.

"In your case, they made an exception?"

"I'm guaranteed one last thing in this life, and that's a public audience when I'm executed. They don't want me saying anything too awful about my imprisonment. A lady maniac is still a lady, after all."

"Are you?"

"A lady or a maniac?"

"I care very little for the former, but the latter holds some interest."

Tears welled up in Billings' eyes and she collapsed down into her hands. "What does it matter now?"

"It matters a great deal to me, and to others who value the truth. Believe it or not, it matters quite a bit to Detective Shea, for he hired me to continue the investigation."

"Hired you?"

"Yes, my name is Samuel Baker and I am a private detective. Detective Shea, despite his misgivings, is bound to serve his superiors, who in turn serve theirs. With the eyes of the world watching the police often settle for the convenient answer for which the public so clamors. I, by nature of my independence, am subject to no such restrictions."

"You aren't?" Her face turned up and for a moment Holmes saw hope cross it.

"Let me be perfectly clear, I am not here to clear your name or prove your innocence. To be honest I am not particularly convinced of your innocence. I am, however, convinced of the need for unimpeachable justice. To let an innocent person hang while a murderer goes free would be unconscionable. Simply to let doubt eat away at the conscience of an excellent policeman would be tragic. So, here I am to discover what I can."

"Even my champion has no faith in my innocence, perhaps it is for the best that I soon leave this world."

"I assure you my mind is open to the facts, and to whatever truth they might reveal."

"Where shall I begin?"

"Why not with the bundle of clothes you were found burning in the furnace?"

"My last act as an innocent woman."

"Is that so?"

"Yes. I realize the timing is dreadful, too dreadful to explain away, but when I put that bundle in the furnace I had no idea what had happened to my father, and to Abigail."

"What were you doing, then?"

"I was mad, maybe the maddest I've ever been."

"You are not helping your supposed alibi."

"It's the truth, do you want to hear it or not?"

"Please continue."

"The bundle, it was a dress, but wrapped within were some mementos."

"Mementos of what?"

The girl hesitated, then, feeling the cold bars in her hands, resigned herself to her circumstances. "A failed affair."

"Oh," said Holmes with disappointment, "a romantic intrigue. So you were spurned and in spite, you destroyed the material effects of your tryst."

"You make it sound petty. Firstly, it was more than a tryst, at least to me. Secondly, a lady in my position needs to protect her prospects."

"With whom was this relationship?"

"That is personal, and rather the whole point of my burning the things."

"Miss Billings, at this juncture proving your innocence would not be enough. I'm afraid we must find another neck for the noose. Your paramour has something approaching motive."

"My love... will never hang." For a moment her eyes were rimmed by tears before a furrowed brow drove them away.

"I have heard accusations of a secret affair within the Billings house."

"My father would never have dishonored my mother. He only had eyes for her while she lived. It was his great attachment, and his great loss, that left him such easy prey."

"For Abigail."

"Yes."

"You do not think very highly of her."

"When I think of her all I feel is betrayal."

"Maids are often dear to the children in their households."

"I knew her my whole life or thought I did anyway. She was only a few years older, so we often played together, took our lessons together."

"Sewed dresses together, perhaps even as gifts for the other?"

Billings was silent.

"She was dear to you. Perhaps more dear than your father may have realized?"

"She is dead and I am falsely convicted. Where does this line of inquiry lead?"

"By your own account, you were upset enough by your recent romantic upset to burn your mementos to ash."

"Is *cue bono* not an axiom of your profession? Who benefits from my father's death? Clearly not me. Who will benefit from my death? Abigail's sisters will inherit all of the Billings estate and the Moore estate. Not a bad recompense for only a year or two of scheming."

"You believe Abigail's sisters would kill her rather than share with her?"

"That family is a viper's nest. She would tell me about it as a child and I would pity her. The awful life she had at home, the way her parents took all of her earnings and gave her none of it. Those girls were raised hungry and vicious."

"Yet they were not present to swing the axe. They were more than a day away when they were contacted by telegram."

"You asked me if I thought they were capable of murdering their own sister over money, my answer is yes. It is beyond me to discover how," she shook her cage.

"What of your uncle, John Moore?"

"He was there to argue about the disposition of the former Moore estate. He was incensed that his family's property was being given to Abigail's sisters."

"Does he not strike you like a more likely suspect? He was known to be present, he was incensed over money, propriety, and the memory of his deceased sister. It is also much more probable for an axe murderer to be a man."

"That was a cornerstone of my defense. You see where probabilities have gotten me."

"He has also hired Bette Salz as his own maid. Not to be indiscreet, but I rather believe their relationship is intimate past the point of impropriety."

"Yet I am locked in a hole awaiting my execution. There is no justice in this world, only grasping avarice and duplicity. I did not see that in time, and neither did my father and now I shall join him in death, the Billings clan done in by misbehaving maids."

"One last question, Miss Billings. If you were going to hide two heads in or around Billings Manor, where would you do it?"

"You are perverse and grotesque, Mr. Baker."

"I have been accused of worse."

"There is a place that comes to mind. Along the front stairs, the paneling can be pried away. I believe it had something to do with the way the house was built, first as a cottage and then expanded out."

"How much room is behind the paneling?"

"I haven't looked there in years, but as I child I could fit inside completely."

"Could one seal himself inside?"

"I don't think so. The opening isn't meant as a door. The panel can simply be jarred loose, but must be pounded back into place until it stays."

"Who knows of it?"

"Living? To my knowledge, I am the only soul."

"I give you my solemn promise that I will investigate this case thoroughly. If you are innocent, be glad. If you are guilty, well, you are beyond trembling." Holmes turned to leave.

"Wait!" Billings pulled at his sleeve. "More water, please. For all I know I won't see another person until a week hence."

Holmes took the cup back to the repugnant valve and filled it, and then filled the other five and carefully carried them over to the girl. On impulse, he also left his cigarettes and lucifers.

"I don't smoke tobacco," the girl said.

"In a pinch, they may serve as tiny torches. Do you know how to light them?"

"I have seen it done a thousand times."

"Farewell, Miss Billings."

"Thank you, Mr. Baker."

As Holmes carefully shut the great red door behind himself he heard the guards shouting back and forth about the missing keys. They would be on alert for strangers now. He quietly exited the stairwell and observed the cells on each side. In one a man slept heavily in the corner. In the other, the prisoner was climbing the bars and hissing at Holmes. Holmes chose the latter and unlocked his cell door. The hissing man dropped to the ground and silently looked at Holmes with his head cocked. "I am going to drop these keys," Holmes said. "You are going to pick them up and release some of your fellows. That is your only chance of escape. Do you understand?"

An unsettling smile spread across the prisoner's face. Holmes gently dropped the keys and began walking purposefully towards the exit. He heard the rattling of cell doors opening behind him.

"Hey, you there!" the guards across the block shouted. "Who are you? Come back here!"

Just as they began to move towards Holmes the loose prisoners began to riot. The guards blew their whistles and raised their blackjacks, preparing for the onslaught. Holmes began to run for the door. As he burst through he called out a warning to the other prison staff. "Jailbreak! Jailbreak!" He had no desire to meet the lunatic he had just liberated out on the streets. Taking advantage of the first waves of confusion Holmes slipped outside and, as calmly as he could manage, strolled back to the bathhouse.

Back in his own clothing, he tossed the bag containing the uniform down the charwoman's alley as he passed and then, two more blocks up hailed a cab. When he asked to be taken to the Billings homestead the cabby launched into a rant against sightseers treating the lives of real people like a carnival show. Holmes plunked triple the fair down on the man's bench and the carriage began rolling.

The Billings homestead was smaller than John Moore's home but somehow more substantial. Even had Lisa Billings not mentioned the way the house had been built out it would have been obvious to Holmes. The original cottage that constituted one corner of the house was squat and rough, while the rest of the house was more refined. For all that, it was solidly built with hand-turned beams and thick shingles. A frill of brightly colored moss had begun to lend age and dignity to the place. Nearby was a stone wall and surrounding the home were overgrown fields. A year ago it would have been quite picturesque, warm light from the windows cast out upon the wildflowers, a wisp of smoke billowing from the chimney. Holmes looked down at the ground and despaired. It had been trampled by a hundred pairs of shoes. As a last resort, he might start at the perimeter and try to work his way in looking for stray prints, but that was a fool's errand and Holmes was not desperate yet.

He approached the main door to the newer expansion of the house and found it to be suspiciously unlocked. Holmes reached for the revolver in his pocket only to remember he hadn't dared take it on his expedition to the jail. He listened for any sign of movement within the house but heard none before being startled then by the sound of his cab leaving. The driver had been paid to wait but apparently to no avail. As he watched the carriage leave he thought he saw movement in the trees. Waiting for a few minutes didn't reveal anything else, inside or outside the home, so he entered, locking the door behind him. He could see the chaise upon which Andrew Billings' body had been found, encrusted in dry blood in the adjoining salon. The blood on the floor had only been superficially cleaned, and half the dried stain was cut off in a neat right angle where someone had removed the rug. The blood splatter suggested a short attacker, but also that Mr. Billings had been viciously felled where he stood by a rapid series of axe strokes. For just a moment Holmes thought he saw a shadow from outside move across the curtains next to the body, then he chided himself for being spooked so easily.

He moved up the stairs and first looked into the bedroom where Abigail Billings had met her fate. The bedclothes had been stripped, but the mattress still held a great copper stain. The floor looked as if it was still crusted with old blood. Whoever had been given the task of cleaning up appeared to have surrendered here. The home would probably sit empty in probate for years and be uninhabitable by the time anyone had an uncontested legal claim to it. His curiosity satisfied for the moment, Holmes descended halfway down the stairs and began tapping upon the wall. Lisa had opened the space when she was a child, and most people would jostle something open by pushing up, so Holmes knelt and shoved up on the paneling until he found a spot that gave. He lifted the section away and was facing a hole just slightly too small for him to squeeze into. It opened onto a shaft that ran both up and down into the darkness. Directly ahead a nail held up a rope. Pulling up on the rope revealed a dangling satchel, too light to hold a pair of skulls. Really, in this enclosed space the smell of any kind of human remains should have been prevalent. Opening the satchel Holmes found a poisoner's dispensary. Hemlock leaves, cyanide powder, some noxious paste he was hesitant to open, pills, any number of nefarious items. What a morbid collection for such an idyllic house, Holmes thought. The satchel was made of well worn roughspun, more likely to belong to a servant than any other occupant of the house. Surely Bette Salz would have disposed of this had it been hers, she had unfettered access to the house for weeks after the killings. That suggested Abigail had her own plans at one point after Lisa had stopped playing here.

While there was still daylight Holmes decided to search the exterior of the property. He went back outside and saw the barn door was swinging. Was there enough wind to cause that? Holmes wondered. Cautiously he stalked over to the wooden building and threw the doors open wide. A cloud of flies swarmed over him and a strange smell hit him, disorienting him for a minute. There was the rank smell of decay, but it was also strangely sweet. The heads must be here, he thought. Why that cloying, sweet odor? He had seen a thousand bodies in as many states of decay and never had he smelled this. As his eyes adjusted to the dark he saw the interior of the barn was covered with a brown, pulpy mass. Had there been more murders here? As he stooped down to poke at it he saw fruit stems poking out, all over. The Billings must have been storing the harvest from their orchard in here. Everything was covered in a sticky, gritty slime. Finding any evidence here would be a Herculean effort, so Holmes decided he could return later if he must. As he went back outside, walking into the afternoon sun he found himself temporarily blinded. Shielding his eyes he also heard someone run around the back of the house.

"Hello?" Holmes cried. "I am here peaceably, I mean you no harm." There was no response. A deer now scampered across the field. Holmes laughed at himself. The next most promising spot seemed to be the well. Holmes leaned over it and looked down into the darkness. There was a gentle flickering where the unseen water caught the waning sunlight. Holmes tossed a rock in for good measure. One rod deep, he estimated. A rope holding a bucket had been staked to the ground. Holmes yanked on it, then leaned back pulling on the rope with all of his strength. It held, so Holmes tossed the bucket into the well and then climbed down the rope. He found solid ground beneath his feet once he was waist-deep in the water. He felt about the base of the well with his feet and failing to find anything began to plunge himself under, feeling around with his hands. Coming up the third time he noticed the well had dimmed. Looking up Holmes saw that the circular opening above him was now a crescent and closing.

"Hello up there, there's a man down here."

"A man who has no business being here," came the response.

"Let me come up and we'll discuss it face to face."

"There's nothing to discuss. You are malingering in business that isn't yours."

"May I ask what business it is of yours?"

"This here is my land, or will be soon enough."

"I find that to be highly unlikely, and more so the only people in a position to make such promises are feckless liars and remorseless murderers."

"You watch your mouth. That's my mama you are talking about."

"Oh, an inheritance then, from your departed aunt to your mother to you. I just don't foresee that transaction taking place. Even less so when yet another murder victim is found here and you and your reprehensible family go to jail."

"You are a stranger out here. No one is going to miss you, and no one will ever know what happened to you."

"I am here on an investigation commissioned by Police Detective Gus Shea," Holmes revealed. "More to the point, I communicated my findings to date to him before I left Fall River proper," Holmes lied. "Tomorrow morning he shall read my daily report, and, unable to reach me, the police will be out here in force."

The voice was silent for a minute. "I'm going to think on it overnight. Maybe I come back and get you out tomorrow, maybe I don't." The crescent hole started closing again. Holmes began to scramble up the rope.

"Stop that!" the voice said.

Holmes was nearly at the top. He could see the boy now, wearing not much more than rags, he was worn out already with not even a score of years to his name. The boy saw Holmes, too. He sneered and brought up an axe, decisively chopping the rope in one swing. Holmes fell to the bottom and found himself struggling under pitch-black water.

"I've done decided, before your detective friend can bring his police, I'm going to bring mine. My mama is real good friends with Judge Thornton, if you know what I mean. He put Lisa down, and he's going to put you down, too. Nice and legal so don't nothing mess with my inheritance." With one more shove, Holmes was in complete darkness.

He regretted gifting his Lucifers to Lisa Billings now. He felt the walls of the well, rough but steep, and of course, Holmes was soaking wet. In the water with him was the severed rope and bucket. Holmes pulled the folding knife from his pocket and cut the rope into four lengths, binding them around his feet and hands. Then he hooked the bucket on his arm and spread his hands wide to touch opposite sides of the well. Convinced of his plan, Holmes floated face down in the water and pressed his rope wrapped hands to one side and his feet to the other. With the prodigious strength for which he was famous, he pushed out on all four limbs and raised his body above the water as if he were in a horizontal stoop. Hand, then foot, other hand, then other foot, he worked his way up the well. So focused was he on the mechanics of his movements that it almost came as a surprise when his back bumped against the well cover. At first it would not budge, and Holmes feared it was somehow locked, but finally, it proved to be merely staggeringly heavy. Flashes of light from the setting sun showed him he was able to break the embrace of the cover and the well. His arms and legs trembling with fatigue Holmes threw all of his strength into one last heaving of his entire body, shoving the bucket into the gap he forced open. He worked his hands over the lip of the well and let his feet drop beneath him. He scrambled up the last few feet of the well, knowing that if he fell down he would not have the strength to make the ascent again. His clothes were in tatters, his extremities numb, his back bruised and possibly even sprained, but he was above the ground again and free. Holmes rolled painfully over onto his back and took deep, calming breaths. As he regarded the well, the bucket suddenly splintered and the cover collapsed with a decisive finality.

It had taken much of the night to walk back to his rooming house in Fall River on rubbery legs, and the mood of the landlord had immediately gone from anger when he had opened the door to bafflement when he had seen the sorry state of Holmes. He called upon the landlady to draw Holmes a bath and fetch him the remains of dinner, while he looked Holmes' injuries over and prescribed a healthy dose of whiskey. Holmes thanked the pair and asked to be awoken at their earliest convenience after daybreak. He tottered to his room and fell into a deep, dreamless sleep. Much to the landlord's surprise Holmes was awoken quite easily just a few hours later and appeared freshly shaven and neatly dressed at the breakfast table within minutes of being roused. He wolfed down the eggs, meat, and bread meant for the half a dozen boarders in residence before proceeding to the courthouse and demanding a meeting with Judge Thornton. In response, the secretary had moved himself bodily in front of Thornton's chambers but stuttered and stumbled before the focused will of Holmes.

"The judge is not in yet, and may not be for some time. His first case is not until noon."

"I shall wait in his office."

"You can't... Are you an attorney?"

Holmes laughed, "No, my knowledge of jurisprudence far exceeds that of a mere attorney."

"I see, but nonetheless... May I ask to what this is in regards?"

"I think Judge Thornton will have already been apprised."

"This is most unusual, I really must object."

"I will gladly affirm that you did everything in your power to stop me. Now, I shall take my place and wait."

With a movement that the befuddled clerk could not precisely recall later, Holmes snaked around him and slipped through the door, locking it behind him. When the clerk made to unlock the door and throw this impudent intruder out once and for all he found his keyring missing from his pocket. He rattled the knob and pounded upon the frosted glass but to no response. Holmes, ignoring the ruckus, was sizing up this new opponent. The office was lined wall to wall in legal tomes, of course. But beyond that, the man had a surprising interest in phrenology, the science of discovering the inherent traits of a person by measuring their skull. Model heads lay about, as well as some facial castings. Behind Holmes when he entered, right where Thornton would be gazing when seated, was a glassed-in display of skulls. Small monkey skulls leading to larger primate skulls leading to ape skulls, with the last two covered in velvet. Holmes easily picked the lock and opened the glass case, gently whisking away the velvet covers. Beneath were two skulls, human, male and female. The bone was new, and unlike the others in the case, never subjected to the harsh elements of nature. The flesh had been cleanly removed. Boiled, holmes wondered? Picked clean by insects? Keeping his hands covered he gently turned the skulls around to find the gashes of an axe blade. Holmes returned the covers to the skulls and reclosed the case, leaving it unlocked.

Holmes picked up the telephone handset resting on Thornton's desk. When the operator responded he asked that Detective Gus Shea of the Fall River Police Department were dispatched to Judge Thornton's chambers straight away. Outside he heard the clerk being harangued by a gravely voice. As scraping came from the keyhole of the door, Holmes replaced the handset and leaned casually against the desk.

The judge came bursting in, red-faced and bellowing. "What is the meaning of this? Do you know who I am? I can hang you with a jot of my pen!"

"Yes, I visited your handiwork in the cellar of the jail."

"Oh, you're that damned Mr. Baker who has been stirring things up. I have to admit that this is not where I expected to find you, but no matter. All your escape has won you is a shorter trip to the gallows."

"People hang in this state for trespassing?"

"In a judge's quarters, most certainly!"

"That is your conception of justice?"

"In Fall River justice is whatever I say it is!"

"Lisa Billings might disagree with you."

"Miss Billings was convicted in a court of law in accordance with the laws of this great state."

"Is it the law of this great state that an innocent girl must hang so that her parents' murderers may pad their purses?"

"Slander is most certainly illegal in this state. Besides, a jury was convinced."

"By you, not by the evidence."

"I'm glad you raised the issue of evidence because I've plenty of evidence of your crimes," he gestured to the gathering crowd outside the office door. "Do you claim to have any support for your allegations, Mr. Baker?"

196

"Of course, but I plan to give it to the police."

"Rest easy on that account, they are on their way."

"Oh, I know, I called for them myself." Thornton choked on his own outrage. "I'm sorry, did you have certain policemen in mind. I suggest you check your pockets, their hands might still be there."

"This is outrageous!"

A shock-white Detective Shea now sidled into the office.

"Mr. Baker, you called for me?"

Thornton interjected, "Detective, arrest this man! I caught him in the act of burglarizing my office, after which he has threatened me and attacked my good character."

Shea looked back and forth between the two men, helplessly.

"Don't just stand there," Thornton continued. "I can be a valuable friend or a bitter enemy."

"I think both you and the judge will find his capacities rendered moot quite shortly, Detective."

"Please tell me you have unassailable reasons for harassing the judge, Mr. Baker." The words seemed even-keeled but there was a despair in Shea' eyes as he looked at Holmes.

"I do. I should like to ask all of our witnesses to step into the office."

"Absurd!" cried Thornton.

"Necessary," rebutted Holmes. "For there is vital evidence in this very room, and I want there to be no doubt of what it is or where it came from. Press in, please."

In addition to the various clerks and other employees of the courthouse, Thornton's policemen had now arrived. Everyone stood pressed shoulder to shoulder in the office expectantly.

"Officers," the judge pronounced. "Have your handcuffs ready. The very instant this folly is over I want this man arrested." He pointed at Holmes.

"I concur, officers, ready your manacles. The very moment this folly is revealed I want this man arrested." He pointed back at the judge. The policemen looked at each other uneasily.

"Now, for the definitive stroke of justice in the case of the murder of Andrew and Abigail Billings." Holmes tossed open the door to the glass case. "The victims themselves are here to testify." Thornton became apoplectic and had to be held down by his own men. With a flourish, Holmes revealed the skulls. The crowd murmured. "From this morbid display most of you must know that Judge Thornton is an enthusiast of phrenology, that is, rendering judgment upon a person based upon the signature marks upon the cranium. I, myself, find the so-called science lacking in general, but in this specific case I do indeed find the practice useful." Holmes scooped one of the skulls up in its velvet cloth and turned it to display the axe mark to the assembly. "I believe you will find that these gashes and ridges reveal the character of a murderer in their owner. That owner, of course, being Judge Thornton." One of the women fainted. The rest of the crowd cried for a noose.

As Thornton was hauled away Holmes turned to Shea. "Do you have an honest judge in this town?"

"A few are honest enough, as judges go."

"Then with all haste hurry to have Lisa Billings' release ordered."

Holmes thought it best to be on the first train out of Fall River after that. He watched the papers with great interest for the next week as Abigail's murderous sister and nephew were captured. With little prompting, they turned upon each other, and Thornton upon all of them. The hangman would have to wait, but he'd get paid two additional necks in interest. A special commission was created to reexamine all of the corrupt Judge's rulings, with hundreds of convicts protesting their innocence anew. Detective Billings found himself newly promoted and had publicly declared a new initiative to stamp out corruption in law enforcement. Finally, Lisa Billings had written to Mr. Baker of New York City, thanking him for his exemplary service. She was even now on a ship to the Continent, which she planned to tour until the interest in her case ceased. She asked Mr. Baker for any travel recommendations he might have. Holmes replied with a brief telegram, simply indicating that had found the Reichenbach Falls in the Swiss Alps were a nice place for an escape.

That damned ring, Jefferson Hope thought to himself. It was cursed and he should have known it. He'd found it, out there, in the desert. He'd lit out from St. Louis looking to make his fortune in the mountains of the West. Instead, he'd found her, out there, in the desert. A gentle rose among the prickly scrub of that wasteland. It was destiny, he thought, the girl and the ring waiting for him on the parched sands beneath the wind-sculpted arches and purple skies. It had been destiny, all right. Just not the happily-ever-after kind. Jefferson Hope and Lucy Ferrier have been two halves of one soul, but that soul wasn't made for bliss. It was bound for damnation and that ring was the anchor meant to pull them down, down into those infernal depths. Hope had carried that ring after Lucy's death, the same as he carried her memory, dear to his heart. It pained him like the horsehair shirts penitent monks used to wear. That the ring could cause pain had given Hope an idea. That ring, that damned ring, it was a weapon, and he reckoned that like most weapons found lying on the desert floor, any man who laid hands on it could use it. And so he had, brandishing it against Enoch Drebber, the unscrupulous rake who had kidnapped Lucy from her adopted home, killed her only family and forced her to marry him so that he could inherit the land of the very man he and his partner, Joseph Stangerson, had just murdered.

Drebber had been true to himself, at least, even if he wasn't true to anyone else. Not even a flicker of remorse crossed his face when he was confronted with Lucy's ring, the one from her true engagement. The one she chose from love. No, what passed that clammy puss was avarice, reptilian in its malice. Drebber had licked his lips and made to snatch the ring right from Hope's fingers.

"If it belonged to my wife then it belongs to me," Drebber had hissed.

Hope had answered that claim with a pistol. Drebber, having played at landed gentry in England, had grown soft, and slow.

"We'll let your God decide," Hope had offered. Drebber had laughed. Hope had cocked the hammer.

"Let's let God decide," Drebber agreed.

Hope had produced one of the little boxes of pills he'd concocted back in New York. One pill contained deadly alkaloid poison, the other was a placebo. Even to Hope they looked identical. Drebber saw them and a cruel smile pulled at his lips. This fool, he thought, would never poison himself. Drebber decided to play along with the little melodrama, and then swipe the other man's gun at the first chance. Hope was surprised to see how cavalier Drebber was in plucking a pill from the box and placing it upon his own tongue. The effect was instantaneous. The dark mirth in Drebber's eyes was replaced by a moment of shock, and then void. Drebber's body collapsed upon Hope, who circled the dead man with his arms and laid him to the ground. Hope had understood the chemistry, and on an intellectual level he had understood what was going to happen, but the actual event left him uneasy. He'd seen men die before, but there had always been a sense of passing, a moment of leave-taking from the body. The life in Drebber had simply vanished like a soap bubble. Hope's reverie was broken by the taste of blood upon his lips. He dabbed at his face with his fingers. They came away red and he laughed. He'd successfully committed a bloodless murder and now this. In a strange fit of pique, he wrote "RACHE" upon the wall in his own blood. He'd read about a murder where that very inscription had left the police in New York baffled. A false clue couldn't hurt. Finding himself giddy, he had stumbled out into the night, only realizing too late the ring was missing. The police had arrived by the time he returned. That damn ring, he thought. His breast pocket felt empty without it, his heart felt empty without it. It had served as the corporeal manifestation of his beloved Lucy these many years. Jefferson Hope had wept.

The next day found Hope driving his cab once again. He still had a living to make in London, and Joseph Stangerson, the other man who'd help kidnap Lucy and murder her adoptive father, still needed killing. He was here, in London. Drebber and Stangerson had been traveling together, still thick as thieves. Between fares Hope hungrily read of his own dark deeds in the daily newspapers his passengers left behind. Finally exhausting the press coverage he read the rest of the papers through and through, as did most cabmen on most days. The job was as much about waiting as driving. It was thus he chanced upon the "Found" column where a certain Doctor Watson advertised having found a gold wedding ring. Hope wondered if it was possible that he had dropped the ring outside. It seemed impossible, ridiculous even, but the ring had found him before. Lucy had found him before. He committed the address, 221B Baker Street, to memory and vowed to call this evening as the ad instructed.

The papers had indicated that an amateur detective by the name of Sherlock Holmes had somehow given the Yard a description of the perpetrator. Hope was surprised that the description was fair, and he decided that he should not show up to this appointment as himself, on the small chance it was a trap. Besides, he reckoned, a lone man calling to claim a woman's ring would surely be suspicious. His landlady, an ancient crone always shrouded from head to foot, had left her washing hanging in the garden to dry. Hope pilfered the clothes, meaning to return them before morning so none would be the wiser. He wrapped himself as she did, and affected her arthritic stoop and trembling voice. Hunched over like this he thought he could keep his face out of view. His hands he soaked in water until they were wrinkled. He observed himself in the mirror. The illusion would not hold up for long, but on a darkened stoop he thought it might pass.

Hope flagged down a cab and, in his pitiable old lady character, told a story of a theft of a family heirloom, and an extortion scheme that was draining her of every last cent. He told the driver he meant to snatch back the thing tonight, and so he desperately needed the man to wait at their destination, and then to speed away when she returned. Hope knew that cabmen heard many strange stories and that, as such, they were both very good and very bad at discerning truth from lie. The man proved incurious enough, and sympathetic enough, for a price. Hope paid it and soon found himself standing at 221B Baker Street. As if unable to read the address he turned and looked up and down the street but saw no obvious policemen. Hope then gave the bellpull a sharp yank. A few moments later a serving girl cracked the door open.

"Does Dr. Watson live here?" With the thrill of the moment upon him, Hope's assumed voice came out harsher than he expected. The girl flinched, but then nodded and gestured Hope in. Now with an audience, he made great pains to totter slowly up the staircase. At the top, the flickering of a fire cast its light under the door and the rich smell of tobacco hung in the air. Hope tapped lightly at the door, just like his own landlady did upon his.

"Come in," cried a voice.

Hope threw open the door and was dazzled by the sudden blaze of light. Suddenly at a loss for what to do, he managed a strangely misplaced curtsey and then fumbled in his pocket, his hands shaking and his eyes blinking uncontrollably. "It's this as has brought me, good gentlemen," he said, dropping another curtsey; "a gold wedding ring in the Brixton Road. It belongs to my girl Sally, as was married only this time twelvemonth, which her husband is steward aboard a Union boat, and what he'd say if he come 'ome and found her without her ring is more than I can think, he being short enough at the best o' times, but more especially when he has the drink." The lies bubbling from his lips surprised even him. "If it please you, she went to the circus last night along with——"

"Is that her ring?" one of the men asked, holding a gold circle aloft. Backlit by the fire it was impossible to see, but it seemed right. If only he could hold it and be sure, but Hope was acutely aware of the men staring at him and he knew this interview must be brief lest his disguise fails him.

"The Lord be thanked!" Hope cried; "Sally will be a glad woman this night. That's the ring."

"And what may your address be?" The man inquired, taking up a pencil.

"13, Duncan Street, Houndsditch. A weary way from here."

"The Brixton Road does not lie between any circus and Houndsditch," said the other man sharply.

Hope did not like the tenure of the situation. These men did not appear to be police, exactly, but he hadn't expected this interrogation, and the second man's eyes seemed to burn right through Hope's disguise. Hope knew he was supposed to be playing frail and feeble, but his blood was up now. He faced round and looked keenly at the second man from his little red-rimmed eyes. "The gentleman asked me for *my* address," he said. "Sally lives in lodgings at 3, Mayfield Place, Peckham."

"And your name is——?"

"My name is Sawyer—her's is Dennis, which Tom Dennis married her—and a smart, clean lad, too, as long as he's at sea, and no steward in the company more thought of; but when onshore, what with the women and what with liquor shops——"

"Here is your ring, Mrs. Sawyer," the first man interrupted, in obedience to a sign from the second; "it clearly belongs to your daughter, and I am glad to be able to restore it to the rightful owner."

Hope could hardly believe it. He had been sure the caper was up and now the ring was in his hand again. With many mumbled blessings and protestations of gratitude, he packed it away in his pocket and shuffled off down the stairs. His cab was waiting at a discreet distance down the street. Hope's legs and back had begun to protest the new posture he had adopted. He had just stood to his full height and stretched when he heard the door of 221B open and close again behind him. Quickly he returned to his aged hobble. Finally, Hope came to the carriage and hopped in, crying out, "Drive to 13, Duncan Street,

Houndsditch," to throw his pursuer off the trail. A moment later the whole carriage rocked as someone hopped on the back. Hope slipped out of the landlady's garb and waited for a distraction in the street. When they passed a pack of feral dogs harassing a butcher's shop Hope lithely stepped out the opposite side and simply walked away into the crowd. In the reflection of a window, he saw the second man clinging to the back of the carriage as it continued down the street. Jefferson Hope smiled to himself.

"London black shag, please."

"Mr. Holmes, couldn't I interest you in this Turkish blend? I concoct it myself, here on these premises. I've yet to find a dissatisfied customer."

Holmes sighed. He had chosen his new quarters in Montague Street because of the proximity to the British Museum, a whole building of novelties to amuse his easily bored mind. Yet the public displays had provided scant clay for his mental kiln. Infuriatingly the curators would not allow him access to the storerooms and laboratories where the real treasures and mysteries lay. Instead, he found himself in a neighborhood where the local tobacconist, used to dealing with self-professed scholars and xenophiles, proved overly ambitious in pushing exotic blends over reliable British tobacco.

"I have no interest in Turkish leaf and I don't believe I ever shall."

"Someday I'll slip it into your pouch and you will thank me. I am an artist with cured tobacco leaves. It is in my blood." The tobacconist accepted Holmes payment and then sighed heavily just as Holmes was walking through the door. For reasons he couldn't explain, Holmes turned back.

"Is something the matter, Mr. Wilshire?"

"What's that?"

"That sigh just now caught my attention. Usually, you are an irrepressibly jovial sort. Too much so for some people's taste."

"Ta, sir. It just that... Well, nevermind. Challenges of the trade."

"I've nowhere pressing to be, and could lend a sympathetic ear." As much as the man grated on Holmes, being on friendly terms with one's tobacconist could pay dividends. Maybe each pouch is a little fuller, the tobacco a little fresher, the price a little less dear. Holmes, having ended his time at university only recently, was still living on a student's budget.

"It's a bit embarrassing, to be honest. You see, one of the costs of running a shop in London is paying for insurance."

"This tertiary business expense is what has you troubled?"

"It's just that, well, the cost of this insurance has suddenly increased. I'm having trouble affording it."

"Can you not negotiate with your current insurer? Or simply change to another."

"It's not that kind of insurance."

"Ah, I see. You are being extorted by criminals, and these criminals have become more greedy. Surely Scotland Yard handles these sorts of things."

"Other shopkeepers have complained, of course, but fruitlessly. The police here are not well-suited to dealing with subtle crimes; crimes of accounting, that sort of thing. A smashed window, an armed robbery, that they are prepared for. They need crimes they can see with their eyes and bludgeon with a truncheon."

"Surely you give them too little credit. London is the finest city in the world, it must have the police force to match."

"It may be the world's finest police force for all I know. I'm still having my pocket picked every month." Wilshire sighed.

"If they had the criminal delivered to them, they would affect the arrest?"

"They would have to, I should think."

"How, exactly, does this criminal transaction take place?" Holmes approached the counter, his eyes now intently focused on the tobacconist.

"She comes to collect in person. I don't think she trusts any intermediaries. No honor among thieves and all that."

"She? You mean to tell me you are strong-armed by a woman?"

"A woman who can hire a criminal gang at a moment's notice and for a pittance, what with times in London being what they are. Besides, it was her husband that forged the arrangement."

"Where is he now?"

"On the run. While he is enough to do for me, in the grand scheme he is a small-time crook, who answers to another, who answers to another and so on right back to the top."

"The top of what?"

"There are whispers that one man in London, one master, manages all of the crime in the city."

"Absurd," Holmes scoffed.

"Nonetheless true."

"I should like to meet this nefarious genius for myself."

"That day would be your last."

"So this man, your insurance agent, goes missing and is replaced by his wife, who presses you for an unsustainable amount of money. All this under the nose of some shadowy villain-general. I shall take the case."

"What case? What are you talking about?"

"Back in university, I would amuse myself by solving little problems for my fellows. I wouldn't mind taking those faculties back out of the stable for a little trot."

"These are dangerous people, Mr. Holmes. Genuine criminals. That's why I just pay them and go about my business. Please leave and forget all that we spoke of today."

The bell on the front door rang as someone entered. The blood drained from Wilshire's face. "Madame Withers, back so soon?" He shooed Holmes away with his hands.

Holmes tipped his brim to the lady as he passed. Her gaze passed over him uninterrupted, her eyes betraying no spark of life. He made sure to jangle the bell on the door loudly and to close it with a definitive bang. He then strolled casually past the front windows and, as soon as he was obscured from the people inside, crossed the street and angled himself so that he could observe their transaction in the reflection of the store window in front of him. The tobacconist was waving his hands in refusal when suddenly Madame Withers seized him by the shirtfront and pressed the point of a blade to his neck. Wilshire relented and the lady released him, letting him drop back down to the floor behind the counter. The tobacconist opened his till and the lady began seizing handfuls of money out and shoving them into her dress. It looked a lot less like a payoff and a lot more like a stickup. Miss Withers brandished her knife at the tobacconist again and then swept out of the shop.

Holmes gave her half a block and began following her, fearing she might hop into a passing cab. To his relief, she instead entered the Grand Royal Hotel. Watching her through the entryway Holmes saw her proceed to the reception desk, where she surrendered much of the money she had just stolen. The manager retrieved, a bit too graciously, one might almost say obsequiously, a key from the cabinet behind him. Holmes carefully noted which hook the key came from. After Madame Withers disappeared up the lift Holmes proceeded into the lobby, where he picked up a newspaper and propped himself against a column in easy sight of the key cabinet. A few minutes later an arriving guest prompted the cabinet to be opened again and Holmes saw that Madame Withers had received the key for 307. When the manager was free again Holmes approached.

"I say, would it be possible to have a message dispatched to one of your guests?"

"But of course, one of our waitstaff would be happy to oblige. May I ask to whom you wish to send a message?"

"To the gentleman in Room 307. We were meant to meet here this afternoon so that we might settle the matter of his boasting in regards to the snooker table. He was an unbearable boor at dinner and I mean to put him in his place."

"My apologies, sir, but there is no gentleman in Room 307."

"Are you absolutely certain?"

"Most assuredly. A woman has been occupying that room alone for a week. She rarely leaves but for brief constitutionals and the maids say she has a widow's attire hanging in the wardrobe. I dare say she is in tragic and dire circumstances. She had not paid since the first night, until today when I began, however regretfully, to evict her. Suddenly she was able to satisfy her bill, and pay for another week besides. That ends the matter as far as I am concerned. Listen to me, gossiping away. Perhaps if you described the man to me I might be of further assistance?"

"No matter," Holmes said. "He's half an hour late as it is, and gave me a false room number to boot. There's no need to humor a liar and a coward any further. You've been a great help." Holmes tipped his hat and was out the door before the manager even realized the interview was over. On the way home Holmes stopped into the offices of the London Times to place an ad:

Mr. Withers - I have found what you left behind at the Grand Royal Hotel. Please apply S. Holmes, Montague Street.

The next day Holmes lay in his flat sprawled across his favorite chair, watching the waning afternoon sun filter through the blue haze he had spent all afternoon assiduously puffing from his pipe when the knock came. Really it was more like a slow, steady pounding set to rattle his door from the hinges should it continue. Holmes released the latch on the window. The drop from the first story to the street below would be jarring, but it had been of use on previous occasions. He palmed his faithful riding crop from its place on the mantle and prepared to face whatever ogre was battering his ramparts. Puckishly, he timed the opening of the door to coincide with the next pounding so that the assailant would be thrown off kilter when his fist met nothing but air. To his surprise, it was not some hulking lout who stumbled in, but rather the diminutive gloved hand of Madame Withers. Her head and torso followed, but somewhat disconcertingly the rest of her did not, as if every part of her below the waist were firmly bolted to the landing. Her top half righted itself and she strode in without an invitation.

She turned back towards Holmes but only incrementally, first her head, then her body, and finally her feet. The strange action reminded Holmes of a cobra uncoiling. He renewed his grip on the riding crop but kept it tucked up his sleeve.

"Mr. Holmes, the gentleman from the tobacconist's."

"I was not certain you had seen me, Madame Withers."

"Of course I saw you, I simply did not notice you. Until your little missive in the paper."

"I thought that might catch your attention. Locked up in your room all day, I assumed you must take the paper the hotel subscribes to."

"Indeed, I am a lonely woman."

"I understood you to be married."

A smile pulled at the woman's lips but did not affect her eyes. "You are a clever lad. It would be more accurate to say I am a woman alone in the world."

"Your husband has abandoned you?"

"I fear my husband has abandoned this mortal coil."

"Suicide?"

"Never!" Now some emotion did reach her eyes; fury. "My husband would never leave me like that. However, he has had some difficulties in his line of business."

"I understand it is now your line of business."

Again came the mirthless smile. "I have not heard from my husband in a week. Even under our current circumstances that is unexpected and distressing. Since you feel the need to interject yourself into my business, I thought you might at least make yourself useful."

"A gentleman is always at the service of a lady."

"I fear for my safety as well as my husband's, and so I am hesitant to leave the hotel for any prolonged period of time. Even this interview distresses me greatly." Holmes noted her relaxed pupils, the gentle pulse in her throat, the soft breath on her lips. "There's a place we used to live, a place I think he might retreat when in fear for his life. We are too well known in the area, which is full of cutpurses and cutthroats, for me to dare venture there. Might you check and see if Mr. Withers is present and safe? It would bring some small relief to my fevered mind. I could pay you, of course."

"No need, dear lady. I am honor-bound to see this through, and besides, you make the destination sound so alluring."

"Here," she handed Holmes a note already written. "This is the address. Be sure to check thoroughly, even if there is no answer. I hate to think of my poor husband lying undiscovered in some back room."

She left then, without another word. Holmes examined his trusty map of London, memorizing three different routes to and from the address. He then exchanged his current clothes for a threadbare suit from his days before university. It was moth-eaten and well out of style. Rubbing up against the walls of a few alleys would complete the desired effect. There was an important difference between a country squire with empty pockets and a genuine unfortunate. One would attract much less notice than the other where Holmes was heading. He secured the crop inside the jacket, as well as putting his lockpicks, a folding knife and a whistle in his pockets. He left all but a pittance in his room. Duly prepared he slipped out into the flow of London, the streets becoming darker and the people more desperate as he went. Overhead the sun dipped below the rooftops and Holmes found himself relying on ever sparser gaslights, and spillover from the windows of homes, pubs and other, less reputable establishments.

The streets were nearly abandoned by the time Holmes arrived at the address Mrs. Withers had given him. He began to have the uncomfortable suspicion she had sent him to his own execution, and like a lamb, he had let himself be led merrily along. The address was for a defunct milliner's. Holmes easily found the door to the residence above and even in the dark, he could see the grime covering the rest of the door had been wiped away from the knob. It wouldn't budge so Holmes turned to scan the street. There were the ambient sounds of city life all around him, but no obvious eyes upon him. He fished the picks from his pocket and went to work on the lock. Sweat ran into his eyes and his hands throbbed with the beating of his heart. He had trouble finding the pinion points for the tumbler but at last the lock was sprung. Holmes eased the door open, it's whining creak seeming as loud as a constable's whistle to Holmes.

Inside he found candles in fixtures along the wall. He broke the first one free and lit it with a lucifer from his pocket. The pasteboard walls bulged under the bubbling wallpaper. The building had been cheaply constructed and poorly maintained. In the brighter parts of London, these tenements had long since been burned to the ground and replaced. The stairs creaked beneath his feet and one fully snapped, sending Holmes reeling for a moment. At the top of the stairs, in the candlelight, Holmes could clearly see recent footprints in the dust. There were a few going in every direction, but most carried through down the hall to a back room. Cautiously Holmes followed the trail and looking through an open doorway Holmes saw trash and fallen plaster from the walls and ceiling. In the middle of the room, he saw a pile of discarded clothes. Then he noticed the flies buzzing about it. He stepped closer in, now smelling a pungent, fetid stench, much stronger than the odor of mold and dust in the rest of the building. Tentatively, Holmes nudged the pile with his shoe. Something solid was inside so he heeled the top of the bundle over and it collapsed out into a body. A man whose flesh, that not eaten away by vermin, was a nauseous rainbow of purples and greens. Holmes' stomach lurched and somehow he was on the floor himself now.

Leaning heavily on the walls Holmes staggered down the stairs and into the relatively fresh air of the slums of London. At least it was cold, and that snapped his rational mind back into action. He breathed deeply and walked away in disgust. There was one thing he was sure of. Madame Withers had sent him there knowing he would find the body. He was a pawn in her game, and Holmes would be a pawn for no one. More than the decaying body, more than the probable murder, what really rankled Holmes was that anyone would take him for a fool. He had been attending some esoteric lectures during his time in London, and at those lectures, he's made some eccentric contacts. Not friends exactly, Sherlock Holmes would never go down in the annals of friendship, but like-minded individuals. Others for whom the spirit of inquiry trumped the demands of propriety. One of these was a coroner, a freelance ghoul who would relish an invitation to macabre intrigue. Holmes proceeded at a quick step, now oblivious to the everyday predators stalking London's shadows.

"Young Sherlock, won't you come in?" Hershel Glave had his smock on. To little effect, Holmes thought. Glave was soaked in effluvia up past his elbows. The stench from inside his morgue was almost unbearable. Looking past Glave's shoulder Holmes saw the mangled cadaver the coroner must be working on, with two more set off to the side. There were always more bodies in London. Some Glave examined for the police. Others he merely disposed of. Yet others... Holmes had gathered enough oblique references to know that Glave earned most of his coin as a kind of purveyor-cum-broker. The demands for human remains are myriad, and to let good produce go to waste in a potter's field ran contrary to Glaves' eminently practical sensibilities. The man repulsed Holmes to the quick, but his absolute detachment from all human sentiment was also fascinating in its own way. The things this man accomplished due in part to his radical emotional disassociation were remarkable. Perhaps it was possible to become morally disentangled while retaining one's ethical self, Holmes thought.

"Doctor Glave, I'm afraid I cannot stay long and I do not wish to impose upon your hospitality."

"No one ever does," a grin split the man's face, revealing rotten brown teeth, worse than most of his subjects.

"I know the location of a body that the Yard doesn't even know it is looking for yet. I promise you that in a couple of days it will be quite valuable. It is associated with a lurid scandal that will make the front page of every rag in London."

"Oh you do, do you? This isn't your handiwork is it, young Sherlock?"

"Of course not! Why would I come and admit murder to you?"

"You'd be surprised at how understanding people think I can be. How understanding I can be for the right price."

Holmes' lip involuntarily curled. "You'll get your pay from the Yard, assuming you agree to my conditions."

"Haha! And what are those, praytell?"

"You will keep the body secret until I tell you otherwise. That means waiting after the reward is announced. Maybe a day or more."

"Why would I do that?"

"Because I'm giving you a gift. Fast, clean money and some favor from the Yard besides. You can have this body in your cellar within the hour. It is good business."

"Haha! Okay, it is a deal." Glave held out a filthy, repugnant hand.

Without hesitation Holmes took it. "To cross me would be bad business."

"Yes, yes, very bad business. Ho-ho!"

Holmes began crushing the man's hand in his grip and boring his hawk-like gaze into the other man's eyes. The coroner faltered and went slack.

"Yes, bad business. I understand, Mr. Holmes."

"See that you do."

Holmes helped Glave haul a hand cart back to the millenary. It was pitch black inside the flat now, but Holmes fumbled for the next candle along the wall and up they went. As they transferred the corpse onto a sheet Graves pulled his hand away from the body's neck and sniffed at his own fingers.

"Hmm. Swine fat," he observed.

They wrapped the body like a mummy and hauled it downstairs and onto the cart. No one looked twice at them on the way back to the coroner's office. The kind of Londoner out at this hour was the kind who knew not to ask questions about the relocation of bodies. Holmes left the coroner at his doorstep, reminded him again to keep the body secret until Holmes directed him otherwise.

Back in his room, Holmes bathed himself in near-boiling water, running through three kettles worth and scrubbing until his skin was red.

The next morning he called upon Madame Withers at the Grand Royal.

"Mr. Holmes, were you unable to find the address?"

"I found it without difficulty."

"Oh, I almost expected to open the paper this morning and read that you had discovered my husband's body." Her soulless eyes searched Holmes' face. "I am relieved, of course, that is not the case."

"Of course. I regret to report that I searched the premises thoroughly and found no sign of your husband."

"No sign at all?"

"Well, there was some scraps and rubbish that suggested someone occupied the flat on occasion, but last night there was no one."

"You checked the flat above the milliner's shop, front to back, every room?"

"Every room, dear lady. Rest assured he was not there."

A wave of panic washed over her face. "That's impossible! Where could...? I know... I just..." Then her face was hard again. "You must leave, Mr. Holmes."

"Is there nothing more I can do to assist you?"

"You can never speak of this, to anyone! Or else..." her hand had slipped down to the knife concealed at her waist.

Holmes managed a nonchalant air. "Or else what, Madame Withers?"

"Never you mind. Just cease your meddling!"

"May I remind you that you came to me?"

Holmes was back in the hotel hallway now, the door to 307 resolutely closed to him. As he walked back to the stairs he found a pair of maids making up one of the rooms.

"Pardon me, do you know when Room 307 might be cleaned?"

216

One of the maids consulted a list in her pocket. "Eight in the evening, as per madame's request. Has there been a change?"

"I hope not," Holmes said, skipping down the stairs. He spent an hour in the lobby reading the paper, just to be sure Madame Withers wouldn't rush right out in her panic. Satisfied that she was in until the evening Holmes went home for a nap and a light dinner. At half seven he was up to the street from the Grand Royal Hotel, feigning an interest in the wares on display in the windows of various shops. When Madame Withers emerged her serpentine gait was unmistakable. She slithered up into a waiting carriage and set off. Holmes hopped into the cab nearest to him and set off after her. In the yellowbacks, carriage chases seemed so exciting, but in reality, the two conveyances simply clattered along at a moderate speed. Madame Withers seemed unaware that she was being followed. Her cab clattered along to the millinery flat. After a few moments inside she came out rending the sleeves of her dress. Her already pallid face was drained of all color. Next, her cab stopped at a cemetery and Holmes had his driver pull to the side of the road so that he might disembark unobserved. The coins Holmes left on the seat seemed to silence whatever qualms the man might have had. Cabmen probably aid in a lot of suspicious behavior, Holmes mused.

Madame Withers moved through the cemetery with great certainty. Having to engage in various little subterfuges along the way, Holmes almost had trouble keeping her in sight. Finally, she arrived at a fresh grave, where she stomped upon the ground. It seemed rather undignified to Holmes until a bell propped up by the headstone rang in response. The stomping and ringing went on for several minutes, reaching a crescendo and then seemingly winding down. Madame Withers appeared to be quite dissatisfied with the interview. She stormed back the way she came, forcing Holmes to duck down behind a memorial to remain unseen. He had a moment to decide between

217

investigating the grave further or following the woman, and at that moment he found his feet moving after her.

He lingered near the gate to hear her destination before flagging down his own cab. Holmes emptied his pockets, promising the driver the lot if he arrived at the Grand Royal Hotel before the carriage that had just left, and by an alternate route. The cabman grinned and Holmes suspected he had hit upon some natural rivalry between the drivers. He held to his seat with both hands as the carriage took careening turns through crowded streets, once even taking an ill-advised shortcut under an archway and through a communal garden. When they intersected the street just up from the hotel Holmes clasped the man on the shoulder, shouting that he had well earned his money, and leaped down onto the road. He smoothed his coat and re-settled his hat before calmly strolling into the hotel and ascending the stairs to the third floor. He planned to listen at Madame Withers keyhole to discover what all of that grave knocking was about. As he stepped out into the hall to look for some spot to hide he was surprised to find three men already waiting outside Madame Withers' door. They wore fine suits but had the rough necks and thick hands of laborers. As they whispered among themselves a cruel laugh rippled through the trio. It appeared Madame Withers had been found by her criminal betters. Still unseen, Holmes stepped back into the stairwell.

As he did the lift began moving and moments later Madame Withers emerged, only to be shocked into stillness at the sight of the three men.

"You've been remiss, Madame Withers."

"I didn't know how to find you. My husband is missing and he handled all the business affairs."

"Tsk, tsk, and now you're a liar too. You've been hiding from us, Madame."

"No, truly, I've tried but it has been so hard, all alone and bereft. You don't know what it is like for a lady in this city."

"You're no lady." The man who had been talking now cuffed Madame Withers and she was knocked against the wall.

Her head coiled back to face him, all the more haughty for the blood trickling from her mouth. Through a sneer, she said, "More's the pity for you." Her blade was in her hand then, slashing up at the brute, drawing a red line across his white shirt that didn't end until the point of her knife was caught under his chin. She laughed. The second man wrenched her arm around until she dropped the knife. The third seized her by the throat, his fingers disappearing into her flesh.

That's just enough, Holmes thought. He sprung forth from the darkness. "You there, stop harassing this innocent woman!" The men turned and bared their teeth at Holmes, even the one lying on the floor pressing his hands against his bloody chest. Holmes banged upon the hotel room doors as he passed, hoping at least some were occupied. "This kind of violence is unacceptable!" Holmes shouted.

The men dropped Madame Withers to the floor and she gasped frantically for air. The two brutes standing began to advance on Holmes, who raised his fists. He had been a champion in the school boxing ring. It appeared he would discover how well that translated into the real world. Just as the blows were about to begin there was a ringing behind Holmes, and then all around him. Out of the corner of his eye, he could see some of the room doors were ajar. The other guests were yanking on the service bells in their rooms.

"With enough witnesses, it won't matter if the police actually catch you here." Holmes spat through gritted teeth. The thugs silently consulted each other and then let their fists drop. They heaved their injured partner up between them and moved for the stairs. Holmes watched them until they were out of sight.

"May I call upon the ladies of this floor to tend to this stricken woman?" Holmes called out.

"That is really unnecessary," Madame Withers objected as she was corralled back into her room by half a dozen clucking hens. A contingent of hotel staff arrived on the lift.

"What's all this then?" the manager cried.

"The woman in 307 has been grievously attacked in your premises," Holmes declared. "Is it your custom to allow blackguards to roam your halls assaulting your guests?"

"Of course not, sir. We are most apologetic."

"Then I trust you will see Madame Withers to hospital and pay for her to stay there until she is completely recovered?"

"Of course it was Madame Withers," the man sighed. "Such a strange woman!"

"Strange or not, you'll have the police guard her hospital room until she is discharged? If not, perhaps my friend at the Times can whisper in the right ears."

"I assure you that won't be necessary, sir. We will ensure she receives the best of treatment. And there will be no charge for your accommodation here as well, Mister....?"

"Oh, I'm not staying here. Just look at the kind of clientele you court."

"Then why were you here at all?" the man asked as Holmes disappeared down the stairs and out into the London night. On the way home he stopped by the telegram office to express to the hospital Mr. Withers deep concern for his wife's wellbeing, and his desire for her to be observed around the clock for as long as is needed for her complete recovery, no expense to be spared. With her husband's orders and the Hotel liable for the bill no hospital would release such a plum for at least a week. Holmes paid for the telegram from the wallet he had lifted from one of the ruffians as they passed in the hallway. Flipping through he saw that this little adventure would keep him in shag and spirits for a month, and it wasn't over yet.

The next evening Holmes visited the grave again. It was made for a recently deceased Bryan Laramie, according to the inscription a beloved brother now resting in the peace of the Lord. Holmes stomped upon the grave as he had seen Madame

Withers do. The bell gave a tentative half ring. As Holmes moved forward to inspect it something shiny on the ground caught his attention. He stooped over it and was surprised to find a glass aperture looking down a tube to a human eye, which after a moment jerked away to the side.

"Halloa?" Holmes called. "Should I alert the caretaker or do you mean to be down there?" The only response was silence. Holmes dug around the glass with his fingers and found it attached to a brass tube, almost as if someone had buried a telescope vertically and left one end just barely exposed. He next examined the bell, hung from a curved metal stake with a cord running down into another tube in the ground. It was akin to hundreds of service bells he had seen before, with the exception of beckoning for assistance to a very unusual place. What stood out was the odor emanating from the tube. It was rank and all too human, but not that of rotting flesh. No, only a living being produced this smell. The occupant of that box was trapped in his own filth, and assuming he was buried within a few days of the death date on this headstone, he had been for almost a week.

"What are you doing there?" came a raspy voice from behind.

Holmes turned to see a stooped man tottering on stiff legs behind him.

"I thought I heard this bell ring, and then I saw an eye in this porthole."

The gravedigger wheezed and slapped his knee. "People see all sorts of ghosts and hobgoblins and whatnot out here. Unsettles the mind to walk amongst all this death."

Holmes looked at the strange man and silently agreed.

"Take my word for it, there's nothing to it. A breeze tinkled the bell and your imagination put an eye at the other end of that pipe. I've dug up more than a handful of these safety coffins and the result is always the same; gruesome and sad. Was he kin to you?"

221

"No, I am putting my own affairs in order and looking for a likely plot for my eternal rest. I've never seen one of these contraptions put in place. Were you there when it was buried?"

"Dug the hole myself and filled it up too."

"The body was unquestionably dead the whole time?"

"I don't open any coffins I don't have to, but he weren't objecting if that's what you mean. Nice and quiet, like they all are."

"The pipes come out I presume? I don't see any others."

"Normally I give them about a week. Long enough they are dead one way or the other and the family's mind is at ease on the matter, but soon enough the dirt is still soft enough to work them out without redigging the whole bloody grave. Besides, the smell comes right through, as you observe. Vermin can also run down in the pipe, for what little that matters. Matters to some."

"Then you are about to remove this pipe? I see it has been almost a week."

"It's about due but that pretty widow keeps coming, so I might let it sit a little while longer. Once that bell is gone it really hits some people that it is final."

"Most kind of you."

"A little kindness is about all I have to share in this world, but I'm right where people need it the most. Let me know if you decide to plant yourself in my garden. I'll take good care of you." The gravedigger staggered away.

"Did you hear that Mr. Withers?" Holmes whispered down the bell pull tube. "These devices stay in place only as long as Madame Withers continues attending Mr. Laramie's grave. I regret to say that she finds herself otherwise engaged presently and she will not be back. If it is any consolation, this is a lovely spot in which to await eternity." Holmes gave the bell cord a couple of jaunty tugs and headed back to Montague Street.

Late the next afternoon Holmes presented himself at Scotland Yard. "I would like to speak to an inspector," Holmes told the desk sergeant.

222

"Whom might you be?"

"Mr. Sherlock Holmes."

"Who?"

"Sherlock Holmes."

"Never heard of you."

"I don't know why you would have."

"Upon what business would you like to consult an inspector, sir?"

"I have identified an extortionist, and I know the location where he has accidentally confined himself by misadventure."

"Where might that be exactly?"

"Within a coffin."

"So he's dead then?"

"Not as yet, but I suspect he is about at the limit."

"How do you come to know this?"

"It all began in a tobacconist's shop when the extortionist's wife came to wring out the proprietor so she could pay her hotel bill. It seems she was already hiding from a grander criminal organization that was trying to kill her husband."

"The one in the coffin?"

"Correct."

"Who is not actually dead?"

"Yes, you see he had switched places with someone who had actually died, leaving the dead body at his old hideout for these criminal enforcers to find."

"How do you know this?"

"I found the dead body."

"Where is it now?"

"I've hidden it."

"Why?"

"To force the wife into drastic action. I believe both she and her husband were waiting for the other body to be found so that the extortionist would be reported as dead and they could escape to a new life together."

A thought slowly formed in the desk sergeant's brain. "Say, this isn't about a Madame Withers in the Grand Royal Hotel, is it?"

"Yes, that's just the extortionatrix."

"Two of a kind, you are. She's barking mad, too. Escape from the same asylum did you? Come to think about it she was complaining of being harried by some amateur interloper. Just one of many complaints, but we'll have it sorted out soon enough." The Sergeant waved to the constables across the room. "Now, Mister...what was your name again? Why don't you wait back here and you can tell the nice doctor all about it when he arrives."

"This is absurd!" Holmes shouted as he twisted his body around and slipped the grasp of the constables. "I'm giving you the solution to a series of crimes and rather than thank me you mean to lock me up?" Holmes was out the door now and into the teeming crowds of London. He doubled back a dozen times, crisscrossing roads and passing through shops until he finally felt like he was free of any pursuit. Then, circuitously, he made his way back to Montague Street. He had barely closed his door behind him when there came a-knocking. Holmes was flabbergasted to find one of the constables standing outside.

"I guess I'm not as clever as I thought," Holmes said.

"You were clever enough, too clever by half. We'd completely lost you within the first few minutes. I've been waiting here for two additional hours for you to return."

"How did you find me then?"

"Sherlock Holmes, your name stuck with me. Not too many of those in London."

"I am under arrest then?"

"Not quite yet. I'm new to the uniform and maybe I'm naive, but I'll take a look at this buried extortionist."

"That's rather kind of you."

"I've a mind to be an Inspector someday, and if I quietly keep my place I'll be rousting drunks and scrubbing cells until

I'm thirty. I'm looking for an exceptional case to make my name, and it's worth an evening to me to see if this is the one."

"Perhaps the Yard isn't a total loss. Well met, Constable…"

"Lestrade, sir. Constable Lestrade."

Holmes could not ride in a police carriage without raising suspicions, and the same was true of a uniformed constable in a private carriage, and so the two walked all the way. Holmes described his adventures in detection at university and Lestrade talked about his yet meager career.

"You've the makings of a fine policeman, Holmes. I can write a testimonial for you if you wish to join the Yard."

Holmes laughed. "I'm afraid I would be a very poor policeman in fact. I do have a talent for observation and deduction, but I fear a uniform would only stifle me."

"Do you mean to go into business for yourself then? Some sort of private detective?" Lestrade laughed heartily at the idea.

"I don't think I could make a career of it, but an occasional consultation to the police might amuse me."

They had arrived at last, the shadows cast by the headstones lying long across the ground. Holmes led the way to the grave, and they weren't even upon it yet when the bell began to ring frantically.

"Help! Help!" came a muffled voice from the bell pipe.

Lestrade began to dig at the earth with his hands but Holmes gestured for him to stop.

Holmes leaned into the pipe. "Should I address Mr. Withers or Mr. Laramie?"

"I thought you said Mr. Withers had replaced Mr. Laramie," said Lestrade.

"That is true as far as it goes, but I suspect Mr. Withers replaced one Mr. Laramie with another."

"Oh," Lestrade's shoulders slumped. "You are mad. At least there is a living person buried in a coffin, that's something. Wait!" Lestrade unbuckled his manacles from his belt. "Please surrender quietly, Mr. Holmes. I'll see to it they treat you decent enough."

"Save the manacles, you'll need them in a moment. What I mean is that Mr. Withers is a pseudonym for Mr. Laramie."

"Then who is the other body?"

"Bryan Laramie."

"But you just said Bryan Laramie is Mr. Withers, and Mr. Withers is buried right here."

"I said Mr. Withers is also Mr. Laramie. But not Bryan Laramie. Bertrand maybe, or Bartholomew. People always think it is cute to give twins similar names."

"Twins?"

"It's true! I'll swear to it! Just let me out!" said Withers from the tube.

"The man in the coffin looks just like the body you found?"

"I rather hope not. The boy I found was seriously decomposed and ravaged. Besides, I have yet to see Mr. Withers' face."

"Then how can you know they are twins?"

"The fatal mistake Madame Withers made was to give me overly precise directions to a supposedly lost husband. Clearly, she knew where the body was and was distressed that it had not been found quickly enough. Why? Because she wanted it to be recognizable when it was found. She wanted the organization that was hounding her to see her dead husband for themselves. The body was identical to Mr. Withers, a twin. In the meantime Mr. Withers found the perfect place to hide; in the grave of his recently deceased brother. They expected the whole scheme to take but a few days. Bryan Laramie could wake up in his grave and Mr. Withers could rest in peace."

"Remarkable, Mr. Holmes!"

"All too pedestrian, Constable Lestrade, now that I understand it. Perhaps this crime-solving business isn't for me after all."

Lestrade ran to fetch a police wagon while Holmes woke the gravedigger. The stooped man didn't thank Holmes for it but seemed to get into the spirit of the thing as Mr. Withers screamed and pounded under the ground beneath his shovel.

Holmes imagined the man had few good stories to tell since all the drama was generally resolved by the time the digger played his part. As Holmes had hoped, the tobacconist Wilshire became quite liberal with the quantity of shag he dispensed. He also followed through on his threat to substitute his Turkish blend, doing so over the Christmas holiday when his store was closed, leaving Holmes with no choice but to smoke the strange stuff. He found he'd lost his taste for English shag by the time the tobacconist reopened. All seemed right again on Montague Street, yet Holmes could not shake the feeling of being watched, as if some malevolent spider eye had fallen upon him.

The Somme, France, July 1916

When I returned to the King's service, I never thought the most gruesome scene I'd encounter would be in the dining room of a French villa. As a young Army surgeon in Afghanistan, I had seen the unfortunate results of still-living men only partially obliterated by artillery. I had seen the queer bloodless waxen figures left behind after a beheading. I've seen the rainbow hues of women and children stoned to death rather than being left behind to be liberated by His Majesty's fighting men. So many deaths, brutal, savage, but in their own way honest. A rock hurled, a blade swung, even a shell fired. A man had looked at another man and chose to end his life with violence. Nature at its most pure and most ugly. But this dining room tableau was inhuman, unnatural. Twenty mid-ranking members of Ally brass representing Britain, France, Australia, and Canada, blue and contorted, dried trails of every variety of effluvia that seemed to have been squeezed from their bodies by the giant invisible hand of some capricious pagan deity. I said a brief prayer into the scented handkerchief at my nose.

I'm sure my escort, Lieutenant Tuttleton, thought I was calling upon God for strength and mercy. In actuality, I hoped that somehow it was possible for my whispered pleas to reach the ears of my former companion in crime-fighting, the fondly remembered consulting detective, Mr. Sherlock Holmes. I could see upon the eager face of young Lieutenant Tuttleton that he, like most, assumed that Holmes' genius was a torch that had been passed to me. Over the years of our association, I had observed Holmes' methods, learned a few neat tricks, and was now more observant than most, but this strange tragedy demanded more than I feared a second-hand genius could provide.

"Captain Watson?" Tuttleton's faith had begun to falter as my brief pause in the doorway had begun to stretch into a positive halt. "I'm sorry, sir. I should have better prepared you for what you were to see. I just assumed, with your experience, that this would be..." The awkward pause while Tuttleton searched for a word that would end that sentence with both our dignities intact expanded out into the room, pushed up against me and finally shoved me into action.

"Murder should never become commonplace, Lieutenant. If you ever find that it does I beg of you to leave military service and take up some gentle vocation where your soul is not further imperiled by moral deafness. I once knew a man who turned to beekeeping when he felt the last vestiges of his humanity evaporating into the black hole of criminal vice and despair."

"Very good, sir." A confused Lieutenant Tuttleton gave a crisp salute and stepped back to the edge of the room. I could practically hear the monologue in his head as he wondered to himself how this strange, possibly senile, old man was meant to discover the cause of these bizarre deaths. Perhaps all of the deductive ability lay in the other member of the famous sleuthing team, and what he was looking at here was merely a trumped-up valet and scribbler. I sighed. Perhaps I was just projecting my own doubts onto his professionally blank face.

I placed my trusty gladstone down on an open end of the dining room table and began a careful stroll around the room, letting my mind go blank and cataloging as much data as possible. There were fresh cut flowers in small vases placed around the room and on the table. A trite extravagance a mile or less from an active front line in a transcontinental war. Looking out a window I saw the very same flowers dotting the surrounding hills. Cowslips, marguerites, gentians, no doubt collected by one of the servants still acting out a lifetime of instruction in keeping up appearances. For the sake of argument, I carefully wafted a few of the vases but detected no suspicious odors. As I passed by the windows I attempted to open them.

"Sealed shut, sir." Tuttleton offered from the corner. "As you can imagine we made an attempt to air out the room very early on. Staff says the windows have always opened before. Very strange, if I may say so."

"Never tamper with a crime scene until it has been inspected, Lieutenant!" Brusque, but nothing like the tirade Holmes would have brought down upon the man. Closer inspection revealed a caking of a simple flour paste around the seal of the windows. It would be difficult but not impossible to heave them open. A few humid days would break down the paste and the windows would be as through untouched. More pressingly, it would be impossible to trace flour and water. An industrial compound might have pointed at a plumber or a road worker or some other tangible avenue of investigation. "Dust these windows for prints. Eliminate the guests, the staff, and any known military personnel on scene, then send on any unidentified prints to my office with another copy to the Secret Intelligence Service. Maybe a familiar face has been here." I next examined the three doors entering and exiting the room and found that fresh strips of felt had been applied to all of the jambs. Strange to take such a precaution against drafts in July. Of course, I already suspected that the purpose was to keep an airborne agent in rather than keep cold air out. Still, I lacked the delivery method.

"Who discovered the bodies?" I asked as I paced the room again examining the light fixtures for signs of tampering.

"A maid, sir. She was retrieving more ice from the cellar when she entered and found this." He gestured broadly at the room. "You can see there where she dropped the ice bucket in fright." Indeed the overturned silver bucket resting on a damp rug was the only sign of disturbance in the room. Other than the twenty corpses, of course. Whatever happened took them so suddenly that none of them appeared to have even risen from their chair.

"The doors were unlocked?"

"There are no locks on these doors, sir."

Next, I examined the diners themselves. Not medically as it was clear from the moment I entered the room that they had expired from an inexplicably fast deoxygenation of the blood, causing severe muscle contractions, the queer blue pallor each exhibited, and of course death. No, I looked in the hands of each, patted down their pockets and pulled up their sleeves at the wrist looking for any sort of deployment contrivance. A right-thinking Englishman would never forego his honor and his immortal soul by committing a suicidal attack, but all of Europe was at war against strange foreign factions and there was no telling what some Godless Bulgarian or Romanian might get up to.

There were a few oddities. Some German coins, a letter both enciphered and perfumed, a little bone idol, a few cameos. Signs of the men beneath the uniforms, but nothing that would accomplish a mass murder.

Next, I inspected the beverages. There appeared to be at least two varieties of wine, one of beer and one of carbonated water at play. Were multiple beverages all poisoned? But why would any have taken a drink after the first man succumbed? They could have all drank at the same time as a result of a toast, but then I would expect to find spilled glasses fallen from spasming hands and most of the bodies toppled from a standing position onto the floor. For the sake of a complete investigation, I carefully examined a few of the glasses. I gingerly ran my finger across the rims, listening for the telltale squeak of arsenic. Then, from my bag, I retrieved a small satchel of vials containing chemical mixtures devised by Holmes to aid in investigations. I swabbed the glasses in an attempt to identify any foreign substances remaining, but the glasses and their contents appeared to be unadulterated.

I looked without hope at the food. The guests at the head of the table had just begun serving themselves and the majority of the guests had no food yet at all. The roast goose at the center of the table caught my eye. It was finely laid out on a silver tray, wreathed with herbs and berries, brushed to a high gloss with butter. Yet it appeared to have been served with a knife protruding from the top, which rather ruined the otherwise refined appearance of the bird. In my mind's eye, I saw my friend's wolfish grin, the one that signified that Holmes had caught the criminal's scent.

"Clear the room!" I cried. "And put your masks on. Civilians clear the building!" There was a great hubbub as I retrieved my own mask from my gladstone propped open on the table as I slipped it on, it was difficult to see through the small glassed apertures provided for the eyes, but the rough waxed canvas felt like security as it scratched securely over my face. Looking around to make sure I was alone in the room I gave the knife handle a tentative jab. Nothing happened so I gripped it firmly and pulled it from the goose. I heard a strange wheeze and a distinctly mechanical click. Freezing mid-extraction, I held my breath for a count of thirty. When nothing else happened I chanced to remove the knife the rest of the way. Then, gently began pulling the flesh from the bird. Revealed in the cavity where one would expect to find a proper oyster stuffing or rich giblets was a pressurized container capped with a large mushroom-shaped plunger. It appeared that anywhere the bird had been cut would have caused the plunger to depress, presumably ejecting a poisonous gas. I retrieved a waterproof sack from my gladstone and securely enclosed the device. I then used a fine silver knife from the table to chip away the paste around one of the windows and then lever the lower pane up. I waited one minute for the room to air out and then tentatively removed my mask. A few shallow breaths were followed by a few deep ones.

"Tuttleton!" I cried. A masked soldier hesitantly entered the room. "Have this sealed in a metal ammo case and then send it along to SIS. Be sure to warn them that it is the remnants of a chemical bomb that causes instant death." With trembling hands, Tuttleton received the bag seemingly in disbelief of his own actions. "Send our boys here back to England with all due respect and send the others home as well. Let each of the receivers know the bodies may still be toxic and should most likely be cremated."

"Is that all sir?" Tuttleton rasped, still wearing his mask.

"Have some good tobacco and brandy sent to my quarters. I plan to spend the evening in rumination while we wait to hear back from SIS."

The next morning I awoke to a swift rapping on the door. I heaved myself upright on my thin mattress and rubbed at my weary temples. "Stop knocking and come in, blast it!" The door swung stiffly open to reveal a dispatch rider in a surprisingly crisp, clean uniform. He snapped an efficient salute and held a piece of paper out into the room careful to not set even a toe across the threshold.

"I'm an old man forced to sleep on a military cot and keep hours and pace with men a third of my age!" I bellowed, waving the slip of paper away. "Read the damned thing or just tell me."

"Director Holmes orders you to appear at once, sir. I am to escort you directly to a secret location."

"Please remind Director Holmes that the SIS does not command Army doctors."

"He thought you might say that, sir." The messenger reached into his coat and produced an envelope. Unlike the dispatch previously offered, which was typed on thin, coarse wartime paper, this envelope was visibly luxe, thick and soft with a repeating crest watermarked throughout. When the messenger tilted the envelope there was no mistaking the waxen image with which it was sealed. "Director Holmes instructed that you be reminded the King of England does command Army doctors." I sighed and waved that envelope away as well.

"Fine, fine. No need to waste a perfectly good royal warrant on me. I've seen a few in my day and I've no doubt Mycroft has a stack of them at hand." I shrugged my field clothes back on and was led outside by the messenger. "No chance of breakfast, I suppose. A quick cup of coffee before we run?"

"Director Holmes was rather insistent about your immediate retrieval. As is I suspect he'll be rather cross it took this long." We arrived at the soldier's vehicle, a motorcycle with a sidecar.

That blasted contraption was expertly designed to sever the passenger at the wait in the event of an accident and small enough to make you glad when that happens.

"You can't be serious! I'm a decorated war hero! I'm on my way to see the director of the SIS!"

"Director Holmes wanted your retrieval to be quick and discreet. Now, sir, if you would please wear these goggles." At first, I took the lenses to be tinted a smoky black, a wise precaution since it appeared we would be driving directly into the rising sun. However, once I had donned the apparatus I was shocked at what I could see, or rather couldn't see.

"Why these goggles are entirely blacked out!"

"Yes, sir. As I said, this facility is top secret. The goggles completely obscure your vision while being less obtrusive than, say, a sack over your head."

"Knowing Mycroft I'm surprised it wasn't a tranquilizer dart in the neck."

"That was Director Holmes initial suggestion, but I noted the indignities of stuffing an unconscious man into a sidecar. Director Holmes conceded that ultimately he only cared about the result. Now, if you will step into the sidecar, Doctor." Six decades and two wars had taken their toll on my body, and Mary's cooking had expanded my personage beyond what would be generally considered regulation size, so it was with no small effort that I found myself wedged halfway into a metal receptacle whizzing along blindly through war-torn France. My Holmes had many times been unwillingly chauffeured under blindfold and had managed to best his captors by counting cobblestones and listening to church bells. Unfortunately, I had just arrived at The Somme yesterday and had no such facility with the locale. I merely gritted my teeth and tried to not be thrown from the moving bike as it seemed to find every rock and pothole between camp and wherever we were speeding.

At one point I heard gunfire off to our left. "Stay calm," the messenger said. "They aren't looking for new trouble, they've got enough as it is." The dust and clamor of the rough road eventually gave way to a muffled swish and the soft rolling of languorous grass-covered hills and all sounds of war seemed to dissipate. Finally, as the motorcycle slowed the messenger announced, "We have arrived." Without waiting for permission I lifted off my goggles. Before me sat a modest, red brick, country estate. We were coasting up a drive that circled a fountain depicting a nymph eternally pouring water from a jug. Around that was a well-tended bed of flowers. In fact, the entire grounds and the house itself all seemed to be in excellent repair. We came to a stop immediately in front of the main entrance. Two hard-looking men, wearing the suits of country gentlemen but with sidearms on their hips, came out from the door. The messenger saluted. "One Captain John Watson, as Director Holmes requested." One of the men produced a photograph of me and briefly held it up next to my face. He gave a stiff nod and the two country gentlemen saluted the messenger, who then hopped back onto his motorcycle and gunned it into the nearby carriage house.

"Right this way, Captain Watson," one of the men said, gently but irrefutably taking me by the elbow and leading me upstairs.

Mycroft sat enthroned in a velvet dovetail armchair, surrounded by a dozen teletypes all clacking away with their inscrutable messages. Little but his eyes moved, ticking back and forth between the tapes. If it wasn't for the alternating ember smoke of his cigar, one might almost wonder if Mycroft Holmes were even still with us. I stood, hat in hand and counted the stubs in the ashtray, the bottles in the rubbish bin, the plates on the sideboard. Mycroft was a prodigious consumer of all things. I often wondered if that was how he himself kept from being consumed. By any rights, he should never have lived to see the twentieth century. Finally, I forced a cough and declared, "Mycroft, you hauled me out of bed for this."

Mycroft heaved a full-body sigh. "Diphosgene."

"Pardon?"

"The aerosol canister you found. Our lab analyzed it. Diphosgene. You are familiar with phosphene, of course. The Huns began deploying it two years ago, hence the natty gas masks we are all expected to carry. Respiratory agent. Death in twenty-four hours. The Germans call it White Star. Well this new chemical, diphosgene, they call Black Star. Exponentially more potent. Only a dram needed where a quart may have been required before. Death is instantaneous. Passes right through the filters on our standard-issue masks."

"But how…"

"The Allies are playing at war with one hand tied behind our backs by a rope called honor. The Germans and the Austro-Hungarians aren't playing. They are committed to total war. If we lose, it will be our weak constitutions and failure of resolve that does us in."

"Surely you can't be advocating that we develop indiscriminate weapons of mass destruction? That would be unconscionable madness."

"When we face evil we must defeat it by any means necessary. To fail to do so is to be culpable in said evil."

"Now I know you are being supercilious, Mycroft. A man like you, all intellect and no emotion, cannot believe in evil."

"I can see the future in my crystal balls, Doctor." Mycroft gestured at his teletypes. "From a distance, over time, all human behavior is a pattern, and patterns can be deciphered and predicted. Mark my words, if we stay our hands instead of delivering a killing blow we will be revisited with an unchecked aggression the likes of which history has never seen."

"Now, now, Mycroft. It can be hard to see in the middle of a battlefield but I think you underestimate the humanity and fellow-feeling of our German and Austro-Hungarian brothers. The Allies will restore peace, fair accords will be created and we will move hand-in-hand into a peaceful and prosperous twentieth century."

"We can all be thankful your befuddled ministrations can only kill one patient at a time."

"Now see here, Mycroft. I didn't submit to being yanked from my bed and dragged blindfolded across half of bloody France to be condescended to by a bloated, disagreeable difference engine!"

"No, you were brought here to take orders from one! We have been tracking shipments of chemicals and the movements of vehicles and containers thought to be designed to safely transport Black Star. We have found a nexus in Merzig. There is an unusually large theatre there known as the Zeltpalast. Our intelligence reveals around-the-clock activity and evidence that exhaust vents have been built into the roof. I want you to go there, confirm that it is the site of Black Star production, and steal the technical information surrounding the creation of Black Star."

"Why me? Surely you must have any number of crack military squads ready to deploy."

"Firstly, we do not wish to tip our hand yet. Despite the unfortunate dinner party yesterday, we do not believe the Germans are actively deploying Black Star. We believe they are stockpiling in order to surprise the Allies all at once. If anything, we are lucky that someone broke protocol and only killed 20 people. The casualties could have been astronomically higher had this chemical been sprung on us in many locations all at once. We need to know exactly what we are dealing with and exactly what their production scope is."

"Secondly?"

"What's that?"

"You indicated that was your first reason. What is the second."

"It seems that my brother held you and your abilities in great esteem. As much as it pains me to admit it, I do respect his judgment. We need someone with the medical knowledge to understand at what they are looking, the wits to steal the information without leaving a trace, and the wherewithal to manage all of this without support from the Crown."

"I beg your pardon?"

"This war is too tenuous and Black Star too dangerous. Should you be captured you must not reveal your connection to Britain and most especially to the SIS. On our part, we will have no choice but to disavow you. In the event that you should be caught, I wonder if you wouldn't mind-affecting an American accent."

"I don't believe I heard you correctly."

"It is just that, according to my analysis of various scenarios, intervention by the Yanks would be expedient in concluding this war."

"Just to be clear, you are asking me to steal the plans for an egregious chemical weapon from a hostile nation, and, failing that, to draw a friendly nation into an intercontinental conflict that will only escalate the death and destruction?"

"I knew you were smarter than you look, old boy." With that Mycroft returned to the clickity-clack of his teletypes, the world of abstracts and statistics of which he was master. I was escorted back downstairs to the parlor, which was now full of maps and telephones and uniformed men hustling to and fro. A Lieutenant Scarsdale, small and trim, pulled me aside.

"Captain Watson, we have arranged to have you inserted into the crew of a Dutch merchant ship. You will accompany an inland shipment of foodstuffs until you reach Merzig."

"I can't speak a word of Dutch!"

"You shouldn't have to. The crew will be aware of who you are and that you are being secreted into Germany. If you stay inconspicuous and never answer anyone with more than the grunt of a simple laborer the rest should be able to cover for you. Most soldiers aren't suspicious of the Dutch or peasants, and it is easy to keep a hungry soldier from asking too many questions by filling his belly."

I briefly wondered what a man like Mycroft knew of soldiers or hunger.

Thus it was that I found myself trundling along through the country roads of wartime Germany, piled in the back of a flatbed lorry with the rest of the turnips. As predicted, a Dutch laborer was beneath the notice of the German soldiers. I hauled produce by day and slept on the bonnet at night, watching smoke from a dozen conflicts obscure the stars. When we finally reached Merzig, I simply carried a bundle of greens in the front door of a restaurant, went through to the kitchen and deposited my burden, and then walked right out the back door. My fellows made the rest of the delivery and drove off as if nothing was amiss. I found an empty crate on which to sit across the street from the Zeltpalast and settled in to wait until nightfall, making every effort to look idle but not intransigent.

There was a moment of anxiety when a German policeman attempted to roust me but I exaggerated my lame leg and pantomimed to the man that I wanted food, approximating the vocalisms of a deaf-mute. In my head, Holmes critiqued every aspect of my performance, but I didn't need the illusion to last long, just long enough for the policeman to decide I was a harmless hassle and be on his way.

As night fell there was a sudden outflux of people from the theatre. First came a bevy of young ladies in smart suits with hair and makeup that seemed obscene in the face of wartime rationing. I didn't understand a word of German but from their demeanor and tone, I took what they were saying to be the idle chit chat and banal trivialities of secretaries. Certainly, they did not seem to have knowingly just come from a chemical house of horrors. Next came a wave of grim-faced men, their dark attitudes more appropriate for the setting. I took it from their rough trousers and rough faces that these were the factory workers. Skilled tradesmen who now found themselves the nimble hands of war. Finally came a handful of twitchy, dark-eyed men furiously chain-smoking in their rumpled tweeds. These men had a small military escort who guided them just a small way down the street to what I presumed was the finest hotel in Merzig. I could not tell if they were treated as dignitaries or prisoners and I guessed they could not be sure either.

Finally, after all activity had ceased and the block had been quiet for a quarter of an hour I spritely made my way across the street. The marquis for the theatre, though dark, still advertised a musical comedy entitled "Zigeunerliebe". I gently tried one door and then another. They were all locked, but only by simple pin tumblers. The keyholes were so large and ornate I might have been able to pick the locks with my pinkie finger, but instead, I popped free the simple picks embedded in the headband of my hat. It had been thirty years since my friend had drilled me on the art of cracking a lock, but my hands remembered. A quick push and a turn and a lift and the door before me swung open a few inches. With a quick look at the still-empty street, I slipped in and deftly pulled the door shut behind me. The click of the latch seemed to echo loudly in the abandoned lobby.

Lit by a single ghost light, the once opulent lobby now contained only a few empty planters and two folding chairs, one on each side of the theatre doorway. Next to each chair was a pile of cigarette butts piled directly on the rich nap of the carpet. I took it that these were makeshift guard stations. Luckily the guards had escorted the scientists back to their rooms, or gilded cages. If I knew how soldiers posted at remote stations behaved, I suspected the men would be drinking and playing at cards the rest of the night. Still thought it prudent to make haste. Looking into the dark recess of the main theatre I found myself squinting as I moved further into the unknown. It too was sparingly lit, so that I could only catch the general outlines of the various machines insides. A few seemed to quietly hiss or tick, but the factory largely appeared to be shut down for the night. I took a minute to memorize the general shapes so I could report back to Mycroft. Since there had been a clear delineation between the factory workers and the scientists, I suspected the technical specifications I was after would be housed somewhere off of the main factory floor.

The theatre manager's office seemed to be a reasonable guess so I turned back into the lobby and felt along the wall until I discovered the stairway to the staff offices above. Try as I might to quiet my approach the stairs groaned as I ascended. I paused at the top and listened but heard no other sound in the building save my own anxious breath. On a hunch, I progressed to the far end of the hall and opened the door. I had expected a scientific bureaucrat's office filled with schematics, binders, tables of loads and stresses and the like, but instead, I found the workspace of an eccentric chemist. Mismatched glassware and a series of gas burners apparently patched directly into the mainlines of the building through holes seemingly kicked through the wall. A variety of jarred substances, liquids, crystals, powders and presumably gasses, lined every surface of the room. Mycroft had seemed to think that this was merely a production facility, but here I saw clear evidence of ongoing experimentation.

What I didn't see were notes. Every scientist in the world took scrupulous notes. You never knew when you would have to retrace the steps of a major breakthrough. Besides, nearly all scientists were absent-minded and relied on their notebooks as a crutch. I began pulling open drawers looking for any sort of paperwork. Most of the drawers contained inexplicable odds and ends - soil samples, a dozen different brands of German cigarettes, an entire drawer filled with what I hoped were animal teeth. Finally, I found a pile of official-looking documents in two binders. Flipping through, I found mechanical diagrams, chemical figures, and table upon table of data. Other than a few cryptic notations it seemed as if the papers had hardly been touched. It wasn't as if someone could have mastered the contents simply by reading through them once. Must be a backup copy, I reasoned. All the better, perhaps it won't be missed for some time.

Having found what I came for, more than I dared hope, I took one binder under each arm and turned towards the door. I froze dead in my tracks. Before me stood a strange man whose bald head appeared to be covered with burns. He looked at me through black lensed spectacles which sat upon a crooked nose and a long, almost oriental mustache. He was wearing a discolored lab coat but standing in a martial art pose. He was so singularly still I was momentarily unsure if he was even breathing. Flanking this unusual person were the four German soldiers I had seen before. Each had a pistol pointed at me.

"Strange," the strange man said in a heavy German accent.

"How so?" I replied.

"A British spy. The British aren't known for their spies."

"His Majesty's secret intelligence service is the finest espionage agency in the world!" My pride of country had found my lips before Mycroft's directive to pass as an American.

"It is the finest information collation service in the world. Your British intelligence service sits in a leather armchair growing ever fatter and risking naught but an occasional papercut."

"You see before you that Britain still produces bulldogs that are up to an honest fight." I placed the binders on the lab table and brought my fists up into a fighting stance. "These are all interesting criticisms coming for a deplorable bastard who makes chemical bombs that will kill tens of thousands of innocent people you will never even lay eyes upon."

"You have no idea what I am doing here, and yet you meddle. Get out of the way and let genius solve the problems created by fools."

"I don't know what kind of solution you think poison gas is, but as long as there is righteous red blood flowing through these veins I'll not stand aside and make way for evil."

The strange man seemed to slump his shoulders in resignation. "I know." The man took three deep breaths and then suddenly twisted the gun out of the grip of the soldier on his right and tossed it to me. Next, he made a quick finger strike to the throat of the man to his left who crumpled to the ground. He then drove his fist deep into the gut of the first man again. Both men fell to the ground. The two remaining soldiers looked to each other in disbelief. The strange bald man stomped the knee of one while seizing the neck of the other and crushing it against the man's own shoulder. Now all four Germans were on the ground.

"Chip in any time, Watson."

"What?" I stood there thoroughly flabbergasted as the man yanked off his nose and mustache, and then peeled back his scalp revealing a full head of hair.

"I say, Watson, you had me quite impressed up until now. Do finish strong, old boy."

"But how...? I thought...?"

"I was briefly employed as a lecturer at a small university in Austria where I showed some promise in the chemical arts. A few rough sentiments expressed in the right beer halls and I found myself employed by the less reputable underbelly of the German Army. A man of my talents was soon assigned to oversee an entire operation and here I have been slowing the production of Black Star as much as logistically possible without blowing my cover while developing a counter agent to substitute in as many bombs as possible. Imagine the Germans furiously peppering our boys with the antidote to their own poison. I've done so well I've even managed to include some invigorating agents, so not only will the Germans be safeguarding our troops against the very attack they think they are committing, but they will even be putting a little extra pep in our step as we march into Berlin. There are more elegant plans but none half as satisfying."

Sherlock Holmes would later lament that if sentimentality had not gotten the best of him, he could have let me be shot and brought the Great War to a conclusion by Christmas.

London, England January 1917

I sat by the fire in my old familiar club chair watching thick, wet snowflakes coat Baker Street while warming the old wounds in my leg and shoulder. I thought wistfully of dear Mrs. Hudson. She had been one with this old building and had been able to stoke from this hearth a gentle warming cheer that carried through the walls and the floor and bathed the entire parlor in a radiant glow. Alas, Mrs. Hudson's time had passed and so had the age when an eccentric bachelor of sporadic means might employ his own widow landlady as a housekeeper. Thus it was that I had lit my own fire, small and angry, throwing harsh shadows in flickering disarray across the room. The heat barely seemed to escape the confines of the hearth.

A tooting automobile horn brought me out of my reverie. Once upon a time Holmes and I could hear the clatter of a client's hansom from two blocks away. Now, in the regular stream of motorized traffic, we were often caught unawares. Although, really, only Mycroft and a handful of his functionaries knew we were here. 221B Baker Street now went through long, regular periods of dormancy, whenever Mycroft called Sherlock out on a mission, or whenever Holmes simply felt the spur of wanderlust. I understood that Holmes had managed to negotiate with His Majesty for a lease of the premises in perpetuity. While Holmes rarely accepted monetary compensation from the bulk of his clients he also rarely shied from trading favors with the especially rich and powerful. I wondered how much longer his residency here would last. I had noticed that tomes on the flora and fauna and history of Sussex now seemed to stay on top of the stacks of books piled around the apartment. I suspected the end of this war would also see the retirement of the world's foremost consulting detective, but of course I kept such deductions to myself. One of Holmes foibles was his lack of appreciation for becoming the subject of his own techniques.

There was a knock at the door. I turned to look at Holmes perched at his chemistry bench. He appeared to be deeply engrossed in some sort of chemical analysis. Having once found a way to conclusively demonstrate that a sample contained blood, I believed he was now attempting to develop a compound that would reveal minute traces of blood invisible to the human eye. I believed that was what all of the bags of blood in the icebox were for. I believed that it was all pig's blood. I chose to believe a lot when it came to Holmes' cryptic experimentation. Another knock at the door.

"I'll just get that, shall I, Holmes? I only ask because it is traditional for the master of the house to answer a knock."

Holmes made a dismissive wave without looking up from his microscope. "Now, now, Watson, this is your home as much as it is mine."

"Surely, Holmes, I haven't lived here in twenty years!"

"Your presence has ever been felt."

"You converted my bedroom into a canary roost the very day I left on my honeymoon with Mary!"

"I had a need for space and suddenly found myself with said space. You can't begrudge me that."

"When I moved back in after Mary died you let the canaries keep the room!"

"Delicate migratory patterns had developed, Watson. A thousand birds would have been lost from disorientation had they been displaced! Did you want that on your conscience? You may take this cricket bat down to the park and start knocking nests out of trees if you feel you must be an instrument of avian cruelty." A pounding at the door. I heaved myself up and made my way down the stairs, each creaking perceptibly under age and weight. I opened the door and was startled to see Mycroft himself on the landing.

"Ah, Captain Watson, I apologize if I have interrupted a delicate moment." Mycroft and two burly associates pushed by me and up the stairs.

"Mycroft," said Holmes, finally looking up from the beakers in front of him. "I see the Diogenes Club must finally be fumigating the premises to drive out all of the vermin."

"Our consciences can rest easy as it is abundantly clear that all of God's creatures are welcome to take up residence here." Mycroft had produced a handkerchief with an eye to draping it over the seat of a chair but was now engaged in refolding it for his pocket, having apparently opted to stand.

"As usual you are overly presumptuous. There are some forms of invasive mold that even I will not abide. Watson, if you would retrieve the bleach? I believe we have some consumptive rot to root out."

I sighed and fished another cigar from the box on the end table.

"As charming as our family reunion has been I do have a rather urgent reason for subjecting myself to your abode and enduring your inferiority complex. Captain, do you recall the chemical agent Black Star you came across while whiling away your time in France?"

"You mean the Black Star that left a gruesome panorama of horrifying death in the dining room of a French villa and caused me to be sent on an international espionage mission that resulted in my inadvertently exposing Holmes and prolonging the most expansive war in modern history, just a few months ago? It does ring a bell."

"Jolly good. Despite your blundering, we did recover the plans for Black Star and the entire cache on site."

"We did that, did we?" Holmes interjected. "I remember seeing myself there. I remember seeing Watson there. I don't recall seeing a Mycroft Holmes in scenic Merzig. Whatever blunder there was took place between those two ears." Holmes jabbed Mycroft in the forehead. "I have every faith stalwart Watson here did exactly what you told him to do. I discovered the factory. I developed a counteragent. I was on the cusp of neutralizing the entire program from the inside. You, Mycroft, meddled in something you didn't understand half as well as you thought you did. As usual, with the usual results."

"Nonetheless, once the Germans knew that we knew about Black Star and knew we had developed a counteragent they shut down production. Or so we thought. It seems that an especially enthusiastic junior scientist on the project has continued access to Black Star."

"It would be naive to for us to assume that there is no Black Star out there anywhere. I'm sure there is any number of copies of the formula and the specifications for the equipment. It is simply too expensive to make and deploy when we have such a ready antidote available at every military staging area across Europe."

"I don't think you understand. This rogue German is not on some distant battlefield, he is here, in London, right now. He means to deploy Black Star against civilians who have no antidote, no training and no recourse to any gas masks or air-tight bunkers. Logistically we can neither protect nor evacuate the whole city."

"Londoners have bucked up under repeated German bombardment. It takes more than a black eye to dampen the English spirit."

"Those bombs arrive by noisy, slow-moving zeppelin. The papers he left behind indicate that he was working on miniaturizing the aerosol disbursement device Captain Watson discovered. Ostensibly to create grenades for use in trench warfare. As part of this research, he created a miniature rocket that could be used to deploy these grenades at a great distance."

"Sensible in its own macabre way."

"Yes, but in a separate notebook found in his personal quarters, we found plans for linking these rocket-powered Black Star grenades together in a sequenced cluster. Theoretically, his design would launch dozens of grenades in every direction. And since the outer grenades are on a delay and first propelled by the inner grenades, the maximum reach of the final rocket grenades to be deployed is as much as a mile. A single strike with this weapon could envelop all of London at once. And it can be contained in a relatively nondescript satchel."

"I see. So you are heading out for a holiday in the countryside, are you? Watson found your choice of French retreats to be gauche but perhaps your poor taste in abandoning the city will be offset by better taste in lodgings?"

"Yes, very good, you observed the luggage in my automobile and surmised you are receiving a visit rather than a summons only because I am relocating out of London for the present. I dare say any middling mind could have done the same, is that not so, Captain Watson?" I ground the stub of my first cigarette into the ashtray rather more than absolutely necessary and sparked a fresh sprig of tobacco.

"It takes a rare breed of man to run and cast aspersions at the same time." Holmes spat.

"Don't be petulant, Sherlock. Honor is no defense against the Reaper's scythe. Now, SIS keeps a list of personages of value and against my advice you are on it. Grab your coat and hat and we shall away."

I sprang from my chair and lunged at Mycroft with the blazing cherry of my cigarette. His subordinate started to move against me but Mycroft called them off with a minute flick of his fingers. "This is too much!" I bellowed. "You are honestly going to abscond in the night with a chosen few and leave London to die with nary a word? Is that what the British Lion looks like now, a whipped tabby cat willing to settle for surviving on a fishmonger's scraps?"

"Calm yourself, Doctor. As you are here as well I suppose I cannot stop you from coming."

"Can't stop me from coming? You blighter! You couldn't make me go! I've got a smarmy ponce who needs a swift punch in the face and then I've a rogue bomber to stop! Shall we, Holmes?"

"Now, now, Watson. We must not let our emotions rule us and drive us to make rash mistakes."

"Holmes, you can't be seriously considering..."

"Oh, I most certainly am, dear Watson. A punch in this vacant visage would do little." Mycroft gave me a superior smirk as Holmes continued. "He cares not for vanity and besides has developed steel cheeks from a thousand justified slaps. A hardened oak cane to the stomach, on the other hand, will hit him where it hurts." Holmes seemed to produce his trusty walking stick as from thin air and drove the head deep into Mycroft's ponderous belly. Mycroft's fellows, slow to react to these ever stranger circumstances, found themselves swept off their feet by a low kicking motion from Holmes. As Mycroft tried to wheeze himself into an upright position Holmes held one man about the neck by an armlock while fending off the other with swift kicks. "I hate to bother you, Watson, but if you would be so kind?" I tapped the second assailant on the shoulder and he swung at me with animal ferocity. I lunged towards him with the full ashtray that had been my constant companion all night. The ash blinded him a moment before the glass tray smacked his temple, flattening the nerve and causing a temporary paralysis as he slumped to the ground. In the meantime, Holmes had rendered his man unconscious by means of oxygen depletion. We soon had Mycroft and his men handcuffed to each other and around a radiator pipe. "It really is quite noble of you to stay here and sink or swim with the proverbial ship, Mycroft."

"You'll pay for this, Sherlock!"

"I shall gladly suffer for my actions if only London does not suffer for yours. Quickly, tell us everything you know, however little it may prove to be."

By Mycroft's reckoning, the bomber would be looking for a wide-open space to maximize dispersal, hard to come by in cramped London. "My analysis suggests he will deploy the gas from an elevated location, The Crystal Palace Towers, the Tower of London, the Clocktower at the Palace of Westminster, maybe the London Bridge."

"Your analysis, as always, is flawed. You, like all pasty, nebbish Englishmen, are subconsciously fixated on asserting your masculinity by means of phallic overrepresentation. Germans don't share that particular subconscious quirk but they do have another. Their fixation with the brute driving force of automobiles, submarines, and most importantly for us, trains."

"What a bunch of Freudian pseudoscience, mumbo jumbo and twaddle."

"To the contrary, men are but animals and animals are but biological machines and machines act as they are designed to act. As we cannot confer with the engineer of the human-machine we must rely on observation to reconstruct the schematic. We have trouble seeing this in ourselves, but if we turn our minds to study creatures we consider to be foreign and simple, like bees, we find it to be self-evident. Also, ask any person out on the street and they will be more than happy to opine on what a Welshman will do in a given situation, or a Hindoo or any other outside group. Behavior is systematically predictable. Your German is going to utilize a train."

"Really, Sherlock. Will you bet our lives upon it?"

"I will bet every soul you were about to forfeit on it. He's looking for an above-ground track that will get him as close to the center of London as possible."

"The London and North Western Railroad runs above ground right into Euston Station."

"My thoughts precisely, Watson. If I were looking to commit such a travesty I would maximize the damage by setting off the bomb at the busiest time of day. Glancing at the clock I see every office worker in London, a not inconsiderable amount, is just about to head home. We've got half an hour by my reckoning and it will take us near that to make the mile up Woburn to get to Euston. There's not a moment to waste, Watson! Flag down a cab for us and I will grab a few necessaries and be with you presently." As I ran down the stairs to the street Holmes turned to the chemistry bench and Mycroft began pleading. Needless to say, Holmes joined me at the curb a few moments later with no sign of Mycroft.

"Euston Station, and stop for nothing!" Holmes shouted tossing a crown on the seat next to the cabby. He held another one up in his fingers so the cabby could see it. "There's another for you if we are standing in the station in ten minutes."

I generally found the enclosed nature of modern cabs to be stifling, but today I was glad of it. The cabbie, already a reckless breed even before the chance to earn a day's wages in a few minutes, swerved in and out of traffic in both directions, jumping up on the sidewalk at times. We had no less than two rocks and five pieces of produce hurled at us, in addition to innumerable colorful phrases. While we did not collide with anyone during the hectic sprint if you told me there was a fatality or two from shock, I would not have been surprised. Holmes had plunked the second crown down on the cabbie's seat and was out the door while I was still trying to get my head and stomach to settle. The station was in full bustle, with thousands of commuters milling about. Holmes ran to the station manager's office and I trotted up behind, trying to stay upright as the ground seemed to heave beneath me.

"What you ask for is impossible, sir."

"You fool! There are four and a half million lives at stake!"

"There's my job at stake, and I'd lose it if I acquiesced to every insane demand of every deranged person who comes pounding on my door."

"What's all this, then?" I asked.

"I have made the very simple and expedient request that all trains be stopped below ground as quickly as possible."

"Firstly, it's impossible. The signals aren't set up to convey that bizarre command. Secondly, it is completely mad."

"What if I assured you we are here operating under the auspices of His Majesty's Secret Intelligence Service and that it is absolutely vital that action be taken."

"Then I would politely direct you to the queue over there right behind Napoleon, and Ramses and Moses who all also have apocalyptic business to conduct on the Metropolitan Railway today." He gestured towards two drunks and a man who appeared to be barking at the ceiling, who were all seated in a secluded corner of the station. "I'm sure the police will be very interested in your statement when they arrive and will treat your information with all due diligence."

"We haven't time for this!" Holmes declared, snatching a train schedule from the station master's desk and running back out into the station. "Track number three, Watson!" Holmes shoved a path through an increasingly hostile crowd and we found ourselves at Track Three just as the train arrived. "Blast it!" Holmes cried. "Give me a hand, Watson." I boosted him up so that he could scramble on top of a newsstand. The proprietor grumbled until Holmes announced his identity and promised to return the next day to autograph every copy of the morning papers, all of which would be describing the shocking event about to take place. The newsman seemed unconvinced but was unwilling to blow even the chance of such an opportunity. Holmes intently scanned the crowd. "Stay sharp, Watson! We are looking for an agitated German scientist lugging around a parcel likely much too heavy for him." I looked through the crowd as they passed around me. Most of the commuters carried some sort of bag, a purse or a briefcase, but none of the bags seemed especially heavy, and most of the commuters were either making idle chit chat or distracting themselves with an evening paper. I saw no one who appeared to be especially anxious.

"Say, Holmes. You don't suppose that instead of carrying a dozen grenades in one bag the bounder has distributed the grenades amongst a dozen comrades?"

"We can only hope not, Watson. We have no hope of stopping or even anticipating a dozen different strikes by a dozen different people. However, while Mycroft's conclusions are often wrong his data rarely is. Everything we know about this scientist suggests he made a spontaneous decision to attack England and that he knows neither the language nor a single person here. I suppose it is not impossible that he could have walked into any German restaurant or tavern and tried to recruit sympathizers, but the timeline doesn't suggest that. Besides, I suspect there are very few people just lounging about waiting to be asked to become suicide bombers for the fatherland."

"Sometimes I fear we are underestimating the Germans."

By this time most of the commuters had disembarked and neither Holmes nor I had seen anything sufficiently suspicious. Across the station came the final boarding call. Holmes clapped his hand to his forehead. "I'm a damned fool and now it may have cost everything!"

"What is it, Holmes?"

"I suppose because this problem arose in a military setting I was thinking of it as a military problem. I pictured the grenade-loaded satchel as a payload and the train as a missile. Naturally, one fires a missile away from oneself and the explosion is at the end of the trajectory. As such, I had subconsciously fixed on the idea of a train as a missile being fired at the station. What if we think like a criminal rather than a soldier. The train isn't the delivery method, it is the escape method! Our scientist sets off the bomb at the beginning of the journey as the train speeds away. If the delay is long enough it is even possible the piloting engineer won't even know anything has happened until the train stops again. According to this schedule, the train departing now is a direct route to Carlisle. Our man can slip out into the crowd in the confusion and be in Ireland in a day. Sinn Féin or any of a dozen other Irish nationalist groups would be happy to provide amnesty to the man who destroyed London. Quickly Watson!"

We dashed across the tracks, to the consternation of the station workers, and ran after the train. Thankfully it was still getting up to speed and we were able to pull ourselves up onto the last car before the train had reached traveling speed. "You take the low road and I'll take the high road," Holmes said, doffing his hat at me and beginning to climb up the service ladder to the roof of the car.

"You can't be serious!" I shouted, grabbing at his pants leg. Holmes shook off my grip.

"The German's best bet is to deploy from atop the train. That being said, he may choose to deploy from a window or from between the carriages. We must find him, Watson. We literally have minutes, if that. Go!" Holmes clambered on top of the train and began crawling forward into the fearsome air draft. I yanked open the carriage door and entered what appeared to be a service compartment. The next two were cargo departments, the last staffed by a very surprised guard. I yelled something about national security and pushed past him while he rubbed the sleep from his eyes.

I entered a dining car only to hear gunshots on the roof above. In response to the diners' screams, I pulled my trusty service revolver and assured them that everything was well in hand. I leaned over the nearest table and lowered the window causing a torrent of wind to send the tableware flying. Leaning out the window and looking up I could not see anything happening on top of the car nor hear anything over the rushing wind. "Pardon me," I said as I climbed up on the table and worked the top half of my body out of the car so that I was seated on the windowsill with my legs inside and my upper half clinging to the outside of the car. I could now hear the altercation above. A shrill voice was screaming in German. Then came Holmes' voice.

"There, there, old boy. You are not thinking clearly. Setting off these bombs in London will only kill more families. You'll be as bad as the bombardier that destroyed your home, but by a magnitude of a million." More German screaming, "Wars are only ended by diplomacy. An act of aggression on this scale will never end a war, it will only strengthen your enemy's resolve. Launch those grenades and you will only sign the death warrant of every German, Austrian and Hungarian while most likely launching the entire globe into a war that will lead to the extinction of mankind. Now, put the gun down." Hearing that the firearm was still in play I pulled myself up the side of the train so that my feet now stood on the window sill and my head and shoulders were above the roof. The German scientist was a small, shrew-faced man with tinted glasses and a dark trench coat whipping in the wind. He struggled to stay upright against the tumultuous gusts and the revolver in his outstretched hand bobbed erratically. Between the scientist and Holmes sat a unique cluster of strange devices. It appeared the scientist had built some sort of frame to attach the individual rocket grenades together. It looked like he had mounted the frame to the top of the train and had been in the process of running some sort of cord, or maybe fuse, down to the passenger area. Holmes had correctly surmised that our genocidal maniac intended to survive the attack and escape by train. Holmes hovered over the device, his cane in a defensive stance so that the German may not touch it. I guessed Holmes had shoved him away from it when the confrontation had begun. I could see a black hatred rise from the man's collar up into his face. Suddenly, instead of staggering, he was quite rigid. The gun, formerly pointed in the general direction of Holmes, now found an unwavering target in the strange device.

"Foolish. That won't get you the millions you hoped for. The explosion might take out a handful of people in the carriage below. Not enough to turn the tide of the war but just enough to see you hanged." The German roared with rage. Before I knew what I was doing I had steadied my elbow on the roof of the carriage and fired three shots center mass. The man toppled and bounced before he dropped from the train.

Quickly Holmes fell upon the strange device. On hands and knees, he inspected the frames, the grenade, the cord. "Watson!" he shouted down to me. "You must have the train evacuated at once! There is a spring-loaded timing device at the center of this mechanism. I fear our German was even more resolute than we thought." Holmes began gently probing the device as I slid back in the window. The engineer and two railway guards were just arriving, summoned by the distraught passengers of this car.

"Now see here!" the engineer cried, lunging at me with a baton, attempting to rap the gun from my hand. "There's a dozen military-trained men on this train, so if you have a mind to hijacking or robbery or some other mayhem you've got another thing coming." I gingerly laid my sidearm on the nearest table and slowly raised my hands.

"Gentlemen. If one of you would be so good as to inspect the top of this car I believe you will find my associate, Mr. Sherlock Holmes, attempting to defuse a poison gas bomb."

"Bloody likely. I suppose you have Florence Nightingale on call should anyone require medical assistance."

"It would cost you nothing to look." The engineer thought for a moment and then nodded back at one of his fellows. The man exited the car, stepped off onto the external utility ladder and then we heard the clunking of his boots up the metal rungs, followed by a shout of "Blimey!" The guard slid back down the outside of the ladder and popped back in the door.

"Well?" asked the engineer.

"That's bloody Sherlock Holmes on the roof!"

"Are you certain? Any jackanape could throw on a deerstalker cap and Inverness cape. The better to distract us and rob the train or worse."

"He ain't got none of that getup, sir, but I swear it is him. Me mum were a maid and our family was almost ruined when she was accused of stealing from her mistress. Mr. Holmes swooped in and proved it were the lady's own jilted childhood sweetheart what done it. Me mum kept every newspaper clipping on Mr. Holmes after that. I saw them pinned to the wall every day. Me pa wasn't quite so chuffed by it, but I can swear to you that is Mr. Sherlock Holmes." The engineer turned back to me.

"Dr. Watson, I presume?"

"Very glad to make your acquaintance, sir." I proffered a handshake, which he reluctantly returned. "I'm afraid the situation is most urgent. That bomb is set to explode at any moment and it will be most disastrous when it does. We must evacuate everyone from the train."

"An evacuation will take upwards of thirty minutes after we find a suitable place to stop."

"No good! We are talking about moments!" The engineer thought for a moment and then whispered to one of the guards who marched to the back of the car.

"Your attention please!" The engineer needlessly cried to the passengers. All eyes and ears were already on us. "Will you kindly proceed to the car ahead of us. I'm afraid we have a small situation that must be attended to." There was some grumbling and griping but the remaining guard and the engineer efficiently corralled all of the passengers out of the car. Suddenly there was a mechanical squeal and a lurch that almost knocked me off of my feet. The train sped up. I turned to see the cars behind us falling away.

"What's happening?" I shouted.

"I can't get the people out of the train quickly enough, but I can get the rest of the train away from this car, though not in one piece, as you see."

"The section you scuttled was already empty! All of these people are still trapped with a moving bomb!"

"Now we simply detach this car from the front and speed away before the explosion."

"I'm afraid it is not that simple, old man. This isn't just an explosive. The bomb contains a powerful German poison that will spread over all of London."

"A poisoned gas attack on a civilian city! The curs!"

"So you see, simply abandoning the bomb in an open area is not sufficient. In fact, it may only assist the German's aims. I'm afraid we find ourselves shackled to death." The engineer pounded his fist then whispered instructions to a shocked guard. The man began to protest but the engineer waved him away.

"Only momentarily. My man has run ahead to notify the assistant engineer of my plan. I must get prepared for my role immediately. There is no time to waste. There is a short track divergence ahead that leads into a disused quarry. I intend to detach this car just before the fork and then flip the switch as we go by. With any luck, this car will divert and fly safely inside the quarry before the bomb explodes."

"That is insane, man!"

"Do you have any better suggestions?"

"I shall fetch Holmes immediately!"

The engineer exited the car to the front and pried what looked to be a giant hook from the side of the carriage. He wedged the tip of the hook in the coupling mechanism and then leaned out from the train, presumably looking for the switch. I exited the back of the car, now also the back of the train. I pulled myself up the utility ladder to find Holmes sitting cross-legged by the device, manipulating imaginary objects in the air as he puzzled out a solution. I shouted to him, "Holmes! The conductor is going to shunt this car off from the rest into an enclosed quarry!" Holmes looked up and seemed surprised to see me.

"Watson! What have you been doing with yourself? Stop this train and get the people off!" Again I yelled the gist of the plan. Holmes cupped his hand to his ear and then shrugged and returned to his work. Sighing, I climbed the rest of the way up onto the car roof. On hands and knees, I scrambled over to Holmes. "Watson! This is no time to be contrary! This bomb is so haphazardly constructed by some inscrutable Teutonic logic that I dare not tamper with it. I regret that the most favorable solution I can come to is to absorb as much of the explosion as possible with my body. By dampening the charge at the point of ignition I believe I can significantly reduce the ultimate range of the gas disbursement. It won't save London proper but Greater London will be raising a glass in my honor tonight, I wager."

"There is no need, Holmes. The engineer knows of something even denser and obstinate than you. Up ahead there is a split onto a side track that used to service an old enclosed quarry. He means to divert this car and send it sailing into the old quarry where the blast, and the gas, will be mostly contained."

"A neat trick if there were a dozen trained railway men well-versed in the procedure standing ready. How does he plan to manage it?"

"He stands now with his hand upon the lever that will release this car. He will do so shortly before the split and then leap off and flip the switch."

"Impossible! We are moving too fast and none of the systems in question are designed to react with that speed. The man would have to be prescient to correctly time the release and an Olympic athlete to manage the jump and pull. Even if he did, this car wouldn't stay on the tracks. No, Watson. I will not trust the fate of London, and indeed the world, to the hubris of a delusionally proud man."

"Yes, Heaven forbid we rely on such a character."

"I'm staying, Watson. It is time for you to leave."

"This is it, boys! Jump now or forever hold your peace!" called the engineer from below. With a screech, we felt the car lurch. As the train pulled ahead we watched transfixed as the engineer leaped, rolled and came back to his feet just before the switch. We watched him heave at the lever with his entire body and heard the rusty track groan as it switched for the first time in years. The ticking of the device became louder. Holmes' eyes went wide.

"Be rational, Watson! Jump! You have no reason to be here!"

"I have every reason to be here," I said clapping my hand on Holmes' shoulder. A final protest fell silent on his lips and we took our places, side by side, hunched over the bomb. In a strange way, I found it comforting that the gas would ensure that we would not suffer long. Not strange at all, I found it comforting that I was shoulder to shoulder with Holmes, the defining person of my life, racing headlong into danger to save the day. It was the ending he deserved, and I felt I had earned it also.

As Holmes had predicted, the car began to lose its grip on the track. It began wobbling and we grabbed onto the mounting frame for the explosives, for fear of being thrown onto the tracks and crushed. Then the car flipped onto its side at a cross angle to the track, throwing up sparks as it slid along, the unstoppable force of thousands of pounds in motion pushing us along. Holmes, now above me, had clamped onto my arm to keep me from falling. Ahead we saw the track terminating before the entrance to the quarry. I was relieved to see there was no question the train would make it. As the track ended and the train hit the ground it shook me loose. There was darkness and then I was under stagnant water. In vain, I thrashed around looking for Holmes. Then there was a strangely muffled boom as the bomb finally exploded under the water above me. I saw the bubbles and the shock wave coming for me and then I saw nothing.

London, England, June 1920

I had feared that retirement would prove to be insufferably dull but after that day every criminal triviality that crossed my threshold just seemed more and more tedious. There was always another missing jewell, another faithless spouse, another international catastrophe to be averted. It was all so small and banal and pointless I couldn't fathom how I could ever have been so occupied. So engaged. Without Mrs. Hudson placing toast and jam in one hand and Watson taking the needle out of the other I found myself wasting away physically and mentally, watching the mold spread across the ceiling of my Baker Street apartment. Once I passed out from hunger for so long that I woke up sober. In the morning light filtering through the gaps in the drapes, I watched a bee for what must have been hours. At first, its ponderous, slow flight seemed to rely purely on happenstance, to and fro, here and there. All of a sudden my starved brain painted a pattern in the air as if the bee left a golden trail behind it. This simple creature was painting the room with Euclidean geometrics and it was beautiful. I could not remember the last thing of beauty I had beheld. I had spent so much of my life peering intently at the ugliness of man I had forgotten there was a whole world that man did not touch, did not taint. For just a moment the bee landed gently upon my forehead and I had a second of clarity. Baker Street was a poor bodhi tree and I was a poor Buddha but I had been enlightened. At first, I could not so much as turn my head or lift my arm I was so weakened by hunger. Through sheer force of will, I rolled over and pushed myself up. Finding support in a chair, then a table, then a door frame I staggered into the kitchen. The first cupboard was bare, then the second. In the third, I found a packet of Watson's old tea biscuits and with this sacrament, I was saved.

Now in my small cottage in the Sussex countryside, I tended my apiary, studied the physical transformations of clouds, and kept a detailed catalog of the wildflowers. Rather than being bored I was so utterly absorbed that I often found myself going days at a time without thinking of crime, or war, or mankind at all. Once the local merchants became accustomed to my retiring persona I found I could go without speech for months. Not knowing my name many assumed I was some sort of religious pilgrim, and in a way I was. Others assumed I was deaf or mute, and in a way, I was that too. They either said nothing around me or everything around me. Either way was informative or would have been had my mind still been collecting information about humanity. It was from this blissful reverie that I was cruelly yanked by the long arm of my brother Mycroft.

He sent first one telegram I refused to accept, and then another. The third he paid the telegraph company to shout aloud from just outside my door. He asked that I come back to London out of brotherly love. I kept tapping away at the beehive frame I was mending. He asked the I come out of fellow feeling for my countrymen. I planed the last rough edges off the contraption. He asked that I come on behalf of Watson. I pulled on my coat and hat and joined the telegraph man outside.

I stepped off the train in Victoria Station to find post-war London sunnier than the place I had left. The clothes brighter, the laughter louder, the mood lighter than London had ever been. These people had lost years of their lives to the Great War and now they endeavored to get them back with relish. Feeling an unanticipated sense of nostalgia I elected to walk to the Diogenes Club. After years in the country, the hard, smooth concrete of the sidewalks felt strange under my feet. I listened to my heels and my walking stick clack-clack-click through the streets, reminding me of the Vaudeville follies of my youth. I saw more people before I had left the train station than I had since leaving London. My head swam as the loose voices assailed my ears, the mostly unfamiliar faces pulled at my eyes, and the close, rank smells of a city stopped up my nostrils. For a few moments, the heart of London seemed entirely alien to me. Had I ever truly known this place?

Then, somehow, I found myself standing in front of Baker Street. The drapes were closed and the building gave off that strange sucking aura of emptiness that all abandoned spaces share. I approached the door and reached into my pocket for the key. What a fool! I chided myself. I had no intention of seeing Baker Street again and had not brought the key with me from Sussex. In fact, standing there, I could not remember if I even possessed a key anymore. After my enlightening episode with the bee in Baker Street and all it contained had simply ceased to matter. I had long ago secured by royal decree a lifetime lease of the property. Had I left a key with a caretaker or had I simply walked out of Baker Street with nary a thought to its disposition? I grasped at the knocker and for a moment heard an echo of Mrs. Hudson's cheerful chatter as she lit the hearth. I heard Wiggins bare feet slapping up the stairs with the unbridled enthusiasm of youth. I heard Watson chuckle in amazement at his own retelling of some adventure or another. Even the great logician Sherlock Holmes knew better than to stir the dust of a haunted house. I released the knocker again unswung and made my way on to the Diogenes Club.

Mycroft sat behind his desk reading dispatches and then throwing them into the wastebasket one after another like playing cards. In addition to the teletype machine clacking away, the office contained a buzzing telegraph machine, three radios broadcasting in Dutch, German and Hindi, and a dozen different clocks ticking smartly. This tussy mussy of information all spilled directly into my brother's head. I closed my eyes and filled my ears with the gentle buzzing of bees dancing across lilac blossoms in the warmth of the morning sun.

"Sherlock! You damnable rascal, this is no time for a nap!" My eyes drifted open again to see Mycroft puffing away at a cigarette like the London Express climbing a hill. After regarding me with hard eyes for a moment his entire countenance softened. "Still shell shocked I see. More's the pity. England needs the famous Sherlock Holmes, the hero of the British Empire. Is he still in there?"

"I've done my bit for King and Country and there no one who can say I haven't. I've been very clear that I am not fighting any more wars, Mycroft. You mentioned Watson? That is the only reason I'm here."

Mycroft deftly slid a file folder out from the middle of one of the many stacks of paper growing up out of his office like bureaucratic stalagmites. "Yes, well, it seems that the last case of yours and Watson is not yet closed."

"If there is a new threat from Black Star you have all of the technical specifications Watson recovered. You have my antidote. There is no need for me to further revisit those events."

"Believe me we have made every effort not to involve you. Your current mental state makes you compromised, to say the least. But I'm afraid your months of hands-on expertise with Black Star is just too valuable and our time too short. You know, of course, of this business with the Turkish rebels?"

"I neither know nor care for anything to do with international politics. I am focused purely on natural science now and I fear you have brought me here under false pretense. I'll not respond to a summons from you again, whether or not you invoke the name of Watson."

"Now, now, Holmes. Steady on. Your research into Black Star has been stolen by a British defector and handed over to the Turkish rebels, and thus since the rebels have not the resources to take advantage of it, to the Russians."

"Again I tell you that politics don't concern me."

"We believe they now possess the ability to create a gas against which your antidote does not work."

"War is a notoriously dirty business but it is your business, not mine. Good day."

"Dr. Watson sacrificed all to put a stop to this. You can't leave his work unfinished. Perhaps it will bring you some solace as well."

"Do you truly believe you can trade on sentiment with me?"

"Then let's talk numbers. There are 485 million people in Europe. 138 million in Russia and another 18 million living in the bullseye that is the Ottoman Empire. You and Watson went to superhuman lengths to prevent a bomb filled with Black Star gas from killing 4 million in London. I assure you that this new gas, Red Sword, conservatively has a ten-fold killing power. With weapons like that the next great war will be over before it begins, very much to the detriment of Great Britain."

"This is madness, Mycroft! Madness created by men like you. Why did we ever allow bureaucracy into warfare?"

"Recriminations can wait. Only a select handful of scientists were ever allowed to study Black Star. It was both a security risk and a low priority considering we thought that threat to be held in check. Those scientists are spread across the continent, attached to Guards regiments actively searching for the traitor and the plans for Red Sword. To put it bluntly, we have not enough resources and what few scientists we have are in all probability inadequate to the job once the Red Sword is found. We need a detective of the finest mind and a scientist of the finest caliber. Once upon a time that was you. Will you finish Captain Watson's mission?"

Ankara, Ottoman Empire, June 1920

The city of Ankara lies in the shadow of the Augusteum, essentially a building-sized tombstone for Augustus, the first Emperor of Rome. The man's body was entombed in Rome but the legacy of this world conqueror is enshrined here. A fitting spot for the genesis of the first weapon that could literally lay waste to nations with the push of a button, I thought. Scanning the city from the window of my quarters provided for me by the

Secret Intelligence Service I noted that most other traces of Augustus' reign had been supplanted by the domes and spires of dozens of mosques, giving the city a decidedly foreign feel. Everywhere the world was in flux and even the largest splash eventually dissipates into nothing. I found myself staring at my own reflection in the window.

A knock at the door broke my reverie. Beyond it, a man stood stiffly. The rich embroidered fabrics of his suit and the distinctive Ottoman tailoring was belied by the white flesh of an Englishman, seemingly unable to absorb the Mediterranean sun. He gave a reflexive salute when I opened the door and announced himself as Mr. Smith Perhaps my brother's aura of authority had clung to the Holmes name. Perhaps he simply couldn't remember a time he didn't begin every interaction with a salute. I had the briefcase out of his hand before the door was fully opened. As I closed the door again I heard a brief protest escaping his lips. I carried the briefcase over to the bed and subconsciously listened to the muffled creaking of the floorboards in the hallway. The man shifted his weight, turned to leave, turned back to the door again, and then finally left. The case was locked with tumblers. They turned easily, freshly lubricated to avoid being cracked by feel. I turned them to read JHW, Mycroft, of course, aware of my unique motivation in this matter and flipped the clasps open.

Inside was paperwork. Ledgers. Charts tracking purchases and people and properties and itineraries. "Tut, tut, dear brother. If the answer was here you would have already found it." I shook the papers on the bed like ash from a plug and retrieved my pipe from my luggage. One good thing would come of this trip. In Sussex, it was impossible to obtain a good Turkish blend of tobacco. I began eyeing the items in my valise, pondering what could be sacrificed so that I may pack more tobacco home. Then I had a sudden flash of inspiration. I lept back to the papers on the bed. I found the report of chemical substances traded by volume. I flipped through the folders detailing the various investigations Mycroft had directed. He had run down the top 10 largest trades by volume, except number four. Why not number four? Because butyrylcholinesterase is not an ingredient of Red Sword, or Black Star or any other poisonous gas. It is a chemical prophylactic against poisoned gases. The Turkish rebels aren't creating the disease, they are making the cure. Mycroft was so focused on looking for a sword he didn't even consider looking for a shield.

"Hello!" I shouted to the empty room. "Mr. Smith, I have a lead but I need more data. I know you are there!" I sat in silence for a moment and then heard the door to the suite next door open. A moment later there was a key in my own lock. The pasty false Ottoman from before entered sheepishly. I circled the chemical name on the sheet. "I need to know where this has been going. As quick as you can." The man saluted, with less snap this time, and left the room.

I ate an early dinner of stuffed noodles in cream anticipating taking action the same night but found myself awakened by knocking the next morning. A combination of travel and heavy food must have put me to sleep, I reasoned. It had been a dead, pleasant sleep as sweet as opium and I did not mind the rest.

My faithful SIS contact now handed me a new report, but only after deftly stepping inside my room. I scanned the report and saw that a sweets factory had suddenly and inexplicably began receiving shipments of butyrylcholinesterase. "This is it!" I cried.

"Director Holmes quite agreed. The site was contained last night."

"Last night? I've just been waiting here! Why was I not informed?"

"I'm afraid you were quite incapacitated last night." Smith would not meet my gaze.

"But I consumed nothing but a noodle dish and… do you mean to say you drugged me."

"It was Director Holmes' orders, sir. He felt that you were too unpredictable and that it was best the situation was resolved without your intervention."

"That is absolutely the limit! The train station, now. I am going home."

"I'm afraid the train station is off-limits, sir. The terrorists we captured are being transported from there at present."

"Transported to where?"

"Sir?"

"To where are these so-called terrorists being transported?"

"Back to England, sir. For interrogation."

"It just so happens that England is my destination as well. Shall we?"

"Sir, these are prisoners of war. We have our orders."

"Then slap the handcuffs on me, my wrists have been chafing metaphorically anyway since this whole ordeal began. I knew better than to leave Sussex. It appears vulgar sentimentality has become a failing in my old age."

"I really can't take civilians on a military charter, sir."

I punched the man in the nose, grabbed a handful of papers from the bed and tossed them out into the street. "There, I have assaulted an official of His Majesty and I have distributed state secrets to nationals of a hostile foreign nation. May I be arrested now?" I finally received the handcuffs I had been asking for, though they were tightened more than absolutely necessary. On the way back to the train station no one seemed to see the metal shackles hanging from my wrists. Or rather, they did not observe. Observation can be a dangerous avocation in a land of warring factions.

A short train pulling only a few unmarked cars sat waiting at the station. The caboose carried a machine gun mounted to the back railing. For a moment I saw a makeshift missile frame and heard the screech of bending tracks, but I quickly shoved that memory back to the dark corners of my memory attic. The train's windows were fitted with steel plates with only a small slit for peering out and too high up for me to peer into them.

The middle car was a simple boxcar and into it were being loaded a hundred or more men. I did not look forward to a two-day trip standing on my feet. Smith brought us to a stop at the back of the line of rebels. I scanned the container looking for sources of fresh air. At least being loaded last would put me by the door. Perhaps there would be options there. Though could a retired sexagenarian hold a desperate battalion of militants at bay for very long? My thoughts must have crossed my face because Smith smirked and then yanked me by the arm.

"Worry not, Mr. Holmes. You are still a British citizen and still afforded some small dignities." We proceeded to the first car, unmarked and refitted with at least the basic armor similar to the caboose. My escort helped me step up the stairs and into the darkened interior. He prodded me down to the far side and pushed me down onto the padded banquette. He then took a seat opposite me and lit a cigarette. My eyes were reflexively drawn to the flame and I was momentarily blinded when he shook out the match. "You be happy to know we caught the traitor. He'll be joining us shortly. Perhaps you can perform some deductive magic on him during the journey home, eh? A positive effort might soften whatever blow is coming to you." He rubbed his own still-swollen nose.

The carriage rocked as the traitor and his SIS escort climbed aboard. They were only silhouettes as they came towards us. The end of Smith's cigarette bloomed and faded as he absentmindedly puffed away. The new SIS man shoved his prisoner down next to me. With a metallic screech, the train lurched and pulled away from the station. The two agents nodded at each other knowingly. The cigarette bloomed again and I looked upon my neighbor, a heavily bearded man wearing second-hand clothes tailored for a bigger build, designed for office work but with wear at the cuffs, knees, elbows, and shoulders showing they had been worn in the course of manual labor. The man looked at me agape in astonishment. The cigarette had faded again. In the dim light, I tried to place the face. He clearly recognized me but I had never conducted business in the Ottoman Empire before. A foreigner I had captured in London, or more likely a Londoner that had followed his criminal fortunes to this strange backwater.

"Sherlock?" he gasped.

"The same, and whom am I addressing?"

"You may know me as Boswell," replied the voice of my friend Watson. The cigarette bloomed again and there in the light of the cherry embers I beheld that familiar smile once more.

"If you mean I may know you as overly dramatic and dead you are half right, and until a moment ago I would have picked the wrong half,"

"Now, now, Holmes. You slipped off the moral high ground at Reichenbach Falls."

"I'm sure the devotees of your narratives will be quite pleased by your return from the grave. It will save me the trouble of replying to all of those letters, anyway."

"Very good, gentlemen. We've heard what we needed to." The other SIS man grabbed Watson by the arms and heaved him to his feet."

"What's all this, then?" Watson said.

"Director Holmes just wanted to be sure that there was no collusion. Mr. Holmes appears to be legitimately aggrieved." Smith smirked at me. "You'll be separated for the rest of the journey, and, well, considering the Crown still hangs traitors, you'll likely not see each other again in this life." The other SIS man began dragging Watson to the far end of the car.

"I have stared a thousand reprobates in the eye," I said. "I know a guilty man when I see one. After all of these years, I can smell crime on a man like a bloodhound. That is not a guilty man!" I pointed at Watson after slipping my hands from the shackles with no small amount of pain.

"Bloody hell!" Smith shouted as he rushed at me. Even after being dormant for a decade my baritsu training took immediate hold and I had my adversary braced up against the wall in moments. Watson fell back on his man pinning him to the ground. I snapped one end of the cuffs around the railing encircling the interior of the car and the other on the wrist of my captor. Turning to Watson's man I fished his keyring out of his coat and removed the handcuffs from Watson, replacing them on the unconscious man's wrists. "Now would be an excellent time for answers, Watson."

"When I walked away from the train accident relatively unscathed Mycroft had me transferred directly to the SIS laboratories so I could help document Black Star. You were in the hospital and had not even regained consciousness yet, otherwise, I wouldn't have..."

"Never mind that. The facts of the situation, please."

"I naturally thought that after I completed my report on Black Star I would be free to go, but Mycroft kept me securely contained in their facilities. I was given the choice to assist in their research or rot in a prison cell. At the time I had no idea what they were up to so I begrudgingly kept working, hoping for an opportunity to leave."

"What exactly was my dear brother up to?"

"I was told that we were developing a better antidote that could be distributed more widely, in case of another bomber. I later found out my research was being perverted into an even greater poison than Black Star. Worse, other than my test batches, no antidote was being produced. Had anything gone wrong there was absolutely no recourse."

"That seems rash, even for Mycroft."

"He is not the same man. He has developed a select corp of people in the military and government. Those who believe England must strike first to protect itself. I believe he has had some kind of psychotic break and is now operating in a state of total paranoia."

"That has always been his natural state, but please continue."

"I demanded that production be halted and he simply removed me from the project and left me alone in my cell for days. I pleaded to at least be allowed to build a reserve of antidote and was summarily denied. So I settled in and waited. Over time my guards grew bored, and then lax. I managed to keep a butter knife at one meal and with that, I managed to tease open the latch of my door in the middle of the night. These were not true cell doors but merely regular office doors tinkered so they locked from the outside. Because the entire lab building was designed to keep people out rather than in I was able to enter the lab with ease. I recovered my notes on the antidote and set fire to the rest of the research by throwing everything I could in the lab furnace. No doubt his men can recreate their work but it was a symbolic gesture anyway and perhaps will slow them down a little. Knowing that their target was Russia I began heading east like a tramp, hopping trains and riding on the back of trucks. Eventually, the Turkish Resistance captured me and I managed to get them to pass my formula along to their Russian contacts. They are mass-producing it but that is like being prepared for the swing of an ax by having a bandage in your pocket."

"As you say, Mycroft's scientists can and no doubt are already producing more Red Sword, the charming code name for my brother's little project. What can we do? However dreadful, this horrible knowledge is already in the world and we cannot stop it."

"Perhaps we can't stop the science but we can stop the men."

"How so?"

"On this very train, we have a hundred or more witnesses. With any luck, the SIS men hold incriminating orders. Let us cast this clandestine project into the light. What these people are doing is unconscionable and, once known to the world, the Crown will put a stop to it."

"You place too much faith in those who hold absolute power."

"Kings, Ministers, heads of state all serve at the forbearance of the people. The people will not stand for this large-scale warfare."

"All of this talk is for nothing. We are locked in a metal box being delivered directly to my brother. If he has truly become our enemy it is already too late."

"Nonsense! We are already out of our handcuffs. Nobody's the wiser or we would have heard by now. Let us bide our time. I served in northern France during the Great War. The crossing will be made at Calais, where Mycroft will no doubt have an entire Battalion waiting to take the rebels, and us, into custody. However, this rail line runs straight through Reims, a city thick with Allied sentiment but with loose ties to England. If we stop the train there we can pass our intelligence along to the Deuxième Bureau."

"I realize that you are accustomed to taking great liberties with trains, Watson, but the two of us are hardly suited to commandeering a hostile armored transport."

"We can be thankful then that Mycroft packed us an army."

I don't know if it was the shock of finding my old friend alive or the stress of re-entering the world of espionage after years in the peaceful countryside, or if I was simply becoming muddleheaded in my old age but I found myself hanging from the side of an armored boxcar speeding through the French countryside trying to pick a massive padlock one-handed. Every time my body was tossed against the side of the car by the jarring motion of the train I could feel a dozen angry hands striking the inside. I almost fell off completely when the lock suddenly gave and came loose. Gasping for breath I let the open lock dangle on the latch as I clung to the side of the container. I tried to focus my mind with the slowing of my breath as I waited for Watson to do his part. I could hear the sounds of an altercation up ahead and then I saw two men lying on the ground shouting as the train whizzed past them. There was a large clank then a hiss and the train lurched and slowed and came to a halting stop.

I yanked the lock-free from the latch, leaped down and quickly backed away from the car. From the armored caboose in the rear came shouts from the guards demanding to know why we had stopped. The doors of the boxcar flew open and a hundred enraged faces glared at me. I raised my hands in supplication and did my best to wrest some remedial Turkish from the far corners of my mental attic. "Bekle! Arkadaşınım! Korumaları tutuklayın! Biz özgürlük için bir planı var!" The men looked at each other confused. One stepped to the front.

"What are you saying?" the man snarled. His compatriots shouted.

"My name is Sherlock Holmes. I am freeing you so that you may tell the world of the English plot and the poison gas."

"Lies! This is a trick. You will shoot us if we run!"

"I and my friend are prisoners, like you. We overpowered our guards and have been in hiding the last day, waiting to reach friendly territory. Please, check for yourself," I gestured toward the passenger car where the SIS men were restrained.

"All Englishmen look the same."

I thought of Mr. Smith in his Ottoman suit and wondered if I was truly indistinguishable. It was a humbling thought. "If you do not like my words or my appearance please consider my actions." I gestured at the open land around us. "You are free to leave." A bullet thudded into the ground by my feet.

"Not so fast!" The guards in the caboose had taken up a defensive position on the ground by the rear of the train. "Nobody is going anywhere. Close those doors quietly and no one gets shot." A soldier moved towards me, rifle aimed at my chest. "As for you, I don't care what special instructions Director Holmes gave. I see an escaped prisoner on the ground. My responsibilities are clear." He cocked the rifle. A shot rang out. I found it strange that I felt nothing, only a ringing in my ears but dismissed the phenomenon as shock. Through the ringing, I thought I heard a familiar voice telling me to get down. In the strange silence, I watched as the Turkish rebels lept from the boxcar and swarmed over the handful of British soldiers like bees erupting from a newly smashed hive to punish the petulant schoolboy who threw the rock. Suddenly Watson was in front of me, shaking me by the shoulders. All of the sounds rushed back into my ears as if I had just broken the surface of the water after a deep dive.

"Holmes, Holmes, can you hear me?" Watson was now dragging me back into our train car. He laid me down inside and pulled a revolver from his belt, taking a place between myself and the door. The Turkish man who spoke English appeared in the doorway.

"Is this true, that we are free to leave?"

"It is true, my friend, but I beg of you to listen for a moment. You and your men, you make the anecdote for the English poison?"

"Not us, we guard it and transport it only. Our scientists we moved in secret when we saw the English coming. This gas you English make, it is terrible. An unimaginable horror."

"England does not do this. A small group of fanatics is responsible. We want to stop them before they use the gas. We are going directly to the French authorities. We want to make this terrible weapon known so that military action can be taken."

"I will come with you to see that this thing is done."

"What of your men?"

"They will disappear into the wild and be home in a week. They will spread the warning far and wide."

We feared to leave the armored caboose and we needed to keep an eye on Mycroft's men, who the rebels had thrown in the armored boxcar, so instead of hiking into Reim, we waited for authorities to investigate the stoppage. Watson and the Turkish man, whose name was Mahmed, exchanged war stories and we all smoked some fine Turkish tobacco, watching the blue smoke curl up into the darkening sky.

Paris, France, July 1920

A few weeks later Watson and I sat sipping thick, black coffee at a cafe overlooking the Seine. I watched the boats drift up and down the muggy river and found myself lamenting the end of our recent adventure. Or at least lamenting the size of my suitcase, as I had just finished off the last of the tobacco. Still, after all was said and done, I supposed the coffee would do as it was slightly more invigorating than a cup of Earl Gray. Watson, however, looked the worse for it. He appeared to be strangling the copy of *The Times* he was reading. In place of the expose of corruption and fanaticism, he had hoped for was a photo of a smiling Mycroft and a congratulatory article about the retirement of one of Britain's finest servants. "For King and Country" read the headline. Instead of a bullet, Mycroft was being knighted. Instead of knighthood Watson and I were now *persona non grata* in our native land.

"Dash it, Holmes! This is the most repugnant scene I've ever encountered! The traitor is a hero and the heroes are traitors!" Watson fumed.

"We were never after accolades, Watson. Besides, we know the truth. Those in the dark corridors of power know the truth. Most importantly Mycroft knows the truth. His failure and our triumph will agonize him for the rest of his days." I found myself humming an upbeat little tune as my fingers played out the fingering on the table's edge.

"As long as we did all this for the right reasons." Watson shook his head. "Still, to never see England again…"

"If this case has proven anything it is that our England is gone. It exists only in memories." I glanced at Watson. "Or stories."

"Are you suggesting I shouldn't try to tell our side of things? That I should let this rubbish stand?"

"I'm simply suggesting, my dear Boswell, that the machinations of criminal masterminds like Moriarty, the greatest criminal in London, are simply quaint in this new age, and the same must be said of the greatest detective in London as well. We could adapt, like Mycroft."

"The unscrupulous cur!"

"I am relieved to hear you find that proposition as odious as I do. We can simply step out of the pages of history and disappear into an anonymous retirement. I to my nature studies, you to your medicine, or your writing, or whatever fancy takes you. Or…"

"Or what?"

"Or even to fiction. I have been compiling my notes on Red Sword and I fear the entries read less like science than science fiction. Less like the diary and ruminations of a genius than the daydreams of a poor Austen scullery maid or schoolmarm."

"Fiction? What's the use? Really Holmes. I thought you of all people would despise a word committed to the page for such a capricious purpose."

"I fear I may be a changed man in my old age. You know none of your contacts in journalism would risk it. And none of our countrymen, none of our so-called friends, would even believe it. Are we really willing to put ourselves through that? I think not. But a well-timed serial might catch the public's eye…"

"I'll stop you there. You may plan to live forever, but the rest of us must spend our remaining minutes wisely and I'll not seek my vengeance in sensational literature. Still, seeing Mycroft hacked to pieces over and over, if only on the page, is tempting. But it wouldn't do for you at all. Not with your history…"

"Ah." Even after such a short foray into the art of systematically cataloging my own narrative like a madman, like every nuance mattered and would be endlessly interesting to an audience, even now I could feel the pen calling like a needle and I knew he was right. My Boswell. "No matter. Take heart, old boy. I have secured us a cottage near Lorraine from an old client. Perhaps we shall assist the Sûreté every once in a while, just as a diversion. You'll be back to your old ways in no time."

"Now, now," Watson said, as he gingerly lifted another croissant from the pile of pastries tableside. "Nothing so rash as that. I daresay I've finally had my fill of murder. Wars, espionage, freedom fighters, and the like. It will be nice to get away from all of it out in the French countryside where there is nothing but peace and tranquility."

ORIGINALLY PUBLISHED

"The Bogus Laundry Affair" appeared in *The MX Book of New Sherlock Holmes Stories Part XI*, MX Publishing

"A Change of Art" appeared in *The MX Book of New Sherlock Holmes Stories Part X*, MX Publishing

"The Mystery of the Pharoah's Tablet" appeared in *The MX Book of New Sherlock Holmes Stories Part XIII*, MX Publishing

"The Adventure of the Twofold Purpose" appeared in *The MX Book of New Sherlock Holmes Stories Part XV*, MX Publishing

"The Adventure of the Two Patricks" appeared in *The MX Book of New Sherlock Holmes Stories Part VI*, MX Publishing

"The Adventure of the Gnarled Beeches" appeared in *Sherlock Holmes: Adventures Beyond the Canon* Vol. 3, Bellanger Books

"Sherlock Holmes and the Sharpshooter" appeared in *Proceedings of the Pondicherry Lodge* Vol. 4 Issue 2

"A Case of Juris Imprudence" appeared in *Holmes Away from Home*, Bellanger Books

"How Hope Learned the Trick" appeared in *NonBinary Review: A Study in Scarlet*

"The Adventure of the Dead Ringer" appeared in *Before Baker Street*, Bellanger Books

"For King and Country" appeared in *The Science of Deduction*, 18th Wall Press

Also from MX Publishing

MX Publishing is the world's largest specialist Sherlock Holmes publisher, with over a hundred titles and fifty authors creating the latest in Sherlock Holmes fiction and non-fiction.

From traditional short stories and novels to travel guides and quiz books, MX Publishing cater for all Holmes fans.

The collection includes leading titles such as *Benedict Cumberbatch In Transition* and *The Norwood Author* which won the Howlett Award (Sherlock Holmes Book of the Year).

MX Publishing also has one of the largest communities of Holmes fans on Facebook with regular contributions from dozens of authors.

www.mxpublishing.com

Also from MX Publishing

The Detective and The Woman Series

The Detective and The Woman

The Detective, The Woman and The Winking Tree

The Detective, The Woman and The Silent Hive

The Detective, The Woman and The Pirate's Bounty

"The book is entertaining, puzzling and a lot of fun. I believe the author has hit on the only type of long-term relationship possible for Sherlock Holmes and Irene Adler. The details of the narrative only add force to the romantic defects we expect in both of them and their growth and development are truly marvelous to watch. This is not a love story. Instead, it is a coming-of-age tale starring two of our favorite characters."

Philip K Jones

www.mxpublishing.com

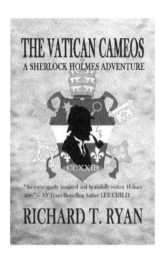

When the papal apartments are burgled in 1901, Sherlock Holmes is summoned to Rome by Pope Leo XII. After learning from the pontiff that several priceless cameos that could prove compromising to the church, and perhaps determine the future of the newly unified Italy, have been stolen, Holmes is asked to recover them. In a parallel story, Michelangelo, the toast of Rome in 1501 after the unveiling of his Pieta, is commissioned by Pope Alexander VI, the last of the Borgia pontiffs, with creating the cameos that will bedevil Holmes and the papacy four centuries later. For fans of Conan Doyle's immortal detective, the game is always afoot. However, the great detective has never encountered an adversary quite like the one with whom he crosses swords in "The Vatican Cameos.."

"An extravagantly imagined and beautifully written Holmes story"

(**Lee Child**, NY Times Bestselling author, Jack Reacher series)

9 781787 055186